# Disney
# 365
# Bedtime Stories

# PaRragon

Bath New York Singapore Hong Kong Cologne Delhi Melbourne

This edition published by Parragon in 2008

Parragon Books Ltd
Queen Street House
4 Queen Street
Bath, BA1 1HE, UK
ISBN 978-1-4054-8025-3
Printed in Malaysia

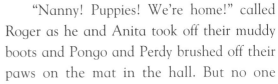

## New Year's Day

It was the first day of the new year, and Pongo and Perdita were out for a walk with their pets, Roger and Anita. The morning fog was beginning to part, and the air was clear and cold. "Oh, Pongo." Perdita sighed happily. "What a wonderful year we've just had – 15 puppies to be thankful for!"

"Yes, darling, and think of all we have to look forward to this year," said Pongo.

"Can you believe they all stayed up till midnight last night to ring in the new year?" Perdita cried. "And still awake when we left! I do hope they don't tire out dear, poor Nanny."

"Yes, that was quite a party we had at the flat last night," Pongo agreed. "And Lucky would have spent the whole night watching television if we had allowed him to."

"Perhaps we should be getting home now," said Perdita. "I am so afraid that Cruella De Vil may come around while we're out. I dread the way she looks at our puppies."

"I suppose we should," said Pongo. "But I'm sure Nanny has been taking good care of them." Pongo and Perdita gently pulled on their leads to let Roger and Anita know it was time to go home. The four of them walked towards home just as a new sprinkling of rain began to gently fall.

"Nanny! Puppies! We're home!" called Roger as he and Anita took off their muddy boots and Pongo and Perdy brushed off their paws on the mat in the hall. But no one answered.

"Pongo!" exclaimed Perdita, her panic rising. "Where are the puppies?"

Pongo raced up the stairs and began searching the rooms one by one. Perdita went to check the kitchen. Roger and Anita exchanged concerned looks, but tried to remain calm.

Pongo hurried into the sitting room to rejoin Perdita, who was on the brink of tears. "Oh, Pongo!" she cried. "Where can . . ."

"Hush, darling," said Pongo, his ears pricked intently. The two dogs fell silent. Then they both heard it: a tiny snore coming from the direction of the couch. There, nestled among the cushions, the puppies were sound asleep!

"I found Nanny!" Roger called. "She fell asleep in her chair!"

Perdita was busy counting the sleeping puppies. ". . . 12, 13, 14 . . . Oh, Pongo! One of the puppies isn't here!"

But Pongo had trotted into the next room. "Here he is, darling!" he called. "It's Lucky, of course. He's watching the New Year's Day celebration on television."

# Three Cheesy Wishes

Long ago, before there was an Aladdin, a Jasmine, or even a Sultan, the magic lamp was making its way towards the Cave of Wonders, where Aladdin would one day find it. A travelling merchant had bought the lamp, along with some other 'junk.' Not knowing its value, he sold it to a cheese seller for some lunch.

Hassan the cheese seller looked at the lamp sceptically. He sighed, and began to shine it up. In a puff of smoke, the Genie appeared.

"Hello there! I'm the one and only magical Genie!" the big blue spirit announced.

"Excuse me?" said Hassan.

"Nice to meet you," said the Genie. "And what do you do here in Agrabah?"

"My name is Hassan, and I'm a – "

"Wait!" cried the Genie. "Let me guess! They say I'm a little psychic, you know!"

The Genie put his hand over his brow as he secretly looked around the man's shop. "You sell . . . cheese! Am I right or am I right?"

"You are right," said Hassan. "But that's an easy guess. Not very magical."

"You're very observant, Hassan," said the Genie. "So I'll give you three wishes."

"Three wishes, eh?" Hassan thought for a few minutes. Then he said, "It's hard to get enough good milk to make the best cheese. I wish I had many, many goats so I would always have enough milk."

*Poof!* In a flash, thousands of goats filled the streets of Agrabah. Goats were everywhere! They crowded the little shop, and knocked over the stalls in the market.

"Goodness!" Hassan cried. "I would have to wish for the biggest cheese shop in the world to sell the cheese from so many goats."

*Poof!* All of a sudden, Hassan's store began to grow and grow! His cheese shop was even taller than the highest sand dunes outside the city.

"This is terrible!" Hassan cried. Far below, the people looked like tiny ants. "I can't live and work in such a monstrosity. All I wanted was to make the finest cheese in Agrabah."

Hassan turned to the Genie. "I wish I'd never met you!" he cried.

*Poof!* Suddenly, the Genie was gone. Hassan found his shop back to normal. Outside, the marketplace was completely goat free.

Hassan searched high and low for the lamp, but it was already tucked into a little boy's pocket. Where would it end up next?

"It must have all been a crazy dream," said Hassan.

But, from that day, everyone said Hassan's cheese was the finest in all of Agrabah!

# An Elephant Lullaby

Mrs Jumbo was very sad. More than anything else in the world, she had been longing for a baby elephant of her own. Many other animals in the circus had babies and, as she watched the mothers with their infants, she grew sadder and sadder. Then one day, a stork delivered a baby elephant to Mrs Jumbo! The tiny elephant was the most beautiful creature she had ever seen, and she was the happiest animal in the circus. But then it happened: her baby sneezed, causing his ears to unfold. They were extremely large ears, and the other elephants laughed at him in a way that was not nice at all.

"Instead of calling him Jumbo Junior," one elephant said drily, "he ought to be called Dumbo!" The others laughed loudly at this.

Mrs Jumbo ignored their taunts and curled her trunk around her beloved baby.

As the days went by, Mrs Jumbo grew to love her baby more and more. She played hide-and-seek with him, pretending to be surprised when he hid behind her legs. She played peeka-boo with him. She sang him lullabies at bedtime, and danced around with him when he woke up.

One evening, Mrs Jumbo found her precious baby looking terribly sad. She guessed that the other elephants had been taunting him again, and her eyes flashed with indignation.

But she tenderly put him to bed, tucking his large ears around him to keep him warm. "Don't mind what the others say," she whispered softly. "You are going to grow up to be a fine elephant! Shall I sing you a lullaby, darling?"

As Dumbo nodded, Mrs Jumbo heard the other elephants talking in low tones in the next stall. "Honestly!" one of them was saying. "You'd think he was the only elephant left on earth, the way she pampers him! She spoils him terribly, she does!"

But Mrs Jumbo ignored their whispers and began to sing:

*Hush, little baby, don't you cry.*
*Mama's gonna sing you a lullaby.*
*And if someone should laugh at your ears,*
*Mama's gonna be here to dry your tears.*
*And if your tears can't be extinguished,*
*Mama thinks that large ears are really*
  *distinguished.*

Then she continued to hum and rock her son until his eyelids grew heavier and heavier, and he fell asleep.

Mrs Jumbo hummed for a little while longer, then stood up. But wait – why was it so quiet?

All along the elephant stalls, soft snoring could be heard. Mrs Jumbo's lullaby had put all the elephants to sleep!

Disney · PIXAR
FINDING **NEMO**

# Marlin's Story

"P. Sherman, 42 Wallaby Way, Sydney . . . P. Sherman, 42 Wallaby Way, Sydney." Dory kept muttering the address. She and Marlin were searching for Marlin's missing son, Nemo. They had just escaped an angry anglerfish, and now they were trying to find someone who could give them directions to Sydney. That's where Nemo probably was.

"P. Sherman, 42 Wallaby Way, Sydney . . . P. Sherman, 42 Wallaby Way, Sydney," Dory continued to chant.

Marlin had the address memorized and thought he would go crazy if he had to hear it again. "Dory!" he said with a sigh. "I know you just want to be helpful, but do you really need to keep talking?"

"I love to talk," said Dory. "I'm pretty good at it. Hmm . . . what were we talking about?"

"I just want to find Nemo," Marlin said.

"That's right, Chico," said Dory.

"One time, Nemo and I . . ." Marlin began.

"Go on," Dory said. "Is this going to be exciting?"

"Yes, it's an exciting story," said Marlin, relieved that he had got her to stop reciting the address. "Well," Marlin began, "one time, I took Nemo to the other side of the reef, to visit a relative of mine who was known as the fastest swimmer of all the clownfish, in his day. But when we visited him, he was getting on in years."

Dory yawned. "When's the good part?"

Marlin sighed. "I was just about to get to it!" he said. "So, anyway, on the way back home, guess what we ran into?"

"What?" asked Dory, confused.

"A huge jellyfish! It was hovering in the water, blocking our way through two big tufts of sea grass."

"Uh-huh," said Dory. She seemed to be trying to remember something. "P. Sherman . . ." she muttered softly.

"For a moment there I thought we were goners," said Marlin. "But then . . . a huge sea turtle swam up and swallowed the jellyfish in one gulp!"

"Did you say thank you to the sea turtle?" asked Dory, who seemed back on track.

"Well, no," Marlin replied. "I was afraid he would eat us, too, so Nemo and I hurried on our way. But, ever since then, I have been fascinated with sea turtles. And I hope I never have to meet another jellyfish!"

"Say, I've got a story too!" said Dory excitedly. "It takes place at 42 Wallaby Way, Sydney. At P. Sherman. Now, at P. Sherman, 42 Wallaby Way, Sydney, there was this, um, fish . . . and . . . well . . ."

Marlin just groaned and kept swimming.

Disney's
THE
LION KING

# Scaredy Cats

"Nala!" Simba whispered. "Are you awake?"

"Yes," Nala whispered back, stepping out of the dark cave where she slept with her mother. "Why are you here? You're gonna get us in trouble . . . again."

Earlier, Simba and Nala had gone to explore the forbidden Elephant's Graveyard, where they'd been trapped by hyenas. Simba's father, Mufasa, had rescued them.

"Come on," Simba hissed. "Follow me."

Soon the two cubs were on the dark savannah near the base of Pride Rock.

"What do you want, anyway?" Nala asked.

"I just wanted to make sure you weren't still scared," Simba said.

Nala scowled at him. "Scared?" she exclaimed. "*I'm* not the one who was scared!"

"What?" Simba cried. "You're not saying *I* was scared, are you? Because there's no way I'd be scared of a few stupid hyenas. I wouldn't have been scared even if we ran into *ten* hyenas."

"Well, I wouldn't have been scared even if we found *20* hyenas and an angry water buffalo," said Nala.

"Oh yeah?" Simba said. "Well, I wouldn't have been scared of *30* hyenas, an angry water buffalo and a – "

"FURIOUS HORNBILL?" a new voice squawked from the darkness.

"Ahhhhhh!" Simba and Nala cried, jumping straight up in the air.

Just then, a brightly coloured bird stepped out of the shadows. It was Zazu, Mufasa's most trusted adviser.

"Zazu!" Simba cried. "You scared us!"

"I wasn't scared," Nala put in indignantly.

"Me neither!" Simba added quickly.

Zazu glared at both of them over his long beak. "Not scared, were you?" he said drily. "That certainly explains the shrieking."

"You just startled us," Nala mumbled.

Zazu fluffed his feathers. "Listen up, you two," he said. "There's no shame in admitting you're scared. Even King Mufasa wouldn't deny that he was terrified when he found out you were missing. And, if it's good enough for him, it's good enough for a pair of scrawny cubs like you. Right?"

"I guess so," Simba said as Nala shrugged.

"Everyone gets scared," Zazu went on. "It's how you respond to it that counts. That's where *true* bravery lies. Get it?"

"Got it," Simba and Nala said.

"Good." Zazu marched towards Pride Rock. The sun was coming up and it was time for breakfast. "Now let's get you back home posthaste . . . or I'll *really* give you something to be scared of!"

# Tree Trouble

Toulouse and Berlioz scampered out by the back door of Madame Bonfamille's house. Behind them, Marie trotted in a more ladylike manner, her long white tail swishing back and forth. But even she couldn't stop herself from launching a surprise attack on her brother Toulouse when his back was turned.

"Here I come!" shouted her other brother, Berlioz, as he pounced on his two siblings. Marie escaped, but Berlioz and Toulouse began to wrestle in the leaves.

"I got you both!" Berlioz exclaimed proudly. "I'm clearly the superior pouncer."

"Oh, yeah?" said Toulouse. "If you're so great, let's see you climb to the top of the oak tree." He raised his chin, gesturing to the towering tree above them.

"Gladly," Berlioz replied. He nimbly leaped onto a low branch and began to climb up, up, up the huge tree.

"Be careful!" Marie called. He was climbing awfully high. Soon he was perched on the highest branch.

"Don't you worry about me," Berlioz called down. He was so far up it was hard to hear him.

Toulouse licked his paw. "All right, so you're a good climber," he called up to his brother. "You can come down now."

Berlioz didn't move.

"I said you can come down," Toulouse repeated.

"I – I can't," Berlioz replied. His voice sounded shaky. "I'm stuck." He began to howl. Soon his brother and sister were yowling too.

It only took a few minutes for Madame Bonfamille to open an upstairs window. She and Duchess stuck their heads out to see what all the noise was about.

"My goodness!" Duchess cried when she spied Berlioz. "What on earth are you doing up there?"

"M-eee-ooo-www!" the kitten replied.

"Don't you worry, we'll be right there to help you," Madame Bonfamille said reassuringly. A few minutes later, she and Duchess appeared in the yard, followed by a very grumpy looking Edgar carrying a long ladder.

"Just climb right up and get him, won't you, Edgar?" Madame Bonfamille asked.

Edgar scowled and mumbled something about foolish felines. But he leaned the ladder against the tree trunk and began to climb. Before long, Berlioz was safely on the ground once again.

Madame Bonfamille smiled at Duchess. "Edgar is *so* devoted to you precious cats," she said. "It warms the cockles of my heart."

## Walt Disney's Cinderella

# A Tiny New Friend

It had been a week since Cinderella's stepmother had forced her to move out of her bedroom and into the attic of the old house. But still Cinderella was not used to her new sleeping quarters. It was a cold, bare, lonely little room. The only other soul around to keep Cinderella company was a skittish little mouse who she had seen scurrying in and out of a hole in a corner of the room.

She had always been fond of animals, and mice were no exception. But how could she let the little fellow know that he shouldn't be afraid of her?

Well, thought Cinderella, he must be cold . . . and hungry.

So one day, at suppertime, Cinderella slipped a piece of cheese into her apron pocket.

And that evening, when her work was finished, Cinderella hurried up to her room and pulled out her sewing basket. She used some scraps of fabric to make a mouse-sized suit of clothing: a red shirt and cap, a tiny orange coat, and two brown slippers.

"A tiny outfit for my tiny friend," she said.

Cinderella carried the clothes over to the mouse hole and knelt before it. She pulled the cheese out of her pocket and placed it, with the clothes, in the palm of her hand. Then she laid her open hand just in front of the mouse hole.

"Hello in there!" she called.

A mouse cautiously poked his head out of the hole and sniffed the air. Seeing the cheese, he inched out of the hole and over to Cinderella's hand. He paused and looked up at her questioningly.

"Go ahead," she said kindly. "They're a gift just for you."

Seeming to understand, but still skittish, the mouse scampered onto her palm, picked up the cheese and the clothes, and hurried back into the mouse hole.

Cinderella chuckled, then waited patiently for a few minutes, still kneeling in front of the hole.

"Well," she called after a short while, "let me see how they look on you!"

Timidly, the mouse came out in his new outfit. Cinderella clapped her hands.

"Perfect!" she said. "Do you like them?"

The mouse nodded. Then he jumped, as if an idea had just occurred to him. He scurried back into the mouse hole. Cinderella frowned. Had she frightened him?

But her worries vanished when the mouse reappeared – along with several other mice, who followed timidly behind him.

"More friends!" Cinderella cried. She hurried to get her sewing basket, delighted to have found the warmth of friendship in the cold attic room.

Disney·PIXAR
## MONSTERS, INC.

# Mike's Worst Nightmare

"AAAAAAIEEEE-AHHHH!" Sulley sat bolt upright in bed. The anguished yell was coming from his friend Mike's bedroom. Sulley raced out of his bedroom and threw open Mike's door.

"Hi," said Mike in a shaky voice. "I guess I must have had a bad dream." He swallowed hard, then sat up in bed and gave Sulley a sheepish grin. "I haven't had one since I was little."

Sulley nodded. "Okay, well, good night, Mike."

"Uh, Sulley, don't you want to hear about it?" Mike asked with a hopeful grin.

Sulley came over and sat down on the edge of his friend's bed. "Okay," he said.

"I dreamed . . ." Mike began. "This is going to sound really, really crazy, I know, but . . . I dreamed that there was a kid, a human kid, in my closet over there!" He pointed across the room and laughed nervously.

"Now, now," said Sulley good-naturedly. "Maybe it was the movie you watched tonight."

"*Kidzilla?*" Mike scoffed. "Nah. I've seen it a dozen times and it's never bothered me before."

"Well, why don't you try to go back to sleep?" said Sulley, suppressing a yawn.

Mike cleared his throat shyly. "I remember when I was little, my mum would bring me a sludgesicle when I had a bad dream," he said.

Sulley sighed patiently, then went to get Mike a sludgesicle from the kitchen.

"She would sing me a little lullaby too," said Mike.

In his low, scratchy voice, Sulley began to sing:

*Rock-a-bye, Mikey, Googley-Bear,*
*With sharp little fangs and shiny green hair!*
*Morning will come when the sun starts to rise,*
*You'll wake up and open those googley eyes!*

"Googley *eye*," Mike corrected his friend, snuggling under his blanket. "Uh, my mum also always checked the closet."

With another patient sigh, Sulley opened Mike's wardrobe door and stepped inside. "Nope. Nothing in here!" he called. Suddenly, there was a loud clatter and a landslide of junk spilled out of the wardrobe door. A yellow mop fell out. It looked just like blond hair!

"AHHHH!" shrieked Mike, leaping out from under the covers. Then he relaxed. "Oh, sorry, pal. In this dim light, I thought that mop was, you know, a human child!" He shuddered and gave Sulley another sheepish smile.

Sulley chuckled at the idea. "Don't be silly, Mike," he said. "A kid will never get loose in Monstropolis – what a disaster that would be!"

"No, you have a point," Mike agreed sleepily. "Good night, Sulley."

"Good night, Mike."

THE EMPEROR'S
NEW GROOVE

# Kuzco's Guide to Life

Hellooooo, all you underlings out there! The name is Kuzco. *Emperor* Kuzco to you, my friend. Welcome to "Kuzco's Guide to Life," otherwise known as rules to live by, *if* you're me! I wouldn't try to follow these rules at home if I were you. I'm an emperor, which means that, besides being rich and powerful and full of charisma, I have everybody in my kingdom doing *exactly* what I want them to do. You, on the other hand, probably don't have that kind of pull at your house. I mean, right now, your mum or dad or aunt or uncle or babysitter or . . . anyway, *someone* is probably telling you that you can only read this one story, and then it's time to get into bed and turn off the light. If you were me, you could have them banished for saying that! You could make them read all 365 stories in a row to you if you wanted to!

So, here are my rules. Read them and weep, and wish that you too were a rich and powerful emperor like me!

**Rule 1:** Do not allow anyone or anything to mess up your groove. By 'groove' I mean the rhythm in which you live your life. For instance, when I feel like dancing around my throne room, that's what I do. And trust me, no one messes up my groove. Of course, a weird thing happened today when I was dancing. Several enormous stone statues fell over and nearly crushed me. Freak accident probably.

**Rule 2:** Never consider anyone's feelings except your own. The other day, a huge, folksy peasant visited the palace and tried to talk me out of building my summer palace on the top of a hill where his family has lived for six generations. Boo hoo, right?

**Rule 3:** Always put your own needs first. When you're hungry, clap your hands and your servants will bring you a meal. When you're tired, snap your fingers and they'll bring you a bed. And when you're bored, lift your little finger and they'll bring in a circus show.

Of course, the other day, when my servants brought in my food, I fed a piece to my dog and he turned into a rhinoceros. And, while I was sleeping in my royal bed, I was sure I heard someone sawing a hole in the floor all around me. And the day the circus came to entertain me, my royal adviser Yzma 'accidentally' dropped the snake charmer's cobra into my lap! But maybe I'm just imagining things.

You don't think people are out to get me, do you? No. That's a crazy idea, isn't it? I mean, nothing bad could possibly happen to me, right?

Whoever is reading you this story is just about to tell you it's time for bed now. Good night!

*Disney's* *Beauty*
AND
THE *BEAST*

# Just Desserts

**B**elle walked to the village, thinking about the wonderful book she had just finished reading. It was full of fire-breathing dragons, magical wizards and brave princesses. She sighed happily and turned her attention to more practical matters – whether she should get treacle or apple tart to enjoy with her father that night after dinner.

All of a sudden, Belle's thoughts were interrupted by a great crashing noise. Even before he spoke a word, Belle knew who was walking behind her. She could recognize that stomp anywhere.

"Gaston," Belle muttered.

"Belle, is it true?" Gaston said. "Have you come out from behind a book?"

"Bonjour, Gaston," Belle said. She was tempted to open her book again on the spot.

"Off to market, eh? I shall accompany you," Gaston announced.

Keeping up a steady stream of chatter about himself and his exploits, Gaston followed Belle into shop after shop.

"My, Gaston, you certainly do boast well," Belle said in a flattering tone.

"Yes! Thank you!" Gaston replied before realizing Belle was not complimenting him. His smile disappeared briefly as he opened the door to the bakery.

Belle stepped inside and quickly asked for an apple tart before Gaston could begin speaking again. When the tart was in her basket, she waved to Gaston and the shopkeeper. "Goodbye!" she called, walking quickly towards the forest path. She sighed in relief. It seemed she was rid of her annoying companion.

"Belle, wait." Gaston caught her arm.

"I really have no time to linger, Gaston," Belle replied. "I must get home to make dinner."

"I can walk you home," Gaston said, puffing out his massive chest. "I insist upon it. You need protection."

"Protection from what? These woods are my backyard!" Belle laughed.

"From predators. Monsters. Thieves," Gaston said dramatically.

Belle sighed and shook her head.

Then, suddenly, Belle and Gaston did hear something on the path ahead. Something large!

Quickly, Gaston pushed Belle out of harm's way. Belle tumbled to the ground. Her basket went flying.

"Look out!" Belle yelled. But it was too late. The 'predator' emerged. It was her father's horse, Phillipe! For the first time that she could remember, Belle smiled at the sight of Gaston. The apple tart had landed right on top of his head!

# Spaghetti and Meatballs

Tramp had just escaped from the dogcatcher – again. He'd taught that dogcatcher who was boss!

Tramp could smell wood burning in fireplaces, dinner cooking . . . his stomach suddenly rumbled. Escaping from the dogcatcher always made him work up quite an appetite!

But where would he go for dinner tonight? He usually stopped by the Schultzes for some Wiener schnitzel on Monday, he had corned beef and cabbage with the O'Briens on Tuesday . . . but what he was really craving was some spaghetti and meatballs.

So, Tramp headed to Tony's Restaurant. He scratched at the back door, as was his custom.

"I'm coming! I'm coming!" Tony shouted. He appeared at the door wiping his hands on a towel. He pretended not to see Tramp, as he always did.

"Hey, nobody's here!" Tony shouted. "It must be April Fools' Day!" He pretended to think for a moment. "No, it's not the first! It's not even April! It's January!"

Tramp couldn't take it any more. He was so hungry! He barked.

"Oh, there you are, Butch my friend," said Tony. Tramp, aka Butch, jumped up and down. "I'll get your dinner," said Tony. "Relax, enjoy yourself."

Tramp sat down and looked around the cluttered alleyway. This was the life!

Just then Tony appeared with a plateful of pasta. He had given Tramp two, no make that *three* meatballs! This was quite a special night.

Tony stood and chatted with Tramp as he ate his meal, telling him about his day – the late delivery of fish, the customer who had complained that the tomato sauce was too garlicky, the trip that he and his wife were planning to take . . . .

Tramp finished eating and gave the plate one last lick. It was sparkling clean.

"That reminds me," said Tony. "There's something I've been meaning to talk to you about. It's time you settled down and got a wife of your own."

Tramp gave Tony a horrified look and began to back out of the alleyway.

Tony laughed so hard his sides shook. "Goodbye, Butch!" he called. "But mark my words, one of these days, you're going to meet the dog you can't resist! And, when you do, I have a good idea – you bring her to Tony's for a nice romantic dinner!"

Tramp barked his thanks to Tony. He walked down the block, shaking his head. He was footloose and collar free! Settle down? That was never going to happen!

# A Never Land Story

It was a cold winter night, and John and Michael just couldn't get to sleep. They climbed onto the bed of their older sister, Wendy.

"Oh, tell us a story, Wendy!" said Michael.

"Yes, please. A Peter Pan story!" pleaded John.

"Certainly," said Wendy. "Have I told you about the time that Peter Pan outsmarted the evil Captain Hook?"

"Yes!" said Michael eagerly. "And we want to hear it again!"

Wendy laughed and began her story. "Well, one night, Captain Hook moored his ship in a secret cove close to the island of Never Land. He and his men rowed ashore quietly, for he was intent on discovering the hiding place of Peter and the Lost Boys. Captain Hook hated Peter Pan because the boy had cut off his hand in a duel and fed it to a large crocodile. And now that crocodile was determined to swallow up the rest of him. Luckily for Captain Hook, however, this crocodile had also swallowed a clock, so the pirate would always be alerted to the crocodile's presence by the sound of the ticking clock.

"Fortunately for Peter Pan," Wendy continued, "his dear friend Tinker Bell learned of Captain Hook's evil plan ahead of time. She flew to Peter and warned him that the pirate was coming. 'Oh-ho!' laughed Peter. 'Well, we shall be ready for him then!' He found a clock just like the one the crocodile had swallowed. He whistled up into the trees, and a group of his monkey friends appeared. 'Here's a new toy for you!' Peter shouted, and tossed the clock up to them. 'Stay out of sight, now!' Peter told the monkeys, and then he and the Lost Boys hurried to their hiding places.

"When Hook came to the clearing, the first thing he heard was the ticking clock. The sound seemed to be coming at him from all sides! The monkeys were having a grand time, tossing the clock back and forth, and creeping up behind Hook. Seized with terror, Hook and his men raced to their boat and rowed madly back to their ship."

Just then, the Darling children's parents came in to check on them. "You're not telling more of these poppycock stories about Peter Pan, are you, Wendy?" their father asked.

"Peter Pan is real, Father!" cried the children. "We know he is!"

As the parents kissed their children good night, they didn't see that a boy in green was crouching just outside the nursery window. He had been listening to the story, and he would be back again – soon.

# A New Job

**B**ernard was a simple mouse. He liked his nice, quiet job as a handymouse, he liked to eat a nice hunk of cheese for dinner, and he liked to fall asleep reading a nice book each night. He didn't like the number 13, black cats (or cats at all, actually!) or the colour green. Another thing that Bernard didn't like was danger of any kind. He liked to play things safe. None of those daredevil mouse exploits for him. Bernard steered clear of all animals bigger than him, any cheese he had not purchased himself, and anything vaguely resembling a mousetrap.

So, when the office he worked in announced it was moving its location from the basement of 1515 Hudson Street to 1313 Hudson Street, he knew it was time to find a new place of employment. One '13' in the address would have been bad enough, but *two*, well, it just would not do!

That afternoon, he bought himself a copy of the *Rodent Report* newspaper, and while munching on his Limburger sandwich, he read the Help Wanted section.

"'Stunt mouse needed,'" he read. He shuddered. "Oh no, that's much too dangerous." He read some more. "'Steward for Albatross Airlines.' Oh no, that's wrong, just wrong!" He sighed. This was harder than he thought.

"'Cheese tester,'" he read. That looked promising! But then he took a closer look at the advert and saw the words 'experimental' and 'hazardous.' Bernard shook his head. He was never going to find a new job!

He put the paper down next to him, when an advert caught his eye. DESPERATELY SEEKING HANDYMOUSE, it read. EXPERIENCE REQUIRED. APPLY AT UNITED NATIONS BUILDING, SUB-BASEMENT. INTERNATIONAL RESCUE AID SOCIETY.

"That's it!" he cried. He headed there right after work. And since Bernard had the most experience of any of the applicants, the job was his!

"Congratulations!" said the French delegate. *"Bon chance!"*

That night, Bernard's friends took him out to celebrate his new job.

"The International Rescue Aid Society," his friend said. "Wow. Could be exciting, don'tcha think?"

"Oh, no," replied Bernard. "I'm going to be the handymouse. No danger. No intrigue. I'll be mopping floors. Fixing leaks. No adventure at all, you can count on that."

His friend raised his glass for a toast. "To your new job," he said.

"To my new job," said Bernard. "May it be safe, quiet and nonadventurous. Just the way I like it!"

### DISNEP's THE LITTLE MERMAID

# Sebastian's Big Day

It was Sebastian's big day. As composer for the court of King Triton, he had been working very hard on a new piece of music, and that evening he was going to conduct the royal orchestra as they played his song before everyone for the first time. At last, thought Sebastian, his true genius would be fully appreciated!

That afternoon, in preparation for the concert, Sebastian went over every detail. He perfected the positioning of the musicians' chairs on stage. He prepared extra copies of the music in case any of the musicians forgot their own. He even had his bow tie washed and pressed.

Then, just before the curtain went up, the musicians began to gather backstage. Music filled the air as the trumpet fish and the conch shell players tuned their instruments.

Benny the octopus, the orchestra's drummer, was the last musician to arrive.

"Sebastian!" he exclaimed, rushing over to the conductor. "I – I can't play tonight!"

Sebastian stared at Benny in shock. "What do you mean? You *have* to play!"

"You don't understand," Benny replied. "I *can't*. I took a nap this afternoon and fell asleep on my tentacles, and now they're all tingly! I can't hold my drumsticks!"

The gravity of the situation hit Sebastian hard. "What am I going to do?" he exclaimed, looking around at the musicians. "My composition calls for eight drums. Benny has eight tentacles – one for each drum. Where will I find enough hands to take his place?"

Just then, Ariel and her six sisters swam backstage to wish Sebastian luck.

"Ariel!" Sebastian cried. "Am I glad to see you!" He explained his problem to Ariel and her sisters. "Could each of you help by playing a drum in the concert?" he asked.

"Of course!" the mermaid sisters replied.

Sebastian breathed a sigh of relief. "Okay, we have seven drummers. We just need one more!"

All the musicians stared at Sebastian.

"*Me?*" he said. "But I am the composer and conductor! This is the day my true genius will finally be appreciated. I cannot be hidden in the drum section. I must be front and centre!"

But, wouldn't you know it, when the curtain went up minutes later, there was Sebastian, drumming away. His day in the spotlight would have to come another time. As he played, he shrugged and smiled.

"Well, you know what they say," he whispered to Ariel, who drummed at his side.

"The show must go on?" Ariel guessed.

"No," Sebastian replied. "A true genius is never fully appreciated in his own lifetime."

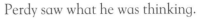

# Pongo Carries a Tune

"I don't know what we're going to do," Roger Radcliffe told his wife, Anita. "We have all these puppies to feed, and I don't have *one* song to sell!"

"Don't worry," Anita told him. "I'm sure you'll be inspired soon."

"I'm glad *you're* sure!" said Roger. "Because all I've got is a bunch of used paper." He pointed to the overflowing wastebasket.

"Don't give up," said Anita. "I know that you can do it."

After Anita left, Pongo watched his pet pace in front of his piano.

"Pongo, old boy, I must have written ten songs in ten days. But they're all terrible," said Roger, pointing to the wastebasket. "What am I going to do?"

Pongo wanted to help his pet, but he didn't know how.

That night, Pongo talked to Perdy about Roger's dilemma. They sat in the middle of the living room, surrounded by puppies.

"Roger has already written ten songs," explained Pongo. "He just doesn't think they're good enough to sell. But I know they are – I've heard him play them, and you don't have a songwriter for a pet without developing a good ear for hit songs. The songs are right upstairs, stuffed inside his wastebasket."

Perdy saw what he was thinking.

"Do you know the way to the music publisher?" she asked.

Pongo nodded. "I've taken Roger for walks there dozens of times."

"I think you should try it," said Perdy.

After Roger and Anita had gone to sleep, Pongo padded into the music room and gathered up the sheet music from the wastebasket. Then he sneaked out of the house, carrying the music to the publisher's office. Pongo pushed all the pages under the door, then trotted back home.

The next day, the phone rang. Roger answered.

"You what?" Roger said into the receiver. "You did . . . ? But how did you . . . ? Oh, I see . . . well, thank you. Thank you!"

Anita rushed over. "Who was that?"

"My music publisher," said Roger. "He's buying ten of my songs."

"Ten songs!" cried Anita. "I thought you didn't even have *one* to sell."

Roger scratched his head in confusion. "I didn't think I did."

"So, what happened?" asked Anita.

Perdy looked at Pongo and barked. Her husband could carry a tune too – all the way across town to Roger's publisher!

### DISNEY'S
# POCAHONTAS

# Listen With Your Heart

It was a clear, crisp day, and Pocahontas had decided to climb to the top of a high mountain with her friends Meeko the raccoon and Flit the hummingbird. She hadn't climbed this mountain since she was a little girl.

They came to a fork in the path. "Which direction should we take, Meeko?" asked Pocahontas. The raccoon pointed to the gentler, flatter path, which made Pocahontas laugh.

"Let's try this one!" she said, pointing to the narrower, steeper route. They climbed and climbed, and the path grew steeper and narrower. Meeko chattered away nervously, and even Flit seemed anxious. As Pocahontas sat down on a large tree stump to catch her breath, the winds suddenly picked up. Then the clouds moved in, and rain poured down on them.

"Uh-oh," said Pocahontas, jumping to her feet. "We can't stay here, and it's too slippery to climb back down. We need to keep moving!" Pocahontas didn't let on to Meeko and Flit but, as the water streamed down the steep path, she grew frightened. The footing was even more slippery, and she was getting colder and colder. Then she remembered something that her Grandmother Willow had told her.

"I need to listen," Pocahontas said to herself. "I must listen to the spirits all around us, and they will keep us safe." She tried to listen, but it was hard to hear anything over the pouring rain and rushing winds. Meeko chattered nervously and clung to Pocahontas.

"I must listen with my heart!" she said. And, suddenly, she heard them. The spirits spoke to her. They told her to climb a little higher, just a bit, and there she would find shelter.

"Come on, Meeko! Come on, Flit!" she called over the wind and rain. "We'll find shelter just a little way up!" Sure enough, they found an opening in the rocks just a bit higher up the path. Between the rocks was a small cave, and inside it was warm and dry. The three of them made their way into the cave and sat, listening to the rain and wind.

The storm soon passed, and the sun came out. "Come on!" Pocahontas cried to Meeko and Flit. "Let's go see what it looks like at the top!" They hurried the rest of the way up the trail until they came out on a wide, flat ledge. Far below, they could see the forest and, beyond it, the sparkling blue sea.

"You see, Meeko? See, Flit?" said Pocahontas. "We're seeing the world a different way. Isn't it beautiful? And just think," she said, more to herself than to the other two, "if I hadn't chosen that unexplored path, I would never have heard the spirits talk to me!"

# A Winter's Tale

One bright, sunny January day, Winnie the Pooh was trudging through the Hundred-Acre Wood on his way to visit his good friend Piglet. Piglet was ill in bed with the sniffles. Overnight it had snowed heavily, and the woods were blanketed in beautiful, fluffy snow.

"Poor Piglet," Pooh said with a sigh. "What a shame he can't come outside to play in this lovely snow." His boots crunched on for a few more steps, and then the bear of very little brain came up with a perfectly wonderful idea. "I know!" he exclaimed. "I will bring some snow to Piglet!" He scooped up a mittenful of snow and formed a snowball. He dropped it into his pocket, and then he made another, and then another. Soon he had three snowballs in each pocket, and another on top of his head, underneath his hat. He hurried on to Piglet's house. When he was nearly there, he passed Tigger, Rabbit, Roo and Eeyore, heading the other way.

"Hello, Pooh!" called Roo. "Come and build a snowman with us!"

"I'm sorry, but I can't," said Pooh wistfully. "You see, I am bringing some snowballs to Piglet, who is sick in bed with the sniffles." He said goodbye and hurried on his way.

Piglet was indeed not well, but he was very happy to see his friend. "Hello, Booh," he said snuffily. "I'b glad you cabe. *Ah-choo*!"

"Poor Piglet," said Pooh. "I'll make tea." He was just putting the kettle on when a large drop of icy water rolled out from underneath his hat and down his nose. This reminded Pooh of something.

"I brought you a present, Piglet!" he cried, snatching off his hat. But there was nothing there. Puzzled, Pooh ran to his jacket, which he had hung on a hook near the door. There were no snowballs in either of the pockets! But there was a sizeable puddle of water on the floor underneath Pooh's coat.

"I don't understand it!" Pooh remarked, scratching his head. "I brought you some snowballs, but they seem to have disappeared."

"Oh d-d-d-dear," Piglet said with a sigh. "Well, thanks for thinkig aboud be. I do wish I could go outside and blay. Could you bull back the curtains so that I can see the snow?"

Pooh hopped up and did what his friend had asked. Both of them gasped when they looked outside.

There, just below Piglet's window, Tigger, Rabbit, Eeyore and Roo had built a beautiful snowman, just for Piglet!

"Oh, friends are wonderbul!" Piglet said happily. "*Ah-choo*!"

# A Bedtime Story

It was bedtime in the little cottage in the woods. Snow White kissed each Dwarf good night and tucked them into bed.

"Wait! Wait!" called out Happy before she blew out the candle. "Please tell us a story!"

"Very well," said Snow White, smiling. She settled down at the foot of the beds and began . . .

"Once upon a time, there lived a happy little princess – or rather, a mostly happy little princess, but for a single person: her stepmother, the Queen."

"Bah!" grumbled Grumpy with a sneer.

Snow White sighed. "You see, no matter what the Princess did – no matter how hard she worked or how good she tried to be – the Queen did everything in her power to make her sad."

"Poor Princess," murmured Bashful.

"Oh, but don't worry," Snow White assured him. "Mostly, the Princess was jolly! She found that if she whistled and sang while she worked, her work would fly by and her mood would be sunny. And then, there were always her daydreams – for she truly believed that if she wished for something hard enough, it surely would come true."

"What did sh . . . she . . . *ah-choo*! . . . wish for?" asked Sneezy.

"Well," began Snow White, "for one thing, she wished for a charming and dashing prince to find her and whisk her away. And then, one day, a prince did find her!"

"Really?" exclaimed the Dwarfs.

"Yes!" Snow White told them. "He rode right up to her castle and even scaled the wall to meet her. And, oh, was he ever charming! But here is the sad part. The very next day, the Queen's Huntsman took the Princess into the forest and told her to run far away and never return."

"So, did she?" Sleepy asked sleepily.

"Yes," Snow White replied. "She ran until she could run no farther. Only then did she realize she was terribly lost and lonely – with no friend in the world and no place to go."

"Poor Princess," whispered Bashful.

"That's what the Princess thought too," Snow White said. "For just a minute. But then she discovered she wasn't alone at all. There were chipmunks and squirrels and deer and rabbits and birds . . . all sorts of forest creatures there to help her. They took her to the sweetest little cottage you ever did see, and the most faithful friends a princess could ever have."

"And what happened next?" grumbled Grumpy.

"Well, they lived happily ever after, of course!" Snow White replied. "What did you think?"

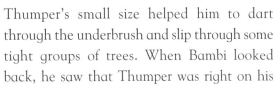

# Walt Disney's
# Bambi

## The Race

"Good morning, young Prince," Thumper greeted Bambi one bright winter day.

"Good morning, Thumper," Bambi said.

"I have a great idea, Bambi. Let's have a race," Thumper said. "We'll start from here." He drew a line in the dirt. "And whoever makes it to that big pine tree over there first, wins the race."

"But it would be silly for us to race," Bambi told his friend.

"Why's that?" Thumper asked, confused.

"Because I'll win," Bambi said.

"What makes you so sure?" Thumper challenged, puffing up his chest.

"Because I'm bigger and faster than you," Bambi explained.

"If you're so sure you'll win," Thumper said, "why are you afraid to race me?"

Bambi paused to think about this. He didn't want to hurt the little rabbit's feelings. "Fine," he said at last. "Let's race!"

"Great!" Thumper exclaimed. "Ready?"

"Ready!" Bambi said.

"Okay," Thumper said, crouching down. Bambi crouched down too. "On your mark. Get set. Go!" cried Thumper. They both took off as fast as they could.

Bambi, with his long legs and big, wide stride, immediately took the lead. But Thumper's small size helped him to dart through the underbrush and slip through some tight groups of trees. When Bambi looked back, he saw that Thumper was right on his heels. Thumper took the opportunity to hop past Bambi. Bambi paused to jump over a tree that had been knocked down, blocking the path. Thumper was able to wriggle under it. He popped up in front of Bambi and took the lead.

Bambi took longer and longer strides, running faster and faster. Soon he had passed Thumper. But, in his hurry to go as fast as he could, he got tangled up in a bush. As Bambi struggled to free himself, Thumper hopped past him again.

They were quickly approaching the big pine tree. Bambi was running as fast as he could, jumping over logs and bushes. Thumper hopped as quickly as his bunny legs would carry him, ducking and weaving through whatever obstacles were in his way. As they crossed the finish line, they were in a neck-and-neck tie.

"See!" Thumper said, panting. "Little guys can keep up!"

"You are absolutely right!" Bambi said, also panting.

And the two friends, both winners, sat down together to catch their breath.

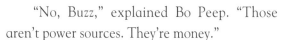

# Money Matters

"Greetings, slotted pig," said Buzz.

"Hello, Buzz," said Hamm the piggy bank. "How are you getting used to life here in Andy's room?"

"Life on this planet is quite interesting," Buzz said. "I look forward to giving a full report to my commander upon my return to base."

Hamm rolled his eyes. Andy's newest toy was a little bit bonkers, in his humble opinion. Buzz had no idea he was not an actual space ranger. It would be funny if it weren't so . . . annoying.

"So, pig," Buzz continued. "Today I noticed Andy placing several round silvery discs into the slot on your back."

"Yes," began Hamm, "that was . . ."

"And now these silver discs reside in your stomach cavity?" Buzz interrupted.

"Well, yes," began Hamm, patting his full belly. "But . . ."

"Aha!" Buzz cried. "I have determined your power source! What an interesting life-form you are! This will definitely make it into my report!"

Hamm shook his head as Woody and the rest of the toys walked up to join them.

"What's going on?" Woody asked.

"Greetings, cowboy," said Buzz. "I was just inquiring about the pig's power source."

"He's talking about the coins in my belly," Hamm explained.

"No, Buzz," explained Bo Peep. "Those aren't power sources. They're money."

"What's money?" Buzz wanted to know.

"It's what people use to get the things they need – like food, or toys, or comic books," said Woody. "Andy's taken me with him to the candy store before. He gives the shopkeeper some of those round things, and the shopkeeper gives him some candy. It's kind of like a trade."

Buzz thought for a moment. "Perhaps I need to procure some of this power source. . . um, I mean money, for myself," he suggested thoughtfully.

The rest of the toys started chattering excitedly. They had never thought about what they would do if they actually had some money!

"I would get myself a new staff," said Bo Peep. "This one's seen better days."

Woody started daydreaming about what *he* would buy. "I guess I could use a new hat and some boots," he said. But then he looked around and laughed out loud. "Look at us, we're being silly!" he said. "We're toys! Toys can't just go to the store and walk up to the counter to buy things!"

"Speak for yourself, cowboy," said Buzz. "Perhaps you've forgotten – I am not a toy!"

Hamm shook his head at the crazy mixed-up space ranger. "I give up!" he said.

# Sleepless Beauty

"Oh, there, there, little Aurora. There, there," cooed Flora, trying to calm the crying, fussy baby Princess. Flora and her fellow fairies, Fauna and Merryweather, stood huddled over the cradle of tiny Aurora and looked down anxiously and helplessly at their royal charge.

But Aurora's cries only grew louder. In fact, she had not stopped crying since the three fairies had arrived with the baby earlier that day at the secluded cottage in the woods.

"Oh, goodness!" cried Fauna. "What have we got ourselves into? We promised the King and Queen that we would hide Aurora out here in the woods, and raise her without magic. But we don't know the first thing about taking care of human babies!"

Flora gave Fauna a comforting pat on the back. "Now, now, don't panic, Fauna," Flora said. "It may be harder than we expected. But this is the only way to keep the Princess safe from Maleficent."

Merryweather and Fauna knew Flora was right. So, one after another, they tried different things to get the baby to stop crying and go to sleep.

"Well," said Flora, "fairy babies are soothed by a sprig of dandelion root placed in their cradle. Let's try that!" Flora hurried out of the cottage and returned minutes later with the sprig. She laid it at the baby's feet.

But the baby cried on. "Perhaps she needs to be entertained!" suggested Fauna.

So, Flora, Fauna and Merryweather locked arms and danced a little jig. They kept it up for quite a while, until they were out of breath and could barely stand up.

But baby Aurora took no notice – and carried on crying.

Now Fauna was getting desperate. "Come on," she said to the others, "let's use a little magic. Just to help her sleep. I can't bear to see her so upset!"

"No! It's much too dangerous!" cried Merryweather.

"Oh, fiddle-faddle!" shouted Fauna, who began to wave her wand over the sleeping child. Just then, she accidentally nudged Aurora's cradle, causing it to rock gently back and forth. Soothed by the rocking, the baby's cries slowly grew softer and softer.

"Fauna!" cried Flora. "You've done it!"

"Look how much she likes the rocking!" added Merryweather.

So, the three fairies continued to rock the cradle gently back and forth, and soon Aurora drifted off to sleep.

"Well," Fauna whispered to the others, once the baby was sleeping soundly, "that wasn't so hard, now, was it?"

# Home Is Where the Heart Is

Tod, an orphaned baby fox, was still getting used to his new surroundings in the Widow Tweed's house. Why, Tod was so young, he was still getting used to being a fox! Imagine how extra-confusing it was for him to find himself in a human's house, where everything he saw was strange and unfamiliar. In the kitchen, Tod's attention was caught by the large box with a door that the Widow Tweed kept opening and closing. Each time she opened the door, Tod caught a glimpse of the box's brightly lit interior and got a whiff of all kinds of delicious treats inside!

But, when Tod hopped into the box, unseen by the Widow Tweed as she was closing the door, he got a surprise. It was cold inside! And as soon as the door closed, Tod found himself sitting in complete darkness.

Luckily, the Widow Tweed heard Tod's whimpers and opened the refrigerator door. "Why, Tod, how did you get in there?" she said.

Tod hopped out and darted away. He wandered into the living room and jumped onto a windowsill. Outside, Tod could see his friends Big Mama the owl and Dinky the sparrow chatting on a tree branch. Tod leaned forward to hop outside and join them. But he bumped into something! Tod was confused. He didn't see anything blocking his way. He leaned forward again. His nose bumped up against something smooth, hard and solid, but it was clear; he could see right through it.

The Widow Tweed chuckled as she looked on from the living-room doorway. "Discovered glass, have you, Tod?" she said with a kind smile.

Whatever glass was, thought Tod, he supposed he'd have to stay indoors. He hopped onto a table and studied a small square object with some knobs on it. He batted one of the knobs. It turned a fraction of an inch. Intrigued, Tod batted it again. This time, the knob turned all the way around, and a loud noise blared out. Startled, Tod bolted under the sofa.

The Widow Tweed rushed over to the object and turned the knob. The noise stopped. Then she coaxed Tod out from under the sofa. "There, there, Tod," she cooed, cradling him in her arms and patting his head. "That's just the radio. You're having a hard time getting used to everything in this strange new place, aren't you? Here, let's have a snack."

It had been a rough morning for the baby fox. But there, in the Widow Tweed's arms, Tod felt a comforting, familiar feeling at last. It was the feeling of being warm and cared for.

All of a sudden, Tod's new home didn't feel so strange after all.

Walt Disney's
# ALICE
in
WONDERLAND

# A Tiny Tale

One day, Alice was sitting in the garden, listening to her older sister read a book out loud. It was lesson time and, as her sister's voice droned on about the ancient Greeks, Alice's mind wandered. She wondered if it was nearly teatime. She had smelled scones baking earlier, and her stomach rumbled in anticipation. She watched a little caterpillar climb a blade of grass, its tiny body scrunching and straightening as it moved up the leaf.

"What must it be like to be as tiny as that?" Alice wondered to herself.

The next thing she knew, she *was* that tiny! In an instant, the garden had grown higher and higher until the grass towered over her head, as tall as trees. The caterpillar, now half as long as Alice, waved its antennae at her and continued its climb.

"Oh, my!" cried Alice. "I must get back to the house. If I don't start out now, I shall never be back in time for tea!" She began to make her way through the forest of grass, until she arrived at the garden path. The path, which formerly had seemed to slope ever so gently, now appeared as a mountain in front of her, and the house was not even visible.

"I shall never get home in time for . . . *WHOOPS*!" Alice felt herself suddenly on her back, travelling feet first up the path.

She looked down and gasped. Three ants were carrying her on their backs! "Put me down at once!" she said to them crossly, but the ants took no notice of her. With a quick twist of her body, she managed to tumble to the ground. The ants appeared not to realize that their load had vanished, and continued up the hill.

"Well, at any rate I am now a good deal closer to home," said Alice, gazing up at her house.

She found herself standing at the edge of a huge puddle. "However shall I get across?" she wondered. Then a large leaf blew off a tree and landed in the puddle directly in front of her. She stepped onto the leaf and let the breeze blow her across. "I am nearly there!" she said triumphantly. But, a moment later, a huge blackbird swooped down and plucked her up by the sleeve of her dress. She felt herself airborne. "Oh, bother, now I shall never get home for tea," she said.

The next thing she knew, her sister was plucking her sleeve. "Wake up, Alice! You've fallen asleep again!" With an exasperated sigh, her sister stood up. "We may as well end the lesson for the day, as it's time to go in and have our tea."

Enormously relieved to be her usual size again, Alice followed her sister up the garden path and into the house.

# Mango Hunting

Once upon a time, long before Mowgli came to the jungle, Bagheera the panther met Baloo the bear for the first time.

This is how it happened.

Bagheera was younger then, but no less grave. He took himself very seriously indeed. When Bagheera hunted, he moved silently, with grace and speed. He never tripped, and he certainly never fell. When he slept, he kept one eye open. When he spoke, he chose his words carefully. And he never, ever laughed.

One day, Bagheera was edging along the branch of a mango tree leaning out over a river. There was one perfectly ripe mango right at the end of the branch, and Bagheera loved mangoes. The only problem was, the branch was slender, and, when Bagheera moved towards the end of it, it began to creak and bend alarmingly. The last thing Bagheera wanted was to break the branch and go for an unplanned swim in the river. His dignity would never allow such a thing.

So Bagheera, crouched on the middle of the branch, was just coming up with a clever plan, when he heard a "harrumph." He looked down and saw a great big grey bear. "It looks like you could use a hand," said the bear.

"No, thank you," said Bagheera politely. "I prefer to work on my own." But the bear paid him no heed, and began climbing up the tree.

"I'll tell you what," huffed the bear. "I'll just sit at the base of that branch and grab your tail. You can climb out and grab the mango, and I'll keep a hold of you in case the end of the branch breaks off. Then we can share the mango!"

"No, I don't think that's a very good idea," said Bagheera impatiently. "I doubt this branch can hold both of us any – "

*Snap!*

The bear had, of course, ignored Bagheera and climbed out onto the branch. And the branch had, of course, snapped under their combined weight. And now a very wet, very unhappy panther sat in the river next to a very wet, very amused bear.

"Oh, ha-ha-ha-ha!" hooted Baloo (for it was Baloo, of course). "Oh me, oh my, that was an adventure! Oh, come now," he said, seeing how angry Bagheera was, "it's not a total loss, you know." And Baloo held up the broken branch, with that perfect mango still hanging from the end of it.

"I'll tell you what," said the bear, "let's go climb onto that rock and dry off in the sun while we eat this mango. I'm Baloo. What's your name?"

"Bagheera," said the panther, as they climbed up onto the warm, flat rock. And then, almost despite himself, he smiled. And then, very much despite himself, he laughed. And Baloo laughed right along with him.

Disney's
## Lilo & Stitch

# Show-and-tell

"Please?" pleaded Lilo.

"No way, Lilo!" Nani replied.

"He'll be good. I promise!" Lilo said.

"Oh, all right!" Nani said crossly.

Lilo had been pestering her big sister all morning, begging Nani to let her take their pet, Stitch, to dance class for "show-and-tell." Nani was worried it could cause a lot of trouble. The girls her age were not kind to Lilo, who had a lot of trouble fitting in. As a result, Lilo tended to lash out at them and get herself into trouble. And the problem was, her strange pet, Stitch, was just like her. Nani was convinced that the awful-looking creature they picked up at the pound wasn't even a real dog. Just like Lilo, Stitch didn't seem to fit in very well, either. The other dogs at the pound had certainly shunned him.

When they arrived at dance class, Nani gave her little sister a quick hug. "You behave yourselves!" she said.

"You'll behave yourself," Lilo said to Stitch. "I know you will."

Some of the girls sniggered as Lilo and Stitch walked in and sat down.

"All right," said the dance teacher. "What have you brought today, Lilo?"

Lilo stood up. "This is my dog. His name is Stitch. I got him at the pound."

"He sure is ugly!" said Myrtle.

"Now, Myrtle, be nice," the teacher said.

"Can he fetch?" Myrtle asked. She threw a water balloon that she had brought for show-and-tell right at Stitch!

Stitch caught the balloon neatly, then threw it back at Myrtle. "No!" yelled Lilo, and threw herself in front of Myrtle, accidentally knocking the other girl over. The water balloon hit Lilo and broke, sending water flying everywhere!

"Oh, Lilo," said the teacher, "I think it's time for your pet to go home." Lilo picked up Stitch and ran outside.

Lilo sat down at the kerb. Stitch sat down too. "You got us in trouble today," Lilo said to him. "Why did you hit Myrtle with that water balloon?"

Stitch growled.

"Oh, that's right," said Lilo, "you don't *do* fetch. How could I have forgotten?" She looked thoughtful. "How about we play catch, instead? That's almost the same thing as fetch, but there's an important difference. Fetch is something you play with a pet, and catch is something you play with a friend. I think you're more my friend than my pet, Stitch."

Stitch nodded eagerly and held up a ball. Lilo smiled, and the two friends spent a lovely afternoon together playing catch.

**DINOSAUR**

# Jungle Race

Aladar raced through the jungle, sprinting forward on his powerful legs. His heart pounded in his chest. Tree branches and vines swatted his face, but he ignored them.

"Faster, friend!" Zini cried in his ear. Zini was riding on Aladar's back, clinging tightly with his lemur paws. The two were playing Jungle Race, one of their favourite games. With Zini on his back, Aladar ran from one end of Lemur Island to the other as fast as he could.

"Look out!" Zini suddenly cried. But it was too late. Aladar didn't see the thick, rope-like vine across the path. A split second later, he tripped and fell, sending Zini flying through the air.

Aladar went down hard, knocking against a tree trunk. Catching his breath, he blinked and sat up slowly. For a minute everything looked topsy-turvy. Then the familiar jungle path swam slowly into view.

The only thing that didn't swim into view was Zini. Aladar got to his feet and looked around.

"Zini!" he called. "Zini, where are you?"

Aladar stood completely still and listened. But he heard nothing.

Panic began to well up in Aladar's chest. Where was his friend? What if he was badly hurt?

"Zini!" he called again, louder.

Aladar began to search the area, pushing branches and leaves and vines aside. Unlike him, Zini was small. If he didn't search carefully Aladar might overlook him.

Aladar was several feet down the path when Zini zoomed in, swinging on a vine. He landed on a nearby tree branch.

"That was amazing!" Zini cried in excitement. "First I flew through the air like a meteor. Then I grabbed hold of a vine and swung halfway through the jungle. I practically made it all the way to the ocean!"

Aladar gave a big sigh of relief. He was so happy to see his friend! "I was worried about you," he said.

Zini leaped onto Aladar's back and wrapped his long, furry arms around his friend's neck. "Sorry, Aladar. But I couldn't resist the opportunity for a flight like that. I felt like a bird! Let's do it again!" he cried.

Aladar rubbed his head. There was a small bump where he'd hit the tree trunk. Luckily, it didn't hurt too much.

"I think I need a little rest," Aladar said.

Zini let out a disappointed sigh. "Oh, all right," he said.

Aladar grinned. "But maybe we can do it again tomorrow."

"Excellent!" said Zini.

# Geppetto's Gift

One day, Geppetto was in his workshop painting a clock, when he had an idea. "I know what I will do with that pine log I just found," he told his little cat, Figaro. "I will make a splendid puppet!"

He put down the clock and got to work. When he had finished making the puppet, he got out his jars of paint and some fabric. "Now," he said to Figaro, "should my puppet's eyes be blue or green? Should her hair be yellow or brown or black? Should her dress be red or purple?"

Suddenly, Geppetto heard a noise outside. He went to the window and looked out. He saw groups of children on their way home from school. Geppetto watched them skip past, laughing and shouting and swinging their schoolbooks. He sighed sadly. "How I wish I had a child of my own," he said.

Just then, he noticed a little girl walking quietly with her mother. Like the other girls, she carried a schoolbook under her arm. When a group of girls skipped by her, she looked at them shyly.

"That little girl must be new in town. She looks like she could use a friend," Geppetto said. Suddenly, he had an idea.

"Excuse me, young miss," he called from the window. "I wonder if you could lend me a hand?"

The girl hurried over, tugging her mother after her. Why, an invitation to Geppetto's workshop – how grand!

"As you can see, my friend here needs some eyes," Geppetto said, pointing to the puppet. "But I don't know what colour her eyes should be."

The girl thought hard. "Green," she decided.

Geppetto picked up his pot of green paint and painted two big green eyes onto the wooden face.

"Now, what colour do you suppose her hair should be?" Geppetto asked.

"Brown," the little girl said with a smile.

Carefully, Geppetto painted brown curls on the puppet's head. "She'll need a dress," he said next. "What do you think? Red? Green?"

The girl looked down at her own blue dress. "Blue," she told Geppetto.

So Geppetto made a little blue dress for the little puppet. Then he added a smiling red mouth to the puppet's face.

"Now there's just one last thing," Geppetto said. "I'm busy in my shop all day long, and I'm afraid this little lady might be lonely. Could you take care of her for me?"

The girl's face lit up with delight. "Thank you!" she cried. Hugging the puppet in her arms, she carried her out of the workshop.

"Thank you," the girl's mother said. "You know, you'd be a wonderful father."

Gepetto smiled. If only! he thought.

Disney's
# ROBIN HOOD
## Bows and Arrows

"Thanks, Mr Hood!" Skippy Bunny hopped around holding the bow and arrow Robin Hood had just given him. "This is the best birthday present in the world!"

"Want me to show you how to use it?" Robin asked.

"Yes!" cried Skippy.

"See, you put this here." Robin lined the arrow up with the bow. "Then pull here and let it fly." The arrow soared through the air and landed in the centre of a tree trunk across the yard.

"Wow!" Skippy cheered.

"That's nothing!" Robin said. "Here," he said, handing an apple to Skippy. "Put this on the head of that scarecrow."

"Sure thing, Robin!" Skippy hurried off.

As soon as the apple was in place, Robin let his arrow fly. It zipped through the air and hit the apple, neatly slicing it in two.

"Wow!" Skippy cheered again.

Robin picked up one of the apple halves and bit into it. "Nothing to it," he bragged.

"Can I try?" Skippy asked.

"All right," Robin said, placing a new apple on top of the scarecrow's head.

Skippy pulled back the bow. But, when he let go, the arrow landed only a few inches in front of him.

"That's okay," Robin said. "It happens to the best of us!"

"Even you?" Skippy asked.

"Well, not me. I never miss!" Robin boasted as he pulled back his bow. Just as he did, Maid Marian's carriage rolled by. Robin's head turned and his hand slipped off the bow. The arrow fell to the ground a few inches in front of him. Skippy giggled.

"What's so funny?" Robin asked crossly.

"Nothing!" Skippy said, hiding a smile.

"Ahem. As you can see," Robin said, "even the most experienced archers lose their focus occasionally. But it helps if you think of a goal, and keep your goal in mind while you draw the string back, aim and let go. I find that thinking about setting the Sheriff's pants on fire is a wonderful help for me when I'm shooting."

"Okay," said Skippy thoughtfully. "I'll think about how someday, when Prince John isn't taxing us for so much, maybe my family can have enough to eat for dinner every night."

Skippy pulled the string back and back and back, and then he let it go with a *twang*. The arrow sailed through the air and split the apple in two.

"Young rabbit," said Robin, "with archers like you on our side, Prince John won't stand a chance. Soon your family will have plenty to eat for dinner . . . . And, who knows, maybe I'll get to set the Sheriff's pants on fire too!"

DISNEP'S
**TREASURE
PLANET**

# Jim's Vow

It had been a very odd night for Jim Hawkins and his mother. A mysterious alien named Billy Bones had crashed his ship near their inn, the Benbow. Before he died, Bones had given Jim a strange treasure map, thought to be the key to finding the riches of the notorious pirate Captain Flint – the loot of a thousand worlds! Jim had just taken the map out of the dying alien's hands when a gang of murderous alien pirates had arrived at the inn, searching for that very same map.

Jim and his mother had barely had enough time to escape with their friend, Dr Doppler, before the inn had been destroyed.

Once they had arrived at Dr Doppler's house, Jim had somehow convinced his mother to allow him to accompany Dr Doppler on the search for treasure. It would be the adventure of a lifetime! They would set off in the morning.

There was so much to do to prepare for the journey. But for now Jim lay in bed, safe for the moment at Dr Doppler's house, and thought about what he would do if he had all the money in the galaxy.

"Well, for one thing," he said to himself, "I'd buy myself a cool new solar surfer and be the envy of all the other guys." Jim was an accomplished surfer, but he knew his mother wished he worked as hard at his schoolwork as he did at his surfing.

"And for another," he went on, "I'd buy myself a fleet of private robots and program them to do all my chores without ever talking back to me." His mind was racing now, as he thought of more and more possibilities. "And I'd quit school and buy myself the latest-model space navigator and go off exploring the galaxy!"

Jim sat up in bed. He took the treasure map from under his pillow and looked at it closely, thinking hard. Then he replaced it carefully.

"But I don't need any of those things," he said quietly to himself. "If I find any treasure at all on this trip, I'm going to give it to Mum so she can rebuild the inn." He swung his legs over the side of the bed and stood up. He tiptoed to the room where his mother was sleeping. In the dim light, he could see that her face looked pale and lovely. The lines of worry seemed to have smoothed out in her sleep. He bent down and kissed her cool brow.

"I'm going to make you proud of me, Mum," he whispered to her as she slept. "Just you wait and see."

He smiled to himself. He was sure of it.

# Crack the Whip!

Mickey woke up and looked outside. It had snowed last night! "It's a perfect day for ice skating!" he cried. "I'll invite all my friends to come."

On the way, Mickey picked up Goofy, Donald, Daisy, Huey, Dewey, Louie and Minnie. When they got to the pond, everyone laced up their skates and made their way to the ice. It was as smooth as glass. The friends began skating around and around.

"Hey, I have an idea!" shouted Mickey. "Let's play crack the whip!"

Nobody else knew how to play, so Mickey explained the game. "I'll start out as the leader," he said. "We all join hands and form a line. Then we all skate around and around in a big circle. Once we get going, the skater at the end of the line lets go!"

"That sounds like fun!" said Goofy.

"Cool!" cried Huey, Dewey and Louie.

They all joined hands and began skating in a circle. Around and around and around they went. Donald was at the end of the line.

"Okay, Donald, let go!" shouted Mickey. Donald let go and went sailing away.

Around and around and around the rest of the gang went.

"Now, you go, Daisy!" cried Mickey. Daisy let go and went flying away across the ice.

Next went Huey, then Dewey, and finally Louie. Goofy followed them.

Now just Mickey and Minnie were left. Around and around they skated. Then Mickey shouted, "Let go, Minnie!"

Minnie let go and zoomed off with a squeal.

Mickey was having a fine time. Now all alone, he began to spin around and around and around. When he finally came to a stop, it took quite some time for his head to stop spinning. "Wasn't that fun, guys?" he said. "Want to do it again? Guys? Where is everyone?"

Mickey looked around. Where had everyone gone? And then he saw them. Seven pairs of ice skates at the ends of seven pairs of legs were sticking out of seven different snowbanks, kicking away.

"Uh-oh," said Mickey. He dashed over to the side of the pond and, one by one, he pulled all of his friends out of the snow.

"Gee, sorry about that," said Mickey.

Goofy shook his head, and snow flew everywhere. "That was fun!" he said cheerfully. "But I sure could use a cup of . . ."

"Yoo-hoo!" came a cheerful cry. It was Grandma Duck, standing at the edge of the pond. She was carrying a flask filled with hot chocolate!

"Hooray!" cried all the friends.

# Palindrome-mania!

"Hey, Atta," Flik said. "Did you know that your name is a palindrome?"

Atta gave him a strange look. "What's a palindrome?" she asked.

"It's a word that reads the same forwards and backwards," Flik replied. "Spelled forwards, your name is A-T-T-A. Spelled backwards, your name is also A-T-T-A. See?"

"Oh," Atta said. "That's neat. I've never heard of palindromes before."

"Really?" said Flik. "I love them. There are other names that are palindromes, like *Bob*."

"Or *Lil*?" tried Atta.

"Right!" said Flik. "And *Otto*."

"And *Nan*!" added Atta. "This is fun!"

"What's fun?" said Dot, who had just run over to them.

"Thinking of palindromes," Atta replied.

"Huh?" said Dot.

"Exactly!" said Flik. "*Huh* is a palindrome!" Together, Flik and Atta explained to Dot what a palindrome was.

"Oh!" said Dot. "Wait! Let me see if I can think of another one." Dot looked around, hoping that something she saw would spark an idea. She spotted her mother, the Queen, off in the distance, lounging in the shade.

"*Mum!*" cried Dot. "That's one, isn't it?"

"Not bad," said Atta with a wink, "for a *tot* like you!" Atta giggled, pleased that she had got another palindrome into her sentence.

"Oh, yeah?" replied Dot with a mischievous grin. "Well, you ain't seen nothin' yet, *sis!*"

Taking turns, Dot and Atta challenged one another to think of more and more palindromes. Dot came up with *eye*, *pop* and *toot*. Atta countered with *gag*, *noon*, *did* and *redder*.

"Yes," Flik interjected, "*redder* is a nice, long one! It's harder to think of palindromes that have more than four letters. Believe me, I've spent hours on that. But there's always *Aidemedia* – that's a type of bird, you know. And *Allenella*, of course, which is a category of mollusc . . . ." Flik went on to list a longer palindrome for just about every letter of the alphabet – most of them sciencey words that Atta and Dot had never heard before. As he droned on and on and on, Dot and Atta looked at each other and rolled their eyes. Now they were both thinking of the same word, and it wasn't a palindrome: B-O-R-I-N-G.

When Flik had finally finished with his list, he looked up at Dot and Atta with a self-satisfied smile. Each of them had a palindrome ready.

"*Wow*," said Atta flatly, sounding more bored than impressed.

"*Zzz*," snored Dot, who had drifted off somewhere between *V* and *W*.

# Rolly's Midnight Snack

"Time for bed!" called Pongo.

"Aw, Dad," complained Patch, "we're not tired!"

"No arguments," said Pongo. "Little puppies need their rest."

With a sigh, Patch joined the line of puppies climbing the staircase.

"I'm hungry," Rolly complained as the puppies settled down for the night.

"You're always hungry," said Patch.

"And you always want to stay awake and have adventures," said Rolly.

Patch sighed. "Too bad we never get what we want."

Hours later, Rolly felt a tap on his shoulder. "Is it morning?" he asked with a yawn.

"No," said Patch. "It's midnight. Wanna explore? I'll get you a snack."

"A snack!" cried Rolly excitedly.

"Shhhhh!" said Patch. "Come on."

Rolly followed Patch to the kitchen.

Patch nodded towards the table. "After dinner, I saw Nanny put some juicy bones up there. She's saving them for tomorrow's soup."

"Soup!" cried Rolly. "What a waste! Bones are for chewing on!"

So, Patch and Rolly came up with a plan.

First, Patch climbed onto Rolly's shoulders to reach the table.

Everything went fine until Patch threw

down the first bone and it landed in the dustbin. Rolly took off after it and leaped inside!

Rolly was stuck. Patch tried hard not to panic. He thought and thought until he came up with another plan – a Rescue Rolly Plan!

Patch went upstairs and woke Lucky and Pepper. The two puppies followed Patch into the kitchen. Then Patch found his father's long lead and tossed one end into the dustbin.

"Take hold of the leash!" Patch told Rolly.

"Okay," said Rolly.

Patch turned to the other puppies and said, "Now, let's all pull on this end of the leash, on the count of three."

The three puppies pulled. The dustbin fell over and Rolly tumbled out onto the kitchen floor.

"Thanks!" said Rolly.

The puppies licked their brother, and they all returned to bed.

Before Rolly drifted off to sleep, he whispered to Patch, "Guess you finally got your adventure."

"Yeah," said Patch. "But I'm sorry you didn't get your snack."

"Sure, I did," said Rolly. "While I was waiting for you to rescue me, what do you think I was doing? I was eating that juicy bone. And, boy, was it good!"

# Groundhog Day

Winnie the Pooh pounded on Piglet's front door. "Wake up! Wake up!" he called to his friend. "Today is Groundhog Day!"

Piglet dressed quickly and, moments later, the two friends were hurrying to the homes of their other friends who lived in the Hundred-Acre Wood. "Today is Groundhog Day!" shouted Pooh and Piglet together as they roused Tigger, Rabbit, Owl, Eeyore, Kanga and Roo. Then the whole group proceeded to Christopher Robin's house to wake *him* as well.

But where are we going to find a groundhog? wondered Piglet. Soon, they arrived at the Thoughtful Spot, and everyone sat down to wait.

"Um, exactly what is it that we are waiting for?" asked Piglet after a few moments.

"Why, groundhogs, of course!" said Pooh.

"But what is it that is supposed to happen on Groundhog Day?" Piglet persisted.

Being a bear of little brain, Pooh was unsure how to answer. He looked expectantly at Christopher Robin.

"There is an old tradition," Christopher Robin began, "that says that 2 February is the day that the groundhog comes out of his hole after a long winter sleep, to look for his shadow. If he sees it, he decides that there will be six more weeks of winter and returns to his hole. If he doesn't see it, he decides that spring will soon be here, and stays above ground."

"I see," said Pooh, who, truth be told, did not really see at all.

A few more moments went by, and then Rabbit cleared his throat. "Pooh," he said. "Do you expect that the groundhog will take much longer to appear?"

"Oh!" Pooh replied, looking at his friends. "I haven't got the faintest idea how long it will take to see a groundhog, as I don't know any groundhogs personally."

This news came as a bit of a shock to the group. But, all of a sudden, Gopher's head popped up from the ground in front of them.

"Aha!" shouted Pooh triumphantly.

"It's only Gopher," said Rabbit.

"I believe Gopher will do quite nicely today," said Christopher Robin. "Gopher, do you or do you not see your shadow?"

Gopher blinked in the sudden sunshine, then looked down at the ground. "I sssssay," he said. "I ssssupose I do ssseee my ssshadow."

"Well, that's that, then," said Christopher Robin. "Six more weeks of winter. Thank you very much, Gopher."

"You're welcome," replied Gopher, who seemed a bit confused by the whole thing. "Happy ssspring, everyone!"

# Disney's Aladdin

# Pesky Princes

Jasmine's father, the Sultan, was growing impatient. "My dearest daughter," he said pleadingly, "the law states that you should be married before your 16th birthday, and that is coming up soon. Must you be so picky? There are many princes who would love to marry you."

Jasmine sighed. "So far they've all been so . . . pompous," she said. "But I promise to try, Father."

The very next day, Prince Sultana arrived, carried on a litter and accompanied by a huge group of camels, trumpeters and servants. He bowed down low before Jasmine. "I know you will be pleased to hear that I have selected you as my bride," he said in a tone Jasmine didn't like one bit. "Shall we discuss our wedding?"

Jasmine tried to hide her dislike. "I was just about to take my pet for a little walk around the palace. He needs his exercise, you see. Why don't we discuss it while we walk him?"

The Prince readily agreed.

With a sly smile, Jasmine whistled. Out bounded her pet tiger, Rajah. When he gave a snarl of welcome, the Prince ran away.

"Well, he didn't last long," said Jasmine happily, as she gave Rajah a big hug. "Nice work, Rajah."

The next day, another suitor arrived, this time with an even bigger group of servants in tow. "Announcing . . . Prince Habibi!" the footman called out, as the procession arrived.

Jasmine poked her head out of her bedroom window and called down, "Hi! Sorry, I can't come down. The, uh, stairs are being polished. Do you mind taking my laundry to the royal cleaners? Catch!"

Prince Habibi stood below the tower, arms outstretched. *Boom!* A big laundry bag knocked him flat. "Harumph!" he cried, and off he went.

The next day, Prince Baklava arrived. "The Princess is at the royal pond, sire," the footman said. Prince Baklava headed there, with three servants holding up his cape so that it wouldn't get muddy. Upon arriving, he saw Jasmine, reading a book on a little island in the middle of the pond. All around her, huge alligators waited in the water, looking hungry.

"Hello!" Jasmine called to him. "Would you mind coming out to fetch me?"

Prince Baklava stared at Jasmine and then at the alligators. With a shriek of terror, he turned and ran as his servants jogged behind him, still holding up his cape.

Jasmine giggled and stood up. Then the Princess stepped daintily across the pond on the backs of the alligators. "Thanks, guys," she said with a wink as she headed back to the palace.

# Disney's MULAN

## Soup's On!

Mulan stood in the kitchen, moodily stirring a pot of soup for supper. Grandmother Fa sat at the table, sorting through grains of rice. Neither one of them spoke. They were both lost in thought at the recent news they had received: Mulan's father, Fa Zhou, had been ordered to join the Chinese army in order to help protect the Emperor from the invading Huns. One male out of every household was expected to report for duty. As Mulan had no brother, it was her father's duty to join. But though her father had been a great warrior in his day, Mulan knew that he was no longer young, and was not strong enough to withstand any more battles. Mulan was distraught, for she knew that if her father joined the army and went into battle, he would surely die.

"Why must my father fight?" Mulan asked her grandmother suddenly. "He is but one man, and the Emperor would never know the difference if he didn't join. Yet what a difference to our family it would be if he were to die!" She sighed heavily.

Her grandmother also sighed and continued to sort the rice silently for a few moments. Then she stopped and turned towards Mulan. "You are partly correct. One grain of rice, such as this one that I have in my hand, is small and insignificant." Then she held out her hand and tipped the grain into the large bowl of rice she had been sorting. "Yet together, you know, all the grains of rice in this bowl could feed many people. The Emperor needs an army of many, many people in order to defeat the invaders."

Mulan shook her head miserably, afraid that if she spoke she would cry. She was young and stubborn, and it was difficult for her to accept the sacrifice that her father was expected to make.

Grandmother Fa was just as unhappy as Mulan. But the older woman realized that it was useless to protest against some things. She stood up and walked silently out of the kitchen.

Mulan continued to stir the soup, even though it didn't need stirring. Next to the pot sat a small bowl, which contained a peppery red spice. She picked up the small bowl and looked at it thoughtfully. "One grain of rice is small and insignificant," she said to herself. "And yet, a tiny pinch of the spice from this little bowl could change the flavour of this whole pot of soup. Perhaps," she went on, "one person *can* make a difference, if she follows her heart."

Mulan dumped the whole bowl of spice into the pot, and smiled.

"Soup's on!" she cried.

# Hide-and-seek

For quite a while, Dumbo was the newest baby in the circus. But then, one day, the stork arrived with a brand-new delivery – a baby girl giraffe.

"You know, Dumbo," said his friend, Timothy Q. Mouse, "I think we should ask that new baby to play with us."

Dumbo nodded. He loved making new friends!

So together, Timothy and Dumbo made their way to the giraffes' pen.

"Hello, Mrs Giraffe," Timothy said. "Can your lovely new baby come out and play?"

Dumbo gave Mrs Giraffe a big, hopeful smile. "Well . . . I suppose so," she said.

She gave her baby a kiss, and sent her off in the care of Timothy Mouse – and Dumbo.

"Okay, kids," said Timothy, standing before the two, "what do you feel like playing?"

Dumbo and the baby giraffe stared back at him blankly.

"Hmm . . . I see," said Timothy. "You don't know that many games. May I suggest hide-and-seek?"

Dumbo and the giraffe nodded happily, as Timothy closed his eyes and counted.

"Ready or not," he said finally, opening his eyes, "here I – hang on! Don't you guys know you're supposed to hide?"

No, actually, they did not.

"Okay," Timothy sighed. "Let's take it from the top. When I close my eyes, you guys hide. You find a place where you can't see me and I can't see you. Like this . . ." Timothy ducked behind a popcorn tub. "Get it?"

Dumbo and the giraffe slowly nodded.

"Okay then, let's try this again. One, two, three . . ." Timothy counted to 20, then opened his eyes. "No, no, no!" he groaned. "You can't hide behind the popcorn. You're too big. Let's try this one more time."

Again, he closed his eyes and counted. Then, very slowly, he opened them and looked around. "Much better!" he said, surprised. Of course, it didn't take him long to find Dumbo's wide body behind a narrow tent pole, or the giraffe's tall neck sticking up from behind the clowns' trunk. But they were getting closer!

"This time, guys, try to find a place for your whole body to hide," Timothy said.

So, Dumbo and the giraffe waited for Timothy to close his eyes once more, then they quietly sneaked behind the pole and trunk again. This time, the tall, skinny giraffe hid behind the tall, skinny pole. And short, wide Dumbo hid behind the short, wide trunk. And do you know what? They were hidden so well, Timothy Q. Mouse may still be looking for them to this very day!

![Disney · PIXAR FINDING NEMO]

# The Induction

Nemo still had a satisfied smile on his face from the previous night's induction ceremony. I'm part of the club! he thought.

"So, Shark Bait, what did you think of that ceremony last night?" Gill asked.

"It was the best!" Nemo exclaimed.

"If only we could get Flo to be part of the ceremony," Deb mused. "But she never seems to want to come out at night."

"So, kid, what was your favourite part?" Jacques wanted to know.

"I think my favourite part was swimming to the top of Mount Wanna ... wannaha ... ha ..." Nemo tried unsuccessfully to pronounce it.

"Wannahockaloogie," Bloat said.

"Yeah," Peach reminisced. "I have a soft spot for my first climb too."

"I wonder," Nemo said. "Who came up with that name?"

Bubbles pointed at Gurgle, who pointed at Bloat, who pointed at Peach, who pointed at Deb, who pointed at Flo.

Deb shrugged. "I guess we came up with it together," she said.

"Why do they call it the Ring of Fire if there's no fire?" Nemo asked.

"Well, you see, it's like this – I don't know," Peach had to admit.

"But who made it up, then?" Nemo asked, confused. "Didn't you guys *invent* the ceremony?"

"I think Bubbles came up with the Ring of Fire," Gurgle offered.

"Aren't they beautiful?" Bubbles mused.

"I find it very unsanitary to swim through others' bubbles," Gurgle complained. "Which is why I came up with the chanting part of the ceremony. It's very cleansing both for the body and the mind, and circulates carbon dioxide through the gills."

"That makes sense," Nemo agreed, although it really didn't.

"Don't forget about the kelp fronds," Peach piped up.

"Oh, there's no big secret there," Deb confided. "I just like giving a good whack with the old kelp fronds every now and then." And she demonstrated by whacking Bloat, who immediately began to swell up.

"Was that really necessary?" Bloat asked as he floated away.

"What can I do in the next ceremony?" Nemo asked eagerly.

"Hopefully, we won't have another one. Not if we break out of here first, Shark Bait," Gill answered.

"Well, you never know," Deb said forlornly. "Maybe Flo will come around."

Everyone rolled their eyes, including Nemo.

Disney's
# BROTHER BEAR
# And They're Off!

"What are you doing, eh?"

Kenai looked up to see Rutt and Tuke standing and staring in disbelief. The two goofy moose were trying to determine just what Koda, the young bear cub who was travelling with Kenai, was doing.

"Koda is watching those centipedes," Kenai replied.

Koda looked up. "They're racing," he said. Rutt looked surprised. "Gee, I didn't think centipedes knew how to race."

"Everybody knows how to race," Tuke told Rutt. "Even a hoof-for-brains like you."

"That's a great idea!" Koda's eyes sparkled. "You guys should have a race!"

"It'll be great, eh," Rutt said, stretching his gangly legs. "The Great Northern Moose Race of – er – what year is it, Tuke?"

"How should I know?" Tuke replied.

"Guys!" Koda shouted. "Come on, focus. Ready – set – go!"

Both moose stood still, staring at him. "Where are we going?" Rutt asked.

"You're just supposed to go!" Koda cried. "You're racing, remember?"

"Oh, gee, that's right." Tuke stepped forward. "Come on, Rutt. Keep up."

"No! You're not supposed to tell him to keep up!" Koda cried. "You're supposed to run away from him! How else are you going to win?"

So Tuke took off at a gallop. Rutt just stood there.

"Well?" Kenai said. "Aren't you going to run after him?"

"Run after him? Why would I do that, eh?" The moose looked confused.

Koda growled with frustration. "Because that's what you do in a race!"

"Oh!" Rutt nodded. Then he ambled off after Tuke.

The two bears glanced at each other. "Even the centipedes could beat those two," Koda whispered to Kenai.

Kenai laughed. "Let's follow them."

First they came upon Tuke, who had stopped to eat twigs. Then they found Rutt rolling in the mud. Then Tuke caught up with Rutt, and started gossiping about some squirrels they knew.

Finally the bears gave up. "Maybe some animals just aren't meant to race," Koda said sadly.

Kenai could tell the little bear was disappointed. "You may be right," he said. "But I have an idea."

"What?" Koda asked.

Kenai grinned. "Race you to the river!" he cried. He took off with Koda chasing him happily, laughing all the way.

# Tag!

Early one morning, Simba woke up ready to find Nala and continue their game of Tag. The night before, when their mothers had made them stop ("Time for bed, Simba!" "Time for bed, Nala!"), Simba had been It – which is a terrible way to go to bed! – and he was eager to tag Nala and make *her* It as soon as possible. But, when he arrived at the pride's meeting place, everyone, it seemed, was there except for Nala.

"Where's Nala?" he asked his mother.

"Oh, I heard her mother say she wasn't feeling well," she replied. "So they're staying in the cave and resting until she's better."

"But she has to come out," protested Simba. "I'm It and I have to tag somebody!"

His mother smiled. "I'm afraid you'll just have to wait, little Simba," she said.

"But that's so boring!" Simba groaned.

"You can play by yourself, Simba," she reminded him.

"Aw, all right." Simba sighed. First, he tried hunting grasshoppers. But they jumped so high and so far – and so fast! – he soon grew tired and frustrated.

Then he tried climbing trees. But the birds didn't much like a lion cub messing around among their branches and shooed him away.

Finally, he tried just lying down and finding pictures in the clouds. But that was Nala's favourite game, and it made him miss her.

He rolled over and swatted a bright wildflower with his paw. "Tag, you're It," he said half-heartedly. Then, suddenly, an idea popped into his head. What if he picked some wildflowers and took them to his sick friend? It might even make her feel better!

With newfound energy, Simba picked as many flowers as he could carry in his mouth and made his way back to the pride's cave.

"Dees ah fur Nana," he said, dropping the flowers at Nala's mother's feet. "These are for Nala," he repeated. "I hope she feels better really soon."

"Oh, thank you, Simba," the lioness said. "But why don't you give them to her yourself? She seems to be feeling much better. Nala!" she called. And out came Simba's friend, smiling and looking very glad to see him.

She sniffed at the pretty flowers. "Are these for me? Gee, thanks, Simba." Then she turned to her mother. "Can I go out and play with Simba now, Mama?"

"I don't see why not," said her mother.

"Grrreat!" said Nala.

"Yeah, grrreat!" said Simba. Then he reached out and gently tapped her with his paw. "Tag! You're It!"

# Dear Sisters

"I had the strangest dream," Cinderella told her mouse friends one morning while she was getting ready for another day of drudgery. "My Fairy Godmother sprinkled happy dust over Anastasia and Drizella, and they were so nice to me."

"But that was only a dream," Jaq warned her.

"I know," Cinderella told him, "but it was so nice, that I think I'll try to pretend that it really happened. Whenever they're horrid to me, I'll pretend they actually said something sweet and kind."

"They don't seem so sweet and kind to me," Jaq told Gus as the three went downstairs. Gus nodded in agreement.

"Wash my dresses." Drizella threw her laundry at Cinderella.

"And polish my shoes." Anastasia opened her wardrobe door. "All of them."

"Do the dishes!"

"And mop the floor!"

"Draw the curtains!"

"And clean the rugs!"

"Right away, sisters!" Cinderella sang out, as sweet as you please. "Thank you!"

All day long, Drizella and Anastasia barked orders at Cinderella. But, no matter what they asked her to do, Cinderella always sang back, "Right away, sisters!" or "You're too kind!"

Finally, Anastasia pulled Drizella aside.

"No matter what we tell Cinderella to do, she stays happy," Anastasia said. "She acts like we're doing her a favour. It's making me nervous!"

"Do you think she's gone mad?" Drizella asked. Anastasia looked worried. "She could be! Who knows just what she's capable of!"

Just then, Cinderella walked in. She stopped, surprised to see her stepsisters looking at her as though she were crazy.

"Why, my dear sisters, whatever can be the matter? I do hope you're not ill," she said.

"*D-d-d-dear* sisters?" quavered Anastasia. "You called us your *dear* sisters?" She and Drizella edged towards the door.

"Of course," said Cinderella. "I adore you both. I'm the luckiest girl in the world to have such kind, caring siblings."

That did it. Convinced that Cinderella had lost her mind, the two stepsisters turned and ran. Cinderella listened as her sisters' doors slammed shut. Then she smiled at Gus and Jaq, who had been watching the whole time.

"They may not actually be caring or good-natured," Cinderella said to the mice, "but they'll be too frightened to come out of their rooms for at least a few hours. Who's up for a game of hide-and-seek while we've got the run of the house?"

The mice squeaked happily, and the friends spent a lovely afternoon together while Anastasia and Drizella cowered under their beds.

Disney·PIXAR
## MONSTERS, INC.

# Relaxopolis

It was another cold blustery day in Monstropolis. Sulley and Mike were on their way to work. Mike sighed heavily.

"What's wrong, little buddy?" asked Sulley.

"I'm sick and tired of winter!" Mike replied. "It's cold, it's windy and it gets dark early." He thought for a moment. "Sulley, I think I have the winter blues!"

"Sure sounds like it," said Sulley. "Only a month or so to go, though."

Mike sighed again. A month or two more of winter sounded like an eternity! But a big smile spread across his face when he looked up and saw an advertising board. On it was a big pink monster sitting in a lounge chair on the beach, wearing sunglasses and sipping what looked like an ice-cold booberry slushie. In big letters it said: BEAT THOSE WINTER BLUES IN RELAXOPOLIS!

Mike stopped in his tracks and grabbed Sulley's furry arm. He pointed at the sign, too excited to say a word.

"That's a great idea!" Sulley cheered. "A week on a tropical island is just what we need!"

As soon as he and Sulley got to work, Mike filled in their holiday forms. They would be on their way to Relaxopolis first thing Saturday morning!

When they arrived, they didn't even unpack their bags. They went right to the beach where they each ordered an ice-cold booberry slushie.

As they lay down on their deck chairs on the sunniest part of the beach, Mike said, "This is the life!"

"You bet," said Sulley. "Do you think you need some of this Monster Tropic sunscream? You'd better be careful. You don't want to get too much sun on your first day!"

"I'll just soak up the rays for a little while first," said Mike happily. "My winter blues are just melting away." He slipped a big mirrored sunglass over his eye and put his arms behind his head. This was paradise!

After a while Sulley got bored with sunbathing and decided to go for a swim. Then he joined in a game of beach monsterball. Then he let some little monsters bury him in the sand up to his neck. A couple of hours later, he returned to the deck chairs, where Mike was sound asleep. Sulley took a closer look. His little green friend had not changed position since Sulley had left. Mike had burned himself in the sun!

Sulley covered Mike with a towel and ran over to get him a refreshing booberry slushie. When he returned to the deck chairs, Mike was just waking up.

"Hey, little buddy," said Sulley. "Guess you chased those winter blues away, huh?"

Mike just looked at Sulley sleepily.

"You aren't blue any more," Sully explained. "Now you're bright red!"

*Disney's* Beauty AND THE BEAST

# Snow Day

One cold February day, Belle sat on the windowsill in her room in the dreary castle, sad and homesick, watching the snowflakes swirl outside. She had agreed to remain in the Beast's enchanted castle in exchange for her father's freedom. How she missed her little home and her dear father! The Beast tried to be kind to her, but he was gruff and had such a terrible temper.

Suddenly, she jumped. The Beast had appeared, trudging through the snow beneath her window. She thought she saw him glance quickly up at her, but she wasn't certain. "What on earth is he doing?" she asked out loud. She watched him scoop up an armful of snow and try to form it into a ball, but it fell apart, spraying snow right in his face. Belle giggled to herself. "Why, I think he is trying to build a snowman!" she cried. "But he has no idea how to begin!"

Next, the Beast made a smaller snowball. This one managed to hold together, and he began pushing it around the courtyard. It grew bigger and bigger. Soon it was so big even the strong Beast could hardly move it. Belle watched him struggle to push it, and then suddenly fall headlong over the top of it, his enormous feet kicking vainly in the air. At this, Belle let out a peal of silvery laughter. It was the first time she had laughed since she had arrived in this dreary old castle.

A few of the servants heard Belle's laughter and ventured cautiously into the hallway outside her room. They, too, were under the enchantment and dearly wanted their master and this beautiful girl to fall in love, as that was the only way to break the spell.

"Do you suppose she is starting to like him?" Mrs Potts whispered to Lumiere.

"I don't know!" he whispered back. "I hardly dare to hope! But just in case, I must arrange for another romantic dinner for two this evening!" He hurried in the direction of the kitchen, already thinking about foie gras, flambé, soufflé and crème brûlée.

Belle watched the Beast slowly climb to his feet. Scowling, he began to roll another snowball. This time, he slipped on some ice and fell flat on his back.

With another laugh of delight, Belle jumped to her feet and threw on her cloak. She raced out of her room, and hurried outside to join the Beast in the snow. She even showed the snowy beast how to make a snow angel.

The servants all ran to the window to watch the two new friends play in the snow together. Maybe, just maybe, something good was about to happen!

Walt Disney's
# Lady and the TRAMP
# A Lady's Touch

Late one night, Lady's ears perked up and her eyes flew open with a start. The baby was crying! Lady had grown to love the new baby in the house, and she was very protective of him. If he was crying, she was going to find out why. She climbed out of her basket, pushed open the swinging door with her nose and tiptoed up the front stairs.

Meanwhile, Jim Dear and Darling were trying to calm the baby. "Oh, Jim, I just don't know what's the matter with him!" said Darling. She was holding the baby in her arms, trying to rock him and soothe him, but his little face was a deep red and covered with tears. Jim Dear sat groggily at the edge of the bed and looked at his wife helplessly.

"Well, we know he isn't hungry," said Jim Dear, "since we've just given him a bottle." He massaged his temples as though they hurt. Then he noticed Lady, who had walked tentatively into the bedroom. "Hello, Lady," he said to her.

Lady took a few steps closer to the cradle, where Darling was laying the baby down. His little fists were closed tight, and his shrieks had turned to loud sobs.

"We just don't know what's the matter with the little guy," Jim Dear said wearily to Lady. "We've fed him and changed him, and I've sung him every lullaby I know. Maybe you can figure out what's bothering him!"

That was all the invitation Lady needed. She jumped up onto the bed and peered into the cradle. The baby's eyes were squeezed shut and his cheeks were wet with tears. His little legs were kicking the covers. Lady reached in and tugged at the covers to smooth them out. The baby opened his eyes and looked at Lady. His cries dropped to a whimper, and he reached out to touch her. His tiny hand grabbed hold of her ear and tugged. Lady winced but held still. With her chin, she began to rock the cradle and, with her furry tail, she beat a rhythmic *thump, thump, thump* on the bedcover.

"Ga!" said the baby as he broke into a gummy smile, his big blue eyes looking like wet forget-me-nots. Still holding Lady's ear, the baby giggled.

"Oh, look, Jim Dear!" cried Darling delightedly. "Lady has got him to stop crying!"

"I just don't know what we'd do without you, Lady!" Jim Dear said gratefully.

*Rock, rock, rock* went the cradle. *Thump, thump, thump* went Lady's tail. Soon the baby's eyelids grew heavy, and then his eyes closed. Tears still streaking his little round cheeks, he relaxed his grip on Lady's ear, smiled and fell asleep.

# Disney's HERCULES

## A Growing Boy

The mortal parents of Hercules, Amphitryon and Alcmene, had known he was a special child from the moment they had found him, alone and crying in the wilderness, wearing a medal that bore the symbol of the gods. But, as the baby grew, they were surprised to see Hercules' superhuman strength grow stronger and stronger with each passing day. He could tie poisonous snakes into knots and lift grown-ups high into the air.

"Ma," said Hercules, one day when he was five years old, "I'm bored."

So Alcmene handed Hercules a clay spinning top. With one mighty spin, Hercules launched the top into the air. It whizzed around the room, smashing several jugs. Alcmene ducked as the top flew over her head and crashed into a wall, breaking into several pieces.

"Sorry, Ma," said Hercules, wincing.

"That's all right, Hercules," Alcmene replied. "It was an accident. But perhaps you should play outside from now on."

The next day, Alcmene gave Hercules some marbles to play with. She showed him how to use his thumb to shoot one marble at another.

Hercules shot tentatively at first. But soon he grew more confident. Lining up a shot, he flicked his thumb as hard as he could. The marble flew out of his hand, sending the target marble rocketing towards the horizon.

Luckily, the nearest neighbours lived a few miles away. But, one by one, all of Hercules' marbles were lost this way.

"Amphitryon, I simply don't know what to do with Hercules," Alcmene said to her husband the next day. "He's too strong for ordinary toys. And, if he plays with the other children, I worry he may hurt them without meaning to."

"Hmm," Amphitryon replied. "Yes, the boy is stronger than he realizes. Why, I do believe he's got to be as strong as an ox!"

That gave Amphitryon an idea. That afternoon, he walked to the marketplace. When he returned to the farm, he was leading an ox by a rope.

"Hercules," he said, leading the ox over to his son, "come meet your new playmate." Amphitryon took the rope lead from around the ox's neck. He handed one end of the rope to Hercules. He offered the other end to the ox, who took it between his teeth.

Within seconds, the two had fallen into a friendly game of tug-of-war.

Hercules laughed.

The ox twitched his tail playfully. Hercules' parents looked on and smiled.

"That's our boy," Alcmene said proudly.

### Walt Disney's
# Snow White
### and the Seven Dwarfs

# Happy Valentine's Day

"Whatcha doin', Doc?" Happy asked.

Doc was hard at work carving a heart out of a piece of wood. "I'm making a present for Snow White," he replied.

"A present for Snow White?" Happy exclaimed. "Oh, dear! Did I miss her birthday?"

"No, silly," Doc said. "It's Valentine's Day."

"Valentine's Day?" Happy turned to Dopey. "Have you ever heard of Valentine's Day?"

Dopey shook his head.

Doc cleared his throat. "Valentine's Day," he began, "is a very special tradition that gives people the opportunity to let loved ones know how important they are."

"I'm giving Snow White these handkerchiefs," Sneezy said as he sneezed into one of them. "Well, maybe not *this* one."

"That's very thoughtful," Doc answered. "I'm sure she'll be able to use them."

"If he has any left," Grumpy moaned.

Then Bashful shyly held out a paper flower he had made.

"Wonderful! And you?" Doc asked Dopey.

Dopey held up a paper aeroplane he'd just made for Snow White.

"You know what I'm going to do? I'm going to juggle for Snow White for Valentine's Day," Happy offered.

"She'll love that!" Doc said.

Sleepy yawned as he held up a pretty card he made.

"And you?" Doc asked Grumpy.

"Well, all right," Grumpy confessed. "I wrote Snow White a poem."

"A poem! Really? Can we hear it?" Doc asked.

"Don't push your luck!" Grumpy snapped.

Just then, the cottage door opened. Snow White had arrived!

"Happy Valentine's Day!" the Seven Dwarfs sang, each holding up his gift for Snow White to see.

"What a wonderful surprise!" Snow White exclaimed. She was holding a bundle of valentines – pretty red and pink hearts on lacy doilies – and handed them out to the Seven Dwarfs, placing a kiss on each of their cheeks. The Seven Dwarfs all thought they were the most beautiful valentines they had ever seen. Even Grumpy was pleased. Bashful blushed an especially bright shade of red as Snow White kissed him on the cheek, and Sleepy started yawning before Snow White could hand him his card. Then Sneezy sneezed, blowing his card into the air. Happy laughed, and Dopey smiled too.

If you asked any of them, he'd tell you it was the best Valentine's Day ever!

## Walt Disney's
# Peter Pan

# Peter Pan's Visit

John and Michael Darling sat, silent and still, on Michael's bed, listening intently as their big sister, Wendy, told them yet another story about their favourite hero, Peter Pan.

Meanwhile, their dog and nursemaid, Nana, dozed peacefully under the open window of the Darling nursery.

". . . And then," Wendy was saying, "with a quick slash of his sword, Peter Pan cut the evil Captain Hook's hand right off!"

Michael and John gasped. Nana started too, and jumped to her feet. But Nana wasn't alarmed by Wendy's story. She had heard a strange noise coming from just outside the window. Nana faced the window, listening carefully for the sound to repeat itself.

There it was again!

Unnoticed by the children, who were caught up in their story, Nana scurried over to the window and poked her head outside.

And there, just to one side of the window and crouched on a narrow ledge, was a red-headed boy dressed in green from head to toe.

Nana froze, then leaned towards the boy slowly, growling a low warning growl.

"There, there, Nana," the boy whispered softly. "Please, don't bark."

At the sound of her name, Nana froze again, then tilted her head to one side, as if trying to figure something out.

"You're wondering how I know your name," the boy whispered. "Well, I know a lot about you and Wendy and John and Michael. You see, I've been coming here, now and again, for quite a while to listen to Wendy's stories – stories about me!" He stood up straight and puffed his chest out proudly. "I'm Peter Pan, you know!"

Now, Nana was not a mean dog. But there was one thing – well, three things, really – that she was very protective of, and they were the three children inside that nursery. Nana knew it was up to her to make sure they were safe and sound. She also knew that strange boys crouching outside the nursery window – Peter Pan or not – were not to be tolerated.

And so, with another low growl, Nana suddenly lunged further out of the window and snapped her teeth at Peter Pan. The boy flew out of the way just in time, but his shadow was not quite so fast. It struggled to get loose, but it was held tight in Nana's mouth!

Startled, Peter Pan flew off into the darkness and began his journey home to Never Land. But he knew he had to get his shadow back. He would have to return to the Darling nursery – and soon! And *this* time, he would need to go inside....

# Fish-in-the-box

"Ariel?" Flounder called out timidly, poking his head inside Ariel's secret grotto. Ariel had told Flounder to meet her there, but she hadn't arrived yet. "I guess I'll wait for her inside," Flounder said to himself. He swam around slowly, gazing at Ariel's collection of things from the human world. The rock ledges were filled with various objects the Little Mermaid had found in sunken ships and up at the surface – everything from a clock to a music box to a knight's helmet. It was Ariel's favourite place.

But, without Ariel there, Flounder found the place lonely . . . and quiet . . . and . . . creepy.

"Yikes!" Flounder screamed, startled by the sudden appearance of another fish as he swam past a piece of a broken mirror. When he realized it was just his own reflection, Flounder breathed a sigh of relief. "Oh, Flounder, don't be such a guppy," he told himself, repeating the line Ariel always used on him.

Flounder swam past one object that he had never noticed before – a square metal box with a handle on one side.

"I wonder what that thing does," said Flounder, staring at the handle. After a few moments' hesitation, Flounder summoned his courage. By flapping his tail fin and pushing the handle with his nose, he managed to turn it around once . . . twice . . . three times. Nothing happened. Flounder was halfway into the fourth turn when –

*Boing!*

The latch to the top of the jack-in-the-box released and the spring-loaded jester inside popped out of the box and lunged at Flounder.

"Ahhhhhhhhhhhh!" Flounder screamed as he raced backwards away from the jack-in-the-box and collided with the lid of an open treasure chest. The force of the collision caused the lid of the chest to slam shut, trapping Flounder inside.

Moments later, Ariel swam through the door of the secret grotto.

"Flounder?" she called. "Are you here yet?"

From inside the chest, Flounder yelled to Ariel. *"Mm-nn-eer!"* came the muffled cry.

Ariel followed the sound of his voice and swam over to the chest. Lifting the lid, she found her friend inside. "What are you doing in there?" Ariel asked with a giggle.

Thinking quickly, Flounder replied, "I'm about to do my imitation of that thing." He pointed at the jack-in-the-box. Then Flounder sprang suddenly out of the chest, raced out of the door . . . and kept on swimming.

He'd had enough of Ariel's secret grotto for one day!

# Albatross Taxi Service

Orville the albatross was feeling low. His maintenance job at the Central Park Zoo (hours: 9–3; duties: eating all the popcorn, pretzels and half-finished hot dogs that the little children dropped) had just ended for the season. What would he do next?

Orville sighed and leaned against a lamppost at the busy junction of 45th and Broadway. He liked to watch the cars zoom back and forth. Just then there was a tap on his wing. He looked down to see an elderly mouse couple. "Excuse me, sonny," said the grandfather mouse. "Would it be possible for you to help us cross this busy street?"

Orville looked confused. "You want me to go in the middle of the street and stop traffic?"

"Perhaps you could give us a lift . . . *over* the traffic," the grandmother mouse suggested. "We'll buy you a hot dog as payment."

Mmmmm! Orville couldn't say no to the promise of a tasty hot dog with mustard and sauerkraut, so he readily agreed. Besides, it was the right thing to do, lending another animal a helping wing. "It's a deal!" he said.

Just then, the grandmother mouse whistled to a group of mice standing nearby. "Harvey, Mildred, Polly, Carl – let's go. We have a ride!"

"Wait!" Orville said. "I can't give *all* of you a ride. Just how strong do you think I am?"

"Think about it this way," said the grandfather mouse. "The more mice, the more hot dogs."

Well that was certainly true. With that in mind, Orville agreed to help all the mice across the road. It took three trips. The mice held on just a bit too tightly to Orville's feathers, and Orville's landings left something to be desired, that was certain, but soon everyone was across the road, safe and sound.

"Here are your hot dogs!" the mice said. Orville was disappointed to see that they were offering him hot dogs from the mouse hot-dog stand, which were considerably smaller than the human kind. Still, a deal was a deal, and Orville was not one to look a gift horse – or mouse – in the mouth.

Orville then found a discarded sardine tin, which he used for seats, and thus began the Albatross Taxi Service for Mice. Word spread, and soon Orville couldn't keep up with the demand! He was a very successful businessbird.

Then one day it hit him – he was selling himself short! Forget about Albatross Taxi Service – it was time to think bigger. He'd get himself a scarf and goggles and start Albatross Airlines! He sold his taxi business to an entrepreneurial pigeon and set up shop at the airport.

Now, if he could only learn how to land, everything would be perfect!

Walt Disney's
# Bambi

# Practise Doesn't Always Make Perfect

One day, Bambi and Thumper were playing in the meadow.

"Look, Bambi!" exclaimed Thumper.

A herd of stags was thundering towards them.

"I wish I could be a stag!" Bambi exclaimed.

"Well, you know what my father always says," said Thumper.

"I know," said Bambi. "'Eating greens is a special treat. It makes long ears and great big feet.'"

"No, not that!" said Thumper. "I mean, he does say that, but he also says, 'If you want to hop well, but your hop is all wrong, then you have to practise all day long!'"

"I have to hop all day long?" asked Bambi.

"No!" cried Thumper. "If you want to become a stag, you have to practise!"

Bambi glanced back at two big deer. They suddenly ran towards each other, locking horns to test their strength. They looked so powerful and majestic. Bambi wanted to be just like them!

"Okay," Bambi told Thumper.

"Okay," said Thumper. "Follow me."

Thumper hopped to the edge of the meadow. He stopped by a big oak tree. "Lower your head," he told Bambi.

Bambi lowered his head. "Now what?" he asked, staring at the ground.

"Run straight ahead," said Thumper.

Bambi ran straight ahead – towards the trunk of the old oak tree! But, before he got there, a voice cried, "Stop!" Bambi did, skidding to a halt only a few inches from the tree trunk.

Thumper and Bambi looked up. Friend Owl looked down at them with big curious eyes. "Bambi, why were you going to butt my tree trunk with your head?" asked Friend Owl.

"I'm practising to become a big stag," said Bambi. "Stags butt heads to show their strength."

Friend Owl laughed and said, "Bambi, the stags have antlers to protect their heads! And becoming a stag is not something you can practise. It's something that will happen to you with the passing of time."

"It will?" said Bambi.

"Of course!" Friend Owl assured him. "Next summer, you'll see. You'll be bigger and stronger. You'll also have antlers – and, I hope, enough sense not to butt heads with an oak tree!"

"Yes, sir," said Bambi.

"Now go on, you two," said Friend Owl. "And don't be in too much of a hurry to grow up. You'll get there soon enough, I promise you!"

"Okay," said Bambi and Thumper. Then the two friends returned to the snowy meadow to play.

# Holiday Shopping

Jack Skellington, the Pumpkin King, came upon four doors – one decorated with a shamrock, another with a heart, a third with a turkey and another with an Easter egg. He walked from door to door to door, staring at each of them, searching for some meaning. All the while, Jack's ghost dog, Zero, was right beside him. Finally, Jack turned to Zero.

"What is a door," Jack said, "but a chance for something more!"

Zero nodded, so Jack swung open the first door with the shamrock. There was a noisy crowd of people inside – all wearing green. They were busy cutting shamrocks out of thick green paper. Zero was ready to dive right in, but Jack pulled him back by the collar.

"How bizarre!" Jack exclaimed. "It's not shaped like a diamond, or a star."

Zero was a little let down but, as Jack approached the door with the heart on it, Zero's spirits began to lift.

Inside, things were very red. There were lots of boxes of chocolates and tons of roses being arranged in vases of all shapes and sizes. As Zero was about to sink his teeth into a chocolate, Jack pulled him back.

"Oh, no!" Jack began to blush. "All this romance is a no-go!"

Zero slunk away with his tail between his legs. Still, there was hope. Jack was already standing in front of door number three – the door with the turkey. He opened the door with a flourish. You wouldn't believe what he found inside! There were people roasting turkeys, mashing potatoes and whipping cream for pumpkin pies. It smelled delicious, but the room was as hot as the inside of one of the ovens, from all the cooking. Jack quickly closed the door again. This time, even Zero was relieved.

They stood in front of the last remaining door. The egg painted on it was staring back at them in all its colourful glory. Jack looked at Zero, who nodded reassuringly. Then Jack opened the door.

There were people painting eggs and filling baskets with bright green grass, multi-coloured jelly beans and chocolate bunnies. Zero barked gleefully. He was about to follow the white rabbit hopping past him, when Jack caught hold of his tail.

"I'm not sure about that bunny," Jack warned. "To me, he seems sort of funny."

Zero looked up. They had tried all the doors. What would they do now? Jack looked at him knowingly.

"You know what this means?" Jack asked Zero. "I think we'll have to stick to Halloween!"

# TOY STORY

## Dino-scare

"I'm a failure as a carnivore!" groaned Rex the dinosaur. "I'm just not scary, Woody!"

"Now, now," said Woody soothingly. "Remember what's really important here. The main thing is that Andy plays with you, and you should be happy about that! Not like that new guy," scoffed Woody, darting a look over at Andy's newest toy, Buzz Lightyear. "He doesn't even realize he's a toy!"

"Red alert! Red alert! Andy's coming!" shouted Sarge, the Green Army Man sergeant. With a mad scramble, all the toys assumed their positions. The door burst open and Andy raced in. Looking quickly around the room, he grabbed Buzz off the bed, and then Woody from the floor.

"Sheriff Woody, I have a special assignment for you today," said Andy, holding Woody in front of his face and assuming a grave look. "You're going to team up with Buzz Lightyear, Space Ranger!" He held Buzz up in front of Woody so that they were face-to-face. "We have an invasion of alien dinosaurs from another planet!" he said. "This is big, Sheriff." Dropping Buzz and Woody on the floor with a loud clatter, Andy raced over to where Rex the dinosaur lay next to the toy box. He picked him up and stomped him across the room, roaring menacingly.

"Andy!" Andy's mother called from downstairs.

"Yeah, Mum?" Andy shouted in reply.

"I need you to gather your dirty clothes for me! I'll bring you a basket!" she called.

"Okay, Mum!" Andy called back. Then an idea struck him. With a little chuckle, Andy scooped up Rex, then stood next to the door, waiting for the sound of his mother's footsteps on the stairs.

"RAAAH!" roared Andy, jumping into her path as she came in. "I'm an alien dinosaur, here to take over your planet!"

"Gracious!" she said, taking a small step backwards in mock terror. "You certainly did scare me! Now, here." She thrust the basket into his arms and went into the laundry room.

Andy did as he was told. Scooping up big armloads of clothes, he tossed them into the basket. "Be back soon, Buzz and Woody," he said to the toys as he staggered towards the door carrying the basket. "Keep the universe safe while I'm gone, okay?"

As soon as the door had closed and the coast was clear, the toys began to stir. Rex hurried over to Woody. "I scared Andy's mum, didn't I? Didn't I?!" he said excitedly.

Woody grinned. "I think you really did scare her, Rex. Nice going, big guy."

# Chaos in the Kitchen

"Now, now, dearie," said Aunt Flora to little Aurora, "it's time for your nap." Flora had just given the baby (who was now named Briar Rose) her bottle and settled her in her cradle.

"Time to make supper!" Flora said to Fauna and Merryweather, turning away from the snoozing baby Princess and clapping her hands together purposefully.

Flora, Fauna, and Merryweather gave each other uneasy grins. It was the first meal the three fairies had to prepare in the little cottage in the woods, where they would live until Aurora's 16th birthday. The King and Queen had sent their beloved daughter into hiding to try to protect her from a curse laid on the Princess by the evil fairy Maleficent. In order to be sure to keep Aurora well hidden, the three fairies had vowed to give up their magic wands and live as ordinary humans. None of them had ever cooked, cleaned or cared for a baby before. This was going to be quite an adventure!

"Now, remember, dearies," said Flora firmly, "we're to use no magic when preparing this meal!"

The three fairies sighed. This was not going to be easy! "I shall cook a stew," announced Merryweather. The others thought that was a wonderful idea. What a cosy meal for their first night in the cottage! Stew sounded hearty and delicious!

"I'll bake some blueberry biscuits and mash the potatoes!" said Flora.

"Are you sure you know how?" asked Fauna.

"How hard could it be?" said Flora. "Fauna, why don't you make a salad?"

"I'll try!" said Fauna brightly. So Merryweather chopped meat and vegetables, Flora mixed flour and water for the biscuits, and Fauna shredded, chopped and diced the salad vegetables.

But, an hour later, dinner still wasn't ready. Merryweather's stew smelled like old boots. Flora opened the oven and pulled out her biscuits, which were not only blackened, but also as flat as pancakes. The mashed potato was terribly lumpy. And somehow most of the salad greens had ended up on the floor.

The three fairies looked at each other in dismay. "Back to the drawing board, girls," said Flora. "But let's not be too hard on ourselves – after all, we've got 16 years to learn how to cook without magic!"

"And that's how long it's going to take!" replied Fauna.

Merryweather laughed. Fauna was obviously joking – wasn't she?

Walt Disney's
# ALICE
in
WONDERLAND

# So You Want to Write a Poem

One day in Wonderland, Tweedledum and Tweedledee decided to write a poem about writing poems. So, they put their heads together and set to rhyming. Soon they had quite an amusing poem composed. It even had a title – "So You Want to Write a Poem." The only thing they just couldn't agree on was how to end it.

"Read what we have so far, would you?" said Tweedledee.

So Tweedledum began:

So you want to write a poem.
You do? Is that true?
Writing poems is usually
Easy to do.
Sun rhymes with fun;
Dew rhymes with shoe;
End sounds like friend,
And other words too.
Breezy is easy;
It rhymes with queasy.
Pet sounds like net;
That one's no sweat.
Many a word
Will rhyme with day.
Like hay and say
And even bouquet.
Words with long 'e' sounds
Are always a cinch.
Bean tree and sweet pea
And flea, at a pinch.

But then there are toughies
Like cousin and buzzin'.
There are rhymes for them,
But they're not dime a dozen.
Also tricky is icky
And apple and stronger.
Although you can rhyme 'em,
It may take you longer.
There's whoozit and whatsit
And hogwash and hooey.
You try to rhyme those,
And your brain goes kablooey.
So, when writing a poem,
Keep one thing in mind:
Avoid all the hard words
And you'll do just fine!

This poem is over.
This poem is penned.
This poem is finished.
So this is the ...

Tweedledum looked up. "That's it," he said.

Tweedledee racked his brain. "What rhymes with 'penned'?" he said. "'Bend'?" He tried it out: "'This poem is finished, so this is the *bend.*' No, no, that doesn't seem right."

Tweedledum took a stab at it. "There's 'pretend'. 'This poem is finished, so this is *pretend.*' Nah, I don't like it."

Tweedledee sighed. "We'll never think of a good rhyme for the end of this poem."

"You're right," said Tweedledum. "I guess we'll have to leave it unfinished."

So that's what they did.
And that was the end.

Disney's
**OLIVER**
&
*Company*

# Homeward Bound

"**W**elcome back to our humble abode," Dodger told Oliver. He and his friends had 'rescued' the little kitten from the town house he had been living in with his new owner, Jenny, and brought him to the barge where they lived.

"But I want to go back to Jenny's," Oliver explained.

"Jenny? So, all of a sudden you have a thing against dogs?" Dodger was offended. "And after all we've done for you! Why, don't you remember what it was like before you met us? You were all alone, cold, wet and sad. You were a friendless little kitten in a soggy cardboard box until you met us. And now you're too good for us dogs?"

"No, no, I don't have a thing against dogs," Oliver explained. "Honest!"

"Then why in the world would you pick Jenny over New York's coolest canine?" Dodger asked.

"It's not you – " Oliver started to say.

"Oh, I get it," Dodger interrupted, circling around Oliver. "You're all about money now. Got a taste of the finer things in life, and now you wouldn't want to be seen slumming with the likes of us dogs."

"That's not true – " Oliver began.

"Well, I'll tell you one thing money can't buy," Dodger barked. "Freedom!"

"Freedom?" Oliver asked.

"Yeah, on the street you can do what you want, when you want to. Then, if you want to just kick back with the gang at Fagin's, that's cool too. See what I mean? The freedom to choose instead of being locked up in that big house, doing whatever Jenny wants when she wants it," Dodger said.

"It's not like that!" Oliver protested.

"You could have all the freedom in the world but, instead, you're leaving us for a better cut of prime rib," Dodger said accusingly.

"No, that's not it at all," Oliver explained to his friend. "I like it at Jenny's. It's comfortable, and I get lots of love. Jenny needs me, and I need her, too!"

Dodger thought about this for a moment, then gave in. "You know what, kid? I can't argue with that. Stay with Jenny if you want."

"Okay." Oliver suddenly felt sad. "We can still be friends, though, right? Even though we see things differently?"

"Sure," Dodger agreed.

"And, you'll come visit?" Oliver asked.

"Visit?" Dodger considered this for a moment. "Absatively posolutely!"

Oliver grinned. It was the best of both worlds. What more could a kitten ask for?

# Go Fish!

"Okay, small fry," said Baloo the bear. "Today I'm going to teach you to fish like a bear!"

Mowgli was delighted. He loved his new friend Baloo. Unlike Bagheera the panther, who kept insisting that Mowgli should live in the Man-village for his own protection, Baloo made no such demands on Mowgli. Baloo was much more interested in having a good time living in the jungle, and so was Mowgli.

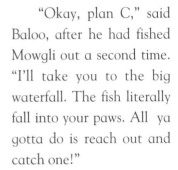

"Now, watch this, kid," said Baloo as they arrived at the riverbank. "All ya gotta do is wait for a fish to swim by and then . . ."

*Whoosh*! Quick as a flash, Baloo held a wriggling silver fish in his paw. "Now you try it!" he said to Mowgli.

Mowgli sat very still, waiting for a fish to swim by. Then – *splash*! – he toppled headfirst into the water.

"Hmm," said Baloo after he had fished Mowgli out and set him down, dripping. "Now I'll show you my second technique."

Baloo and Mowgli walked towards another part of the river. This time, the fish could be seen occasionally leaping out of the water as they swam down a little waterfall. Baloo waded a few steps into the water, waited for a fish to jump, then – *whoosh*! – he swiped a fish right out of the air. "Now you try, buddy."

Mowgli waded in just as Baloo had done. He waited for the fish to jump and then leaped for it. *Splash*!

"Okay, plan C," said Baloo, after he had fished Mowgli out a second time. "I'll take you to the big waterfall. The fish literally fall into your paws. All ya gotta do is reach out and catch one!"

Mowgli followed Baloo to the big waterfall. Sure enough, silvery fish were jumping all the way down the fall. Catching one would be easy!

In the blink of an eye Baloo held up a fish for Mowgli to admire.

"I'm going to do it this time, you watch me, Baloo!" said Mowgli excitedly. He scrunched up his face with concentration. Then – *flash*! – for an instant, Mowgli actually had a silvery fish in his hands. But, a second later, the fish shot out of his grasp and jumped into the water again. Mowgli looked down at his empty hands with a sigh.

"You know what, kid?" said Baloo, clapping a huge paw on Mowgli's skinny shoulders. "I think you're working too hard. That's not how life in the jungle should be! It should be fun, happy and carefree. So, come on. Let's go shake a banana tree instead!"

And Mowgli cheerfully agreed.

# Stitch Upon a Time

"Once upon a time," read Lilo.

"Wait," said Stitch.

"Wait for what?" asked Lilo.

"Snacks," said Stitch. He climbed off the bed and scampered to the bedroom door.

"You better not let Nani hear you," warned Lilo. "She thinks we went to bed."

Stitch crept into the hall, lifted his big ears and listened.

"No Nani," he whispered. Then he dashed downstairs and into the kitchen.

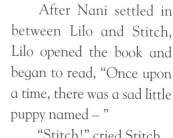

"Soda, pineapple, pickles, coleslaw," recited Stitch, peering into the fridge. "Hmm . . . pineapple-pickle-coleslaw sandwich . . ."

Lilo tiptoed up behind him. "You can't put all that in a sandwich," she whispered.

"*Yaaaaahhhhh!*" shouted Stitch.

"Sorry," whispered Lilo. "I didn't mean to startle you."

"*What* is going on in here?" demanded Nani, storming into the kitchen.

"Stitch wants a snack," Lilo explained.

"It's not time for snacks," Nani said. She shut the refrigerator door and marched them both back up the stairs. "It's time for bed."

"*Story*," said Stitch as he climbed into bed and held up the book. "Time for story."

"Please?" Lilo asked. She and Stitch both blinked their big dark eyes at Nani.

Nani sighed and said, "Oh, all right. But it had better be a short one."

"Goody!" cried Stitch as Nani climbed into bed too.

After Nani settled in between Lilo and Stitch, Lilo opened the book and began to read, "Once upon a time, there was a sad little puppy named – "

"Stitch!" cried Stitch.

Lilo continued, "There was a sad little puppy named . . . *Stitch*. He was sad because he was lost."

"Lost," repeated Stitch.

Lilo passed the book to Nani and said, "Your turn."

Then Nani began to read, "But one day, he met a little girl named – "

"Lilo," whispered Lilo.

Nani smiled. "He met a little girl named . . . Lilo."

Then Nani continued reading the story, until she reached the very end.

". . . and they lived happily ever after," Nani finished, shutting the book.

"Ever after," murmured Stitch, closing his eyes.

"Ever after," echoed Lilo, closing her eyes.

Nani waited until they were both sound asleep, then headed downstairs for a snack. Maybe she'd have a pineapple-pickle-coleslaw sandwich!

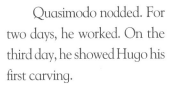

# The Sweetest Songs of All

"Why is Quasimodo so sad?" asked Hugo. "Judge Frollo has commanded that he never leave Notre Dame Cathedral," answered Victor. "He's lonely because he has no friends."

"But I'm his pal. And so are you," Hugo said.

"We're made of stone," Victor said. "Quasimodo needs living friends."

"But gargoyles make great friends!" Hugo exclaimed. "We're always there, and you can't break our hearts, because they're hard as rock!"

"Hush! Here he comes now," said Victor.

"Good morning, Quasi!" Hugo cried. "Nice day for ringing bells."

"I guess so," Quasimodo replied, staring at the people far below.

"Cheer up! What do they have down there that we don't have up here?" Hugo asked.

Quasimodo frowned. "I don't know, because I've never been there. But I hear people laughing and singing."

Then Victor spoke. "The sweetest songs of all can be heard in this tower, if you do what I tell you to."

"I will!" Quasimodo cried.

"It will take a long time, so you must be patient," warned Victor.

"I will! I will!" Quasimodo promised.

"Then fetch a piece of firewood and a knife from the kitchen," Victor commanded.

Quasimodo quickly returned with both.

"I want you to carve a statue of a dove," said Victor.

Quasimodo nodded. For two days, he worked. On the third day, he showed Hugo his first carving.

"Wow, that really looks like a dove," said Hugo.

"I'm going to carve a finch tomorrow," Quasimodo vowed.

For many weeks, Quasimodo carved hundreds of birds out of wood. Larks and thrushes and robins and sparrows. Each statue was better than the last. He worked so hard that he nearly forgot he was lonely.

Finally, he showed Victor and Hugo a carving of a beautiful nightingale.

"It is your best work of all," said Victor.

Quasimodo was so proud that he set his bird on the highest tower so they could all admire it.

The next morning, he was surprised to see two real birds perched next to his statue. More birds soon arrived. Some even built nests. Soon, hundreds and hundreds of birds lived in Notre Dame. They woke Quasimodo with their songs in the morning. They sang him to sleep at night.

As Victor said, the sweetest songs of all had come to Notre Dame. Since that day, birds have always lived in Notre Dame Cathedral.

# Walt Disney's
# Pinocchio

## Follow Your Star

Jiminy Cricket was a wanderer. He loved the independence, the excitement and the simplicity of his way of life. For many a season, he had roamed the countryside, stopping to rest in towns along the way, and moving on when he grew restless.

But lately, Jiminy Cricket had noticed that there was one thing missing from his vagabond lifestyle: a purpose. Camping one night by the side of the road, he sat on his sleeping bag and gazed into his campfire.

"I wonder what it would feel like to be really helpful to someone," he said.

Jiminy lay on his sleeping bag and tried to get comfortable on the hard ground as he gazed up into the starry night sky. As his eyes scanned the many tiny points of light, one star to the south jumped out at him and seemed to shine brighter than all the rest.

"Say, is that a Wishing Star?" he wondered aloud. Since he couldn't know for certain, he decided it would be best to make a wish on it, just in case. "Wishing Star," he said, "I wish to find a place where I can make a difference and do a bit of good."

Then, his wish made, Jiminy Cricket suddenly felt a strange impulse: an urge to get up, gather his things and follow that star – the Wishing Star. He couldn't quite explain the feeling, but he felt it just the same.

So do you know what Jiminy Cricket did?

He put out the campfire. He gathered his things. And he took to the road. He followed that star all through the night. He walked for miles along highways and byways, across fields and over hills. He walked until the sun came up and he could no longer see the star to follow it. Then he made camp and he slept.

He did the same thing for several more nights and several more days.

Then, one night, he came to a village. Looking up at the Wishing Star, Jiminy Cricket noticed that it seemed to hang directly overhead.

It was very late at night as Jiminy Cricket walked into the village and looked around. Every window of every house was dark – except for one window in a shop at the end of a street. So Jiminy Cricket hopped over to the window. Peering inside, he saw that it was a woodcarver's workshop, dimly lit by the embers of a fire dying in the fireplace. It seemed a warm and pleasant place to stop for the night.

Little did Jiminy Cricket know that it was the home of Geppetto, a kind old woodcarver who had just finished work on a puppet he called Pinocchio.

And little did he know that he had just found a place where he would do more than just a bit of good.

**Disney's**
# ROBIN HOOD

# A Royal Pain

"Sir Hiss, wake up! Wake UP!" Prince John shouted into the face of his slumbering royal adviser. Sir Hiss awoke with a start and sat bolt upright in his tiny cradle at the foot of Prince John's bed.

"Wha-what is it, Your Highness?" Hiss replied. He shook his head and tried to shake off his sleepiness. "Is everything all right?"

"No, everything is NOT all right!" Prince John snapped. He sat on his bed, crossed his arms and pouted. "I don't know how you can sleep while I lie here wide awake, tossing and turning!"

It was very late. All of Nottingham was quiet and still. No other candles were burning in the kingdom. Since the greedy Prince over-taxed all the poor people of Nottingham, he had every comfort, including the largest and softest bed in all the land. Yet, that night, Prince John could not get to sleep.

And Sir Hiss realized that he would not sleep until Prince John fell asleep. So he sprang into action, trying everything *he* could think of to send the Prince off to dreamland.

First, he brought the Prince something to drink from the castle kitchen.

"*Ugh!*" Prince John spat out his first mouthful. "This milk is WARM!"

"Well, yes, Your Majesty," replied Hiss. "Warm milk will help you get to sleep."

"Take it away!" the Prince ordered.

Next, Sir Hiss tried singing a lullaby. He crooned, "*Go to s-s-s-s-sleep, little prince-s-s-s-s . . .*"

But Prince John scrunched up his face, wiped it with the back of his hand, and yelled, "Say it! Don't spray it!"

Sir Hiss was annoyed. But he had one more idea. "Why don't you try count-ing sheep?" he suggested.

Prince John did as he was told. But, before he had counted to ten, he had lost his patience.

"Oh, I don't CARE how many sheep there are!" he thundered.

Sir Hiss was at the end of his tether. And he was completely out of ideas. Then he spotted the Prince's money bags, piled high in one cor-ner of the bedroom . . . and he knew what to do.

"Okay, sire," said Sir Hiss. "Then how about counting your money?"

Sir Hiss opened one of the money bags and pulled out a handful of gold coins. As he dropped a coin back into the bag, it made a soft clinking sound. He dropped another, and then another . . . and Prince John closed his eyes and began to count each clink.

"One . . . two . . . three . . ."

Before he got to ten, Prince John was fast asleep . . . wearing a huge grin.

# Leaping Leap Year

It was a sunny morning, and Mickey and Pluto were outside playing catch. Mickey threw Pluto a ball. Pluto took a deep breath, did a fancy spin and leaped into the air to catch it.

"Nice job," Mickey said, cheering him on. "Great catch! Great leap!"

Great leap? Mickey's words echoed in his head. "Oh, my goodness, do you know what today is?" he asked Pluto.

Pluto leaped into the air again and again. He wanted Mickey to take the ball from him and toss it again.

"I almost forgot. Today is leap year!" Mickey exclaimed.

Pluto dropped the ball at Mickey's feet.

"I mean, today's not actually a year – it's a day," Mickey continued, talking to himself.

Pluto wasn't sure Mickey understood him. He wanted to play! So he leaped into the air again and again.

Leap! Leap! Leap!

Leap! Leap! Leap!

"That's the spirit!" Mickey encouraged him. "Leap year is something to be excited about! After all, it happens only once every four years. Well, almost every four years."

Mickey took a pad and pencil out of his back pocket and started working out figures. "There's a mathematical equation to figure this out if you really want to be exact." He scribbled some notes. "That's zero divided by . . . hmm, let me see here . . . carry the . . ." Mickey started blushing. "Maths is not really my thing." He put the pad back in his pocket. "Let's just say once every four years! Imagine if your birthday were on 29 February – 29 February only comes once every four years. So instead of being 12, you'd be three!" He laughed. "Just kidding . . . I think!"

Pluto sat down, panting with exhaustion, as Mickey continued explaining it to him. "Every four years, there's an extra day in the calendar – 29 February – and that's today!

"Do you know why we have leap year?" Mickey asked. "Because we have 365 days in a year, but it actually takes the earth a little longer to orbit the sun. So we have to make up for lost time!"

The excitement in Mickey's voice got Pluto excited again. He was back on his feet, tail wagging, ball in his mouth, leaping up and down.

"That's right," Mickey agreed, and joined Pluto in his leaping.

Leap! Leap! Leap!

Leap! Leap! Leap!

"Hooray!" shouted Mickey. "It's leap year!"

# Month-o-grams

"What are you doing, Dot?" Flik asked. Dot was sitting on the floor surrounded by acorns, leaves, dried flowers, rocks, pebbles, sap and little pots of berry juice.

"Oh, no, don't tell me, it's Princess Atta's birthday, and I forgot!" Flik cried.

"Nope," Dot answered. "I'm making month-o-gram cards for everyone!"

"Oh, right, excellent!" Flik exclaimed. "Month-o-gram cards, of course!" Then his smile faded. "Uh, Dot, what's a month-o-gram?"

"You've never made a month-o-gram?" Dot asked.

"Apparently not." Flik was beginning to feel sheepish.

"Well, don't worry," Dot told him. "We're in luck! Today's the first of the month, and that's exactly when month-o-grams are sent out."

"Really?" Flik said.

"Really," Dot said. "So grab some stuff and get started." She thrust a handful of leaves, some berry ink and a writing splinter at Flik.

"What do I do?" Flik was nervous.

"Just take the leaf." Dot demonstrated. "Decorate it and write something nice on it."

"Who do you send month-o-grams to?" Flik wanted to know.

"Everybody!" Dot exclaimed. "The Blueberries send them to our family and friends

every month to let them know we care."

"That sounds like an excellent idea!" Flik said. "I'm going to make one for the Queen and Atta and one for you, of course . . ."

Flik and Dot got down to work. Hours later, they were surrounded by piles of month-o-grams, enough for everyone in the entire colony.

"Flik, it's getting late," Dot said. "We had better start delivering these."

Just then, two worker ants rounded a corner and bumped right into each other. They tumbled down, tangled up in a jumble of legs and antennae.

"Hey, watch where you're going," they growled at each other.

"Let's give them each a month-o-gram," Dot whispered.

So, Dot and Flik walked up to the ants, helped them untangle themselves, and handed each of them a month-o-gram of his own. "Happy March!" Flik and Dot cheered.

The ants smiled broadly. They hugged each other. They hugged Dot. They hugged Flik and then they strolled off together.

"See!" Dot told Flik. "It works!"

Flik and Dot set out to make the rest of their deliveries. They handed a month-o-gram to every ant they saw, spreading happiness and cheer throughout all of Ant Island.

# Superhero for a Day

Lucky sat glued to the television set. He was watching his favourite show, "The Thunderbolt Adventure Hour". Thunderbolt always knew exactly what to do to save the day. He was a superhero dog.

"I'm going to be just like Thunderbolt when I grow up," Lucky announced when the show was over.

Patch laughed at his brother. "Thunderbolt can jump clear across a river," he said. "You can barely climb up the stairs!"

"Just wait!" Lucky told him. "You'll see!"

While the other puppies went outside to play, Lucky practised his leaping. He leaped from the arm of the sofa onto the chair. He leaped from the stool onto the sofa. Then he leaped from the chair . . . right into a lamp. *CRASH!* Nanny came running. "Lucky!" she scolded. "Go outside while I clean this up!"

When Lucky went outside, he found Rolly with his head stuck in the bushes. "Don't worry!" shouted Lucky. "I'll save you!" He ran up to Rolly, grabbed him by the leg and pulled. Both pups tumbled backwards. "Ow!" yelled Rolly as he and Lucky collided. "What did you do that for?"

"You were stuck!" answered Lucky. "I was trying to save you."

"I didn't need saving!" complained Rolly. "We were playing hide-and-seek!"

Lucky's brothers and sisters came over to see what all the fuss was about. "Come on," said Patch. "Let's go inside before Thunderbolt Junior tries to save anybody else!"

Lucky stayed behind. He'd show Patch! He could be a superhero dog if he tried. He climbed to the top of the kennel to practise leaping some more. If he practised outside he wouldn't break any more lamps!

Below him, Penny had returned to fetch her bone. But she found it had already been snatched by Bruno, the neighbourhood bully.

Lucky watched from above as the bulldog growled and bared his teeth. The puppy peered over the edge of the kennel, frantically wondering what to do.

"Ahhhhhh!" Lucky screamed, losing his balance and tumbling off the roof.

"Ahhhhh!" Bruno cried when Lucky landed on his back. The bulldog dropped the bone in terror, turned and ran off. By now the other puppies had come running from the house.

"What happened?" asked Rolly.

"Lucky saved me!" Penny said. "You should have seen him! He flew right through the air and scared Bruno away – just like Thunderbolt!"

Lucky puffed out his chest with pride.

"Wow!" said Patch. "Can I have your autograph?"

# Disney's Aladdin

## Grumpy Rajah

It wasn't always so easy being the daughter of a sultan. Sometimes Jasmine thought she would be the loneliest girl in Agrabah – if it weren't for Rajah, her tiger (and best friend).

But, apparently, it was not always so easy being a tiger either. Rajah was having a bad day.

"Grrr," Rajah growled.

"What's got into you?" Jasmine asked him.

Rajah looked at her with a 'none of your business' glare and growled again.

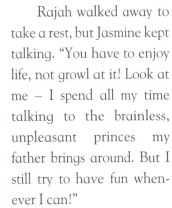

"Hmm," Jasmine said thoughtfully. She was determined to cheer up the tiger. For one thing, he was her only friend, and life gets pretty unpleasant when your only friend is in a bad mood. And, for another, Jasmine just wasn't allowed to do much, being a princess, so she was always glad to have a project. Right now, her project was to make Rajah purr.

"You know what you need?" Jasmine asked. Rajah paced back and forth.

"You need to try to relax!" Jasmine told him.

Rajah looked at her with a raised eyebrow.

"You know," Jasmine explained, "loosen up, have a good time."

Rajah began a low-grade growl again.

"All right, all right!" Jasmine surrendered. "I'll stop."

But she just couldn't let it go. She really wanted Rajah to be happy!

"Rajah, don't be mad." Jasmine patted him on the back. "I wouldn't be saying this if I didn't care about you."

Rajah walked away to take a rest, but Jasmine kept talking. "You have to enjoy life, not growl at it! Look at me – I spend all my time talking to the brainless, unpleasant princes my father brings around. But I still try to have fun whenever I can!"

Rajah lay down and put his paws over his ears.

"Oh, I get it." Jasmine caught on. "You're jealous of all those princes!"

Rajah looked up. Jasmine was right. He *was* sick and tired of all those princes coming around.

Jasmine lovingly scratched Rajah behind the ear. "Jealousy isn't becoming," she teased him, "even in tigers. I know I haven't been spending much time with you lately, Rajah. But it's not like I have a choice. The law says I have to find a prince to marry."

Princes, Rajah thought. Yuck!

"But you know," Jasmine continued, hugging her tiger around his big furry neck, "I like you better than any prince."

Rajah began to purr. Jasmine smiled. Mission accomplished!

"Princes!" Jasmine said. "Yuck!"

WALT DISNEY'S
THE JUNGLE
BOOK

# The Den of Doom

"Where are we going, Baloo?" Mowgli asked. He and Baloo had been travelling through the jungle for a while now.

"Have you ever heard of the Den of Doom, Man-cub?" replied Baloo in a hushed voice.

Mowgli gasped. "The Den of Doom? They say that the Den of Doom is a giant cave filled with bears who will eat anything – or anyone! They say that those bears can hear for miles and see in the dark! They say that even Shere Khan is afraid of them!" he exclaimed.

"Mmm-hmm," said Baloo. "They do say that. They *also* say that all of the bears in the Den of Doom are over eight feet tall, that their teeth are green and razor-sharp, and that their battle cry is so loud that the whales in the ocean hear it and shake with fright. They say all that, and much, much more."

"And we're *going* there?" Mowgli squeaked. "We can't! Baloo, those bears aren't like you! They're dangerous!"

"Too late, Man-cub," Baloo said with a grin. "We're already there!" He picked up Mowgli, whose knees were knocking together so hard he could barely stand, and strode right into a thicket. The bear ducked under a huge palm frond and emerged into a large, sunlit clearing in front of an enormous cave. Baloo put Mowgli down. The boy looked around in complete and utter surprise.

Mowgli had expected to see hundreds of fierce, angry bears. Instead, he saw hundreds of relaxed, happy bears having a really good time. Bears were swimming in a small pond, splashing and laughing. Bears were resting in the cool shadows of the cave. Bears were playing tag out in the clearing and chomping on piles of ripe, delicious fruit. It was, in short, a bear party.

"I don't understand," Mowgli said to Baloo. "This is the Den of Doom?"

"Yep," Baloo said happily, grabbing a palm frond and fanning himself with it. "It used to be called the Den of Delights, but we had to change the name. See, everyone in the jungle knew that the Den of Delights was the most fun place around. We bears never turned anyone away from our party. But then it got so crowded that it just wasn't any fun any more. So we spread a few rumours, changed the name, and *presto* – it's the Den of Doom! Now no one bothers us bears any more."

"But what about me?" Mowgli said anxiously. "I'm not a bear."

"You're an honorary bear, Mowgli," Baloo replied with a smile. "You sure have enough fun to be one!"

# Float Like a Butterfly

One day, Dumbo's best friend, Timothy Q. Mouse, found Dumbo looking sad. "What's the matter, little guy?" the mouse asked the elephant. "Have people been teasing you about your ears again?"

Dumbo nodded. The little elephant looked totally miserable.

Timothy shook his head. The two were very good friends and did everything together. He didn't mind one bit that Dumbo had large ears. In fact, he thought they were great.

Timothy was trying to think of a way to cheer up his dear friend. And then he saw something. "Look, Dumbo!" he cried, racing over to a nearby fence post. Hanging from the fence was a large cocoon. "It's a butterfly cocoon!" Timothy said excitedly.

Dumbo came over to examine it.

"And look – it's about to hatch into a butterfly," said Timothy. He looked thoughtful for a moment, and then he turned to Dumbo. "You know what? You are a lot like the little caterpillar that made this cocoon."

Dumbo looked at Timothy quizzically.

"Yep, it's true. You see, a caterpillar is something nobody really wants around much. They think it's kind of plain looking, and it can't really do anything very interesting. But then one day, the caterpillar turns into a beautiful butterfly, and everyone loves it. And you know what? I think you're going to be that way, too. When you get older, everyone is going to admire you rather than tease you!"

Dumbo smiled gratefully at his friend, and wiped away a tear with one of his long ears.

Suddenly, it started to rain. "Oh no!" cried Timothy. "The butterfly is going to get its new wings all wet. It won't be able to fly if it gets rained on. What'll we do? We need an umbrella!"

As Timothy looked this way and that for an umbrella, Dumbo smiled and unfurled his long ears. He draped them over the fence post so that they made a lovely roof for the insect, protecting it from the falling droplets of rain.

"Great idea!" said Timothy admiringly. The two friends stood there during the downpour, which didn't last very long. While they waited, they watched the beautiful new butterfly emerge from its cocoon and unfurl its colourful wings. When the rain stopped, the butterfly spread its wings (which were quite dry, thanks to Dumbo) and flew away.

"You know, my friend," said Timothy as they watched it fly away, "I think someday you're going to be a big success. You'll be like that butterfly – happy, carefree and floating along. Well, not floating for real, that's impossible. Imagine that, a flying elephant!"

Disney · PIXAR
**FINDING NEMO**

# Homesick

Nemo still couldn't believe everything that had happened to him. First, he'd been snatched up by a scuba diver in the ocean. Then, he'd travelled a long way in a big water cooler. Finally, he'd been dumped in a fish tank in a dentist's office. The other fish in the tank seemed nice, but Nemo missed his dad and his old home. He couldn't think about anything except getting back to the ocean. But would their plan to escape really work? It seemed hopeless . . . .

"Hey, kid," Bloat the blowfish swam over to him. "Are you okay? You look a little down in the gills."

"I'll say," said Nigel the seagull.

Peach the starfish glanced over from her spot on the tank wall. "He's just upset," she said. "It's only natural." She smiled kindly at Nemo. "It's okay, hon. We know how you feel."

"How could you know?" he muttered, feeling sorry for himself. "You weren't grabbed out of the ocean, away from your dad."

"Well, no," a fish named Gurgle admitted. "But we all had families back where we came from. We all miss them."

"Really?" Nemo blinked in surprise. He hadn't thought about that.

"Sure," Peach said. "The lady who sold me over the Internet kept lots of us starfish in her basement." She sighed sadly. "I still wonder where all my brothers and sisters ended up. I'd give two or three of my arms to see them again."

"I hear you," Bloat agreed. "I was hatched in somebody's garage. They sold me and a whole school of my brothers and sisters and cousins to Bob's Fish Mart. Just when we made friends with the other fish there, he came in and bought me." He waved a fin towards the dentist in the office outside the tank. "It could be worse, though," Bloat continued. "You guys are the best friends I've ever had."

A fish named Deb nodded. "I'm lucky he bought me and my sister together. Right, Flo?" She smiled at her own reflection in the glass of the tank. When the reflection didn't answer, Deb shrugged. "I guess Flo is too choked up to talk right now. But I can tell by her smile that she agrees. We don't know what we'd do without each other. But we still miss the rest of our family."

"Wow," Nemo said, looking around at his new tankmates. "I guess you guys *do* know how I feel."

Even though he was sad that the other fish had been taken from their families, it made Nemo feel a little less alone. At least they understood how much he wanted to find his way back to his father. Now, a little braver and more determined than ever, Nemo was ready to escape from the tank – no matter what.

Disney's
The Adventures of
**THE GREAT MOUSE DETECTIVE**

# A Lesson in Confidence

"Oh dear!" Olivia, a very worried little mouse, sat with Dr Dawson next to the fireplace in Basil of Baker Street's home.

"What's the matter?" Dr Dawson asked.

"What's the matter?" Olivia repeated indignantly. "My father's been stolen by a peg-leg bat! Have you forgotten already?"

"No, no, dear," Dawson reassured her. "Of course not. I know you must be quite upset."

"Quite upset!" Olivia cried angrily. "I couldn't possibly *be* more upset!"

"But we're at Basil's now, and he's the best. You even said so yourself," Dawson said.

"But what if he doesn't want to help me?" Olivia asked.

"Why wouldn't he want to help you?" Dawson asked.

"You heard him," Olivia answered. "'I simply have no time for lost fathers,'" she said, quoting the detective.

"He didn't mean it," Dawson said reassuringly. "He's just in the middle of something. Perhaps we caught him at a bad time. But, whatever the circumstances, my dear, you must try not to fret."

"I know you're trying to help me, Dr Dawson," Olivia said, as politely as she could manage. "But I don't know if I can really avoid fretting. My father is out there somewhere, and I just *have* to find him!"

"You're right!" Dawson said. "You do have to find him. You have to help Basil track down your father and, in order to do that, you are going to need a clear mind. Now, can you have a clear mind while you're fretting?"

"Well, it probably doesn't help," said Olivia reluctantly.

"Can you think logically while you're upset?" Dawson asked.

". . . Probably not," Olivia said.

"Can you work side-by-side with Basil of Baker Street, the great mouse detective, to save your beloved father while you are *worried*?" Dawson asked.

"No!" Olivia paused as the truth sank in. "No, I can't. I owe it to my father to be level-headed. I can be sad and scared later – right now I have to be a detective, like Basil!" she finished triumphantly.

"That, my young lady, is the smartest thing you could have said. And, if you can hold on to that attitude, your father will be found in no time." Dawson smiled at Olivia.

Just then, Basil came swooping back into the room. "Of course he will. I never miss my mark. Your father is as good as found, because I am just that good!"

Olivia smiled secretly. She knew *she* was just that good too.

# Just Like Dad

"Dad, when I grow up, I want to be just like you," Simba said to his father.

Mufasa nuzzled his son's head gently. "All in good time, son," he said.

Just then, Simba's friend Nala bounded up to them. "Come on, Simba!" she called. "Let's go play by the river!"

On their way, Simba stopped abruptly. "Listen to this," he said. He threw back his head and roared as loudly as he could. Then he looked at her expectantly. "Do I sound like my dad?"

Nala tried unsuccessfully to suppress a giggle. "Not quite," she said.

Soon they reached the river. The waters were high as a result of the recent rains. Simba found a quiet pool at the side and stared down at his reflection. "Do you think my mane is starting to grow?" he asked Nala.

Nala sighed. "Maybe a little," she replied. "But, Simba, what's the big rush? Let's just have fun being young!"

Simba was eyeing a tree branch that extended over the raging river. "Well, I may not be as big as my dad yet, but at least I'm as brave as he is!" he shouted, and raced up to the tree. Climbing its gnarled trunk, he began walking along the branch over the water.

Nala hurried over. She heard a loud crack. "Simba!" she yelled. "Come back here! The branch is going to break!"

But Simba couldn't hear her over the loud waters. Nala bounded away to get help.

Simba felt the branch begin to sag. "Uh-oh," he said to himself. Suddenly the whole thing broke off and Simba tumbled into the water. The current was strong, and he struggled to swim towards the shore. He was running out of strength, and he realized he might not make it.

Then he felt himself being lifted out of the water and tossed onto the bank. Dripping and coughing, he looked up – right into the angry eyes of his father.

"Simba!" thundered Mufasa. "There's a big difference between being brave and being foolish! The sooner you learn that, the better chance you will have of growing old!"

Simba hung his head. Out of the corner of his eye, he saw Nala, pretending not to overhear. "I'm . . . sorry, Dad," he said softly. "I just wanted to be brave like you."

His father's gaze softened. "Well," he said. "As long as we're soaking wet, why don't we go to a quieter part of the river and do some swimming?" He looked over to where Nala was sitting. "Come on, Nala!" he called. "Come with us!"

"Yippee!" cried the cubs, and they all went off together.

Walt Disney's
*Cinderella*

# Chore de Force

Cinderella watched as a blue-and-pink-tinted bubble floated up from her bucket. "Isn't that pretty?" she said as she watched the bubble float higher and higher and finally pop into nothingness. Gus and Jaq and all the rest of Cinderella's mouse friends nodded in agreement.

"I bet it would be fun to float around in a bubble all day! I could see whole cities at a time, bounce on clouds and soar with the birds," Cinderella said dreamily. Her bird friends chirped happily. They liked the idea of sharing the skies with her.

"What am I doing?" Cinderella suddenly said. "I should stay focused on my chores." She finished cleaning the windows and prepared to mop the floor.

Cinderella plunged the mop into a bucket of soapy water, then dragged it across the floor. At first, she felt worn out. Then it occurred to her, as the mop slid across the slippery floor, "This is like dancing! How I love to dance!" Gus and Jaq copied Cinderella as she twirled around the room with the mop. "What fun!" she cried happily.

"Oh, my," Cinderella caught herself. "Did I say that aloud?" Maybe I just need to get away from all these bubbles, she thought. Ironing should do the trick!

She was ironing away and humming merrily to herself when she realized how dark the sky had grown.

"Look at the time!" Cinderella exclaimed. "I've been daydreaming the day away and haven't even started dinner."

Cinderella hurried to the kitchen where she chopped and minced and grated and stirred. "I don't know where this day has gone," she fretted as she added ingredients to her stepsisters' favourite soup. "I've got absolutely nothing done!" And, just then, Cinderella's stepsisters, Anastasia and Drizella, barged into the kitchen.

"Where's my laundry?" barked Anastasia.

"Done," Cinderella said.

"And my ironing?" Drizella added.

"Done," Cinderella replied again.

"Did you mop the floors?"

"Wash the windows?"

"Make our dinner?"

"Done, done, done!" Cinderella said gaily.

The sisters marched out of the kitchen muttering with displeasure.

And there Cinderella stood, all alone in the kitchen once more. As she stirred the pot of soup, she thought, I guess I did get a lot done, after all! She twirled across the room in celebration – and Jaq and Gus and the rest of her mouse friends joined her.

March
# 10

# Monster Moneymaker

As Mike and Sulley walked through the lobby of Monsters, Inc., to the Scare Floor, they passed the Scarer of the Month photos of Sulley hanging on the wall.

Mike suddenly turned to his big blue friend. "Sulley," he said, "do you ever think that we deserve a little more?"

"More?" Sulley asked.

"Oh, you know," Mike continued. "You're the top Scarer month after month. All you get is a lousy picture in the hallway, and I get nothin'. We should be famous!"

"What have you got in mind?" Sulley asked.

"A marketing campaign," Mike told him.

"How would we do that?" Sulley asked.

"Well, for starters, we'll get you some new head shots, and not just any old head shots but autographed head shots. And we won't stop there." Mike was on a roll. "We'll make mugs, posters – T-shirts even – with all your best poses." Mike demonstrated a few of his friend's Scarer poses for Sulley, including Sulley's personal favourite – the ol' Waternoose Jump and Growl. "We can set up a gift shop right here in the building featuring 'Sulley the Super Scarer' memorabilia."

"Why would we want to bother with all that?" Sulley wondered.

"Money!" Mike exclaimed, rolling his eye.

"I don't know, Mike," Sulley said. "It just doesn't seem right, us making money off these things. But what if we . . . that's it!" Sulley jumped up, nearly knocking Mike over. "We'll donate the money to charity!"

"Who said anything about donations?" Mike asked.

"That's a great idea!" Sulley said, ignoring Mike.

"How will we bask in any glory if we give the money away?" Mike asked.

"Well, we will, sort of," Sulley explained. "We'll make the donation on behalf of Monsters, Inc."

"I don't know about that," Mike said.

"It's a wonderful idea!" Sulley replied. "And when we help the company make a generous donation, Mr Waternoose will be very proud of us!"

Mike was suddenly warming to the idea. "And we'll get lots of press!" he added.

"Sure, why not?" Sulley said with a shrug.

"It's a great idea!" Mike cheered.

"I agree!" Sulley said.

"I'm glad I thought of it!" Mike gave his best friend a huge smile.

"You always have such good ideas," Sulley agreed with a grin.

"It's like I always say," Mike added. "Scaring's important, but it's the brains behind the monster that matter most!"

# A Beastly Makeover

One evening, the Beast was heading towards the dining room when Lumiere suddenly stopped him.

"You can't go to dinner looking like *that*!" Lumiere said.

"Why not?" the Beast demanded. "I'm wearing my best outfit!"

"Clothes aren't enough," Cogsworth chimed in. "You have to make a good impression."

"You always told me looks don't matter, anyway," the Beast growled.

"There's a difference between looks and style," Lumiere told him.

"And you may have no control over your looks," Cogsworth added, "but you certainly can do something about your style!"

"What's wrong with my style?" the Beast said, looking a bit hurt.

"Okay," Cogsworth began, "let's talk hair."

"What's wrong with my hair?" the Beast cried, offended.

"Women like hair long, but neat – not straggly," Cogsworth explained. "When was the last time you combed it?"

"I–" the Beast began.

"You've got it all wrong," Lumiere interrupted. "Women like hair short, closely cropped." He brandished a pair of scissors.

"I don't *want* a haircut!" the Beast said.

"We could always try ringlets," Cogsworth offered, nodding wisely.

"Or braids," Lumiere suggested. At this, the Beast climbed onto a table and, from there, onto a bookcase that swayed dangerously under his weight.

"How about a French twist?" Cogsworth said.

A low growl began in the Beast's throat.

Just then, Belle hurried into the room, interrupting the stand-off, and this is what she saw: the candelabrum and mantel clock brandishing combs and ribbons at the snarling, cornered Beast – who was scrabbling to stay on top of the bookcase. Belle burst into laughter.

"What's going on?" she asked.

"We were just trying to fix his hair," said Lumiere. "It's a dreadful mess!"

"Actually," Belle said, "I happen to like it just the way it is. Beast, are you going to stay up there all night?"

And at that, the Beast leaped off the bookcase and strode towards her.

"Do you really like my hair?" he asked.

"It looks just fine," Belle reassured him. "Now, would you escort me to dinner?"

"I would be honoured," the Beast replied.

Cogsworth and Lumiere looked baffled as the two headed off to the dining room.

"Kids these days," Cogsworth said.

Lumiere just shook his head.

73

# Don't Mock Jock

Aunt Sarah had only just arrived to look after the baby while Jim Dear and Darling were away, but already her Siamese cats, Si and Am, had caused nothing but trouble. When they made a huge mess in the living room, Lady had been blamed for it, and Aunt Sarah had taken Lady to be fitted with a muzzle!

Meanwhile, left alone in the house, Si and Am had discovered the doggy door that led out to the garden.

"What works for doggies, works for kitties, too," hissed Si.

They slunk out to the garden. They dug in the flower beds, scared the birds at the birdbath and chased a squirrel up a tree.

Then they found a small hole in the garden fence. They poked their heads through the hole and spied Jock snoozing by his kennel.

"Time for a wake-up call?" said Am.

Si smiled and nodded. They squirmed through the hole and stole silently across the yard until they were sitting on either side of the sleeping Jock. Then, at the same moment, they let loose a shrill, ear-splitting yowl.

Jock awoke with a start. By the time he had identified the culprits, Si and Am were halfway across the lawn, heading for the fence.

Jock tore after them, barking. But, in a flash, the cats squirmed through the small hole

and were out of Jock's reach. The opening was too small for Jock. He had to be content with sticking his head through and barking at the cats as they strolled casually up the back steps of Lady's house and through the doggy door. Then they collapsed in a laughing fit on the kitchen floor.

"Dogs are so dim-witted." Si cackled.

They waited a while, then crept out through the doggy door again, itching to try their trick once more. Peeking through the hole in the fence, they spied Jock, eyes closed, lying in front of his kennel. They squirmed through the hole and crept towards him.

But, this time, Jock was ready for them. When the cats got within five feet of him, the feisty Scottie leaped to his feet and growled. The cats gave a start, wheeled around and raced for the fence, only to find the way blocked by Jock's friend, Trusty the bloodhound, who stood, growling, between the cats and the hole.

Jock and Trusty chased Si and Am around Jock's garden until Jock was confident they had learned their lesson. Then they allowed the cats to retreat through the hole in the fence.

This time, they didn't stop running until they were up the back steps, through the doggy door, and safely inside.

And inside is where they stayed.

# Bedtime for Duchess

"Come, my precious ones!" Duchess called to Berlioz, Toulouse and Marie. "It's time to go to sleep."

"Oh, Mother!" Toulouse complained.

"But I'm not tired!" Marie joined in.

"I'm not going to sleep," Berlioz added. "Night-time is just when things start happening for us alley cats." Berlioz crouched down low, hindquarters in the air, and pounced on an imaginary opponent.

"Who does he think he's kidding?" Toulouse whispered to Marie, who rolled her eyes in agreement.

"Now, now, it's been a long day," Duchess told them. "I don't want to hear any more protests."

"Mother!" Berlioz whined.

"We need a bedtime story!" Marie insisted.

"A story? My darlings, it's way past your bedtime, and I'm just too tired tonight," replied Duchess.

"Then why don't we tell *you* a story?" Toulouse offered.

"Yeah!" Berlioz chimed in.

"What a lovely idea," said Duchess.

"Once upon a time . . ." Marie began.

"There was a big, mean, ferocious alley cat," Berlioz continued.

"Berlioz!" Marie protested. "It's not supposed to be scary. She'll have nightmares!"

"Sorry, Mama," Berlioz said.

"That's quite all right," Duchess told him.

"Now where were we?" Toulouse asked.

"Once upon a time . . ." Marie began again.

"Yeah, once upon a time there was this amazing kitten," Toulouse said. "And he could paint like no other kitten you've ever seen."

"And that's because the model for his paintings was the most beautiful kitten you've ever laid eyes on," Marie added.

"Give me a break!" Berlioz said, grumbling under his breath. He and Toulouse snickered.

"Very funny." Marie was not amused. "Can we get back to the story?"

"This kitten was a painter by day and a smooth-talking, alley-hanging, danger-seeking hepcat by night," Berlioz continued.

Toulouse tapped Berlioz with his paw. He looked up and saw what both Toulouse and Marie were seeing. Duchess herself had fallen asleep!

Berlioz, Toulouse and Marie each gave their mother a kiss good night.

"Good night, Mama," said Marie.

"Good night, Mama," said Toulouse.

"Good night, Mama," said Berlioz.

Then all three curled up beside Duchess and promptly fell asleep too.

Walt Disney's
# Peter Pan
# Pixie Play

"What do you say, Tink? Can you get it?" asked Peter Pan.

Peter and Tinker Bell were floating high above the streets of London, right outside a large open window. Inside, three children were sleeping soundly.

Tinker Bell made a confident, jingling sound.

"All right, then. In you go!" said Peter.

Tink darted through the window. Then, leaving behind a trail of pixie dust, she flitted around the nursery searching for Peter's missing shadow.

When Peter had last visited this house, the children's nurse, Nana, had spied him outside the nursery window. She tried to grab him, but all she got was his shadow. Tonight, Peter had come to get his shadow back. He knew it wouldn't be easy, because Nana was a Saint Bernard dog. And Peter knew it was easy to fool children but hard to fool a dog. So, for this job, he needed a fairy's help.

Peter watched as Tinker Bell flew around the nursery. First, she flew over the eldest child, Wendy Darling, and then her two younger brothers, John and Michael. All three kept right on sleeping.

But, when Tinker Bell flew over Nana, the dog awoke with a sneeze! Tinker Bell's pixie dust had tickled Nana's nose.

"Woof! Woof!" barked Nana, trying to grab the fairy. All of a sudden the poor dog's feet couldn't find the floor. The pixie-dust magic had lifted her up. Now Nana was floating around the room!

When Peter heard Nana bark, he raced inside. Then he saw Nana floating and started to laugh.

Suddenly, the pixie dust wore off, and Nana's paws hit the floor again. With an angry growl, the dog charged at Peter Pan!

"Yikes!" Peter cried, darting through the window with Tinker Bell right behind him.

"Back to Never Land, Tink!" said Peter. "We'll get my shadow back tomorrow night."

On a twinkling trail of light, Peter and Tinker Bell soared into the sky and vanished.

Back inside the nursery, Wendy suddenly woke up. "What's this!" she cried, touching the window. Her hand sparkled with pixie dust.

"Peter Pan must have come back, looking for his shadow. I'm sorry I missed him," Wendy told Nana with a frown of disappointment.

"Woof! Woof!" said Nana.

"Yes, I know," Wendy replied. "Time for me to go back to bed."

But, as Nana licked Wendy's cheek good night, Wendy promised herself that she would be ready to meet the remarkable Peter Pan the next time he paid her a visit!

DISNEP'S
THE LITTLE
**MERMAID**

# The Wrong Gift

"Wow, Flounder, everyone's here!" cried Ariel. Mermaids and mermen had come from all over the ocean to wish Ariel's sister Aquata a happy birthday.

Unfortunately, Ariel still needed to pick out a gift for her sister. So, Ariel and Flounder left the party and swam to her secret cave.

Together they looked over Ariel's vast collection of bells, clocks, jewellery and other human knick-knacks she'd scavenged from shipwrecks.

"How about this?" asked Flounder, swimming around a ship's wheel.

"Too big," said Ariel.

"Or this?" suggested Flounder, nudging a single gold earring.

"Too small," said Ariel.

Suddenly, Ariel noticed a music box.

"This is it!" she cried. "The perfect gift! I've listened to this one again and again, and it plays a really beautiful song."

Ariel swam back to the celebration. Beside King Triton, Aquata sat on a clamshell, and, one by one, the guests presented her with their birthday gifts.

While Ariel waited her turn in line, Sebastian the crab swam by. "Hello, Ariel," he said. "What gift do you have for Aquata?"

When Ariel proudly told Sebastian, his jaw nearly dropped to the ocean floor. "Are you out of your mind?" he cried.

Ariel's eyes widened. Sebastian was right! King Triton hated humans. And Ariel was not supposed to have anything from their world. That's exactly why she'd kept her cave a secret!

Just then, King Triton's deep voice bellowed, "Ariel, you're next."

Ariel hid the present behind her back.

"What gift do you have for your eldest sister?" asked Triton.

"Uh . . . um . . ." Ariel stammered.

"A song!" Sebastian announced.

Ariel racked her brain for a song to sing, and then she hit on it! She opened her mouth, and sang the melody from the music box.

When she finished, Flounder swam behind her, replacing the gift in her hand with a beautiful starfish for Aquata's hair.

"It's beautiful!" said Aquata. "And so was your song!"

King Triton smiled approvingly, and Ariel sighed with relief. How she wished her father would change his mind about humans!

"I'd give almost anything to see what the human world is like," she told Flounder. "Do you think my father will ever understand?"

"Maybe when he finally sees what it means to you," said Flounder, "someday he will."

# Bagheera Bears Up

**M**owgli danced around, humming happily to himself.

"What are you doing, Mowgli?" Bagheera asked from his perch in a nearby tree.

"Practising being a bear," Mowgli told him. "You should try it."

"Me?" Bagheera said, stunned. "I couldn't possibly do such a thing."

"Why not?" Mowgli wanted to know.

"Well, I'm a panther and I happen to like being one," Bagheera replied. "Why on earth would I want to be a bear?"

"Are you kidding?" Mowgli exclaimed. "Bears have the life! They hang out all day long, and they eat ants!"

"Eat ants?" Bagheera asked. "And that's a good thing?"

"Sure!" Mowgli said. "Well, truthfully, they tickle your throat at first. But you get used to it soon enough."

"Have you?" Bagheera asked.

"Not yet," Mowgli confessed. "But I will!"

"Whatever you say, Mowgli," said Bagheera.

Mowgli thought for a moment. "And if you were a bear, you would eat fruit and drink coconut juice, and you would relax, just like us!"

"If you ask me," Bagheera said. "I don't see anything so bad about being a panther. In fact, I like it very much."

"I think you're scared," Mowgli told him.

"Absolutely not!" Bagheera protested. "What on earth would I have to be scared of?" He stood up, stretched and gracefully jumped out of the tree and onto the ground.

"Exactly," Mowgli said. "So, why not try it?"

"You've got to be kidding me!" Bagheera said.

"You know what your problem is?" Mowgli said.

"I'm afraid to ask," Bagheera said.

"You're like a beehive," Mowgli told him. "You work too hard." He stared at Bagheera. "Come on, dance with me!" he cried, grabbing Bagheera's paw and prancing around the panther. After a bit, Bagheera began to dance too, moving his feet and twitching his tail.

"That's it!" Mowgli cheered.

"You know what?" Bagheera admitted. "This isn't so bad after all."

"Now you're getting it!" Mowgli exclaimed. "Now you see why being a bear is so great!" The Man-cub stopped dancing and threw himself on a soft patch of moss. "It's not so bad, is it?"

"Actually," Bagheera said, scratching his back against a rock, "it's sort of fun!"

"One more time!" Mowgli cheered, and they began dancing again.

# St Patrick's Day Switcheroo!

Huey, Dewey and Louie were getting dressed one morning when Louie had an idea.

"Hey," he said to his brothers, "are you two wearing green for St Patrick's Day?"

"Yes, of course," said Dewey.

"Me too," said Huey.

"Well," replied Louie, gesturing at the green shirt and hat that he wore every day, "then I bet we could really confuse our Unca Donald!"

Huey and Dewey both smiled as they contemplated Louie's sneaky idea.

"He's so used to seeing me wearing red . . ." said Huey.

"And me wearing blue . . ." said Dewey.

"That if he doesn't look closely," said Louie, "he'll be totally confused!"

The three of them chuckled as they headed towards the kitchen. Then, while Huey and Dewey hid in the hallway, Louie walked in and sat down next to Donald Duck, who was reading the newspaper at the breakfast table.

"Morning, Unca Donald," said Louie.

"Morning, Louie," Donald replied. "Will you go get your brothers? Breakfast is ready."

"Okay," Louie replied, leaving the room.

Next, Dewey walked into the kitchen and sat down. "Morning, Unca Donald," he said.

Donald looked up only briefly from his paper. "I thought I told you to go get your brothers, Louie," he said.

"No, you didn't," Dewey replied. "And I'm not Louie."

Donald looked up and scrutinized Dewey's face. "Oh," he said. "I'm sorry, Dewey. Go get your brothers, would you?"

"Okay," Dewey replied.

A few minutes later, Huey walked into the kitchen and sat down at the table.

Donald glanced up from the newspaper. "Well, where are they?" he asked Huey impatiently.

"Where are who?" said Huey.

"Your brothers," Donald replied. "I asked you to go get them."

"No, you didn't," said Huey.

"Yes, I –" Donald looked up from the paper and stared at Huey hard. "Oh . . . Huey," he said, realizing his mistake. "I thought you were . . . hey!" Donald looked at Huey suspiciously. "Are you three trying to confuse me? Is that why you're all wearing the same thing?"

Huey looked up at Donald with a blank stare. "Whatever do you mean, Unca Donald?"

"It's St Patrick's Day," said Louie, coming in from the hallway.

"Yeah," said Dewey, following Louie into the kitchen. "That's why we're all wearing green. Happy St Patrick's Day, Unca Donald!"

# March Comes in Like a Lion

"Oh dear," said Pooh as the wind whipped around him. "It's very windy. Are you sure this is a good idea, Tigger?" He and Tigger were carrying Pooh's kite out into a clearing in the middle of the Hundred-Acre Wood.

"Don't be silly, Pooh Boy," Tigger responded. "Today is the perfect day to fly your kite. After all, what else is wind for?"

"Yes," Pooh replied. "I suppose you're right." He leaned into a particularly strong gust to keep it from blowing him over as they walked on. Winter was on its way out of the Wood, and spring was on its way in – and it seemed the wind was rushing in to fill the space in between, for it was one of the blusteriest days Pooh could remember.

At last, struggling against the wind, Pooh and Tigger reached the middle of the clearing and got ready to launch the kite. Pooh unrolled some kite string while Tigger held the kite.

"Okay, Pooh," said Tigger. "Get ready! You hold on to the string, and I'll toss the kite up into the wind. One . . . two . . . THREE!"

With that, Tigger tossed the kite and it was immediately seized by the strong wind and carried high into the air where it danced and darted this way and that.

Meanwhile, Pooh struggled to hold on to the roll of kite string.

"Let out some more string, Pooh!" Tigger suggested. "Let's see how high we can fly it!"

So Pooh let out some more string. The kite sailed higher into the air and, blown around by stronger and stronger gusts, it tugged harder and harder on Pooh's end of the line.

"Fly it higher, Pooh!" exclaimed Tigger.

So Pooh let out more and more string until he had let it all out. He clung tightly to the end of the line as the kite soared, seeming almost to touch the low clouds.

Then, all of a sudden, a tremendous gust of wind blew through the clearing. At the end of the kite string, Pooh felt his feet leave the ground as the wind grabbed hold of the kite and carried it sharply upward.

"My goodness!" said Pooh, realizing that he was being lifted up. Then, before he could be carried too high, he let go of the kite string and tumbled gently to the ground.

But the kite sailed on – up and away, dancing on the breeze for what seemed like forever, until it came to rest at last in the high branches of a very tall tree at the edge of the clearing. Pooh wondered how he would ever get it down.

"Oh well," said Tigger, patting his friend sympathetically on the back. "Guess you flew it just a little too high there, Pooh Boy."

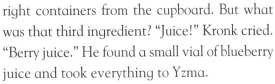

# Potion Commotion

Emperor Kuzco's royal adviser, Yzma, was down in her secret laboratory, mixing potions. She had enlisted her enthusiastic but dim-witted right-hand man, Kronk, to help her in her work.

"Kronk, I need spider legs, one eye of newt and elderberry juice . . . and quickly!" Yzma directed.

"Legs, eye, juice," Kronk repeated. "Right." He hurried across the laboratory to the cupboard that contained all of Yzma's potion ingredients. Inside were hundreds of glass jars, some filled with coloured liquids and powders, others holding creepy-looking body parts of various insects and lizards.

"Let's see," Kronk said to himself as he pored over the containers. "Legs, eye, juice. Legs, eye, juice." He found the 'legs' section. "Newt legs! Check!" Kronk said to himself, confusing Yzma's instructions.

Then he found the 'eye' section. "Spider eyes! Got it!" he said, grabbing the jar. He hurried back to Yzma with the two containers.

"Kronk!" shouted Yzma. "I said spider legs and newt eye! Not newt legs and spider eye! And where's the elderberry juice? Hurry, hurry!"

Kronk hurried back to the cupboard. "Spider legs . . . newt eye . . . spider legs . . . newt eye," he recited as he went. This time, he managed to remember them and took down the right containers from the cupboard. But what was that third ingredient? "Juice!" Kronk cried. "Berry juice." He found a small vial of blueberry juice and took everything to Yzma.

"Not blueberry juice, you numbskull!" Yzma screamed. "ELDERBERRY!"

"Right," Kronk said.

He hurried back across the laboratory and quickly located the 'juice' section. "Boysenberry . . . cranberry . . ." he read, moving alphabetically through the containers.

"ELDERBERRY!" Yzma shouted at him. "Get it over here! *And step on it!*"

Kronk finally located the right bottle. "Got it!" He rushed it across the laboratory. Yzma reached out to take the bottle from him.

But Kronk didn't hand it to her. Instead, he gently placed the bottle on the floor.

Then he lifted his right foot and stomped on it – hard – shattering the bottle and splattering juice everywhere.

"KRONK!" Yzma screamed in surprise. "What are you doing?"

Kronk was confused. "I did just what you said," he explained. "I got the elderberry juice. And I stepped on it."

Yzma let loose a hair-raising scream of frustration and collapsed in a heap on the laboratory floor.

# Walt Disney's
# Bambi

# Spring Has Sprung!

Spring had come at last to the forest. *Sniff, sniff* – Bambi could smell the change in the air. The days were growing longer. The nights were getting shorter. The ice and snow were quickly melting away. Crocuses and daffodils were pushing new green shoots out of the ground.

And the forest didn't feel quite as lonely as it had during the cold weather. In just the last few days, Bambi had noticed that there were more animals peeking their heads out of their holes and burrows and dens.

As he took a walk through the forest very early one morning on the first day of spring, Bambi came upon Mrs Possum and her children hanging upside down by their tails from a tree branch. She and Bambi had not seen one another in a long while. But Mrs Possum recognized him just the same.

"Well, hello, Bambi," said Mrs Possum.

"Hello, Mrs Possum," Bambi replied. "I haven't seen you since autumn. Where have you and your family been all winter long?"

"Oh, we like to spend most of our winter indoors," Mrs Possum replied. "But now that spring is here, it's so nice to be out in the fresh air again." Then Mrs Possum and the rest of her family closed their eyes and dozed off, because they liked to spend most of their days sleeping, you know.

Walking on through the forest, Bambi stopped by a tree filled with twittering birds.

"Hello, Bambi," said one of the birds.

"Hello," Bambi replied. "And where have you birds been all winter long?"

"Oh, we fly south for the winter, to warmer places where we can find more food," the bird explained. "But we are so happy it is spring once more. It is lovely to be back in the forest."

Then the bird joined her voice with her friends' twittering tunes. After so many months without it, the chirps and tweets were sweet music to Bambi's ears.

Bambi walked further, meeting old friends at every turn. He came upon mice moving from their winter quarters back into their spring and summer homes. He noticed the squirrels and chipmunks snacking leisurely on nuts, no longer storing them away in their winter stockpiles. He heard a woodpecker rapping at a pine tree. And he spotted the ducks out for a swim on the pond.

Yes, thought Bambi, it had been a long, cold, difficult winter. But somehow the arrival of spring made him feel that everything would be all right. Everywhere he looked there was life, there were new beginnings . . . and, most importantly, there was hope.

**March**
**21**

# Home Sweet Home

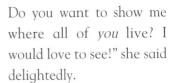

As the sun rose above the Seven Dwarfs' cottage, Snow White was already thinking about what to make for supper that evening. She had arrived at the cottage just the day before, after her evil stepmother, the Queen, had driven Snow White from the palace and the Queen's huntsman had left her alone in the forest. Luckily, a group of helpful woodland creatures had befriended Snow White and led her to the Dwarfs' little cottage. Now, for the first time in a long time, she felt safe and happy.

She was so grateful to the Dwarfs for sharing their cosy home with her, she wanted to give them a special treat.

"Perhaps we'll have gooseberry pie for supper tonight!" she said to her furry woodland friends after the Dwarfs had gone to work. The little animals nodded in agreement. Together they left the cottage and headed to the forest to pick berries. With all her friends helping, Snow White quickly filled her berry basket. Then she sat down among the sweet-smelling flowers with a sigh.

"How different life has become," she said to her friends. "I don't miss the grand castle at all. I love living in this funny little cottage. A home does not need to be grand to be a happy one! Remember that!"

The animals exchanged looks with one another. They began tugging at her skirt to pull her to her feet.

"What is it, dears?" she asked them. "Oh! Do you want to show me where all of *you* live? I would love to see!" she said delightedly.

Two bluebirds were first. Twittering excitedly, they fluttered around their nest, which had been built in a cosy nook of a nearby tree.

"What a lovely nest!" cried Snow White. The birds looked pleased.

The fawns were next. Pulling at her skirt, they brought Snow White to a sun-dappled clearing in a warm glade.

"How cosy!" exclaimed Snow White. The fawns flicked their tails happily.

Next, the chipmunks and squirrels showed her the hollow in an old tree where they lived. Then the rabbits proudly showed her the entrance to their burrows.

"You all have such pretty little homes," said Snow White, as they made their way back to the Dwarfs' cottage. "Thank you for showing them to me. We are all lucky to live where we do, aren't we?" she said with a smile.

And with that, she skipped the rest of the way back to the cottage to start preparing her pie. She could hardly wait until the Dwarfs got home!

# The Chosen One

The green three-eyed alien toys looked up as something moved overhead. They let out soft gasps and murmurs. Was it the Claw? The Claw was their master. It descended from the sky. It decided who would go and who would stay. Every alien eagerly awaited the day that the Claw would choose him.

But this time it was not the Claw. Instead, the small door on the side of their home opened. Dozens of three-eyed aliens just like them poured in.

"Welcome," one of the original aliens greeted the newcomers. "Welcome to the Choosing Place."

Another alien gasped. "Look!" he cried. "One of the new ones is not like us. He is – different!"

The others looked. Then they cried out in surprise and confusion. One of the new aliens had only *two* eyes on his round green head!

"What is the matter with your face, stranger?" one of the three-eyed aliens asked warily. "You don't look like us."

"I – I don't know," the two-eyed one said hesitantly. "I have always been this way. A Voice from above once said that – that . . ."

His voice trailed off with shame. A three-eyed newcomer spoke up.

"I heard the Voice," he said solemnly. "It said that it was – a Manufacturing Defect."

The three-eyed alien toys murmured with astonishment and a bit of suspicion. There had never been such a thing in their world before!

Suddenly there was a great whirring sound from above.

"The Claw!" someone cried reverently. "The Claw – it moves! It descends!"

"The Claw! The Claw!" the others murmured.

"The Claw decides who will go and who will stay," someone said.

They all waited, gazing upwards hopefully as the Claw came closer and closer. Finally, its talons closed over one round green head.

"The Claw has chosen!" they cried.

"Cool!" a child's muffled voice came from somewhere outside. "I got the best one!"

The aliens watched as the Claw raised the Chosen One above the others. They gasped as they recognized the strange, two-eyed newcomer.

"The different one has been chosen!" one of the three-eyed aliens exclaimed. "The Claw has chosen him despite his Manufacturing Defect!"

"The Claw knew that the different one was special," someone else added.

The others nodded solemnly. "We will learn from the Claw," one of them said.

"Yes," another finished. "From now on, we will welcome all newcomers, no matter how different. For the Claw has shown us the way."

# Miss Bianca's First Rescue

The headquarters of the Rescue Aid Society was buzzing with activity. Mice from all over the world had gathered together for an emergency meeting. The Chairman of the Society had to shout to be heard over the hubbub.

"Attention, delegates!" he cried. "I have called this meeting because a canine urgently needs our help." He clapped his hands. "Mice scouts, bring in the distressed doggie!"

Two mice workers hurried into the room, leading a small dog with a long body and short little legs. His head was stuck inside a dog food can.

"*Mama mia!*" cried the mouse from Italy.

"Arooooo!" howled the dog.

The mouse from Yemen suggested pulling the can off the dog. Four muscular mice set to work, pulling and tugging. But it held fast.

The mice finally decided that the can would have to be removed by mechanical means. The Zambian delegate suggested using a can opener.

Suddenly the door to the meeting room flew open. There stood a pretty little mouse. She wore a fashionable coat and expensive perfume.

"Oh, excuse me," she said. "I seem to be in the wrong place. I'm looking for Micey's Department Store?

"Dear me," she said, noticing the delegate with the can opener, "what are you doing to that poor dog?"

"The dog is quite stuck, I'm afraid," the Chairman told her. "But the situation is under control."

The glamorous mouse pushed up her sleeves and marched over to the dog.

She kicked the top of the can three times. Then she gave it a swift twist to the left. And the can popped off!

"Hooray!" the mice all cheered happily.

The little mouse smiled. "That's how I open pickle jars at home," she explained. "Well, I'd best be on my way."

"Ah, Mr Chairman?" a voice piped up from the corner of the room. It was the Zambian delegate.

"Yes?" said the Chairman.

"I'd like to nominate Miss . . . uh, Miss . . ." The delegate looked at the pretty mouse.

"Miss Bianca," she told him.

"I'd like to nominate Miss Bianca for membership in the Rescue Aid Society," he said.

The Chairman turned to the rest of the mice delegates. "All in favour say, 'Aye!'"

"Aye!" all the mice cried.

"Woof!" the dog barked happily.

Miss Bianca smiled. "Well," she said, "I suppose Micey's can wait for another day."

Walt Disney's
**Sleeping Beauty**

# Berry Picking

Once upon a time, in a forest far away, there lived a lovely princess who did not know she was a princess, and three good fairies who pretended to be mortal. (Of course, you know exactly to whom we are referring . . . so let's get right to the story of Briar Rose and her three 'aunts.')

One morning, Flora called the group together to suggest they go out to search the forest for berries.

"What a wonderful idea," said Briar Rose.

"Yes, indeed," said Merryweather. "If we pick enough, we can make a berry pie."

"If we pick enough," declared Fauna, "we can make enough jam to last us through the whole year."

"Well, we'll never have enough if we don't get started now," said Flora. And so they gathered their berry baskets and set out.

They followed a shady path through the forest until they came upon a thicket bursting with berry bushes. And, without delay, the four berry-pickers got to work. But, as you will see, just because they got to work, doesn't mean their baskets actually got full.

Merryweather, for one, had a terrible time keeping her basket upright. Every time she bent to pick another berry, her basket tipped and out spilled all but two or three.

Fauna, on the other hand, had an entirely different problem keeping her berries in her basket – somehow they kept finding their way into her mouth!

And as for Briar Rose, her heart and her mind were miles away from her berry basket . . . dancing instead in the arms of a handsome stranger.

"All right, dearies," Flora called as the sun began to sink. "It's time to start back to the cottage. Let's see what you've got."

"Um, well . . ." said Merryweather. "I don't seem to have many berries in my basket."

Flora rolled her eyes and moved on to Fauna. "Let me guess . . ." she said as she looked from Fauna's empty basket to her purple mouth.

"Ah, yes . . ." Fauna said as she guiltily dabbed at a drop of juice on her lips. "Berries . . . delicious!"

Flora sighed. "And you, Briar Rose?" she asked hopefully.

But Briar Rose just looked down sheepishly at the empty basket in her hands. "I'm sorry, Aunt Flora," she said. "I guess I got a little bit distracted."

"Well," said Flora, shaking her head, "no berry pie for us this week, I guess." Then she shrugged. "But we can always have chocolate cake instead!"

## Meeko's Wild Ride

"What a perfect day for a canoe ride," Pocahontas said to her friend Meeko the raccoon, who lounged in the bow of the canoe as Pocahontas paddled down the river. Flit the hummingbird was flying alongside them.

It was a warm, sunny, early spring day. The chunks of ice on the river had melted away, and there were only small patches of snow here and there along the riverbank. In fact, all of the melted ice and snow had added several feet to the water level. The river was high and moving fast, but Pocahontas confidently guided the canoe downstream.

Soon, they came to a fork in the river. To the left, the river flowed swiftly but calmly as far as Pocahontas could see. But gazing down the other arm of the river, Pocahontas caught a glimpse of white water.

"Ooh," she said, "rapids!" She steered the canoe to the right and headed straight for them, eager for a challenge.

But Meeko, who had been reclining lazily, sat bolt upright. He knew that he was in for a wild ride! He scurried to hide behind Pocahontas, then clung to her as the canoe took a sudden dip and plunged into the rapids.

"Meeko, relax," said Pocahontas with a chuckle. "These are baby rapids."

A small wave sprayed water lightly into Meeko's face. He shrieked, scurried onto Pocahontas's shoulder, and buried his face in the back of her neck.

The canoe bobbed along on the white water. Pocahontas laughed gleefully. But poor Meeko climbed onto the top of her head, trying to get as far from the water as possible.

Then, spying a mini-waterfall up ahead, Meeko closed his eyes and wrapped his arms tightly around Pocahontas's head.

"Hey!" Pocahontas said with a laugh. "I can't see a thing!"

Nonetheless, she piloted the canoe gently and easily down the waterfall and into a calm pool of water on the other side.

Meeko was still clinging to Pocahontas's head with his eyes shut tight, when Pocahontas ran the canoe aground on the riverbank.

"Okay, brave Meeko," she said, teasing him. "It's safe now."

Opening his eyes and spying dry land, Meeko clambered down and raced along the canoe's gunwale toward the riverbank. But, in his haste, he lost his footing. He slipped and landed with a splash in the shallow water.

Pocahontas couldn't help laughing. "Let your guard down too soon, eh?" she said.

Meeko just scowled and decided to keep his paws on land for a while.

# A Party of Three

The Widow Tweed hummed cheerfully as she decorated her cottage. Tod, the little fox she had adopted not long ago, watched with excitement. This was his first birthday in his new home!

"Now, Tod," said the widow, "who shall we invite to your party?"

Tod jumped on the windowsill and looked over at Amos Slade's farm. The Widow Tweed knew what that meant: Tod wanted his friend Copper the hound dog to share in the celebration. "I know Copper is your friend," she said, "but what if Amos catches him over here? There's no telling what that old coot might do!"

Tod jumped on the kind woman's lap and gazed up at her with big, sad eyes. "Oh, Tod! Stop looking at me like that. Well – all right! You can ask Copper over just this once!"

"I'm not supposed to leave the yard," Copper explained when Tod invited him. "I'll get in trouble with my master."

"Don't worry," Tod said. "I've got it all figured out." He lifted up one of the hound dog's enormous, floppy ears and whispered his plan.

Soon Tod showed up in Amos Slade's chicken yard. He ran among the birds, causing them to flap their wings and cluck in panic. That was Copper's signal to bark as loudly as he could. Amos burst out of the cabin just in time to see Copper chasing Tod into the woods.

"Follow me!" yelled Tod to Copper. He led his friend through a series of hollow logs, and then through a long, underground burrow. When the two pals emerged above ground, they were right outside Tod's back door. The Widow Tweed was waiting.

"Quick, scoot!" she said, shooing the two into the cottage.

While Amos Slade wandered around the woods trying to find Tod and Copper, the party festivities at the Widow Tweed's were just beginning. The three played hide-and-seek, pin-the-tail-on-the-donkey and drop-the-clothespin-in-the-jug. Tod won every game. Finally, it was time to cut the cake. After everyone had seconds, the widow spied Slade coming out of the woods. She let Copper out through the back door, where he stood barking ferociously.

"Good tracking, Copper!" Slade cried. "Did you chase that no-good fox all the way through the woods?" Copper looked up at his master and wagged his tail. "Copper," Slade said, "what's that on your face?" The hound turned his head and quickly licked the cake crumbs off his muzzle. "Hmmm," said Slade. "Must be seeing things. Let's go home then."

Inside the cosy cottage, Tod smiled. It had been a wonderful birthday – and sharing it with his best friend had definitely been the icing on the cake!

# The Silent Treatment

The Queen of Hearts loved to shout orders at her royal subjects. She shouted so much, in fact, that it wasn't surprising when she came down with a terrible case of laryngitis.

"There, there," said her husband, the diminutive King. "Rest your voice and let me do the ruling for you, my dear." The Queen hardly let the King get a word in edgeways, so he was looking forward to being in charge for a change.

As they strolled through the royal garden, the Queen noticed that the fence was painted pink instead of the required red. "Off! Off!" the Queen croaked. She wanted the King to punish the royal gardeners with her favourite order, "Off with their heads!"

Instead, the King said, "The Queen decrees that you may have the day off!" The gardeners cheered as steam escaped from the Queen's ears. "You must relax, sweetheart," the King warned her, "or you simply won't get well."

Soon the couple paused to play a game of croquet. The Queen hit the hedgehog ball with the flamingo mallet, and the hedgehog rolled willy-nilly across the lawn. The playing-card wickets knew better than to let the Queen make a bad shot. They jumped all over the grass, making sure the ball passed underneath them. "I'm undefeated!" the Queen rasped triumphantly.

"What's that, dear?" asked the King. He couldn't understand exactly what his wife was saying. "The Queen says she cheated!" he finally announced.

The entire royal staff gasped. Those nearby ducked as the Queen swung a flamingo at the King's head.

"That's enough croquet for today," crooned the King soothingly. "You don't want to tire yourself out."

He led his wife to a bench in the shade. The Queen sat down, pointed to the servants hovering nearby and acted out drinking a cup of tea.

The King stood up and announced, "You're all invited to have tea with the Queen!" Of course, this was not what the Queen had in mind at all.

A table was laid with tea, fancy cakes and sandwiches. Everyone ate, laughed and had a wonderful time. The Queen, ignored by everyone, seethed with anger.

She grabbed one of the flamingo mallets, then charged the table. Unfortunately, she didn't see the croquet ball in her path. As she tripped, the flamingo's beak plunged into the ground, causing the Queen to pole-vault up and over the table of guests and through her open bedroom window.

"A splendid idea, my dear!" called the King. "A nap will do you good!"

# Dance, Daddy-o!

Deep in the jungle at the temple ruins, the monkeys and their ruler, King Louie, were always looking to have a swingin' time.

"Let's have a dance-off!" King Louie suggested to the monkeys one evening.

"Hooray!" the monkeys cheered.

"What's a dance-off?" one monkey asked.

"You know, a contest," said King Louie. "An opportunity for everyone to get down, strut their stuff, cut a rug! And whoever lays down the smoothest moves is the winner!"

"Hooray!" cheered the monkeys.

King Louie rubbed his chin. "The first thing we need is some music," he said, pointing at the monkey musicians. "Hit it, fellas!"

The musicians blasted out a jazzy tune, blowing through their hands like horns, knocking out a beat on some coconuts and drumming on a hollow log. Soon, all the monkeys were gathered around the musicians, tapping their toes and shaking their tails.

"Now," said King Louie, "who will dance?"

All the monkeys raised their hands. King Louie looked around. "Let's see," he said scratching his head, "I choose . . . me!"

"Hooray!" the monkeys cheered. They were disappointed not to be chosen. But, after all, King Louie *was* their King.

So King Louie moved his hips from side to side. He waved his arms in the air. He closed his eyes so he could really feel the beat.

"Dance, Daddy-o!" one monkey cried.

King Louie boogied and bopped like he had never boogied and bopped before. Then, when the song was over, King Louie stopped dancing and scrambled onto his throne. "Now it's time to choose the winner!" he said.

"But King Louie . . ." one monkey began to object. All the other monkeys were thinking the same thing: didn't you need more than one dancer to have a dance-off?

"Oh, silly me," said King Louie with a chuckle. The monkeys looked at each other and smiled, expecting that the King had realized his mistake. But, King Louie said, "Of course, we need a judge! Who will judge?"

Everyone raised their hands. King Louie looked around, then said, "I choose . . . me!"

"Hooray!" the monkeys cheered.

"And as the judge, I will now choose the winner of the dance-off," King Louie continued. He looked around at all the monkeys. "Now, let's see. I choose . . . me! Let's hear it for the winner!"

"Hooray!" the monkeys cheered, because, after all, King Louie was their King – and a pretty swingin' dancer, too!

# DINOSAUR

# Lemur Love

Early one morning on Lemur Island, Plio sat on a branch, trying to groom her daughter. Suri was very fidgety. She was itching to join her friends. But Plio wouldn't let Suri go until her fur was combed and clean.

"Suri, sit still," said Plio as she used her bottom teeth to comb Suri's fur.

"Why do I have to be groomed every single day?" Suri groaned.

"Would you rather I let you swing around with dirty fur?" Plio said.

"Yeah!" Suri exclaimed.

Plio sighed. "All right, all done," she said, giving Suri's fur one last stroke. In a flash, Suri jumped up and hurried off to join her friends.

Plio shook her head as she watched Suri go. "Every morning, it's the same thing: an out-and-out struggle to get that girl groomed," she said to herself. "But if I didn't, I bet she'd get so tired of being messy that, after a few days, she'd be *begging* me to groom her!"

That gave Plio an idea. So the next morning, Plio didn't say a word about grooming. Just as Suri was about to leave her mother's side to go off and play, she hesitated. "I guess you have to groom me first, huh, Mum?" Suri said glumly.

Plio shrugged. "Not if you don't want me to," she replied.

"Really?" said Suri. "Yippee!" And she hurried off to meet her friends.

"Do I have to be groomed this morning," Suri asked the next day, "since you didn't do it yesterday?" She looked down at her slightly matted fur.

"Nope," Plio said. "If you want to be untidy, you can be untidy."

"Cool!" said Suri. But this time she didn't sound quite as excited as she had the day before.

The morning after that, Plio caught Suri looking over at her wistfully.

"Suri?" Plio said. "What's the matter?" But Plio thought she knew what the matter was.

And just as Plio expected, Suri said, "Mum, would you groom me this morning?"

"Groom you?" Plio replied, pretending to be surprised. "But, Suri, I thought you *hated* being groomed. Let me guess: you're tired of having messy fur, aren't you?"

Suri shook her head. "No," she said.

"No?" said Plio in surprise.

"No," repeated Suri. "I miss being fussed over." She hung her head bashfully and wrapped her arms around her mother.

Plio's face softened into a smile as she hugged Suri back.

Then Plio gave Suri a long and careful grooming.

And do you know what? Suri didn't fidget once.

# Walt Disney's
# Pinocchio

# A Helping Hand

"Oh, Pinocchio!" cried Geppetto. "I can hardly believe that my little puppet is alive!" It was the morning after the Blue Fairy had visited Geppetto's house and brought Pinocchio to life. "You must get ready for school, my boy," said Geppetto.

Pinocchio was full of curiosity. "Why must I go to school, Father?" he asked.

"Why, so that you can learn!" Geppetto replied. "Now be a good boy and go make the bed while I clear away these dishes."

Ever eager to help, Pinocchio sprang up from the breakfast table and ran over to Geppetto's workbench. He found a hammer, a nail and a piece of wood, and began to pound loudly with the hammer.

"Pinocchio! Whatever are you doing?" cried Geppetto.

"Well, you asked me to make the bed," said Pinocchio. "So I was starting to make one."

With a little smile, Geppetto patted him on the head and said, "Perhaps it would be better for you to put the cat out."

As Geppetto turned back to the breakfast table, Pinocchio jumped up and grabbed a pitcher of water. Hurrying over to Figaro, Pinocchio threw the water onto the cat.

"*YEEEEOOWWWW!*" shrieked Figaro.

"Pinocchio!" shouted Geppetto. "Why did you do that?"

"You . . . you told me to put the cat out. I thought he had caught fire," said Pinocchio in a small voice.

"Oh, my dear boy, you have much to learn!" Geppetto sighed as he dried off Figaro. "Okay, you can be a helpful boy by helping me to pick up the house a bit before you leave for school."

"All right, Father!" said Pinocchio, and he raced out the front door.

"Where in the world is he going?" Geppetto wondered aloud, as he followed Pinocchio outside.

Pinocchio was crouching at the base of the house, trying with all his might to lift it.

"What are you doing, son?" asked Geppetto with a twinkle in his eye.

"Trying to pick up the house, Father," said Pinocchio, his voice straining with effort.

Geppetto chuckled and gently guided Pinocchio back inside. "My boy, the sooner you go to school and learn about the world, the better for us both," he said. He collected Pinocchio's hat, his schoolbook and an apple for the teacher, and sent him on his way.

As Geppetto watched his new son walk off to school, he shook his head worriedly. "I hope he manages to stay out of trouble today," he said to himself. "My little boy has much to learn about the world."

**ROBIN HOOD**

# A Game of Robin Hood

"Let's play Robin Hood!" Skippy shouted to his friends Tagalong, Toby and Sis. As he did every day, Skippy was wearing the hat and carrying the bow and arrows that the real Robin Hood had given him for his birthday.

"All right," agreed Tagalong. "I'll be Robin's best friend, Little John. Toby can be the mean old Sheriff of Nottingham!"

"Well, then, I will be Maid Marian," said Sis.

The kids adored Robin Hood. He and his band of Merry Men lived in Sherwood Forest, but no one was sure exactly where, which was a lucky thing, since the Sheriff dearly wanted to find and arrest them. Robin Hood was loved by the people, because he robbed from the rich and gave to the poor. Nowadays many people were needy, for they were taxed heavily by the Sheriff of Nottingham. Everyone knew that the Sheriff was in league with the evil Prince John, and that they used the tax money for their own gain. Prince John's brother, King Richard, was the true King of England. But King Richard was fighting in the Crusades, far away.

"Hands up, sirrah!" said Skippy gleefully. He and Tagalong pretended to raid Toby's carriage. "We shall lighten your wallet today and give it away to the worthy citizens you have been taxing so heavily."

"Drat! My evil plans have been foiled again!" snarled Toby, pretending to hand over his money. "One day I'm going to get you, Robin Hood!"

Skippy laughed. "You'll never find me, Sheriff!" he cried. "If you come into Sherwood Forest, we will give you such a whipping that you'll wish you'd never heard of Robin Hood!"

Sis giggled, then ran over to a table and climbed up on top of it. "Oh, Robin! Robin!" she cried. "Help me, my darling, my own true love! That mean old Prince John had me locked up in this high tower! He heard that we are in love, and he intends to prevent us from ever being together! It's he and that horrible old Sheriff who ought to be locked up!"

Suddenly, the children froze. Someone had chuckled from behind the open door of the cottage. "Uh-oh," Skippy whispered. "We're toast. It's got to be the Sheriff of Nottingham!"

"He'll lock us up and throw away the key," Toby said, his voice shaking.

Sis jumped down from the table and hurried over to the others, who all looked terrified.

And then, suddenly, the 'Sheriff' stepped out from behind the door. It was Robin Hood!

"Keep up the good work, kids!" he said with a merry laugh. And then he bounded away into Sherwood Forest.

DISNEY'S
Lilo & Stitch

# Who's Fooling Whom?

Lilo had only had her new dog, Stitch, for a little while. Already he had managed to break just about everything he touched, and got Lilo's sister Nani dismissed from her new job.

Then April Fools' Day rolled around, and Lilo decided that, for one day, she was allowed to be a pain in the neck *back*.

Lilo got started first thing in the morning. She left a whoopee cushion on Stitch's chair at the breakfast table. When he came in to eat and sat down, a very loud and very rude noise reverberated around the kitchen.

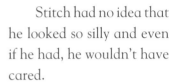

Lilo laughed and shouted, "April Fools'!"

Stitch shrugged. He made rude noises all the time, so he wasn't embarrassed one bit.

After lunch that day, Lilo handed Stitch a cream-filled cookie. She had replaced the filling with toothpaste mixed with pickle juice.

Stitch took a bite.

"April Fools'!" cried Lilo.

Stitch took another bite . . . and another . . . and another, until he finished the cookie. Then he licked his lips. Ugh! thought Lilo. Stitch would eat anything!

Later that day Lilo smeared some of Nani's eyeliner around the eyepieces of her binoculars. She pretended to see something interesting out on the water. "Check out that huge wave," she said. Lilo held the binoculars up to Stitch's eyes so he could look through them. When she pulled the binoculars away, Stitch had a dark ring around each of his eyes.

"April Fools'!" cried Lilo.

Stitch had no idea that he looked so silly and even if he had, he wouldn't have cared.

Stitch also didn't seem to notice the fake blood dripping from Lilo's mouth before dinner, the ping-pong balls that rained down when he opened the bedroom door, or the arrow-through-the-head hat Lilo put on at bedtime.

"You're no fun to fool, Stitch," said Lilo.

Then she pulled back the covers on her bed and climbed in. But, for some reason, she couldn't extend her legs all the way.

"Hey!" Lilo exclaimed. "Someone short-sheeted my bed! Nani!"

Nani poked her head into Lilo's room.

"Very funny," Lilo said to her.

Nani looked at Lilo with a blank stare. "What's very funny?"

Nani looked as if she didn't know what Lilo was talking about. But that only left . . .

No way, thought Lilo. Stitch was just a dog. Lilo looked at him, sitting at the foot of her bed, wagging his tail. There was no way he could have short-sheeted her bed.

Was there?

# Bird Trouble

It was the height of the rainy season, and the roof of the ant colony had sprung a leak. "Bucket brigade!" shouted Princess Atta. The ants obediently lined up and began catching the water in cupped leaves, passing them along the length of the line and dumping them into the stream. It was exhausting, but the ants were used to hard work.

"There's got to be an easier way," Flik said. "Tomorrow I'm going to invent a way to fix the roof!"

"What are you doing, Flik?" Dot asked the next morning. The rain had let up for a moment, and the two were outside. Flik had arranged dozens of torn pieces of leaves along one side of the sloping roof.

"I'm fixing the leak," he said cheerfully. "See, these leaves act as rain deflectors. Then the water will run into these hollowed-out flower stems that will act as gutters."

"Wow," said Dot. She was the only ant who thought Flik's inventions were worthwhile.

"The only thing I'm missing is some sort of deflection device for the ant hole itself," he said. "Aha!" he shouted a moment later. He had spotted a buttercup. "That flower should work perfectly. Come on, Dot. Give me a hand. Boy, oh, boy, is this invention ever going to impress the Princess!"

Together, the two ants dragged the buttercup to the top of the anthill.

"What on earth are you two doing?" It was Princess Atta.

"Flik figured out a way to fix the leak!" shouted Dot triumphantly.

Flik shrugged modestly. "It's very simple, really. See, what I did was . . ."

Suddenly, the ant lookout began shouting, "Bird! Bird! Bird coming!"

Flik, Atta and Dot ran for cover. Sure enough, a hummingbird was hovering just above the anthill.

"It's going for the flower!" shouted an ant. The hummingbird pressed its long beak into the buttercup Flik had dragged over the anthill.

"Avalanche!" shouted the ants. The delicately built anthill began to collapse. Ants scrambled to get out of the way. The bird flew off.

"Nice work, Flik," said Princess Atta. "This is going to take weeks to rebuild."

Flik sighed and hung his head.

"Don't worry, Flik," whispered Dot. "Someday you'll do great things."

"Oh, you're sweet, Dot," Flik said sadly. "If only it hadn't been for that bird. I should have known it would like the flower. Birds are so predictable." Now Flik looked thoughtful. "Maybe someday I could use that to my advantage."

Flik smiled at Dot. "Imagine that," he said. "An ant using a bird in his plan!"

April
**3**

# The Good Thing About Rain

"Rise and shine!" cried Pongo. One by one, he nudged each of his 15 Dalmatian puppies with his nose.

The puppies yawned and stretched.

But Rolly just rolled over and slept on.

"Aw, come on, Rolly," Pongo whispered in the pup's ear. "It's morning! Don't you want to go out?"

At the mention of the word 'out,' Rolly was instantly wide awake!

Rolly was not alone. As if by magic, the sleepy group had become a pack of jumping, barking puppies. They raced together through the kitchen to the back door, where they jumped up and down, waiting for Nanny to let them out into the garden.

"Okay, here I come," said Nanny, as she made her way across the kitchen. Then she flung the door open wide and stepped out of the way to let the puppies race past.

But they didn't move. It was raining!

"Oh, go on," said Perdita, trying to nudge the pups out the door. "It's only a little water."

But they wouldn't budge.

The next morning, Patch awoke with a start. With a few sharp barks, he helped Pongo wake the other puppies. Within seconds, all 15 were crowding around the back door.

Nanny rushed to open the door again.

And once again, the puppies were very disappointed to see raindrops falling.

"Well," said Pongo with a sigh, "April showers bring May flowers!"

The next morning, the puppies weren't in any hurry to go outside. After all, it was probably still raining. They thought that all they had to look forward to was another whole day spent inside.

So, when Nanny opened the door on a sunny morning, the puppies were so surprised that they didn't know what to do.

Then, springing into action, they tumbled over one another in their rush to get out the door. They raced off in different directions, ready to sniff, dig, roll and explore.

But then, almost at once, all 15 puppies froze in their tracks. They looked around at each other, then down at themselves. What was this stuff getting all over their spotted white coats? It was brown. It was wet. It was squishy. It was mud! And it was FUN!

From the doorway, Pongo and Perdita looked out at their muddy puppies and laughed.

"You know what this means, don't you?" Pongo asked Perdita.

Perdy nodded. "Baths."

Pongo smiled, watching the frolicking puppies. "Let's not tell them – just yet," he said.

# Dishes, Dishes, Dishes!

"Hmmph." Jim Hawkins grabbed another plate from the enormous pile of dishes he was scrubbing and dunked it into the soapy water. "This is not the adventure I had in mind," he said grumpily. Jim had been dreaming about travelling into the etherium and finding Treasure Planet since he was a kid. And he was finally doing it! But somehow working in the galley doing dishes for a crazy cyborg had never been a part of his fantasy.

With a sigh, Jim rinsed the plate he was holding and grabbed another one. He wished he was allowed to do something (besides mopping) up on deck. Jim was sure he could do as good a job as Oxy and Moron with the rigging, or at least be as helpful as Birdbrain Mary. But no. He was stuck in the kitchen, washing dishes. Alone.

Being alone was practically the worst part of it all. It was getting to be that Jim even looked forward to Silver's company. Of course, he was a weird old guy with a creepy cyborg eye - and that arm! But at least he told some good tales of spacers, and he was better than no company at all.

"Oh, no. No help for me. Just 'Get to work, Jimbo. I want this place shipshape by morning'," Jim said, doing his best Silver imitation under his breath.

Turning quickly, Jim looked back at the door to make sure Silver hadn't heard him. When he turned back, he saw with relief there was just one dish left. Yawning, he dipped it in the bucket, scrubbed it, rinsed it and wiped it dry. Then he added it to the pile of clean dishes.

"There," Jim said with a sigh. But, when he looked back, another dish was sitting beside his washtub. "Hmm. Must've missed one," he said picking up the plate.

"Now *that's* got to be it," Jim said, drying his hands on a towel. He leaned back on his stool and what he saw nearly caused him to fall over. Another dirty dish was waiting to be cleaned!

"I know I got the last one!" Jim rubbed his eyes. Perhaps he was more tired than he thought. But, when he opened his eyes, the dish was still there. "I've been in the kitchen too long," Jim mumbled. By the time he had cleaned it, another had appeared in its place!

Jim had to get out of the kitchen. He was starting to go crazy. Suddenly, the dish he was scrubbing slipped out of his hands. Then a pink blob burst out of the soapy water, spluttering and giggling.

"Morph!" Jim couldn't help but smile at little blob of protoplasm and his practical joke. "Gee, thanks for all of your help with the dishes," he said with a laugh.

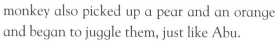

# Monkey See, Monkey Do

"Come on, Abu!" Aladdin called across the busy Agrabah marketplace.

From his perch on top of the basket-seller's cart, Abu barely heard the call. He was captivated by the monkey he had just spotted peeking out at him from behind the fruit-seller's cart. Abu jumped off the basket cart and darted over to say hello.

But the other monkey scurried away and hid behind a wheel. From his new hiding place, he peeked out at Abu.

Abu looked around, trying to think of a way to draw out the monkey. The fruit seller was distracted, talking to a customer, so Abu hopped up onto the cart and picked up an apple. He balanced it on top of his head. Then he scurried over to the edge of the cart and peered down, hoping to attract the monkey's attention.

But he was gone.

Abu heard monkey chatter behind him. He turned around to find the monkey standing at the other end of the fruit cart, balancing an apple on *his* head, just like Abu.

Abu laughed and picked up a pear and an orange. He began juggling them in the air, hoping to amuse the other monkey.

But the other monkey didn't look amused. He looked annoyed! He thought Abu was trying to show him up. Not to be outdone, the monkey also picked up a pear and an orange and began to juggle them, just like Abu.

Abu put the fruit down. He did a handstand on the cart railing.

The other monkey did a handstand too.

Abu grabbed hold of the cart awning, then flipped over and swung from the awning by his tail.

The other monkey did the same.

Abu laughed again. He thought this game was fun. But now he wanted to find a stunt that the other monkey couldn't copy. Abu looked around. He spotted Aladdin coming his way.

Abu had an idea. He jumped off the fruit cart, darted over to Aladdin and scrambled up the length of his friend's body until he was lounging comfortably on top of Aladdin's head.

The other monkey stared in amazement. He didn't know that Aladdin was Abu's friend. How could he copy that stunt? He looked around. The closest human was the fruit seller. Throwing caution to the wind, the other monkey scurried over to him – but he'd only climbed as high as the fruit-seller's shoulder before the man chased him away.

Then, from behind the basket cart, the other monkey crossed his arms, pouted and watched that sneaky Abu laugh and wave good-bye as he was carried away on top of Aladdin's head.

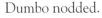

# Walt Disney's DUMBO

## You're Gonna Be Huge!

**D**umbo sat in the corner with a big frown on his face.

"What's the matter, kid?" Timothy asked.

Dumbo just shook his head.

"You've got nothing to be sad about," Timothy continued.

Dumbo didn't say anything.

"Well, if you're not going to tell me what's bugging ya, I guess I'll just have to figure it out for myself," Timothy said. "I know!" he exclaimed. "You're hungry?"

Dumbo shook his head.

"Thirsty?" Timothy asked.

Dumbo shook his head again.

"Concerned about the June-bug population in Saskatchewan?" Timothy suggested.

Dumbo shook his head doubly hard.

"Well, then," Timothy concluded. "It can only be one thing. It pains me to say it, but I think you have a case of 'feeling sorry for myself-itis'."

Dumbo's large ears pricked up.

"Yes," Timothy continued. "It's a dangerous disease that has affected many of us. Even the strongest cannot avoid it."

Dumbo looked to his left and to his right, then pointed to himself.

"Yes, that's right – you!" Timothy said. "I bet I know what's got you down – your above-average ear size."

Dumbo nodded.

"And the fact that people make fun of you," Timothy continued.

Dumbo nodded even more.

"And, on top of all that," Timothy said, "you've been separated from your mother."

A tear started to form in Dumbo's eye.

"Don't feel sorry for yourself!" Timothy ordered.

Dumbo looked up, surprised.

"You know why?" Timothy asked. "Because one day you're gonna be huge!"

Dumbo blinked in disbelief.

"We're talking autographs, your name in lights. They're gonna eat their hats for the way they treated you," Timothy predicted.

Dumbo looked nervous.

"I don't mean eat their hats for real," Timothy explained. "It's just a figure of speech. Not that some of them wouldn't deserve having to eat their hats. But that's not what we're talking about. They're gonna be really sorry they treated you so bad, understand?"

Dumbo nodded his head.

"All right then," Timothy said. "Feeling better?"

And Dumbo nodded doubly hard as visions of success, happiness – and being with his mother again – filled his head.

# Good Luck Charm

In ancient China, it was believed that crickets were good luck. But, on one particular night, long, long ago, Mulan's Grandmother Fa was having trouble remembering that. It was very late. There was a cricket loose somewhere in her bedroom, and every time she was about to drop off to sleep . . .

*Cri-cket! Cri-cket!* the cricket chirped loudly.

"This cricket will bring good fortune to our home," Grandmother Fa said, looking on the bright side.

All was quiet for a few minutes. Grandmother Fa slowly relaxed, wondering if perhaps the cricket itself had finally dropped off to sleep, when –

*Cri-cket! Cri-cket!*

"Ugh!" exclaimed Grandmother Fa, throwing off the covers and getting out of bed. Now she was determined to find that cricket.

She lit a candle and began her search. She looked under the bed. She peeked behind the chest of drawers. She looked everywhere.

But there was no sign of the cricket.

Grandmother Fa blew out the candle. She got back into bed and tried to sleep.

*Cri-cket! Cri-cket!*

Grandmother Fa got out of bed again and relit her candle. She searched in her wardrobe. She looked inside her slippers. She checked under her pillow. But she didn't find the cricket.

One more time, Grandmother Fa climbed into bed and tried to sleep.

*Cri-cket! Cri-cket!*

Grandmother Fa sighed and dragged herself out of bed. She relit the candle. Was there anywhere that she hadn't yet looked?

Just then, a slight movement on the windowsill caught Grandmother Fa's eye. There, sitting on the windowsill, was a tiny cricket. She scooped it up gently and cradled it in her hand.

That's when Grandmother Fa noticed that the window was open. And it looked as if a rainstorm was brewing outside.

"Well, little cricket," said Grandmother Fa, "is that why you were trying to get my attention?" Had the cricket been trying to save Grandmother Fa from waking up to a puddle beneath her open window? "Maybe you're good luck, after all," she said.

She decided that she would hold on to the cricket and see if it brought her more luck. So Grandmother Fa pulled out a bamboo cricket cage, gently placed the cricket inside, and put the cage on her bedside table.

Then, she climbed into bed, blew out the candle and closed her eyes. At last, she thought, she'd be able to get some sleep.

*Cri-cket! Cri-cket!*

Or would she?

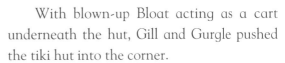
# A Change of Scenery

Dr Sherman had left for the day when Gill called everyone together for a Tank Gang meeting.

"We need to make some changes around here," Gill began. "We've all been living in this glass box for how long now? And every day we stare at the same scenery – the same volcano, the same sunken ship, the same treasure chest and tiki hut. Well, seeing as how we can't change what's in our tank, I propose we rearrange things a little. Who's with me?"

"Great idea!" cried Peach the starfish.

"I'm with you," said Deb. "And Flo is too," she added, pointing at her reflection.

Everyone agreed it sounded like a good idea. "We can completely transform the place," said Bloat.

"All right!" said Gill. "Then how about we start with the tiki hut? Bloat, you hoist it up. Gurgle and I will help you move it. The rest of you guys tell us where you think it should go."

Gill, Bloat and Gurgle swam over to the tiki hut. Bloat wriggled his body underneath it and blew himself up, hoisting the hut a few inches off the gravel. Meanwhile, Gill and Gurgle stationed themselves on either side of the hut and prepared to push.

"Let's try it over there," said Peach, pointing to a far corner of the tank.

With blown-up Bloat acting as a cart underneath the hut, Gill and Gurgle pushed the tiki hut into the corner.

"Oh, no," said Deb, "that's all wrong. Can we see what it looks like over there?" She pointed to the opposite corner of the tank.

So Gill, Gurgle and Bloat worked together to move the tiki hut again.

"That's a disaster!" exclaimed Jacques.

"Yeah, he's right," said Nemo.

Gill, Gurgle and Bloat were getting worn out by all the moving. "Can we all just agree on where it should go?" said Gill. "And quickly?"

"Ooh! I know!" said Deb. "Bring it over this way." She led Gill, Gurgle and Bloat over to a shady spot next to some plastic plants. "Put it down here," she said. So they did.

"I like it!" exclaimed Peach.

"The perfect spot," said Jacques.

"Mmm-hmm," said Bubbles.

Gill stepped back and looked around. "Guys, this is where it was in the first place!"

"Is it?" asked Peach.

Deb giggled. "Well, no wonder it just seems to fit here!"

The other fish nodded – except for Gill, who sighed in frustration.

And that was the end of the tank redecoration for the evening.

# Pictures in the Stars

Ever since Mufasa had died and Simba had left the Pride Lands, Timon and Pumbaa had been Simba's only friends – but what fun the three of them had together. One of their favourite things to do after their evening meal was to lie on their backs in the tall grass and gaze up at the night sky, looking for shapes in the stars.

"Okay, okay, I got one," said Pumbaa, lifting a foreleg to point to one area of the sky. "See, over there, that long, thin, curving outline? It's a big, juicy, delicious slug!" Pumbaa licked and smacked his lips, imagining the taste of a slug snack. "Mmm-mmm!"

Simba chuckled. "Pumbaa, how can you still be hungry? We just ate!"

Pumbaa shrugged. "It's a gift," he said.

Timon cleared his throat. "I hate to disagree with you, Pumbaa my friend, but that's no slug you see up there. That's an elephant's trunk. If you follow that curving line of stars, you see it connects with the elephant's head at one end. And there are the ears," Timon said, tracing it all out with his finger, "and there are the tusks."

Simba chuckled again. "Somebody still has his mind on that elephant stampede we almost got flattened by this afternoon," he said.

"Hey . . ." Timon said defensively, "what's that supposed to mean?"

"Oh, no offence, Timon," Simba replied. "I just think it's funny that the things you and Pumbaa see in the stars just happen to be the same things that are on your mind at the time."

"Ooh! Ooh! I've got another one!" Pumbaa interrupted. "A big bunch of tasty berries right over there," he said, pointing at a grouping of stars. "Don't they look good?"

"See what I mean?" Simba said to Timon, gesturing at Pumbaa.

"All right, all right, Mr Smarty-Pants," Timon replied. "So what do you see in the stars?"

"Well, now, let's see," said Simba, gazing intently at the tons of tiny points of light twinkling down at them. There were so many that you could see practically any shape in them that you wanted to. It all depended on how you looked at them. But just to get Timon's goat, Simba wanted to find something really bright – something really clear. Something Timon couldn't deny that he saw too.

Just at that moment, a shooting star streaked the entire length of the night sky.

"I see a bright streak of light rocketing across the sky!" exclaimed Simba.

"Ooh! Me, too!" said Pumbaa. "Timon, do you see it?"

Timon had to admit that he did. "Yeah, yeah, I see it," he muttered grudgingly. "Ha-ha. Very funny, Simba."

# Piglet's Pink Eggs

Winnie the Pooh had dropped in to visit Piglet, who was busy dyeing Easter eggs. "Easter is coming up, you know," Piglet explained.

On Piglet's kitchen table were six little cups. Pooh peered inside them. Each one held a different-coloured dye: blue, green, red, yellow, orange and pink.

Then Pooh noticed a basket filled with some eggs Piglet had already dyed. Every one of them was pink.

"Would you like to dye the last egg, Pooh?" Piglet asked.

"Oh yes," Pooh replied. "I would like that very much."

So Piglet showed him how to place his egg in the wire dipper, and how to use the dipper to dip the egg into the cups of dye.

"What colour should I dye my egg?" Pooh asked.

Piglet smiled. "That's the fun of it, Pooh," he said. "You can choose any colour you want!"

Pooh looked over at Piglet's basket of pink eggs. Then he looked back at the cups of dye.

"You don't seem to have a yellow egg yet," said Pooh. "So I think I will dye mine yellow."

"Good idea!" Piglet exclaimed.

Pooh dipped his egg into the cup filled with yellow dye. He let it sit in the dye for a few minutes, then lifted it out again.

"It worked!" cried Pooh. "Piglet, look! What do you think of my yellow egg?"

"Oh Pooh, it's great," Piglet said. "It's b-bright . . . a-and it's sunny . . . and i-it's very, very yellow, isn't it?"

Piglet was quiet for a moment. Then he cleared his throat.

"D-do you think . . . I don't know for sure, mind you. But do you think it could maybe use a little bit of, say, pink?" Piglet said.

Pooh took another look at his egg. "I think you're right," Pooh said. So he dipped his egg into the cup filled with pink dye. He let it sit there for just a few seconds before lifting it out. The little bit of pink dye on top of the yellow dye made the egg look pinkish-yellow.

"Hmm," said Piglet. "That's very pretty. But – if you don't mind my saying so, Pooh – I think it could use just a little more pink."

"Okay," said Pooh. So he dipped the egg back into the pink dye. This time he let it sit for five whole minutes before lifting it out. More pink dye on top of the yellow-and-pink colour made the egg look as pink as pink could be.

"Well, what do you think?" asked Pooh.

"Perfect!" Piglet exclaimed.

They let Pooh's egg dry. Then Piglet put it in the basket with all the other pink eggs.

"Well, what do you know," said Piglet. "It fits in so nicely!"

**WALT DISNEY'S Cinderella**

# Of Mice and Rice

"Cinderella! Help!" shrieked Drizella. "And hurry!" yelled Anastasia.

Cinderella dropped the broom she was holding and rushed down the hallway. "What is it, stepsisters?" she called.

"We're stuck!" yelled Anastasia.

Cinderella hurried to the parlour. She barely managed to suppress a giggle at what she saw. Her two stepsisters were stuck in the doorway, so hasty had they both been to leave the room first. Their grand hoop skirts were wedged tightly in the doorway! With a bit of tugging and pulling, Cinderella managed to get the sisters unwedged. Smiling to herself, she headed back to the kitchen.

"*Meeeeeowww!*" came a cry.

"What on earth . . . ?" said Cinderella. She hurried into the kitchen. Lucifer the cat was howling at the top of his lungs. "What is the matter, Lucifer?" she said, running over to the fat feline. "Oh! You silly thing! You've got yourself stuck too!" Cinderella laughed and tugged him out of the mouse hole he had wedged his paw into. With a haughty look at Cinderella, the cat strode away.

"Oh, that naughty cat!" she said. "He got himself stuck chasing after you poor little defenceless mice, didn't he?" She peeked into the tiny mouse hole.

The mice crept cautiously out of their hole. "You little dears," Cinderella said softly. "Why, you're all shaken up! Well, do you know what I do when I feel sad or afraid? I find happiness in my dreams." She picked up her broom. "You see this broom? I like to pretend that it is a handsome prince, and the two of us are dancing together!" She and the broom began gliding around the room.

The mice squeaked with delight. Then suddenly they dashed for their hole. Someone was coming!

It was Cinderella's stepsisters. "What on earth are you doing, Cinderella?" said Drizella.

"I was just, uh, sweeping," Cinderella replied quietly, blushing.

"Well, you looked as though you were having too much fun doing it!" snapped Anastasia. Then a nasty smile appeared on her face. Picking up a bowl of rice from the table, she dumped it onto the floor. "Perhaps you need something else to sweep!" she said with a mean laugh. The two sisters left.

Cinderella's mouse friends rushed out and began to pick up the grains of rice. That gave Cinderella an idea. "Why don't you take the rice for yourselves?" she said. The mice squeaked happily, and Cinderella smiled. "You know," she said, "I think we'll be just fine if we all look out for each other."

# A Monstrous Mix-up

One morning at work, Mike Wazowski opened the door to his locker to find a note taped inside. It said:

*Mike,*
*Roses are red.*
*Violets are blue.*
*I have got my eye on you!*
*Sealed with a kiss from . . .*
*Your Secret Admirer*

Mike's mouth fell open. He showed the note to his best friend, Sulley.

"Who do you think it could be?" Sulley asked.

"I have no idea!" Mike replied. "Hey, you don't think it could be that six-armed cutie down in Purchasing, do you? Or that sassy, one-eyed receptionist, Celia, with the pretty hair?"

"I guess it could be anyone," Sulley said. "But, hey, it's time to get to work."

On the way to the Scare Floor, Mike's mind was racing. Who could his admirer be? Then Mike heard his least favourite voice.

"Wazowski!"

It was Roz, the humourless and strict Dispatch Manager, sliding up behind them. "You owe me some paperwork!" she said.

"Oh . . . right," said Mike. "I'll get that to you ASAP, Roz. See ya." He and Sulley turned on their heels and hurried on down the hallway.

"All right, Wazowski," Roz called out to Mike, shaking her finger. "But remember: I've got my eye on you. I'm always watching . . . ."

Mike and Sulley froze in their tracks and stared at each other.

"Did she just say . . . ?" Sulley began.

"'My *eye* on you?'" Mike said, recalling the wording in the note from his secret admirer.

Sulley gulped. "Your secret admirer is *Roz?*"

"NOOOOOOOO!" Mike's scream filled the hallway just as Celia came sauntering around the corner.

"Hey, Mike," she said batting her eye at him. "Rough morning?"

"Oh. Hey, Celia," Mike replied sullenly, still traumatized by the idea that Roz liked him.

"Gee," said Celia, "I thought my note would make your day."

Mike stared at her. "*Your* note?" he said, stunned. "Celia, you're my secret admirer?"

She sighed. "Wasn't it obvious? 'I have got my eye on you'? As in, I have one eye, just like you?"

A wave of relief swept across Mike's face.

"I was going to ask you if you wanted to go out sometime," Celia continued. "But if you don't want to . . ."

Without a word, Mike leaped into Celia's arms and clung to her. "Thank you, thank you, THANK YOU!" he exclaimed.

Celia giggled. "So . . . I guess that's a yes?"

### Disney's
# BROTHER BEAR

# Hide-and-sniff

Little Koda had been talking . . . and talking . . . and talking for hours. And to tell you the truth, Kenai had stopped listening long ago.

"So!" said Koda. "What do you think?"

"Hmm?" said Kenai, who'd been sleepily digging berry seeds out of his teeth.

"I said," said Koda, bouncing up and down, "what do you think?"

"Oh, I don't know." Kenai didn't have the least idea *what* Koda was talking about. "Whatever you say, I guess."

"All right!" exclaimed Koda. "I *knew* you were ready to play a game. Tag! You're it. Close your eyes and count to 27 – 'cause that's all I can count to – and then try to find me. Good luck! You'll need it – I'm an excellent hider!"

And with that, Koda raced off.

"Excuse me?" Kenai exclaimed. But Koda was already out of view. "Just a minute!" Kenai shouted. "Come back here!"

Playing hide-and-seek with a bear cub was the *last* thing Kenai wanted to do. They had to get to where the lights touched the earth so Kenai could be a boy again. Honestly, if Kenai hadn't needed Koda to help him get there, he probably would have left him then and there. But he did need Koda. And, unfortunately for Kenai, that meant he had to find him.

Now," Kenai said to himself, "if I was a pain-in-the-neck, blabbermouth bear cub, where would I hide . . . ?"

He raised himself up on his two rear legs and assessed his surroundings. Hmm. This wasn't going to be easy. There were bushes everywhere, a whole forest to the south, and what looked like a group of caves to the east. Where to begin? He started with the bushes since they were the closest, but the only thing he found there was an irritable badger.

"Sorry," said Kenai, backing away.

"And just what are you doing nosing around in other creatures' business?" demanded the badger. "You big old bears think you own the whole country!"

"I said I was sorry," said Kenai. "I was just playing a game. You haven't seen a cub about *so* high hiding here, have you?"

"Seen a cub? Thank heavens no!" replied the badger. "But I sure did smell one over yonder. *Whoo!* Can't you?"

Smell? Kenai gave a big sniff and was suddenly aware of how much stronger his sense of smell was now that he was a bear. Yes, indeed, he *could* smell the little cub.

"Gotcha!" he soon hollered, poking his shaggy head into a cave. "You should know better, Koda, than to play hide-and-seek with a bear!"

# Castle Cleaning

It was a particularly warm and sunny April morning, and Belle and Chip the teacup were gazing out of a castle window at the blue sky and the budding trees and plants.

"Well, Chip," Belle said, "it is definitely spring at last. And you know what that means, don't you?"

Chip hopped up and down in excitement. "It means we get to play outside?" he asked.

Belle laughed. "Well, yes, that too," she replied. "But first it's time to do some spring cleaning."

So Belle got together a few cleaning supplies. "I think I'll start in the dining room," she said. Belle pulled the silverware out of the silver cabinet and began polishing a fork.

"Ooh!" exclaimed the enchanted fork. "Careful! Ouch! Not so hard around the tines!"

"Oh, dear!" said Belle. "I'm sorry." She gently polished the rest of the utensils.

Next, Belle gathered all the dishes. But when she dipped the first enchanted dish into the soapy water in the sink, it cried out, "Ahh! Too cold! Too cold!"

Belle gasped . . . and hurried to add more warm water to the sink.

After finishing the dishes, Belle moved to her bedroom, where she began dusting the Wardrobe with the Featherduster.

But the moment the Featherduster touched the Wardrobe, both enchanted objects began to shake with laughter.

"Hee, hee! Ha, ha!" said the Wardrobe. "That tickles!"

"You've got that right!" the Featherduster said.

Belle went to the library to take a break from her cleaning. Chip hopped in. "Oh, Chip," she said wearily, "spring cleaning in this castle is a challenge. I'm not used to cleaning enchanted objects!"

Chip giggled. "And I guess we're not used to it either. We always just clean ourselves!"

"Clean yourselves?" said Belle.

That gave her an idea. If the enchanted objects could clean themselves, they could clean other objects too!

Belle called the enchanted objects together. "I wonder if I could ask your help with a little project," Belle began.

Soon Belle had a small army of enchanted objects cleaning everything else in the castle. In a few short hours, the entire castle had been cleaned, and Belle and Chip were relaxing in the library.

"Well," Belle said as she sank into a comfortable chair, "you know what they say: 'Many hands make light work.' And a little enchantment never hurt either!"

Walt Disney's
## Lady and the TRAMP

# Tony and the Tramp

Tramp licked the last of the tomato sauce from his chin. "So, what do you think, Pidge?" he asked Lady.

"That was the most wonderful meal I've ever had," Lady gushed.

"What did I tell ya?" Tramp boasted. "There's no one in the world who can cook up a meal like Tony!"

"I couldn't agree with you more," Lady said. "Can I ask you a question?"

"Sure thing," Tramp said. "Ask away!"

"I was just wondering," Lady began, "how you and Tony met."

"How I met Tony?" Tramp laughed. "Now that's a story!"

"I bet!" Lady said.

"Well, see, it goes like this," Tramp began. "It was a cold and snowy night. I don't think it had ever been that cold before, and I know it hasn't been since. I had been walking uphill for miles. Icicles were hanging from the tip of my nose."

"Wait a minute!" Lady interrupted. "You were walking for miles – uphill? In this town?"

"That's right!" Tramp said. "You've never seen the likes of it."

"Exactly!" Lady told him. "You know why?" Tramp shook his head.

"Because it isn't possible! There are no big hills around here!" Lady said.

"Not possible?" Tramp said. "Okay, you're right," he confessed.

"So, then, what's the truth?" Lady asked.

"The truth is," Tramp began, "I wasn't always the slick, handsome devil you see before you."

"Is that right?" Lady was amused.

"And this one afternoon I was being harassed by a group of mangy mutts who outnumbered me ten to one. So, I took off as fast as my paws could carry me. And as they were chasing me, along came this dogcatcher!"

"Oh, no!" Lady exclaimed.

"Exactly!" Tramp continued. "The mutts scattered out of sight, so I didn't have *them* to worry about any more. But now the dogcatcher was closing in! I thought I was a goner!"

"What happened?" Lady asked.

"Then Tony came running out with a bowl of steaming hot pasta," Tramp explained. "He told the dogcatcher I was his dog. The dogcatcher didn't believe him. But, when Tony put the bowl of pasta down in front of me, he had no choice. Let me tell you, I thought I'd died and gone to heaven."

"I can relate to that," Lady said, recalling the meal.

"And the rest," Tramp said, "as they say, is history!"

"And a tasty one at that!" Lady concluded.

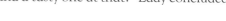

# Should I Stay or Should I Go?

Wendy sat watching Michael and John play with Peter Pan and the rest of the Lost Boys.

"John and Michael seem so happy," Wendy said to herself. "And why wouldn't they? Never Land is such a beautiful place, and the flying is so much fun!

"Still," she had to admit, "it is also dangerous. Who knows what sort of trouble we could get into, especially with Captain Hook running about?

"And," Wendy continued, "I don't think that Tinker Bell likes me very much."

Wendy considered this, then burst out, "What am I talking about? I'm making it sound like it's an awful place, but the truth is, Never Land is the most wonderful place on earth!

"Perhaps that explains it!" Wendy suddenly realized. "Maybe I really want to stay in Never Land, but in my heart of hearts I know I shouldn't. After all, Mother and Father must miss us terribly. And we miss them too! Oh, and what about Nana?" Wendy began to fret. "She must worry about us endlessly!

"That settles it!" Wendy stood up abruptly. "We must leave for home immediately.

"But if I stay – " Wendy stopped herself. "I'll never have to grow up!"

Wendy thought about the pros and cons of never getting old. "Then again, I always wanted to be an adult someday," she concluded.

Just then, Peter Pan swooped down beside her. "What are you doing, Wendy?" Peter asked.

"Oh, nothing," Wendy told him.

"Then why don't you come join us?" he suggested.

"I will," Wendy told him. "In a minute."

"All right! But last one there is a rotten – " Peter took off before he could finish his sentence.

"How can I ever leave Peter and the Lost Boys?" Wendy wondered. "They need me so much.

"But so do our parents," she quickly reminded herself.

"Should I stay?" she wondered aloud. "Or should I go?"

Wendy's eyes fell upon a daisy. She bent over and pulled it out of the ground. "Should I stay?" she asked as she pulled a petal from the daisy. "Or should I go?" she asked as she pulled a second petal from the daisy.

Wendy did this over and over again until there was only one petal remaining on the daisy. "Well," she said, "this flower says we should go back home. And I suppose it's right. We'll go back . . . but maybe not just this minute."

Wendy stood up. "Hey, Peter, wait up!" And with that, she flew off after Peter, her mind at ease at last.

# Ariel Changes the Tune

Sebastian rapped his claw on a piece of coral and cleared his throat. But the mermaids kept talking as if the little crustacean were not even there. With a heavy sigh, Sebastian grabbed a huge conch shell. After a lot of effort he managed to hoist it to his mouth and blow.

The shell sounded like a giant horn. The mermaid princesses looked startled, and, to Sebastian's relief, they stopped talking.

"Shall we begin?" the small crab asked calmly. He was anxious to start rehearsing. King Triton's daughters had amazing singing voices, but they still had not decided on the right song to sing for their father's birthday. And there were just a few days left before the celebration!

Sebastian raised his claw and was about to bring it down to start the vocal warm-up when Aquata interrupted him.

"Ariel's not here," she said.

"Oh, Ariel!" Sebastian cried. Ariel was constantly swimming off on her own and holding things up.

"Do you want us to find her?" Arista asked.

"No." Sebastian sighed dramatically. "Then you will all be lost, and I don't know what I would tell your father."

"We wouldn't get lost," Attina protested.

"We *always* show up on time," Adella added. The other sisters nodded their heads in agreement.

"Why do we have to sit around and wait for her?" Alana grumbled. The rest of her sisters nodded angrily.

"Girls, girls!" Sebastian said, trying to calm them. He wished they could go ahead without Ariel, but her voice was by far the most beautiful.

Suddenly, Ariel swam up with Flounder.

"I hope you weren't waiting for me," she said sweetly.

"Ariel!" Sebastian didn't know whether he should be angry or relieved.

"Where have you been?" Aquata put her hands on her scaly hips.

"We still don't have a song for father!" Attina added.

"We do now!" Ariel said cheerfully. She couldn't tell them, but she had been to the surface. It was forbidden. But she had got something very special from her seagull friend Scuttle today. A new song! Ariel began singing the human tune. After only a moment, Ariel's sisters began to sing along.

Sebastian closed his eyes and listened. The song was perfect! "Where did you learn it?" he asked when they were done.

Ariel looked at Flounder. "A little bird told me," she said with a wink.

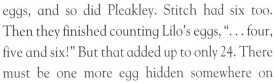

# Easter Egg Hunt!

The Easter holiday was quickly approaching, which meant one thing: the annual Pelekai Easter egg hunt! Lilo couldn't wait to begin painting eggs. First she asked Nani to help make some hard-boiled eggs. Then Lilo found Stitch, Jumba and Pleakley, and everyone took turns painting the eggs.

"This is my favourite part," Lilo said. "I'm going to paint one pink with purple polka dots!"

"I'm going to draw mosquitoes on mine," said Pleakley, grabbing a crayon.

"Blue!" cried Stitch, dunking his egg violently in the cup of blue dye.

While everyone cleared up, Nani went down to the beach to hide the eggs. When everyone got to the beach, Nani announced the rules. "There are twenty-five eggs hidden on this beach. Whoever finds the most eggs will win the prize."

"What's the prize?" Lilo asked.

"Oh, you'll see," Nani replied with a smile. "On your mark . . . get set . . . go!"

The sun shone on the brilliant white sand as Lilo, Stitch, Jumba and Pleakley searched high and low for the eggs. They found one buried under a sand castle, another hidden under a beach blanket, and even one atop the belly of a man snoring on the beach!

As the afternoon sun began to sink, everyone gathered to count the eggs. Jumba had six eggs, and so did Pleakley. Stitch had six too. Then they finished counting Lilo's eggs, ". . . four, five and six!" But that added up to only 24. There must be one more egg hidden somewhere on the beach.

So they split up and went looking for the last egg. Finally, Lilo spotted something under a palm tree. "Everybody, come quick!" she cried. "I think I've found the last egg!"

Nani, Jumba and Pleakley came running. "Look," said Lilo, "it's a huge foil egg. The biggest chocolate egg I've ever seen!"

"It sure is," said Nani. "This is the prize, Lilo, and since you all found the same number of eggs, it looks like you all get to share it!"

"But where's Stitch?" said Lilo. Just then, the huge chocolate egg began to twitch. It rattled and shook, and then –

Stitch popped out of it, yelling, "Ta-daaa!" Bits of chocolate scattered everywhere.

"Wow!" cried Lilo. "Did you guys plan that?"

"No, Lilo," said Nani, looking completely confused and a little disturbed. "I have *no idea* how Stitch got in there without breaking the foil."

"My secret!" said Stitch cheerfully. He began munching on a piece of the chocolate egg.

Nani and Lilo smiled and shrugged, and then they all sat down and ate bits of chocolate egg while they watched the sun set over the water.

# Destructo-boy

"Hercules!" Amphitryon called. "This hay pile is about to fall over. Could you hold it up while I go to get the cart?"

"Sure, Pop!" Hercules told his father.

Hercules was the strongest boy in his village. He could easily hold up the enormous stack of hay bales with one hand.

Soon, another farmer approached, struggling to hold onto a team of six disobedient mules.

"Need any help?" Hercules asked.

"Hercules!" the farmer gasped. "If you'll hold these mules, I can go get my sons to help me get them home."

"Be glad to!" Hercules took the mules' leads with his free hand.

Just then, a woman came by dragging a cart filled with pottery. She was panting.

"Good day, ma'am," Hercules said politely. "Could I give you a hand with that?"

"Why, thank you," the woman replied. "But it looks like you have your hands full!"

"Oh, I'll be finished here in a second," Hercules said. "Then I can . . ."

His voice trailed off. He'd just noticed some children his own age running down the road, laughing and shouting as they tossed a discus.

Hercules gazed at them longingly. For some reason, he'd never seemed to fit in with the other village children. Perhaps it was because they didn't understand him. Or perhaps it was because Hercules had once challenged them to a 50-yard dash – and beaten them all by 49 yards.

"Hey, guys!" he called as the discus sailed towards him. "I've got it!"

He lunged towards the discus. The mules' leads went flying. The haystack teetered.

"Uh-oh," Hercules said.

He tried to grab the hay and the mules at the same time, but he accidentally tripped one of the mules, which crashed into the haystack, which fell right onto the woman's cart, and all over the boys.

Hercules winced at the sounds of breaking pottery and shouting boys. The mules were already running off towards the horizon.

"My pottery!" the woman wailed.

"What's the big idea?" one of the other children demanded, standing and brushing himself off.

"Yeah." Another boy grabbed the discus from Hercules. "Stay out of our way from now on . . . Destructo-Boy!"

Hercules' shoulders slumped. Why did this sort of thing always happen to him? Whenever he tried to help, he only made things worse. But he knew that, one day, his strength would help him be a hero. He just hoped that day would come soon. There was only so much unbroken pottery left in Greece!

# The Prettiest Flower

One morning, Bashful went out to pick the prettiest flower he could find. Suddenly, he heard a noise just over the hill.

"*Ah-choo!*"

Bashful climbed the hill and saw his friend on the other side.

"These darn flowers are making me sneeze," said Sneezy. "But it's worth it – because I've picked the prettiest flower for Snow White's hair." He showed Bashful the white orchid he'd picked.

"That sure is pretty," said Bashful. "But I've got a flower for her too. It's even prettier."

Bashful showed Sneezy the rosebud he'd picked. Then he blushed pinker than its petals.

"*Ah-choo!* Yours is pretty too," said Sneezy. "Let's go home and see which one Snow White likes best."

On the path back to their little cottage, Sneezy and Bashful came upon Doc, Happy and Sleepy. They were all arguing about something.

"Snow White bikes liolets," insisted Doc. "I mean she likes violets!"

Happy laughed. "No. She likes daisies!"

"I think she likes muuuuuums," said Sleepy with a yawn.

"You *would* think that!" grumbled a voice behind them. It was Grumpy. He held a long stem with small pastel blossoms.

"That's the perfect flower for you, Grumpy," said Doc. "Snapdragons!"

"Very funny!" Grumpy snapped.

When they all arrived at their house, they saw Dopey.

"Dopey, what do you have behind your back?" Doc asked.

Dopey showed them a single yellow tulip.

"*Another* flower!" cried Happy.

When the Seven Dwarfs went inside, they found Snow White in the kitchen.

"We all wanted to thank you for being so good to us," said Doc. "So we each picked a flower for your hair."

"Now it's *your* turn to pick the flower you like best," said Grumpy.

Snow White felt terrible. She loved all the Dwarfs and she didn't want to hurt any of their feelings by choosing one flower over another.

"I have an idea," she told them. "Put all of your flowers down on the table, and go outside for five minutes. When you come back in, I'll be wearing the flower I think is the prettiest."

The Dwarfs went outside. When they came back in, they gasped in surprise. Snow White had made a flower crown.

She'd found a way to wear all their flowers!

"I love every one of your flowers!" she told them. "Just like I love each and every one of you!"

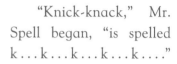

# This Spells Trouble!

"Woody! Bo!" whispered Hamm. "Hey, have you guys noticed anything a little . . . off . . . about Mr Spell lately?"

"What do you mean?" asked Bo Peep.

"His spelling hasn't been so sharp these last few days," Hamm explained.

Woody looked at Hamm in disbelief. "Aw, no, Hamm, that can't be right," he said. "Mr Spell was made to spell. He never gets anything wrong."

Hamm shrugged. "Well, see for yourself," he said. "Come on." They walked over to Mr Spell.

"Hey, there, Spell," said Hamm. "I was, uh, wondering if you could help us out with something. Woody and me, we just made a little bet about how you spell the word 'rutabaga.' Could you help us settle it?"

"Sure thing, Hamm," Mr Spell replied. "Rutabaga. That's r . . . r . . . r . . . r . . . r . . . ."

Woody and Bo Peep exchanged nervous glances. Hamm raised his eyebrows and gave them a see-what-I-mean look.

"Great, thanks," Hamm said to Mr Spell, trying to act naturally. "Oh, hey. And how about the word 'platypus'?"

"Platypus," Mr Spell repeated. "That's spelled p . . . p . . . p . . . p . . . p . . . ."

Woody and Bo Peep stared anxiously at Mr Spell. Could he be losing his spelling edge?

It seemed unbelievable. But how else could they explain what they were hearing?

"Okay," Hamm said. "One more question. How do you spell 'knick-knack'?"

"Knick-knack," Mr Spell began, "is spelled k . . . k . . . k . . . k . . . ."

Oh, no, thought Woody. This was serious. Mr Spell was a really, really bad speller!

"Spell," said Woody, laying a sympathetic hand on Mr Spell's back. "Are you feeling all right? You don't seem yourself."

"Oh, sure, Woody," Mr Spell replied. "I feel fine . . . fine . . . fine . . . fine . . . ."

As Mr Spell continued to repeat the word, Woody suddenly understood the problem.

"Hey! Hamm!" Woody exclaimed. "He's not spelling incorrectly. He just keeps getting stuck. Don't you, Spell?"

But Mr Spell couldn't respond. He was still stuck on "fine . . . fine . . . fine . . . fine . . . ."

Woody gave Mr. Spell a firm slap on the back. It didn't help. So Woody came up and gave him a good whack. . . .

Mr Spell fell over on his side. The cover to his battery compartment came loose. Two corroded-looking batteries fell onto the floor.

"Heh, heh, heh," Hamm chuckled. "Well, this isn't so bad. Mr Spell just needs some new batteries!"

# Walt Disney's Bambi

# First Impressions

Bambi was just discovering the wonders of the forest. His mother had brought him to a little clearing in the woods. The sudden sunshine and bright green grass surprised and pleased him, and he bounded around on his still-wobbly legs, feeling the warm sun on his back and the soft grass under his hooves. While his mother grazed nearby, Bambi began to explore.

He found a patch of green grass and clover, and he bent down to eat. This was not an easy feat, as his long legs made it difficult for his little neck to reach the ground. When his nose was just a few inches from the tips of the grass, he suddenly leaped backwards in alarm. A leaf had just sprung up from the patch of grass and had landed a few feet away. A hopping leaf? he wondered. He followed it and, as soon as he drew close, the leaf hopped away from him again! Bambi looked around at where his mother stood, still grazing. She seemed to think they were in no great danger. So, he followed the leaf all the way to the edge of the clearing, where a wide brook babbled over craggy rocks.

Bambi's fascination with the hopping leaf faded as he approached the brook. Water cascaded smoothly over the rocks, bubbling and frothing in shallow pools. He took a step closer and felt his foot touch a rock at the edge of the water. Suddenly, the rock moved! It shuffled towards the water and then – *plop*! – jumped right in and swam away. Bambi was dumbfounded as he watched it dive beneath the surface and vanish. He stared at the spot where the rock had been for a moment, and then stooped down to have a drink, widening his stance in order to do so.

Suddenly, he jumped back in alarm. There in the water, staring right back up at him, was a little deer! Cautiously he approached again, and there it was!

Bambi turned and bounded back across the clearing to his mother. "Mama! Mama!" he cried breathlessly. "You will never guess what I have seen!"

His mother lifted her head and gazed at him with her clear, bright eyes.

"First," he said, "first I saw a jumping leaf. Then, I saw a rock with legs that walked right into the water and swam away! And then," he he continued in amazement, "and then I saw a little deer who lives right in the water! He's right over there, Mama!"

His mother nuzzled her son, thinking over what he had said. Then she laughed gently. "Darling," she said. "I think you have just seen your first grasshopper, your first turtle and your very own reflection!"

TIM BURTON'S
NIGHTMARE
BEFORE
CHRISTMAS

# Scary Claus

Sally and Dr Finklestein were working in the lab when a package arrived. The label read: A SPECIAL GIFT FOR A SPECIAL PERSON.

"The most special person in Halloweentown is Jack Skellington," said Sally. "This must be for him!"

When Jack arrived, Sally and Dr Finklestein showed him the package.

"Why, it's a gift!" cried Jack. "Let's open it together."

"It's a shame to rip the pretty blood-red paper," cooed Sally.

But they opened it anyway.

"What is this?" said Jack, holding up a string of twinkling lights.

"It's a necklace," said Sally.

"And this?" said Jack. He held up a glass ball. Painted on it was a picture of a chubby ghost with a long white beard. When Jack touched the glass ball it said, "Ho, ho, ho!"

"Eek!" cried Sally. "That's the scariest ghost I've ever seen! It gives me the chills."

"Well," said Jack, "since this is a gift, I guess I should wear it."

He put on the necklace, then hung the ball from it. With every step, the ghost cried its horrid call. "Ho, ho, ho! Ho, ho, ho!"

"How do I look?" asked Jack.

"Very scary," said Sally, trembling.

On the way home, Jack met the Mayor. "Eek!" the Mayor screamed.

"This will be perfect for Halloween," Jack mused.

But, as Jack walked home, everyone was frightened by the scary ghost. His long white beard and red, red cheeks made the citizens of Halloweentown run for cover!

Later that day, Sally visited Jack. "I'm here to tell you that your gift is just too scary, even for Halloweentown," Sally said. "The children are having nightmares about a man with a long beard and red cheeks coming down their chimneys and eating their Halloween cookies!"

"That's terrible," said Jack. He decided to return the package to Dr Finklestein.

"I'll put this gift in a safe place where it won't frighten anyone," said the doctor.

Later that day, there came a knock at the castle door. Dr Finklestein answered.

"It's the scary ghost!" he screamed.

"I'm not a ghost," said the visitor.

"Yes, you are!" cried Dr Finklestein. "I recognize those chubby red cheeks, that long white beard and the blood-red suit!"

Dr Finklestein ran into his castle to hide.

"But my name is Santa Claus," the stranger insisted. "I'm looking for a Christmas package that was delivered here by mistake!"

April
**24**

# Donald Takes Flight

"**D**aisy, I have a surprise for you," said Donald Duck one clear spring day. "I've been taking flying lessons."

"That *is* a surprise," said Daisy Duck.

Donald took Daisy to a nearby airport. On the runway sat an old-fashioned plane with open-air seats. Together they climbed into the small plane. Then Donald started the engine.

"Up, up and away!" he cried as they took off.

"Can you do any tricks?" shouted Daisy.

"Sure!" called Donald. He steered the plane into a loop-the-loop.

"You're a very good pilot, Donald!" Daisy cried, clapping her hands.

Donald was so proud of himself, he told Daisy he would fly wherever she wanted to go.

Daisy thought it over. "Let's go to Paris, France!" she said. Donald was so eager to impress Daisy that he didn't think twice. "Paris, here we come!" he cried. Before long, however, the plane's engine began to cough and choke.

"Uh-oh," Donald said to himself as the plane began to drift towards the water.

"Is anything wrong?" asked Daisy.

Donald knew they were running out of fuel. But he didn't want Daisy to find out.

"Everything is fine, Daisy," Donald said nervously.

Just then, he saw something floating below them. It looked like an airport runway. But what would a runway be doing in the middle of the ocean?

As the plane drifted closer to the water, Donald realized he had no choice. He'd have to land his plane on the floating runway.

Just before he landed, Donald's eyes nearly popped out of his head. It wasn't a runway at all. It was the top deck of a huge ocean liner!

"Duck!" yelled one of the ship's passengers, and a dozen people scattered.

Donald zoomed over their heads and carefully landed the plane on the long, wide deck.

"Hey, it really *is* a duck!" cried one of the passengers.

Just then an announcement came over the ship's speakers. "Good evening, ladies and gentleman. Dinner is served!"

Donald helped Daisy out of the plane. He was sure she would be upset. But she wasn't. "Dinner on a cruise ship!" she cried. "Donald, you're just full of surprises, aren't you!"

"Yes, indeed," said Donald with a huge sigh of relief. "And here's one more surprise: I think this ship's on its way to France!"

"Oh, Donald, you're the best," said Daisy.

No, I'm not, thought Donald, as Daisy hugged him. What I really am is one lucky duck!

Walt Disney's
Sleeping
Beauty

# Fairy Medicine

Deep in the forest, in a humble cottage, the three good fairies had been secretly raising Briar Rose for many years. One morning, the girl woke up with a terrible cold.

"We must nurse her back to health," said Flora.

Fauna and Merryweather agreed. So, while Briar Rose stayed in bed, Flora brought her a bowl of soup. Fauna fetched her a cup of tea. And Merryweather gave her a dose of medicine.

"Ooooh!" said Briar Rose, wrinkling her nose. "That tastes awful!"

"Most medicine tastes awful, dear," said Merryweather. "Just drink it down."

"Would you like anything else?" Flora asked.

The princess blew her nose and gazed out her window at the beautiful spring day.

"What I really want is to get out of bed," she said. "*Ah-choo!*"

"Oh, no, dear," said Flora. "You're far too sick."

Then the fairies left Briar Rose and went downstairs.

"I feel bad for the sweet girl," said Fauna. "Staying in bed all day is boring."

"What can we do?" asked Merryweather.

"I know!" cried Flora. "We'll entertain her!"

"Splendid!" said Merryweather. "I'll fetch my wand and conjure up some fireworks, a puppet show, and – "

"And perhaps that clever dog who jumps through hoops!" added Fauna.

"No!" Flora cried. "We all agreed to give up our fairy magic until Briar Rose turns 16 and she's safe from Maleficent's curse."

"Not even a little magic?" asked Fauna. "Just a few fireworks?"

"No!" Flora said again, stomping her foot.

"Well," said Fauna, "how do mortals entertain themselves when they're sick in bed?"

"I know!" cried Flora. She brought out a deck of cards. "We'll play card games! That will be fun!"

The three fairies then went up to Briar Rose's room and played card games with her all afternoon. Briar Rose won almost every game, too, which really cheered her up.

After a while, Briar Rose yawned and said she was ready to have a sleep. So the fairies went back downstairs.

When Flora went outside to do some gardening, Fauna approached Merryweather. "Tell me the truth," she whispered. "Did you use magic to let the princess win?"

"I just used mortal magic," confessed Merryweather. "No harm in a little sleight of hand. After all, you must admit, if you're feeling down, winning is the best medicine!"

# Funny Faces

Hugo, Victor and Laverne were gargoyles at the great Cathedral of Notre Dame. Most of the time they were stone, but they came to life in the presence of Quasimodo, the bell ringer at Notre Dame. Although they were all good friends, Hugo and Victor were always finding something to bicker over, and today was no exception.

"That's ridiculous!" Hugo snapped at Victor.

"No, *you're* ridiculous!" Victor shot back.

Victor had suggested that Quasimodo tell Frollo, the Minister of Justice and Quasi's master, that he wanted to take some time off. Hugo had pointed out that Frollo would sooner become a gypsy than give Quasimodo a holiday. Then the argument had really taken off.

"Well, you started it," Hugo told him.

"I started it?" Victor asked.

"That's right, stone face!" Hugo shouted.

"Who are you calling stone face? Blockhead!" Victor fought back.

Suddenly, a loud whistle interrupted them.

"May I have your attention, please?" Laverne said. "I would like to propose a way for you to settle this dispute like gentlemen."

"What is it?" Quasi asked.

"A face-making contest," Laverne said. "Here are the rules. You two take turns making faces at each other, and the first to make the other laugh, wins!"

"I'm going first!" declared Hugo, sticking his tongue out at Victor.

"Child's play," said Victor scornfully. He crossed his eyes at Hugo.

"Ha!" said Hugo. "Try resisting *this*!" Hugo crossed his eyes, flared his nostrils, and stuck his lower jaw out, baring a crooked row of teeth in a hideous grimace.

Victor managed to keep a straight face at this, but Quasimodo couldn't help but laugh out loud.

"Shh!" Laverne said. "Frollo's coming!"

"Frollo?" Hugo and Victor grew pale and quickly turned back to stone.

Just then, Frollo marched in. "What's going on up here?" he asked Quasimodo.

"Nothing, sir," Quasi said, trying not to laugh. He was having a hard time keeping a straight face because, behind Frollo, Victor and Hugo were still busy making faces at each other, each trying to make the other laugh.

"Hmm," said Frollo suspiciously. As he turned to go, Victor and Hugo stopped making faces at each other, and began making funny faces at Frollo's back. When he was out of sight, all four friends collapsed with laughter.

"You know what," Quasi told them. "I have so much fun with you guys, it beats going on vacation!"

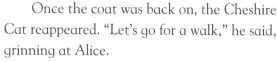

# Sillying the Blues Away

"**O**h, me, oh, my!" the White Rabbit said as he rushed past Alice.

"Wait! Excuse me!" Alice called to him. But he was gone.

Alice sat down. "I'm never going to get out of here," she said worriedly.

"What's the matter?" a voice asked. "You seem blue."

Alice looked all around, but she didn't see anyone. "Where are you?" she asked.

"Is that better?" the Cheshire Cat said as he suddenly appeared out of nowhere.

"Why, yes," Alice replied.

"Would you like some help?" the Cheshire Cat asked.

"You'll help me?" Alice cried.

"Absolutely!" the Cheshire Cat said with a grin. "But you have to do exactly as I say."

"Okay," Alice agreed.

"First," the Cheshire Cat told her, "you have to put on this winter coat."

"But it's spring," Alice protested.

"You promised to do as I say," the Cheshire Cat reminded her.

"Okay." Alice started putting it on.

"Backwards!" the Cheshire Cat ordered.

"But . . ." Alice began. The Cheshire Cat started to disappear. "Wait, don't go!" she pleaded. "Here, I'm putting it on."

Once the coat was back on, the Cheshire Cat reappeared. "Let's go for a walk," he said, grinning at Alice.

"But I'm feeling a little silly," Alice said.

"Don't worry," the Cheshire Cat told her. "No one's looking."

But the truth was, Alice could have sworn she heard the bread-and-butterflies laughing at her.

"Now, drink this cup of apple sauce," the Cheshire Cat said.

"Don't you mean apple juice?" Alice asked.

"No, I mean apple sauce," the Cheshire Cat said. "Drink it while walking around in a circle – three times."

Alice hesitated. "Are you sure about this?"

"It's always worked for the bread-and-butterflies," the Cheshire Cat told her.

"All right, then," Alice said. But, by the time she started her second circle, her doubts grew stronger. "I think you're playing a trick on me," she said. "You're having me do all these things to make me look silly."

"True," the Cheshire Cat agreed. "But it's awfully hard to feel blue when you look this silly!" His smile hung in the air a moment before he entirely disappeared.

Alice thought for a moment, and she had to agree. She was still lost, but now she didn't feel quite so sad about it!

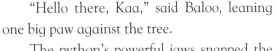

# Snake Eyes

"I'm ssstarved," hissed Kaa the python as he slithered across the jungle treetops. "I need a sssnack . . . ."

Suddenly, Kaa noticed a small figure relaxing on the ground below. It was Mowgli. Kaa slithered over to him.

"Are you feeling sssssleeepy?" hissed Kaa. "You look sssleeepy; jussst look into my eyesss . . ."

Mowgli tried not to look into the snake's eyes, but it wasn't easy. When he turned one way, Kaa was there. When he turned another, Kaa was there too!

"Sssslip into ssssilent ssslumber," Kaa hissed. "And sssleep . . . sssleeep . . . sssleep . . ."

Before Mowgli knew it, his body went completely limp. Kaa had hypnotized him!

Thank goodness Mowgli's friends walked by at that very moment.

"Look!" cried Bagheera the panther. "Kaa's after Mowgli again."

"Get over there and do something," Baloo told Bagheera.

"The last time I interfered with Kaa, he hypnotized *me*," said Bagheera. "*You* do something."

Kaa's fangs watered as he coiled his long body around Mowgli. Then Kaa opened his giant python mouth above Mowgli's head and – hey! Someone had jammed a stick into his jaws, propping them wide open!

"Hello there, Kaa," said Baloo, leaning one big paw against the tree.

The python's powerful jaws snapped the stick. "You sssshould not insssert yourssself between a sssnake and his sssnack," he hissed.

"Oh! Sorry!" said Baloo. "I was just admiring how very talented you are."

"Talented?" Kaa said. "Me?"

"Sure!" said Baloo. "I'm very impressed how you hypnotized Mowgli there. I bet you could hypnotize almost anything in the jungle. Almost . . ."

"What do you mean *almost*?" said Kaa.

Baloo coolly polished his claws against his fur. "Well, let's see," he said. "I bet you can't hypnotize . . . a fish." Baloo pointed to the pond.

"Jusssst you watch me," Kaa told Baloo as he slithered towards the pond.

Hanging his head over the water, Kaa hissed, "Jussst look into my eyesss. You feel sssssleeepy . . . sssssleeepy . . . sssssleeepy. . . ."

Suddenly, Kaa stopped hissing. Or moving. He just stared into the water.

Bagheera stepped up to Baloo and whispered, "What's the matter with him?"

Baloo just laughed. "Kaa was so determined to prove me wrong, he didn't even notice the water was reflecting back his image. That crazy snake hypnotized himself!"

DISNEY'S
## OLIVER & Company

# Oliver Plays Piano

"I've got to get rid of that kitten," Georgette the poodle muttered.

From the time she was a pampered pup, Georgette was used to being the only pet in Jenny's house. Not any more! Nowadays there was also a little lost kitten named Oliver.

Every day Jenny fed him with Georgette's fancy silver bowl, then she brushed his fur with Georgette's special brush. Why, she even played a song for Oliver on her piano!

That gave Georgette an idea. "The piano! Now I know how to get rid of that furry feline."

Georgette waited until everyone had gone to bed. Then she tiptoed over to Oliver, grabbed the sleeping kitten, tossed him inside the big piano, and shut the lid. *Bang!*

Inside the piano, Oliver yawned and looked around. He was surprised to find himself in the dark wooden box. He began to move through the box to find a way out, but every time he moved, his four paws hit the piano strings. *Plink! Plunk!*

He started moving faster, hitting note after note and chord after chord.

"This is fun!" Oliver exclaimed. *Plunk! Bing! Plink!* "I'm playing the piano, just like Jenny!"

*Plink! Plunk! Plink! Plunkity-Plink!*

Soon, the terrible racket woke everyone in the house!

"What is that horrid noise?" cried Winston the butler. He hopped out of bed and hurried into the living room. Georgette was standing nearby and doing her very best to look innocent.

"It's that cat!" Winston huffed. "That creature is just too noisy. It's got to go!"

"Success!" Georgette said to herself – until Jenny appeared in her nightgown. The little girl rushed past the butler and opened the lid of the piano. When she saw Oliver inside, she squealed, "How cute!"

The butler scratched his head. "Cute?"

"Uh-oh," muttered Georgette.

"Oliver is trying to play a song on the piano," said Jenny, "just like he saw me do earlier today. What a wonderful kitty you are!"

Jenny hugged Oliver, and he began to purr.

When the butler saw how much Jenny loved Oliver, his heart melted. "Oh, well," he said. "I guess a little noise isn't the end of the world. Off to bed with you now, Jenny."

"Good night," said Jenny. Then she kissed Oliver's head and told him, "You must go to bed now too. Let me tuck you in."

Before she left, Jenny patted her poodle's head and said, "Oh, Georgette, aren't we lucky to have a new friend like Oliver in the house!"

"Drat!" Georgette said to herself. "I'd say it's that little fur ball who's the lucky one!"

# Look Sharp, Jiminy!

"Gosh." Jiminy Cricket scratched his head between his antennae and yawned a big yawn. Climbing into his tiny matchbox bed, he gazed again at the wooden boy, who was fast asleep.

Jiminy still could not believe his eyes – or his luck. It had been a miraculous night. Not every cricket got to witness a wish granted by the Blue Fairy and see a puppet come to life. And not every cricket was chosen to be somebody's conscience!

Jiminy hopped out of bed. It was pointless to try to sleep. He already felt like he was dreaming. Being a conscience was a big job, but he was just the bug to do it. "Right and wrong." Jiminy looked from one of his hands to the other. "Sure, I know the difference. All I have to do is tell Pinoke. It'll be a snap." Jiminy snapped his fingers. "And I'll even look good doing it."

Jiminy ran his hands down the new jacket hanging by his bed. He picked up the hat and twirled it. "My, my," he said, shaking his head. Then he could not resist any longer. He put on his new shirt, coat, hat and shoes. Then he hopped over to Cleo's fishbowl to see his reflection.

Jiminy whistled low. "Don't you look smart," he told his reflection. "Smart enough to help that wooden boy. Except for that smudge." Jiminy leaned down to inspect a dull spot on his shoe.

He breathed on it and rubbed it with his sleeve. Soon it was shining like new. He looked like a million dollars!

Suddenly Geppetto snored loudly. Jiminy jumped and looked up. Outside the sky was starting to lighten.

"Would you look at that?" Jiminy knew he had to get to bed. A conscience needed to be alert! He hurried out of his new clothes, hung them up carefully, and tucked himself back in bed. "Big day tomorrow." He yawned. "Very big day." A moment later the little cricket was chirping in his sleep.

Jiminy woke to the sound of hundreds of cuckoo clocks. He sat up and rubbed his eyes. He barely remembered where he was. Then the events of the evening before flooded back. Why, he had work to do!

"Get up, Pinoke!" Jiminy called towards the big bed. But Pinocchio was already gone. The bed was made and Geppetto and Figaro were gone too!

Cleo swished nervously in her bowl and pointed towards the door.

"I must have overslept!" Jiminy pulled his new clothes on quickly. "I can't let Pinoke start school without me. You don't have to be a conscience to know that's wrong!" And, quick as a flash, Jiminy hopped out of the door.

# Disney's ROBIN HOOD

# Smitten

Robin Hood straightened his hat and smoothed his whiskers. "How do I look, Little John?" he asked.

"You look like you always do," John replied with a wave of his hand. "Like a regular Casanova."

Robin grinned. "Let's hope Maid Marian agrees with you." He put a hand over his heart. "I just hope she still remembers me."

"Quit mooning and get going, Rob," Little John said. "The day isn't getting any longer."

"Right, right," Robin agreed. But the truth was, he felt a little nervous. Maid Marian was the cleverest and most beautiful maid in the land. And she'd been in London for several years. What if she didn't remember her childhood sweetheart?

"Get going," Little John repeated.

Robin nodded and set off through the forest. He had to be careful, because Prince John had declared him an outlaw. If he or any of his men saw him, Robin would be thrown into jail. Or worse.

"She's worth it," Robin told himself as he hurried towards the castle.

Soon Robin was outside the castle gate. He could hear voices – female voices – laughing and talking. Maybe one of them was Marian's!

Robin's heart pounded in his chest. He had to see! He looked around and spotted a large tree with branches that reached inside the castle grounds. Perfect!

Robin leaped gracefully up to the first branch, grabbed hold and began to climb. When he was nice and high, he worked his way out on a branch. Now he was inside the castle grounds. And, if he moved a few leafy branches aside . . . .

Robin moved a branch and leaned forwards to see who was talking. It was Marian! She was playing badminton with Lady Cluck. And she was a good shot!

"Nice one, Maid Marian," Lady Cluck said, as Marian won a point.

Robin gazed down at the sight below. Marian was so lovely, and so talented!

"Oops!" Marian said as the shuttlecock sailed off the court completely.

Robin saw it fly towards his hiding place. It landed in the tree just above him! Determined to get it for Marian, he got to his feet and reached up. But he lost his balance and fell just as the shuttlecock came loose. The two landed on the ground at the same time.

"Ooof!" Robin didn't mean to make an entrance like this!

"What was that?" Lady Cluck asked as Robin scrambled away and leaped over the fence.

"I do believe it was an outlaw," Maid Marian said with a smile.

# Abracadabra!

Manny was not at his best. Gypsy could tell. Already that day, he had lost two magic wands and stepped on his turban.

And with the matinee show at P.T. Flea's World's Greatest Circus about to begin, Gypsy knew she had to be on her toes. Manny was going to debut his new trick: the Levitating, Flaming and Disappearing Water Torture Chamber of Death.

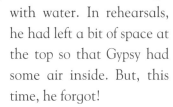

"Ladies and gentlemen," Manny announced, "prepare to be stunned and amazed by the Levitating, Flaming and Disappearing Water Torture Chamber of Death. You will watch as my lovely and talented assistant, Gypsy, climbs inside this chamber" – Manny motioned towards the empty sardine can at his side – "where I will bind her hands and feet. Then I will fill the chamber with water, seal it, levitate it five inches off the ground and set it ablaze. And, finally, you will watch in awe as the chamber disappears before your very eyes!"

Manny and Gypsy had rehearsed the act thoroughly. Everything was planned down to the last detail. But, if one little thing went wrong with the trick, Gypsy could be in big trouble.

As it turned out, one little thing didn't go wrong – three big things went wrong!

Manny made his first mistake when he tied Gypsy's hands and feet together. He was supposed to leave the strings loose so that Gypsy could wriggle out of them once she was inside. But Manny accidentally tied them too tight!

Then Manny filled the chamber too high with water. In rehearsals, he had left a bit of space at the top so that Gypsy had some air inside. But, this time, he forgot!

Manny's third mistake was locking the trapdoor. Together, he and Gypsy had rigged an escape hatch in the back side of the sardine can. Once Manny sealed her inside, Gypsy wriggled out of her bonds, opened the trapdoor, and, unseen by the audience, escaped from the chamber before Manny levitated it, set it on fire and made it disappear. But, this time, Manny accidentally nudged the latch that secured the trapdoor from the outside. Gypsy was locked inside.

Luckily, Gypsy hadn't left anything to chance: she had stowed a sharp shard of glass inside the sardine can. She had learned to hold her breath for ten minutes. And she had put a release latch on the inside of the trapdoor.

She was safely out of the chamber in one minute flat.

At the end of the trick, Manny called Gypsy in front of the audience. "How did you do it, my dear?" he asked dramatically.

"It was magic!" she replied, with a smile and a sigh of relief.

# Patch and the Panther

One dark night, 15 Dalmatian puppies sat huddled around a black-and-white television set. They watched as Thunderbolt, the canine hero, crept through a deep, dark jungle.

Suddenly Thunderbolt pricked up his ears. The puppies held their breath. Two yellow eyes peered out of the bushes. It was a panther!

"Thunderbolt, look out behind you!" Penny barked at the television.

"How will Thunderbolt escape the hungry panther?" the TV announcer asked. "Don't miss next week's exciting episode!"

"Aww!" the puppies groaned, disappointed that their favourite show was over.

"I'll bet Thunderbolt tears that ol' panther to pieces," said Patch.

"I'd be scared to fight a panther," said his brother Lucky.

"Not me!" cried Patch.

"All right, kids. Time for bed," Pongo said, shutting off the television with his nose. He watched as the puppies padded upstairs and settled down in their baskets.

"Good night, pups," Pongo said.

"Good night, Dad," the puppies replied.

Pongo switched off the light. Moments later, the sound of soft snores filled the room. The puppies were fast asleep.

All except for one. Patch was wide awake.

He was still thinking about Thunderbolt and the panther.

"I wish some ol' panther would come around here," Patch said to himself. "I'd teach him a thing or two."

Just then a floorboard creaked. Patch pricked up his ears. Then he crawled out of his basket to investigate.

The floorboard creaked again. What if it's a panther? Patch thought with a shiver. But I'm not scared of any ol' panther, he reminded himself.

Suddenly Patch saw a shadow flicker across the doorway. The shadow had a long tail. Panthers have long tails, Patch remembered. Just then two yellow eyes peered out of the darkness.

"Aroooo!" Patch yelped. He turned to run, but he tripped on the rug. In a flash, the panther was on top of him. Patch could feel its hot breath on his neck. He shut his eyes . . . .

"Patch, what are you doing out of bed?" the panther asked.

Patch opened his eyes. It was Pongo!

"I – I was just keeping an eye out for panthers," Patch explained.

Pongo smiled. "Why don't you get some sleep now," he suggested. "I can keep an eye out for panthers for a while."

"Okay, Dad," Patch said with a yawn.

Pongo carried Patch back to his basket. And in no time at all, the puppy was fast asleep.

Disney's
ATLANTIS
THE LOST EMPIRE

# Out for a Spin

One day, Princess Kida was showing Milo and the rest of the explorers the wonders of Atlantis. Vinny found an ancient gold medallion. Everyone was impressed, and they all decided to search for more treasure.

Milo, however, decided to go exploring with Kida instead. The Princess led him up the staircase of a huge pyramid. When they reached the top, they found a shark-shaped vehicle.

"It's an Aktirak," Kida told him.

"Aktirak must mean shark, because this flyer is shaped like a hammerhead," said Milo. "Can we take it for a spin?"

"If you wish," Kida said. "But you must not wreck this flyer as you did the last!"

Milo blushed. "Sorry about that," he said.

Kida used her crystal to start the engine. Then she and Milo climbed on.

Milo pushed a button and the Aktirak blasted into the sky!

"Wow! This machine looks like a shark but flies like an eagle!" cried Milo. They dived low over the water, skimming the waves.

Suddenly, a school of flying fish burst out of the water and surrounded the flyer. One flapped in Milo's face and he nearly lost control.

"We've got to get back to land!" he exclaimed. The Aktirak shot up into the sky.

"Beware of the cliffs ahead!" Kida warned.

Milo tried, but the Aktirak could not fly high enough. They were about to crash!

"The cave!" Kida cried, pointing to a hole in the side of the mountain.

Milo steered the Aktirak through the entrance. Now they were racing inside a large cavern.

Twisting the flyer, Milo dodged stalactites hanging from the cavern roof. Then he saw the head of a huge stone fish in the cave wall. Its mouth was open, and daylight streamed through it. He twisted the controls, and the Aktirak flew right though the fish's gaping mouth.

"Like threading a needle!" Milo declared.

Just then, the tail of the flyer scraped the stone fish and the Aktirak flew out of control.

"Hang on!" Milo cried.

The flyer hit the side of the pyramid, then bounced. It landed at the exact spot where Kida and Milo first found it.

The others heard the crash and rushed over. They found Milo and Kida standing next to the wrecked flyer.

"What happened?" Audrey cried.

"We went out for a spin," Milo said.

"Are you saying you actually *flew* this wreck?" Audrey demanded.

"I did!" said Milo. "But it's pretty obvious I need to sign up for Atlantean driver's ed!"

# Disney's Aladdin

## Abu's Blues

Abu couldn't believe it. One second he was a monkey. The next – *POOF!* – he was an elephant!

It was all the fault of the genie that Aladdin had found inside a lamp.

Worst of all, nobody seemed to notice that Abu wasn't thrilled about his new shape. Aladdin – now known as Prince Ali – was busy with the Genie and the Magic Carpet. Abu glared at them. Only a few hours ago, Abu had been Aladdin's only friend. Now Aladdin hardly seemed to remember he was around at all.

Abu watched as the Genie waved his arms and – *POOF!* – dozens of exotic white monkeys appeared. Then the Genie conjured up a group of snake charmers.

Abu wandered off, looking for space. He almost tripped over his new trunk a few times as he headed to a quiet spot.

He sat down, wishing he had a nice, juicy melon or a banana. Would he and Aladdin ever wander through the marketplace again, searching for a free meal? Would Aladdin ever pay any attention to him at all, between the blue guy and Princess Jasmine?

Abu scowled. Princess Jasmine. Talk about trouble – that was where this had all started. Ever since Aladdin had met her, it was as if Abu didn't matter any more . . . .

"Abu! Abu!"

Suddenly, Abu realized that someone was calling him. It was Aladdin!

"There you are, Abu!" Aladdin cried. "We were looking all over for you."

Abu glared at him suspiciously. What did he want? Was the Genie going to turn him into something else – maybe a big, ugly cobra for Prince Ali's new snake charmers?

"Come on." Aladdin didn't notice Abu's annoyance. "It's almost time!"

Time for what? Abu had no idea what Aladdin was talking about. He trumpeted at him angrily, complaining about how Aladdin didn't seem to want him around any more.

"Don't be silly, Abu!" Aladdin exclaimed. "You're the most important one in this whole parade! Now come over here . . . ."

"Ready, Monkey-boy?" the Genie said. "Er, I mean, Elephant-dude?"

He waved his arms, and a luxurious litter suddenly appeared on Abu's back. The Genie lifted Aladdin into it.

Suddenly, Abu understood – he and Aladdin were at the head of the parade! Aladdin wasn't going to forget him just because he'd met other friends! Lifting his trunk proudly, he let out a loud trumpet and led the way towards the Sultan's palace.

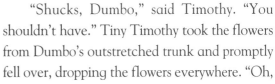

# The Best Gift Ever

Apart from Dumbo's mother, Mrs Jumbo, all the elephants at the circus made Dumbo feel like a nobody. They laughed at Dumbo's large ears and said that he would never amount to anything.

But Timothy Q. Mouse was different. Since the day he and Dumbo had met, Timothy had encouraged Dumbo. Dumbo was so happy to have a friend like Timothy. He wanted to do something nice for him in return.

So, one afternoon, Dumbo decided to give Timothy a gift. At feeding time, Dumbo put aside a bale of hay. Then he lugged the hay behind the Big Top and looked around for Timothy. Dumbo found him lounging in the shadow of the lion cage and plopped the hay bale down at Timothy's feet.

"Hiya, Dumbo!" said Timothy. "What's with the hay?"

Using his trunk, Dumbo nudged the hay bale closer to Timothy.

"For me?" Timothy said. "Wow. Uh . . . thanks. I, uh, wonder what I'll do with it all."

Dumbo's heart sank as he realized that mice didn't eat hay. And he wanted to give Timothy something he'd really like.

The next day, Dumbo came upon a patch of flowers growing just outside the elephants' tent. He picked a nice big bouquet and took it behind the Big Top to Timothy.

"Shucks, Dumbo," said Timothy. "You shouldn't have." Tiny Timothy took the flowers from Dumbo's outstretched trunk and promptly fell over, dropping the flowers everywhere. "Oh, dear, look what I did," said Timothy.

But Dumbo thought *he* was the one who should feel bad. The bouquet was too heavy for Timothy to enjoy.

The next day, under the Big Top, Dumbo spotted a bunch of balloons tied to a seat, left behind by one of the children. Balloons! thought Dumbo. Why, those wouldn't be too heavy for Timothy. They stayed up all by themselves. So Dumbo untied them and brought them to Timothy.

But, when Timothy took hold of the balloon strings, the helium-filled balloons lifted him clear off the ground! Quickly, Dumbo reached out with his trunk, grasped Timothy around his waist, and placed him gently on the ground.

Then, with a disappointed sigh, Dumbo took the balloons back. Would he ever find a good gift for Timothy? he wondered.

"Dumbo," Timothy said, "I wanted to thank you for giving me the best gift ever."

Dumbo's eyes widened in surprise. What could Timothy mean? Every gift he had tried to give him had been all wrong.

"You're my best friend," Timothy said. "And that's the best gift I could ever ask for."

# Disney's THE LITTLE MERMAID

# A History Lesson

"Ariel, what am I going to do with you?" King Triton asked with a sigh. He looked wearily at his daughter. "You know you're not allowed to visit the surface. None of us are – it's just too dangerous!"

Ariel hung her head. She had been caught going to visit the surface – again – to visit her seagull friend, Scuttle. King Triton just couldn't understand the Little Mermaid's interest in the human world. It made him sad that most of his conversations with his favourite daughter involved him yelling and her storming off. Suddenly, the King had an idea.

"You know, Ariel," he said thoughtfully, "you're so interested in learning more about the human world, but I bet you don't know that much about the world you live in!"

Ariel looked up. "What do you mean, Daddy?" she asked, looking confused. "What's there to know?"

"Well," said Triton, "for starters, do you know about the first Queen of the Merfolk?"

"I guess not," Ariel replied.

Ten minutes later, Ariel and her father were swimming slowly through the Royal Merseum (that's a merfolk museum, you know), and Ariel was discovering that merfolk history was much more exciting than she had ever imagined.

"This is a portrait of Queen Fluidia, the first Queen of the Merfolk. She was my Great-great-great-great-great-great-great-great-great-great-great-great-grandmother," said King Triton. He gestured at a sandpainting of a regal mermaid holding a pearl sceptre. "That would make her your Great-great-great – well, you get the idea. Anyway, Fluidia united all the merfolk into one kingdom many years ago, to fight an invasion of sharks. The Shark Army was the greatest, fiercest army the ocean had ever seen, but Fluidia was more than a match for them! She used that pearl sceptre as a club – she was so strong that she could start whirlpools just by swinging it around."

"Wow," said Ariel. "She sounds pretty fierce."

"She was. She drove those sharks off almost single-handedly, and in gratitude the merfolk made her Queen," King Triton said.

"You know, you come from a pretty interesting family," he continued. "And you remind me a lot of Fluidia, Ariel. You have her strength of will. I think you'll do great things – even if you and I won't always agree on *how* you'll do them."

"Thank you, Daddy," said Ariel, giving her father a hug. She decided not to mention to her father how much his trident looked like a dinglehopper. Maybe she would tell him some other time!

# Happy Mother's Day!

One fine May day, Roo hopped over to Winnie the Pooh's house.

"I have a problem," Roo told Pooh. "Mother's Day is almost here, and I don't know what to give my mama. Do you have any ideas?"

"Let me think," said Pooh. He thought very hard (or at least as hard as a bear of very little brain can think). "Think, think, think. A gift for Mother's Day . . . ."

Luckily, Pooh spotted a big pot of honey sitting in his cupboard. "That's it!" he cried. "Mothers like *honey*!"

"They do?" asked Roo.

"Doesn't everybody?" Pooh asked.

So Pooh gave Roo a small pot of honey. Roo bounced over to Rabbit's house next.

As usual, Rabbit was working in his garden. "Hello, Roo," he said. "What's in the pot?"

"It's honey," Roo explained. "To give to my mama on Mother's Day."

Rabbit frowned. "No, no, no," he said. "Mothers don't like honey. If there's one thing a mother wants to get on Mother's Day, it's a big bunch of fresh carrots."

"They do?" Roo said doubtfully.

"Oh, yes," said Rabbit. He reached into his wheelbarrow and pulled out a bunch of freshly picked carrots.

"Thanks, Rabbit," said Roo. Then he hopped to Eeyore's house of sticks.

"What do you have there, Roo?" Eeyore asked.

"Some gifts for my mama for Mother's Day," said Roo.

"I suppose some mothers might like carrots," Eeyore said. "And maybe others might like honey. But, in my opinion, you can't go wrong with prickly thistles."

"Prickly thistles?" asked Roo.

"Yes," replied Eeyore. "Here, take these. Then Kanga will be sure to have a happy Mother's Day. If that's what she wants."

"Well, thank you," said Roo, tucking the prickly thistles into his pocket and heading for home. He thought about his gifts as he ate his dinner. He wondered which gift to give his mother as he put on his pajamas and brushed his teeth.

The next morning, bright and early, Roo bounded into the living room. "Happy Mother's Day, Mama!" he shouted.

"Why, thank you, dear," said Kanga.

"I thought and thought about what to give you," Roo explained. "Pooh said honey. Rabbit said carrots. And Eeyore said thistles. But I decided to give you this," he said, throwing his arms around his mama.

Kanga smiled. "Thank you, Roo. That's the best Mother's Day gift of all."

Disney's
The Adventures of
**THE GREAT MOUSE DETECTIVE**

# Dawson Takes the Case

"My little boy is missing!" a sobbing Mrs Mousington cried to Basil, the Great Mouse Detective. "Can you help me find him?"

"I'm terribly sorry," said Basil. He was examining a brick wall very closely, looking for clues. "But I'm working on an important case for the Queen. I don't have time."

"No, wait!" cried Dr Dawson, Basil's partner. "Madam, if the Great Mouse Detective is too busy, then perhaps I can offer you my services."

"A splendid idea!" said Basil.

Before Dawson left with Mrs Mousington, Basil stopped him. "Don't forget this," he said, handing Dawson an umbrella.

"But it's a sunny day," said Dawson, puzzled. "Why would I need an umbrella?"

"A sunny day can turn dark quicker than you think," advised Basil. "Remember that, Dawson, and you'll do fine."

Dawson shrugged and took the umbrella. Then he turned to Mrs Mousington and said, "Show me where you last saw your son."

Mrs Mousington took him to a shop with a tall tree in front of it. Dawson searched the area and found a long, white hair. But a closer look told him this was not just any hair. It was a cat's whisker!

Calling to a nearby bird, Dawson asked for a lift up. On the shop's roof, Dawson saw a cat dozing, and beneath its paw was a tiny mouse's tail.

The bird set Dawson down on the roof, and he wondered how he was going to lift the cat's heavy paw. Then he remembered the umbrella!

Using one end as a lever, he heaved. Beneath it he found Mrs Mousington's terrified son.

"The cat was saving me for dinner!" the little boy mouse cried.

Dawson pulled the little mouse free. With relief, he waved at the boy's mother, who was waiting on the sidewalk below. But before Dawson could signal another bird for a ride down, the cat woke up.

Dawson saw only one escape – he opened his umbrella and jumped with the little boy mouse in his arms.

Mrs Mousington let out a terrified scream. But the umbrella filled with air and slowed their fall until they landed gently on the sidewalk.

Mrs Mousington hugged her little boy close. "Oh, Dr Dawson, thank you!" she cried.

Back at the Great Mouse Detective's house, Basil was delighted to hear how Dawson had saved the little boy.

"It was easy," Dawson told Basil. "Thanks to your umbrella, I'd call it an open-and-shut case!"

# Finding Ne-who?

"The coral reef is falling down, falling down, falling down."

Nemo was home, brushing up against the anemone, when the most awful singing he ever heard in his life made him cringe. He swam deeper into the anemone, but it didn't help. The song went on.

"My fair octopus."

And there was something familiar about it . . . . Still cringing, Nemo poked his head out of the golden tentacles to see who was making the awful racket.

"Dory!" Nemo should have known. How could he have forgotten that voice? Nemo swam as fast as he could toward the regal blue tang fish. "Dory! Where have you been?" It seemed like a whale's age since Nemo had seen the fish that helped his dad rescue him from the dentist's fish tank. And he couldn't wait to give her a big hug!

When Nemo got closer Dory stopped singing. That was good. But when she looked at him her face was blank. That wasn't so good.

"Did you say something, kid?" she asked.

"Dory, it's me. Nemo," he replied.

"Ne-*who*?" She looked at Nemo blankly. "Sorry, kid, don't know you. I was just swimming by, minding my own business, singing a song. Hey, why was I singing? Am I famous? Maybe that's how you know me."

"Dory! We're friends, remember?" Nemo had been missing Dory a lot. She just *had* to remember who he was.

"Friends? I just made friends with a hermit crab . . . I think." Dory swam in a circle looking for the crab, but got distracted and started chasing her tail.

"Please try to remember, Dory," Nemo asked again. "You helped save me. You helped me find my dad. You know my dad. Big orange guy? Three white stripes? Looks kind of like me?"

"My dad? Looks like you? Sorry, kid, you don't look anything like my dad." Dory looked at Nemo like he was crazy and began to swim away.

Nemo swam after her. "Just think about it for a second," he pleaded. She *had* to remember something. "I'm Nemo!"

Dory did not turn around but she slowed down. Swimming in a wide circle, she came back. She looked at Nemo sideways, and then started laughing so hard bubbles came out of her nose.

"Had you going, huh?" Dory gave Nemo a big hug and smiled at him slyly. "That was just my little joke. You know I could never forget you!"

Nemo giggled and swam circles around his friend. "Good one, Dory!" He grinned.

Dory smiled back. "Good one, *who*?"

Nemo groaned. That Dory!

## Disney's THE LION KING

# Simba's Thank-you Present

Simba lounged in the jungle, feeling happier than he'd felt in ages. After the terrible stampede near Pride Rock, he didn't think he'd ever be happy again. But his new friends Timon and Pumbaa had helped him feel better.

"I should do something to thank them," Simba told himself as he watched his friends splash in the river nearby. "Something really special!"

He decided to make them a present. When he saw a large piece of bark lying on the ground, he had an idea.

"Ta-da!" he exclaimed a while later, leading his friends to the gift.

Pumbaa blinked. "Thanks," he said. "Er, what is it?"

"A scratching spot," Simba said, flexing his claws. He'd used vines to attach it to a thick tree trunk at shoulder height.

"Gee," Timon said. "Nice thought and all, Simba. But it's a little high for me." He stretched to his full height but could barely reach it.

Pumbaa nodded. "And I don't scratch." He held up one foot. "Hooves, you know."

"Oh." Simba hadn't thought of that.

"Thanks anyway, kid," Pumbaa said.

Simba decided to try again by building them a nice, soft bed to sleep in. He dug a cosy hole in the ground, then filled it with soft things – feathers, sand and bits of fur.

"Ta-da!" he cried when he showed his friends. Timon sighed. "What are you trying to do, kill us? Prey animals here, remember? If we sleep on the ground, we become somebody's midnight snack!"

Simba sighed as they left again. Why couldn't he come up with a present they would like?

"I would've loved that scratching spot," he mumbled. "The bed, too."

Suddenly he sat up straight, realizing what he'd just said. All this time he'd been thinking of presents HE would like – but the presents weren't for him.

"I've got to think like they think," he whispered. Slowly, a smile spread across his face . . . .

A little while later he called them over. "I've got something for you." He pointed to a pile of palm fronds. "I think you're really going to like it. Ta-da!"

He pulled back the leaves. Underneath was a mass of wriggling, squirming, creeping, crawling creatures – bugs and grubs and worms of every shape and size . . . and flavour.

Timon and Pumbaa gasped with delight. "Simba!" Timon cried. "You're a prince! It's just what we always wanted!"

"Yeah, thanks," Pumbaa mumbled through a mouthful of grubs. "You're a real pal!"

Simba smiled. "No," he said. "Thank *you*. Both of you. *Hakuna matata!*"

Walt Disney's
**Cinderella**

# A Birthday Surprise

"Get up, Jaq! Get up!" Gus cried.

"Go away, Gus," Jaq mumbled sleepily and rolled over.

"No, no, Jaq. Get up. It's a special day." Gus pulled on his tail. "It's Cinderelly's birthday."

Jaq sat up. "Today?" he asked, wide-eyed. "Today is her birthday?"

Gus smiled and nodded vigorously.

"Well, come on! We haven't got much time!" Jaq cried. "We have a lot to do if we're throwing a surprise party!"

Soon the birds and mice were gathered on the windowsill for a meeting.

"We can make a cake!" Suzy and Perla volunteered.

"Watch out for L-L-Lucifer," Gus stuttered. Baking would mean stealing eggs and butter from the kitchen!

"We'll take care of that cat," Mert and Bert said, crossing their arms.

The birds whistled that they would decorate the room.

"But we still need a present," Jaq said.

"Something pretty!" Gus cried.

"I've got it!" Jaq sat up straight. "I saw some slippers in the garbage last night when I was looking for food. There's a hole in one toe, but the bottoms were okay."

"We can fix them," the mice chorused.

"And I have a bit of ribbon I've been saving. We can use it on the slippers to pretty them up." Jaq pulled a rose-coloured silk ribbon from his small bag. "Now, let's get to work. We have lots to do!"

It took the mice all day to get ready, but everything turned out beautifully. The sun was setting when the mice and birds heard Cinderella's soft steps coming up the stairs.

"Here she comes!" Gus whispered.

Jaq took a match and lit the candle stump that was stuck in the iced cake. Beside it the slippers were mended and wrapped. The ribbon was twirled into two pink roses, one at each ankle.

The door opened slowly.

"Surprise!" the mice squeaked. The birds twittered and dropped confetti.

"Oh, my!" Cinderella gasped. "This *is* a surprise!"

"Happy birthday," Gus said shyly.

"It's all so lovely," Cinderella said. "But I'm afraid it's not my birthday."

"It's not?" Jaq's smile vanished. The rest of the mice and birds were silent.

"I'm afraid not, but that's what makes this such a special surprise." Cinderella beamed. The animals laughed and they all sat down to share the delicious cake together.

# Win Some, Lose Some

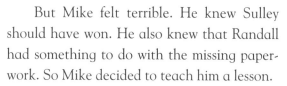

Sulley and his assistant, Mike, were in a race to become the Top Scare Team. But Randall and Fungus were right behind them. So it was lucky that Sulley and Mike were racking up the scares!

"We'll beat Randall easily," said Mike, giving Sulley a high five.

"Just keep that paperwork in order," Sulley warned. "You know how Roz hates when it's late!"

Suddenly, the Scare Floor exploded in panic. George Sanderson had returned from his cupboard with a ball stuck to his foot with chewing gum. Now, special teams from the CDA, the Child Detection Agency, swarmed into the factory to decontaminate George.

During the excitement, Randall crept over to Sulley's workstation. He stole Mike's paperwork and tossed it into a shredder.

After George had been cleaned – and shaved! – the Scare Teams got back to work.

"My paperwork is gone!" Mike cried, his eye blinking in confusion.

"Oh, no!" cried Sulley. "Without that paperwork, none of today's work will count."

"Too bad," said Randall, chuckling. "That makes me today's Top Scarer."

Mike was sad, but Sulley wasn't upset in the least. "Cheer up," said Sulley. "You win some, you lose some. Tomorrow is another day."

But Mike felt terrible. He knew Sulley should have won. He also knew that Randall had something to do with the missing paperwork. So Mike decided to teach him a lesson.

A few days later, Randall was ahead of everyone else in scares.

"This is my best day ever!" Randall crowed to the other Scarers. "Pretty soon I'll be Scarer of the Month!"

But, just then, the alarm went off. George had come back with a lollipop stuck to his ear.

As the teams rushed to decontaminate George, Mike sprang into action. When no one was looking, he hurried over to Randall's and Fungus's workstations and grabbed all their paperwork.

"This is contaminated, too!" Mike cried as he tossed the papers to the floor.

"Burn it!" commanded the CDA decontamination team leader.

With a *whoosh*, a flamethrower burned all of the papers to ashes.

"Where's the paperwork?" Randall cried when he returned to the scare floor.

"Yikes!" Fungus yelped. "Where did it go? It was right here!"

"Well, this is just great," Randall said. "Now my points don't count."

"Looks like you're cooked. Just like your paperwork," Mike said with a chuckle.

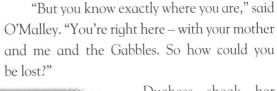

Disney's
*THE* ARISTOCATS

# Wherever You Go, There You Are!

"Oh, dear! Oh, dear!" said Amelia Gabble. The goose and her twin sister, Abigail, had been waddling along the road to Paris, when Amelia suddenly stopped.

"What's wrong?" asked Abigail, bumping into her.

"Just look and you'll see," said Amelia. Stretching out one big white wing, she pointed to the road ahead. Abigail looked, and then the two geese put their heads together and began to argue in low voices.

Behind the geese, Thomas O'Malley, Duchess and her three kittens gathered together.

"I wonder what's wrong," said Duchess.

"Guess I'd better find out," said O'Malley.

He sauntered forward. "Ladies, ladies, what's going on?" he asked the twin geese.

"We know this is the road to Paris," Amelia explained. "But up ahead, the road divides."

Sure enough, the single road split in two.

"I think we should go right," said Amelia.

"And I think we should go left," said Abigail.

The three kittens began to worry.

"Mr O'Malley, are we lost?" asked Marie in a small, frightened voice.

O'Malley smiled down at the little white kitten. "Lost? What's lost? I don't know the meaning of the word."

"I do," said Berlioz. "If you're lost, then you don't know where you are."

"But you know exactly where you are," said O'Malley. "You're right here – with your mother and me and the Gabbles. So how could you be lost?"

Duchess shook her head and said, "Mr O'Malley, if we want to get to Paris and we don't know the way, then I do believe that we are lost."

"But Paris is just a place," said O'Malley. "And places are easy to find."

"Look, Mama, look!" Toulouse shouted. "I see something over that hill. It's the top of the Eiffel Tower!"

"Toulouse, you're right!" said Duchess.

"Nice going, little tiger," said O'Malley. Then he turned to the Gabble sisters. "Well, ladies, looks like Paris is thataway!"

Soon they arrived in Paris, where the Gabble sisters met up with their Uncle Waldo. The geese waved goodbye.

Marie sighed with relief. "I'm glad we're not lost any more."

"Aw, honey," said O'Malley, "someday you'll understand. Places may come and places may go but, when you're a free spirit, you can never be lost."

"Never?" asked Marie.

"Never," said O'Malley. " 'Cause wherever you go, there you are!"

Marie nodded. She liked the sound of that!

Disney's *Beauty* AND THE *BEAST*

# A Little Help

"This is bad," fretted Cogsworth the clock, pacing at the bottom of the castle's staircase. "Bad, bad, bad!"

"What is wrong, my friend?" asked Lumiere the candelabrum.

"The Beast hurt Belle's feelings," said Cogsworth. "Then Belle hurt the Beast's feelings. Now they're sulking in their rooms."

"Ah, that *is* bad," said Lumiere. "We will never be human again unless the spell on the Beast is broken. And the spell won't break until Belle falls in love with him."

"Well, there's no chance of that happening now!" cried Cogsworth.

"Nonsense," said Lumiere. "Sometimes love just needs a little help."

After Lumiere told Cogsworth his plan, they got to work. When everything was ready, Lumiere knocked on Belle's bedroom door.

"*Mademoiselle,*" he called sweetly. "I am here to tell you that the Beast is very sorry about what happened."

"He is?" asked Belle.

"Oh, yes," said Lumiere. "Now do you wish to see your surprise?"

The door slowly opened. "My surprise?" asked Belle.

"*Oui, mademoiselle,*" said Lumiere. "Just follow me."

At that very moment, Cogsworth was standing outside the Beast's bedroom door, his gears quaking with fear. "Darn that Lumiere," muttered Cogsworth. "Why do *I* get the Beast?"

Gathering his courage, Cogsworth finally knocked.

"Go away!" roared the Beast.

Cogsworth wanted to! But, instead, he called, "Master, I am only here to tell you that Belle is very sorry about what happened!"

After a long pause, the Beast said, "She is?"

"Oh, yes indeed," said Cogsworth. "Now follow me to see your surprise."

The door slowly opened. "My surprise?" asked the Beast.

"Yes, Master," said Cogsworth.

Both Belle and the Beast were led into the large drawing room. The room had been filled with fresh flowers from the greenhouse. And there stood Plucky the golden harp.

"Ohhhhh," said Belle and the Beast when they heard the beautiful harp music.

"You're sorry?" asked Belle.

"I am," the Beast admitted.

"I am too," said Belle.

They smiled at each other.

Lumiere and Cogsworth sighed. "You see, my friend," whispered Lumiere, "in their hearts, each really was sorry. They just needed a little help to admit it!"

Walt Disney's
*Lady* and the **TRAMP**

# Howling at the Moon

Lady had been having a really bad day. First, she'd had a run-in with two nasty cats. Then, she'd been put in a horrible muzzle. But, because of Tramp, everything had changed.

"It's amazing how a day can start off terribly but end wonderfully," Lady told Tramp as they trotted through the moonlit park. "Thank you for helping me escape that terrible muzzle – and for dinner at Tony's."

"Aw, shucks, don't mention it!" said Tramp. "Hey, you wanna have some real fun?"

"I don't know," Lady said cautiously.

While she was very fond of Tramp, she also knew they were very different dogs. Tramp was used to life on the streets. So his idea of 'fun' might be very different from hers.

"Don't worry," Tramp teased. "This is something I think you'll enjoy."

"What is it?" asked Lady.

"Well, for starters, you have to look up," said Tramp.

Lady did. The sky was filled with stars and a big, bright moon.

"What am I looking for?" she asked.

"The moon, of course!" cried Tramp. "Haven't you ever howled at the moon?"

Lady laughed at Tramp's suggestion. "What's so funny?" asked Tramp.

"I'm a practical dog," explained Lady. "I bark politely when the situation calls for it, but I don't see any point in howling at the moon."

"Why not?" asked Tramp.

"Well," said Lady, "what's the use of it?"

"You know, Lady," said Tramp, "a thing doesn't have to be useful to be fun. You like to chase a ball, right?"

"Right," said Lady.

"So, there you go," said Tramp. "Sometimes it's good to chase a ball. And sometimes it's good to just let go and howl at the moon, even for no reason."

Lady thought it over. "Okay," she said. "What do I do?"

"First, sit up real straight," said Tramp. "Then, look up at the moon, take a deep breath, and just let all the troubles of your day disappear in one gigantic howl!" He demonstrated: "Ow-ow-OWWWWWWW!"

Lady joined Tramp and howled as loudly as she could.

"You're right!" she cried. "It does feel good to howl at the moon!"

"Stick with me, kid," said Tramp. "I know what's what."

Lady suspected Tramp did know what was what, but there was an even better reason for her to stick with him. He'd become the very best friend she'd ever had.

## Walt Disney's
# Peter Pan

# The Lost Boys Get Lost

The Lost Boys were walking single file through the woods of Never Land, on their way home after an afternoon of adventure-seeking, when Slightly, who led the way, stopped in his tracks on the bank of Mermaid Lagoon.

The others – Rabbit, the Raccoon Twins, Cubby and Tootles – came to an abrupt halt behind him.

"Wait a minute," said Slightly. "We already passed Mermaid Lagoon. What are we doing here again?"

Behind a bush, Tinker Bell giggled as she watched the Lost Boys looking around in confusion.

Tink had spotted them on their march and had not been able to resist playing a joke. So, she had flown ahead of them and used her fairy magic to enchant various landmarks on their route home. She had made Bald Rock look like Spiky Rock, causing the Lost Boys to make a right turn where they should have turned left. Then she had enlisted the help of the sparrows, convincing them to move from their usual perch in the Sparrow Bird Grove to another group of trees, thus tricking the Lost Boys into making another right turn too soon. And finally, she had enchanted the Towering Elm Tree to look exactly like the Weeping Willow, and the Lost Boys had made yet another wrong turn, thinking they were nearly home.

But now, here they were, walking past Mermaid Lagoon, when Slightly remembered passing the same spot a good while back.

"I think we're walking in circles!" Slightly proclaimed. "Lost Boys, I think we're . . . lost!"

Tinker Bell overheard and tried desperately to stifle her laughter. But, before she could contain it, one giggle exploded into a full-fledged laugh and –

"Hey!" said Cubby. "Did you hear that?"

He darted over to a bush growing alongside the path and moved a branch to one side. There was Tinker Bell, hovering in mid-air, holding her stomach and shaking with laughter.

"Tinker Bell!" cried Tootles.

It didn't take them long to work out that Tinker Bell was laughing at *them* – and that she was the cause of their confusion.

Still laughing, Tinker Bell flitted away, taking her normal route home to the fairy glade: left at the Weeping Willow Tree, right just before Sparrow Bird Grove, right again at Spiky Rock, and on towards the Sparkling Stream, which led to Moon Falls and the fairy glade entrance.

But – wait a minute! After turning right at Spiky Rock, Tinker Bell saw no sign of the Sparkling Stream anywhere. Where was she? She had got completely lost.

Do you know how?

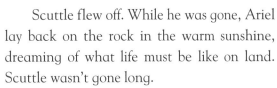

# Dinglehoppers and Jibbermutts

Ariel sat on a rock, talking with her friends, Scuttle the seagull and Flounder the fish. She loved visiting the surface, although she knew it was dangerous for mermaids to venture there. Her father would definitely not approve, but then, these days, he seemed to disapprove of so much of what she liked to do.

"What's it like on land, Scuttle?" she asked.

"Land?" echoed Scuttle. "Oh! Land! Yeah, well, it's great on land. I know all about humans."

"Like what?" Ariel asked eagerly.

"Well! For instance . . . you know all about the dinglehoppers they use to comb their hair, right? And the snarfblatts that they make music with?"

"Yes," said Ariel.

"Well, did you know that they also have these strange rectangular objects with sheets of paper inside? They're called jibbermutts. Humans like to throw them to one another," Scuttle explained.

"Oh, Scuttle," said Ariel breathlessly. "Would you fly up to Eric's window and come back and tell me what you have seen?" Eric was the young prince whom Ariel had rescued after he was shipwrecked during a terrible storm. Even though she had seen him only once, she had fallen head over fin in love with him.

Scuttle flew off. While he was gone, Ariel lay back on the rock in the warm sunshine, dreaming of what life must be like on land. Scuttle wasn't gone long.

"Did you see him?" asked Ariel eagerly. "What was he doing?"

"Yep, I saw him!" Scuttle replied importantly. "He was trying to eat with a dinglehopper! And he had a jibbermutt, but it almost looked like he was trying to read it, instead of throwing it like he's supposed to. Ariel, I don't think your prince is too bright . . . ."

Ariel sighed dreamily, imagining her handsome love. She did wonder why he would try to use a dinglehopper to eat, though. Maybe he was so distracted by thoughts of her, he didn't know what he was doing, the Little Mermaid thought hopefully.

"Don't suppose you'd want his dinglehopper for your treasure chest, would you?" asked Scuttle with a mischievous glint in his eye.

"Oh, Scuttle! You didn't!" shouted Ariel.

"Yup. Just as soon as he set it down, I flew in through the window and grabbed it. Boy, was he surprised!"

Ariel clutched the dinglehopper to her chest. "I'll probably never know what it's like to live on land, but no matter what happens, Scuttle, I will treasure this forever!"

# Baloo's Secret Weapon

**M**owgli and his pal Baloo were taking a lazy afternoon stroll through the jungle. Suddenly, Mowgli stopped in his tracks. "Did you hear that?" he asked.

"Hear what, little buddy?" Baloo asked.

"It sounded like twigs snapping," Mowgli said. "I think somebody might be following us!"

"That was just your old Papa Bear's stomach growling," Baloo told him. "It's time for some lunch."

"And I know just where to get it," announced Mowgli. He shimmied up a tree, plucked a bunch of bananas, and tossed them down to the bear.

"That's my boy!" Baloo cried proudly.

But, as he was scrambling back down, Mowgli spotted a flash of orange and black.

"Shere Khan!" Mowgli whispered to Baloo. "We've got to get out of here!" The tiger had been after Mowgli ever since the boy had first set foot in the jungle.

The two friends didn't know which way to turn. Now that Shere Khan had their scent, it would be almost impossible to lose him. Then they both heard a lively beat drumming its way through the jungle.

"Oh, no," said Mowgli. "King Louie and his crazy band of monkeys. That's all we need!"

Baloo's eyes suddenly lit up. "That's *exactly* what we need, Little Britches!"

Still clutching the bananas, Baloo and Mowgli ran towards King Louie's compound. When they arrived, Baloo disguised himself as a monkey. The orang-utans were so busy dancing and singing they didn't notice his disguise. Then the bear quickly found a huge empty barrel, and filled it with the bananas.

"Look!" cried Baloo, peering into the barrel. "Lunch!" The monkeys ran over and jumped right into the barrel! They greedily ate the feast, tossing peels out as they made their way through the bunch.

Baloo signalled to Mowgli, who came out of hiding. "Come and get me, Shere Khan!" the Man-cub taunted.

Within seconds, the tiger appeared in the clearing, a fierce gleam in his eye. "Hello, Stripes," Baloo greeted him cheerfully. Then the bear picked up the barrel, heaved it, and sent King Louie's troop flying at Shere Khan. The orang-utans landed on the tiger's back, where they frantically jumped up and down, pulling on his tail and ears. Mowgli and Baloo watched as Shere Khan raced back into the jungle, trying to free himself from his shrieking passengers.

"Like I always say," Baloo declared as he grinned at Mowgli, "there's nothing more fun than a barrel of monkeys!"

THE EMPEROR'S
NEW GROOVE

# Superspeedy Spiral Slide-tacular

"Whee!" Kuzco the mighty Emperor ran, jumped and landed the most royal belly flop of all time. And that was only the beginning. Splashing to the top of Kuzco's Superspeedy Spiral Slide-tacular at his very own water park, Kuzcotopia, Kuzco slipped and slid. He descended in circles faster and faster until at last he splashed down into a grand pool. *Thonk!*

"Whoa. Hey. Hang on a second. Did I just get hit in the head with a hoof?" Kuzco sat up and put his hands on his hips. "Because maybe you didn't get the memo, but I'm the Emperor around . . ."

Kuzco's voice trailed off. Something was wrong. Very wrong. The majestic pool was gone. Kuzco was wading in not-so-majestic grass. Kuzcotopia was nowhere to be seen. And, instead of hands, his arms ended in hooves! He had been dreaming! And, worst of all, he had woken to this nightmare: he was still a llama!

Kuzco pursed his llama lips in exasperation. The peasant, Pacha, who had been helping him find his way back to his empire, was eating calmly by a campfire.

Terrific. Kuzco was starving. "What's for breakfast?" Kuzco asked, nosing Pacha's bowl.

"Just a few nuts and berries I found," Pacha said. "You can go get yourself some."

"Why don't you give me yours?" Kuzco asked as he narrowed his eyes.

"Why don't you go get your own?" Pacha pulled his bowl closer.

"Emperors don't eat squirrel food." Kuzco pouted.

"Fine." Pacha turned his back and kept eating. "But you'll be sorry later. We have a long way to go."

The sun grew hot as the pair headed out of camp. Soon Kuzco's tongue lolled out of his mouth. He had no energy. "Carry me!" he pleaded.

"No way." Pacha kept walking down the steep ravine. "Maybe you should have had some breakfast."

"Oh, great, now we get to play 'told you so'!" Kuzco was so busy sulking, he wasn't watching where he was going. He slipped. Frantic, he tried to grab something. Anything!

What he caught was a long, thick, spiralling vine. Kuzco zoomed towards the bottom of the ravine. He descended in circles, faster and faster until – *Thonk!*

"Ouch." The mighty llama Emperor landed roughly in a patch of prickly bushes. But, luckily, they were berry bushes! Quickly, Kuzco began eating the ripe berries. Further up the ravine, he could hear Pacha laughing.

"Go ahead, laugh," Kuzco said. "But you have just seen a preview of Kuzcotopia's Superspeedy Spiral Slide-tacular!"

**Walt Disney's**
*Snow White*
*and the Seven Dwarfs*

# Good Housekeeping

Snow White and the Prince were going to be married. Her dear friends, the Seven Dwarfs, were filled with joy to see Snow White so happy. But they knew they were going to miss her – not to mention her wonderful cooking and how she kept their cottage so clean and tidy.

Snow White was also worried about how the little men were going to get along without her. She decided it was time they learned how to cook and clean for themselves.

"First, let's see you sweep out the cottage," she said. "Remember to push the dirt out the door and not just move it around the floor." The men all grabbed brooms and set to work.

*"Ah-chooooo!"* boomed Sneezy as a huge cloud of dust rose into the air.

"Don't forget to open the door *first*," Snow White added. She moved on to the next task. "Now we'll wash the dishes. First you dunk the plate, then you scrub it, then you rinse and dry it," she said, demonstrating as she went.

Doc stood, holding a dirty plate. "Let's see," he mumbled. "Scrub, dunk, dry, rinse? Or is it dunk, rinse, dry, scrub? Or . . . oh, dear!"

Snow White chuckled good-naturedly. "Never mind," she said. "On to the laundry! First you heat the water over the fire, then you scrub the clothes with a bar of soap, rinse them

and then hang them on the line to dry."

Dopey was first in line. He jumped into the tub and rubbed the bar of soap all over the clothes he was wearing.

"Dopey," said Snow White, "it's easier if you wash the clothes *after* you've taken them off."

A bit later, the Dwarfs trooped into the kitchen for a cooking lesson.

"Today we're going to make stew," said Snow White. "You take a little of everything you have on hand, throw it into a pot, and let it simmer for a long time."

As Snow White was leaving, Doc said, "Don't worry, Snow White. We're going to be fust jine . . . I mean, just fine."

The next night, the Dwarfs made dinner. When their guests arrived, Dopey led Snow White and the Prince over to the large pot simmering over the fire and grandly lifted the lid. An old boot, some socks, a bunch of flowers, and a cake of soap were floating on the top. "We made it with a little of everything we had on hand, just like you said," Sleepy said.

"Perhaps we should go over that recipe again," Snow White said gently. Then she brought out four gooseberry pies from her basket. Ordinarily, Snow White didn't believe in eating dessert before dinner, but this time she would make an exception!

## Rain, Rain, Go Away

*Rrrrumble, rrrrumble, BOOM!* The loud clap of thunder startled Bambi and his friends.

"I don't like thunderstorms!" cried Thumper, looking a little scared.

"I don't like them either!" exclaimed Flower.

"Bambi!" called his mother as the clouds grew dark and the rain began to fall. Bambi followed his mother out of the open meadow and into the woods. From their warm, dry thicket, Bambi watched sheets of rain pour down.

"I don't like thunderstorms," he told his mother, echoing Thumper's words. "I wish the storm would go away and never come back again."

"Oh, my," said his mother. "Do you mean you never again want to drink the cool, fresh water from the forest stream?"

"Well, no," said Bambi.

"Then, do you want the big trees to go thirsty? Their leaves to wither and branches to become brittle?" asked his mother.

"No! Of course not!" cried Bambi. "The trees give us shelter, and their branches give the birds a place to make their nests."

"Then, do you want the sweet grass to turn brown?" asked his mother.

"No," said Bambi. "We eat the grass. We'd go hungry if that happened!"

"Well, then, my son," said Bambi's mother. "I think you'd better not wish for storms to go away forever. Their raindrops fill the streams and water the trees and grass."

"But storms are so scary," Bambi said.

Just then, the rain began to let up, and Bambi's friends scampered through the underbrush and into Bambi's thicket.

"Look at the pond!" cried Flower.

Bambi peered through the thicket. The pond was alive with activity. The frogs were leaping and playing. And a family of ducks was shaking their feathers and waddling into the water.

"Uh-oh," said Thumper. "That old bullfrog's gonna get a surprise."

Bambi watched the lily pad with the big bullfrog drift closer and closer to the line of ducklings. The last duckling wasn't paying attention. The sudden collision sent the frog toppling off its lily pad with a startled *croak!* and surprised the duckling so much it did an underwater somersault!

Bambi, Thumper and Flower laughed.

"I guess I like thunderstorms after all," Bambi told his mother.

"You didn't like thunderstorms?" said Thumper. "That's silly! Why would you ever say a thing like that?"

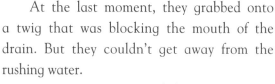

# Spring Time

Outside, it was a beautiful spring day. Inside, most of the toys were busy helping Bo Peep find her sheep for what seemed like the millionth time. Buzz pulled Woody aside.

"Woody," he said. "I need some fresh air. What do you say we sit on the roof for a couple of minutes to enjoy the nice spring weather."

Woody thought for a moment. "Okay," he said. "Let's sit on the roof in the sun. Andy and his mum shouldn't be home for a while. What harm could come of it?"

As it turned out – a lot!

No sooner had the two climbed up onto the roof than the sky grew very dark. Then there was a flash of lightning and a rumble of thunder. Suddenly, the sky opened up and water poured down in buckets.

"Help!" Woody cried. The pounding rain swept him off the roof and into the rain gutter!

"I'm coming!" cried Buzz. But the space ranger wasn't coming to *help*. He was being washed down the gutter too!

Woody and Buzz span head over heels in the rushing water. They sped through the gutter and down the drainpipe. Thank goodness, thought Woody, we'll be on the ground soon. But the force of the water propelled them all the way to the kerb. They were headed towards the . . .

"Storm drain!" he cried.

At the last moment, they grabbed onto a twig that was blocking the mouth of the drain. But they couldn't get away from the rushing water.

Luckily, up in Andy's room, Lenny the Binoculars had been watching the sudden spring storm. He told the other toys, who gathered at the window and saw Buzz and Woody just barely hanging on. "We have to do something!" cried Hamm.

It was Slinky Dog who hopped forward. Rex grabbed his tail and Slinky dropped himself out the window. Then he stretched his spring as far as it would go.

The toys held their breath as they watched.

"He can't reach!" cried Jessie. "We need to form a toy chain!"

Bo Peep held on to Rex. Hamm held on to Bo Peep. The Green Army Men all joined in, and Jessie grabbed on to the last one. Slinky leaned forward, Buzz and Woody grabbed hold of his ears and let go of the twig and – *Boing*! – Buzz and Woody were lifted off the ground and through Andy's window.

Safe and dry again, Buzz and Woody thanked the toys for coming to their rescue. Buzz turned to Woody. "So much for the nice spring weather today," he said.

Woody smiled. "Thank goodness we had a *nice spring* to save the day!"

# Fast Friends

"Here, kitty, kitty," called Penny, peering underneath her bed. "Come on, I won't hurt you." She reached her hand out towards the old orange cat she had seen race into the girls' dormitory room at the Morningside Orphanage and dart under the bed. Now the cat was hiding under there, looking too afraid to move.

Penny had lived at the orphanage for a long time. But, in all her years there, she had never known that a cat lived there too.

"Whatcha doin' under there?" Penny asked.

Surprisingly, the cat answered her. "I'm hiding from the headmistress," he whispered. "Is she coming this way?"

Penny looked up and over towards the door of the dormitory. She saw the headmistress poke her head into the girls' room, glance around hurriedly, then head off down the hallway.

Penny hung down over the side of the bed again. "Nope, she's gone," she said to the cat. "The coast is clear."

Breathing a sigh of relief, the cat ambled towards Penny, came out from under the bed and jumped up onto the windowsill, looking at her. Now Penny could get a better look at him. The cat was wearing a red woollen scarf around his neck and a pair of glasses on his nose, and his long white whiskers looked just like a moustache. He had a very kind face.

"Thanks," the cat said to Penny. "That was a close one."

"Why was the headmistress after you?" Penny asked him.

"Oh," the cat said with a chuckle, "she got me a while back to keep mice out of the basement." He stretched, yawned and jumped down to lie in a patch of sunlight on the floor. "But I don't mouse too well any more. I'm getting too slow to chase anything. I'm not as young and spry as I used to be. Say, my name's Rufus. What's yours?"

"Penny," she replied with a smile. She reached under her pillow and pulled out her teddy bear. "And this is Teddy."

"Well, hello, Penny," said Rufus. "And hello, Teddy."

Teddy just stared back at Rufus blankly.

"Quiet little guy, huh?" Rufus said to Penny. "What's the matter? Cat got his tongue?"

Penny giggled. "Teddy's very good at keeping secrets. And so am I. You can come hide under our bed whenever you need to. We won't tell."

"You won't?" Rufus replied. "Aw, that's mighty good of you." And so, feeling safe and secure by the side of his new friends, Rufus closed his eyes and settled down for a catnap.

# How to Unpack for a Vacation

One morning, Donald Duck heard a knock at the door. When he opened it, he found his friend Mickey Mouse standing there.

"Today is the day!" exclaimed Mickey.

"Today is *what* day?" asked Donald with a yawn.

"Don't you remember?" said Mickey. "You're driving me, Minnie and Daisy to the beach for a week's vacation." Mickey held up his suitcase. "I packed last night. Aren't you packed too?"

"No," said Donald. "I thought we were leaving next week!"

"No," said Mickey. "We're leaving today. And Minnie and Daisy will be here in an hour."

"Oh, no!" cried Donald.

"Calm down," said Mickey. "You have time to get ready. Just pack your things now."

While Mickey relaxed on the porch in a rocking chair, Donald went back inside.

"What do I pack?" Donald muttered to himself as he raced through his house. "I'll need my toys, of course, in case I get bored." Donald ran to his playroom and placed all his toys in boxes.

"What else should I pack?" Donald asked himself. "Clothes!" He ran to his bedroom and took out every suitcase he owned. Then he emptied all his drawers and filled his suitcases.

Finally, Donald calmed down. "That should do it," he said with a sigh of relief.

Mickey couldn't believe his eyes when Donald began packing up his car. Just then, Minnie Mouse and Daisy Duck arrived. They each had one small suitcase.

Minnie and Daisy took one look at Donald's car and gasped. Boxes and baskets were crammed into the back and front seats. Daisy opened the boot and found it overflowing with Donald's suitcases.

"There's no room left for *our* suitcases!" cried Daisy.

"Forget our *suitcases*!" exclaimed Minnie. "There's no room for us!"

Mickey put his arm around Donald.

"It's okay, Donald," he said. "It's hard packing for a vacation. You have to leave some things behind – even some of your favourite things. But they will all be here when we get back. I guarantee it!"

"And besides," added Daisy, "don't you want to leave room in your car to bring back souvenirs, like seashells and T-shirts and salt-water taffy?"

Donald brightened. "Seashells and T-shirts and saltwater taffy!" he cried excitedly. "Oh, you bet!"

"Good," said Mickey. Then he pointed to Donald's overflowing car. "Now let's all help Donald *un*pack for this vacation!"

Walt Disney's
**Sleeping Beauty**

# How Rose Dozed

The moon hung high in the sky, and the stars twinkled around it. It was late at night, and Briar Rose was supposed to be sleeping. But, with all those owls hooting and the frogs in a nearby pond croaking, who could sleep? So, after tossing and turning for hours on end, Briar Rose woke up her three trusted aunties, Flora, Fauna and Merryweather, to see if they could help.

"I've got the solution!" Fauna exclaimed. "You need to count sheep."

"Lie down now, dear," Flora joined in, "and picture a fence. Then imagine sheep jumping over it one by one, and don't lose count!"

Briar Rose lay back and did as they said. But, when she got to sheep 544, she knew it wasn't working. Briar Rose went back to her aunts. "No luck," she said.

"Oh, dear," said Flora. "We'll have to think of something else instead."

"Sleep, schmeep!" Merryweather chimed in. "The night has its own brightness, twinkle and shine. It's such a shame to sleep through it all of the time!"

"You really think so?" Briar Rose asked.

"Absolutely!" Merryweather exclaimed. "Look at the stars burning bright and the moon sending down its own special light."

"That's all well and fine," Flora interrupted.

"But if Briar Rose doesn't sleep at night, she'll be tired during the day."

"Good point," Briar Rose agreed.

"Well, then, try reading a book! Reading always puts me to sleep," Merryweather said with a yawn.

"But I *like* reading," Briar Rose protested. "I'll never fall asleep."

There was a pause, as each of the aunts thought and thought about how to help Briar Rose.

"I know a way to help you sleep!" Fauna said suddenly. "All you have to do," she explained, "is think good thoughts about the day that's passed, and hope for the happy things that tomorrow may bring."

"Is that true?" Briar Rose asked.

"Absolutely!" Flora agreed.

"Now, close your eyes," Merryweather instructed, "and we'll see you in your dreams."

Briar Rose wasn't sure at first, but Flora, Fauna, and Merryweather had never let her down before. So she lay back down and closed her eyes. She remembered her favourite things from that very day, then thought about the wonder tomorrow would bring. Just as she was drifting off, she thought, I hope that never happens to me again. I need my beauty sleep! And wouldn't you know, pretty soon, she was lost in her dreams.

# Walt Disney's ALICE in WONDERLAND

## "R U Slee-P?"

As Alice wandered around Wonderland, she encountered a blue Caterpillar sitting on a mushroom. He was smoking an exotic-looking pipe, and every puff of smoke formed a different letter.

"R U slee-P?" asked the Caterpillar's smoke.

"Am I sleepy?" Alice scratched her head. "I hadn't thought about it – I'm so worried about getting home, it's hard to think about anything else. I don't know, I suppose."

"U kn-O," said the Caterpillar, puffing out a U and an O in red-and-orange smoke.

"I do?" asked Alice.

"Ye-S, U do," said the Caterpillar. "For instance, have U O-pened your mouth without speaking?"

"Oh! You mean a *yawn*?" asked Alice. "No, I haven't yawned."

Then the Caterpillar yawned himself and asked, "Have U felt your I-lids gr-O-ing heav-E?"

"My eyelids growing *heavy*?" repeated Alice. She blinked, trying to determine if her eyelids had gained any weight since the morning.

"No," she told the Caterpillar, "my eyelids are no heavier than usual."

"I C," said the Caterpillar, puffing out a yellow *I* and a lime green *C*. Then his own eyelids began to flutter, and his head began to nod.

"Perhaps *you're* the one who's sleepy," Alice observed, watching the Caterpillar.

"Y?" asked the Caterpillar.

"You yawned, then your eyelids drooped, and you began nodding off," Alice explained.

"I cannot B slee-P," the Caterpillar replied, "because n-O one has sung m-E a lullab-I."

"I can sing you a lullaby if you like," said Alice.

"Pro-C-d," said the Caterpillar.

"Hmm . . . let's see . . . ." murmured Alice. Ever since she'd entered the world of Wonderland, none of the poems and songs she knew came out quite right.

"I'll just try an easy one," she said with a shrug. Then she sang:

*"Tow, tow, tow your rope*
*Slowly up the wall.*
*Merrily, merrily, merrily, merrily,*
*Life is a round ball . . . .*

*"Blow, blow, blow your soap*
*Bubbles in the tub.*
*Merrily, merrily, merrily, merrily,*
*Rub-a-dub-a-dub . . . ."*

After she finished, Alice asked the Caterpillar, "How did you like it?"

"Come back l-A-ter," said the Caterpillar. "U may B right. I am the slee-P one."

And, with that, the Caterpillar fell fast asleep.

### DISNEY'S POCAHONTAS

# Chief Mischief-maker

Like all raccoons, Meeko was curious – and that often got him into trouble. And though Pocahontas had a lot of patience when it came to her small furry friend, other members of the tribe were not as understanding.

"Pocahontas, you must teach that animal how to behave!" Chief Powhatan exclaimed when he caught Meeko playing with the tribe's peace pipe.

"Not him again!" cried the women when Meeko upset the baskets of grain they had spent the entire morning threshing.

"Don't worry," Pocahontas told her friend. "They can't stay mad at you for long. Tomorrow is your birthday, after all!"

Meeko chattered excitedly. He loved birthdays – especially opening presents!

"Now stay out of trouble," Pocahontas warned. "I'll be back soon."

Meeko sat outside the hut Pocahontas shared with her father. He wondered what gift his friend had chosen for him this year. Soon, unable to resist temptation any longer, he slipped inside and spied a parcel. He wasted no time unwrapping it and discovered . . . a feather headdress just his size!

Meeko couldn't wait to try it on. He didn't want to be discovered, so he grabbed his gift and scampered off towards the river. There, he put on the headdress and gazed at his reflection. As he was admiring himself, the headdress fell into the water.

The raccoon fished it out, dragging it through the mud as he pulled it ashore.

Meeko's heart was pounding. He rinsed the feathers as best he could and headed back to the village. On the way, the headdress caught on the bushes. By the time he reached the village, all the feathers except one had fallen out.

Meeko knew what he had to do. He found Pocahontas and showed her what was left of the present. Pocahontas looked at Meeko sternly, but after a moment her face softened. "Meeko, I am proud of you. You had the courage to admit what you have done," she said. "But you must try to do better. No more getting into places where you shouldn't!"

All day on his birthday, Meeko behaved perfectly. That night, Pocahontas presented him with a gift. It was the headdress, but now it had two feathers instead of one. "For every day that you are able to stay out of other people's belongings, we will add another feather," she said.

Meeko was grateful to Pocahontas for being so understanding, and he was determined to make her proud. He would do his best to fill the headdress – but he knew it would probably take him until his *next* birthday!

# A Bear-y Tale

It was time for Mowgli, Bagheera and Baloo to go to bed.

"Good night, Man-cub," purred Bagheera.

"But I'm not sleepy yet," protested Mowgli. "I need a bedtime story."

"Bedtime story?" said Bagheera. "At this hour?"

Mowgli turned to the big bear. "Please, Baloo?"

"A bedtime story, huh . . ." said Baloo. "Now, how do those things begin?"

"Once upon a time . . ." purred Bagheera.

"Oh, right . . . Once upon a time . . . in a house not far from this very jungle, there lived a clan of men," Baloo began.

"Real men?" asked Mowgli.

"Yep," said Baloo. "A father and a mother, and a little cub, just like you. Well, now, this clan, they cooked their food, and one day, don't you know, they made a mighty tasty stew . . . only thing was, when they sat down to eat, it was just too hot. So the mother got an idea. They'd go for a walk in the jungle and, by the time they got back, their stew would be nice and cool. But do you know what happened next?"

"No," Mowgli said.

"Well, that family had barely been gone a minute, when an old bear came wandering up, and stuck his nose into the Man-house."

"He did?" gasped Mowgli.

"Well, now, can you blame him? That stew just smelled so awfully good. And the next thing you know, he was tastin' it – startin' with the biggest bowl, but that was still too hot. So next he tried the middle bowl, but that was too cold. So – he tried the littlest bowl, and, don't you know, it was just right! That old bear didn't mean to, but he ate the whole thing right up!"

"What happened next?" said Mowgli.

"Oh, well, after that, this bear, he started to get tired. Real tired. And, don't you know, Little Britches, that right there in that house, looking so soft and comfortable, were three cushy-lookin' pads . . . I think men call them 'beds.' Anyway, that bear, he had to try them, too. Naturally, he laid down on the biggest one first. But it was too hard. So he tried the middle one, but that was much, much too soft. So, he tried the littlest one, and, son, let me tell you, that thing was so comfortable, he fell asleep right then and there! And he would have slept clear through the next full moon . . . if only that family hadn't returned and . . ."

"And what?" Mowgli asked breathlessly.

"And startled that bear so much, he ran back into the jungle . . . full belly and all."

Mowgli smiled and tried to cover a big yawn. "Is that a true story, Baloo?"

The bear grinned. "Would I ever tell you a tall tale, Little Britches?"

# The Chase

"Whoopee!" Tod cried as he tumbled head over tail towards the water. He hit the surface with a splash. A second later, his friend Copper landed right next to him.

"It certainly is a beautiful day," Copper said.

"Yeah, it sure is," Tod agreed. The two friends swam to the edge and climbed up on the bank. As they sat in the warm sun, a great big blue butterfly landed on Copper's tail.

"Looks like you've made a friend," said Tod.

But the butterfly was frightened away by a booming voice.

"Copper!" the voice rumbled. It was Amos, Copper's master. Amos was usually grumpy, and right now he sounded angry too. "Where are you, mutt?" he shouted.

Tod silently climbed out of the water. He could tell that Amos was nearby, and that his other dog, Chief, was with him.

Copper crept up beside Tod. "I'd better go," he said. "Amos sounds awfully mad."

"Why don't you sneak back to your barrel so you're there when he gets back," Tod suggested. "He can't be mad if you're already home when he finds you."

Copper scratched behind his ear. "But he's right in my path, and Chief is with him. Chief will hear me or smell me for sure."

Tod grinned. "You just leave that to me."

He winked at his friend and dashed up the hill, right past Amos and Chief.

"There's that varmint fox!" Amos cried as Chief took off after Tod, barking like mad.

Amos gave chase, running as fast as he could on his long, skinny legs.

Tod leaped over branches and darted around trees. More than once, Chief got close, his hot breath on Tod's tail. But Tod was smart. He led Chief towards a rocky outcrop and dashed into a small cave. Chief stuck his snout into the opening, growling away. But he was too big to fit.

"Never mind, Chief," Amos said when he finally caught up. "We'll get him later."

Chief gave a final growl into the cave, but Tod had already escaped at the other end and was dashing home.

Exhausted, Amos and Chief started home, too. And, by the time they got there, Tod was napping next door in front of the Widow Tweed's fireplace, and Copper was sitting in his barrel. Next to him, his supper bowl was empty.

"There you are," Amos grumbled. He shook his head. "And I suppose you've been sitting here almost the whole time. We could have used your help catching that dang fox – it's almost as if you're trying to avoid hunting him!"

# Nani and David's Stitched-up Date

Lilo sat at the kitchen table, a frown on her face. "It's not fair that we have to spend the night at old lady Kingsley's house just because Nani and David want to go to a movie," she said.

Stitch nodded.

"How is she going to watch us, anyway, when she can barely see?" Lilo asked. "And," she continued, "do you know what movie Nani and David went to see? *Invasion of the Bug-Eyed Aliens, Part VI: The Sliming* – without us!"

Stitch made a noise of outraged agreement. Lilo stood and said, "Come on, Stitch. Let's go see the movie ourselves."

Lilo and Stitch sneaked past the snoring Mrs Kingsley. Lilo opened and shut the front door as loudly as she could. Then, doing her best impression of Nani, she shouted, "We're back, Mrs Kingsley! Thanks!"

Mrs Kingsley woke up, tottered to the door and peered blindly at Lilo. "Is that you, Nani? Well, I hope you had a lovely time." And with that, the two made a break for the cinema. But, once they got there, they had two problems – money and . . .

"Sorry, kid, no dogs allowed in the cinema," the ticket taker said.

Lilo had to think quickly. "He isn't a dog. He's my teddy bear."

"He sure doesn't *look* like a stuffed animal," the ticket taker said.

"They make them very lifelike these days," Lilo fibbed. "Now, can we go inside? My mother is looking for us and, if we don't find her soon, I think I may start to cry."

"Okay, okay," the ticket taker said.

By the time the two had got into the cinema, the bug-eyed aliens had begun the 'sliming,' and everyone in the cinema was screaming. Lilo and Stitch immediately joined in – perhaps a little too enthusiastically, since Nani and David noticed them right away.

"Excuse me, excuse me," Nani said as she made her way out of her row and down the aisle, cola spilling and popcorn flying.

Nani grabbed hold of Lilo's arm and dragged her out of the cinema. David and Stitch were right behind them.

"I'm so angry with you I'm going to . . . I'm going to–" Nani stuttered.

"–take you out for ice cream," David finished her sentence.

"Out for ice cream?" Nani said.

"It's a beautiful night, and I can't think of anything more wonderful than two sisters having ice cream together." David turned to Lilo and Stitch. "Don't you think?"

**WALT DISNEY'S**
# Pinocchio
# Fish Food

Figaro the cat was scared. He was also hungry. But he knew there wouldn't be any dinner. Figaro, Geppetto and Cleo the goldfish had just been swallowed by a whale!

"Don't worry, Figaro," Geppetto said, seeing the cat's worried look. "We'll get out of here somehow – and when we do, we'll keep searching for Pinocchio. We won't stop until we find him."

That Pinocchio! Figaro growled. After all that Geppetto and the Blue Fairy had done for Pinocchio, he

had run away from home without a care in the world. That was how they ended up inside the whale! Now what would become of them?

Figaro decided then and there that if they ever found Pinocchio, he was going to use both of the wooden boy's legs as scratching posts. It would serve him right.

Meanwhile, Geppetto was peering into the puddle of water at the bottom of the whale's stomach. Figaro watched curiously.

"Let's see," Geppetto murmured, bending over and poking at the water. "There must be something in here . . . ."

"Aha!" Geppetto cried happily. He was clutching a small, soggy clump of seaweed.

Figaro blinked. Seaweed?

A moment later, Geppetto bent down again. "Aha!" he cried once more.

The little cat began to purr, imagining that Geppetto had caught a wonderful snack. But when he peered into Geppetto's hand, all Figaro saw was – more seaweed.

Seaweed was *fish* food, Figaro thought with a scowl. Surely Geppetto didn't expect *him* to eat that for dinner.

But, as he watched, Geppetto carefully divided the seaweed into three portions. He placed one portion in Cleo's bowl. He set one portion in front of Figaro. The third he kept for himself.

"Let's eat!" Geppetto said, smiling bravely.

Figaro sniffed his seaweed. He stirred it around with his paw. But he just couldn't eat the seaweed. With a twitch of his tail, Figaro turned away.

Geppetto watched the little cat with sad eyes. Figaro sighed. He couldn't help but feel ungrateful.

Reluctantly, Figaro turned back to his dinner. He nibbled at the seaweed. It was cold. It was slimy. But it tasted like – *fish*!

Figaro gobbled down the rest of his meal. With his belly full, the little cat felt better. He decided that if they found Pinocchio, he would only use *one* of the puppet-boy's legs to sharpen his claws on.

Probably.

# Disney's ROBIN HOOD

# Easy Come, Easy Go

One day, Robin Hood was boasting to his friends in Sherwood Forest about his skills with a bow and arrow.

"I can take from the rich and give to the poor using only a single arrow," said Robin. "And I'll defeat the greedy Sheriff with that same arrow too."

"With one arrow?" asked Little John. He knew his friend was talented, but that seemed impossible.

"One arrow is all I need," said Robin. "And it won't even *touch* the Sheriff."

"Now, that really *is* impossible!" Little John laughed. He was sure Robin was teasing.

But Robin wasn't joking. "Look," he said, "here comes the Sheriff to collect taxes from the poor villagers. I'll show you how easy it is."

Little John and Robin followed the Sheriff to the village. They watched him knock on the door of the first house.

"I am here to collect the King's taxes!" the Sheriff roared. "Give me the money or you'll be thrown in jail!"

The frightened man opened his door and gave the Sheriff a handful of coins. "It's all we have," said the man.

The Sheriff wrote the man's name in a book. "You still owe more," he said. "I'll be back next month for the rest!"

The Sheriff stuffed the coins into a leather bag hanging on his belt. Then he went to all the other houses and collected more taxes. Soon, the Sheriff's leather bag was bulging with the poor villagers' savings.

As the Sheriff prepared to leave, Little John whispered, "Robin, the Sheriff is taking everything they have. We can't let him get away with this."

"No, we can't," agreed Robin.

Drawing back his bow, Robin took aim.

"You're going to shoot him?" asked Little John.

"No need," said Robin.

Instead, Robin shot the arrow at the bag of coins, putting a hole in it. The Sheriff didn't even notice.

"Why did you do that?" asked Little John.

"Just watch," Robin said with a smile.

As the Sheriff mounted his horse, the coins began to drop out of the hole in the bag. By the time he'd trotted out of the village, all the tax money he'd collected had spilled back out. Robin and Little John collected the money and returned it to the delighted villagers. Little John slapped Robin on the back. "You did it, Robin! You robbed from the rich and gave to the poor – and with only one arrow, just like you said."

"Sure," Robin grinned. "And, as the Sheriff is about to learn, easy come, easy go!"

# Flik Wings It

Flik knew that Hopper and his gang of hungry grasshoppers would soon come to steal all the food from the peaceful ants of Ant Island. So Flik headed off to the big city to find warrior bugs to help fight the grasshoppers.

On his way, Flik saw a shiny dragonfly flutter across the sky.

"Wow, I wish I could fly like that!" he exclaimed.

Suddenly, Flik had an idea. "I built a harvester that harvests pretty well. I wonder if I could invent a flying machine?"

Flik got to work. He gathered sticks and vines and leaves. He found a mushroom cap to use for a seat, and a long red feather for a tail.

When he had gathered all the parts, Flik began to strap the pieces together.

After lots of hard work, Flik took a step back and studied his invention.

"Well, it certainly *looks* like it could fly," Flik said finally. "It has wings that flap and a long red tail."

The frame of Flik's flier was made of twigs, and the wings were made of leaves. The whole machine was tied together with strong vines.

"Time for a test flight," Flik decided.

He climbed onto the mushroom cap seat and used a vine as a safety belt. Then he put his feet on the little pedals and started to pump. Faster and faster, the green wings began to flap. Soon, Flik's flier began to rock; then it leaped into the sky!

"It's working!" Flik cried. He was flying!

With the air racing between his antennae, Flik watched the world flash under his feet. He saw frogs and turtles and other creatures that ate ants.

"Flying is so much safer than walking," said Flik.

But he spoke too soon, for high in the sky above Flik a mother bird was teaching her three little hatchlings how to fly. She spied Flik's strange-looking contraption and thought one thing – dinner!

Flik looked up and saw the mother bird and her babies coming down on him like dive bombers!

"Test flight over!" Flik cried.

Pedalling faster, Flik steered his flier through the limbs of a tall tree. The mother bird and two of her babies were blocked by the branches. But the third baby bird raced between the leaves and caught up with Flik.

Pecking wildly, the little bird ripped a wing from Flik's flier. Spinning out of control, the machine crashed to the ground.

Luckily for Flik, he had also invented a parachute out of a spider's web, and he made a soft landing in the middle of a daisy.

"Another failed invention," Flik said with a sigh. "Maybe someday I'll have a chance to make a flying machine that really works!"

# DINOSAUR

# Raptor Attack!

"Everyone, stand up," said Aladar. "There are raptors around here, and you need to stay with the group where you'll be safe."

"My aching bones," groaned Eema as she struggled to her feet. "Kron hasn't given us much time to rest, has he?"

"No, he certainly hasn't," agreed Baylene. "My feet are so sore, my blisters have blisters. And I know I won't have the strength to get through any more sand bogs like the ones we just got through."

"You girls are doing great," said Aladar encouragingly. He tried to sound cheerful, but he too was exhausted by their recent experience in the sand bogs. Several of the young dinosaurs had wandered too close to the boggy areas and had nearly sunk in the sand. Aladar had pulled them to safety, but it had been a close call.

Although he was young and healthy, Aladar had chosen to stay in the back of the herd with the very old and very young dinosaurs, who needed help to keep up. The leader of the pack, an iguanodon named Kron, had little sympathy for the old and weak. Every dinosaur feared attacks by raptors, the vicious meat-eaters who travelled in packs and who would not hesitate to attack any stragglers at the back of the herd. But Kron was more concerned about getting to the Nesting Grounds – if they lost a few of the herd along the way, so be it.

Aladar gave the two little iguanodons a playful nudge with his nose. "Catch up, guys," he said. "Nobody lags behind."

Suddenly, he heard some rapid footsteps behind him. Wheeling around, Aladar saw three raptors coming over the ridge behind them. "Run and catch up with the herd!" Aladar yelled to the little dinosaurs. "I'll keep them distracted!" The two little dinosaurs scampered away in terror.

"*RAAAAAH!*" Aladar roared. But the raptors looked ravenous and ready to fight. "Think, think," Aladar said to himself, trying to keep a clear head. And then he had an idea.

"Let's see how fast you are!" he roared at the raptors, and took off, back in the direction that the herd had just gone. The raptors pursued him, and he felt them gaining. Then, suddenly, he made a quick turn and doubled back the way he had come. The raptors followed, but then their footsteps stopped. Aladar looked back. They were caught in the sand bog and were starting to sink. Aladar wasted no time rejoining the herd. He looked back to see the raptors barely managing to struggle out of the wet sand. But, for now, the herd was safe.

Walt Disney's
# 101 DALMATIANS

# Lucky's Last Laugh

It was getting quite late at Pongo's and Perdita's house, but their darling little puppies were still not asleep. Not that they didn't want to go to sleep. At least most of them. No, the problem was that one of them wouldn't let them go to sleep – Lucky!

"And then, don't you remember, you guys, the part at the very beginning, when Thunderbolt jumped across that canyon? Whoosh! Like a rocket! Clear to the other side!" Lucky said.

"Yes, Lucky, we remember," his sister Penny said with a groan. "How could we forget? You've reminded us 101 times!"

"Yeah! It was so great! And then there was that part when – "

"Lucky!" wailed Rolly. "We all watched the same episode of Thunderbolt tonight. You don't have to tell us about it."

"Yeah, I know, but I just wanted to tell you about the part when Thunderbolt found the little girl, then ran back to tell the sheriff – "

"Lucky! It's late! We want to go to sleep!" barked Patch.

Lucky laid his head on his paws. "Okay," he said. "I'll be quiet."

All the puppies closed their eyes.

"Oh! But what about the part when the sheriff told Thunderbolt to climb up that cliff, and he got to the top, and he grabbed that rope with his teeth, and he pulled up the little girl – "

"Lucky!" yelped Pepper. "We don't care about Thunderbolt. We want to go to bed!"

"Right." Lucky sighed, lying down once again. "Wait a sec!" He sat up. "Don't care about Thunderbolt? How could you not care that he carried that little girl across that broken bridge and through those raging rapids?"

"We mean," said Freckles, "we want you to be quiet so we can go to sleep!"

"You mean," said Lucky, "you don't want me to tell you about the last part where Thunderbolt ran back to the mountains and into that cave, and found that amazing thing?"

"Yes!" Lucky's brothers and sisters shouted together.

"Why didn't you say so?" said Lucky. "Good night."

And with that, Lucky closed his eyes. For a minute, everyone enjoyed the silence. Then Penny sat up.

"Hey, wait a minute," she said. "What thing did he find?"

"Yeah," said Patch. "I missed that part."

"Me, too," said Rolly. "What was it exactly that he found, Lucky? Tell us."

But there was no answer. Lucky was fast asleep. And now the *other* Dalmatian puppies were wide awake!

# Making Wishes Come True

"Looking good, kid!" the Genie shouted. "Looking good!"

Aladdin adjusted his turban and smiled at the sights that surrounded him. Things in Agrabah certainly looked different from the back of an elephant – even if that elephant was really your transformed monkey!

Abu the elephant raised his trunk and trumpeted as if he could read Aladdin's mind. It really seemed as though Abu was enjoying his bigger size.

Aladdin still couldn't believe he'd found the magic lamp and the Genie inside it. And the three wishes! He'd only used one so far – he'd wished to become a prince. And, as he rode through Agrabah dressed in the finest silk and a jewel-encrusted turban – on an elephant – he definitely felt royal. Nobody could call him a 'street rat' now!

"Princess Jasmine, here I come," Aladdin said as he rode through the crowded streets. He'd wanted to become a prince for one reason and one reason only – to woo the girl who had won his heart. Princess Jasmine was clever and funny and beautiful. And he hoped that very soon she would be his wife.

Abu trumpeted again and the people in the marketplace turned to watch the royal caravan. Aladdin puffed up his chest with pride, then slumped down again as he looked at the people staring up at him. Some of them looked thin. Others were dirty or bedraggled. Aladdin knew what it was like to be poor. How many times had he been in the marketplace with no money for food? More than he could count.

"Abu, Genie," Aladdin said, "we're making a stop."

"But, kid, we've got to get to the palace," Genie objected. "Princess Jasmine might not know it, but she's waiting for you."

For a moment, Aladdin was tempted to heed Genie's advice and forget about his plan. But one look at a hungry little girl gazing at a roasted-meat vendor changed his mind.

"Stop right here, Abu," he told his elephant.

Aladdin got off his mount and proceeded to buy heaps of delicious meats, breads and fruits from several of the vendors.

"This is for you," he told the hungry little girl, as he handed her a loaf of bread and a large piece of roasted meat.

The little girl looked up at him in surprise, then ripped off a piece of bread and stuffed it into her mouth. "Thank you!" she said, her mouth full.

Aladdin handed out all of his purchases to the hungry people of Agrabah. Then, satisfied, he climbed onto Abu the elephant and continued on his way to the palace.

Disney's
**TREASURE PLANET**

# Scary Solar Surfing!

Things were busy at the Benbow Inn – and B.E.N. wasn't helping much! The clumsy robot had already spilled purp juice on a whole family of Cyclops, broken a whole set of Mrs Hawkins's Alponian chowder bowls, and was now chasing a healthy serving of Zirellian jellyworms across the dining room floor.

"Don't you worry, Mrs H.," B.E.N. assured the innkeeper. "Tell those spacers their lunch will be on the table in just one minute . . . *whoops*! Better make that two minutes."

And all this was after Mrs Hawkins had begged him *not* to help her out. You can imagine her relief therefore when Jim walked in, home for the summer from the Interstellar Academy, carrying his solar surfer.

"Jim!" she cried. "Going surfing, I see. Wouldn't you love to take B.E.N. out with you?"

"Huh?" said Jim.

"Did someone say solar surfing?" B.E.N. asked, looking up and letting the worms wiggle away. "I'm in! Let's go! Unless, of course, you really need me, Mrs H."

"Oh, no, no, B.E.N.," she said. "You go have fun. You've helped me quite enough!"

Jim sighed and headed out, with B.E.N. right behind him. He would never have let his mother down, but he was *not* looking forward to surfing with a walking booby trap!

"Oh boy, oh boy! I've always wanted to do this!" said the robot as Jim unfurled the solar sail and they took off. "Where's the steering wheel? Where's the ON button?"

"Hang on, there, B.E.N.," said Jim. "There is no steering wheel. All you have to do is lean – like this. And there is no ON button. In fact, whatever you do, do not touch this button here!"

"Roger that!" said B.E.N. "Stepping on button a no-no. I completely understand and will not, under any circumstances – *Aghhhhhh*!"

To Jim's dismay, B.E.N. kicked the very button he had warned him not to. Instantly, the sail retracted, and the solar surfer began to fall.

"Help! Help! Help!" cried B.E.N., leaping onto Jim's back and holding on with all his might.

It was all Jim could do to balance himself as the surfer spiralled out of control! Luckily, there was no better surfer in all the greater galaxy than young Jim Hawkins, and after a few heartstopping seconds they were back under control.

"Phew!" sighed B.E.N., wiping his metal brow. "That was a close one, huh?"

"Yeah," muttered Jim.

"But it was pretty cool, too," B.E.N. went on.

Jim started to smile. "Yeah," he said.

"Wanna do it again?" asked B.E.N.

Jim's smile widened. "Yeah," he said.

And off they went.

**WALT DISNEY'S**
# DUMBO

# 'Ears a Job for You, Dumbo!

It had been a hard day for little Dumbo. It was bad enough that everyone made fun of his ears except his mother, but then they had put his mother in a cage, so Dumbo couldn't even be with the one person who loved him and treated him decently.

What made things even worse was that Dumbo didn't have anything to do. It seemed that he was the only creature in the circus who didn't have a job. Everyone had a purpose except Dumbo. All he could do was feel sad and be laughed at.

Dumbo heaved a sigh and went for a walk through the circus tents. Soon, he found himself among the refreshment stands. Everyone here had a job too. Some were squeezing lemons to make lemonade. Others were popping popcorn or roasting peanuts. Wonderful smells filled the air.

Finally, Dumbo came to a little candyfloss wagon. The puffy cloud of sugar looked tempting, and Dumbo wanted a taste, but there were so many customers he couldn't get close enough.

Suddenly Dumbo heard a loud buzzing. Then all the customers waved their hands over their heads and ran away.

The smell of sugar had attracted a swarm of nasty flies!

"Scat!" cried the candyfloss man. "Go away before you scare off my customers."

Dumbo reached out his trunk to smell the delicious candyfloss.

"Not you, Dumbo!" the candyfloss man cried. "It's bad enough chasing flies. Do I have to chase elephants too?"

Poor Dumbo was startled. With a snort, he sucked candyfloss right up his nose. *Ahhh-choo*!

When he sneezed, Dumbo's ears flapped – and something amazing happened.

"Remarkable!" the candyfloss man cried. "All the flies are gone. They think your ears are giant fly swatters!"

The candyfloss man patted Dumbo's head. "How would you like a job?"

Dumbo nodded enthusiastically and set to waving his ears. Soon, the candyfloss stand was the most popular refreshment stand in the circus – and had the least flies. But, best of all, Dumbo now had something to do to take his mind off his troubles. He was still sad, but things didn't seem quite so bad. And, who knows, perhaps soon he'd have his mother back.

"I wonder what other amazing things those big ears can do?" said the candyfloss man, giving Dumbo a friendly smile. "I'll bet they carry you far . . . ."

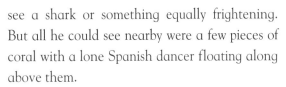

# Hide, Dude!

"Come on, Squirt!" Nemo cried happily. "Race you to the coral shelf!"

Nemo took off, pumping his mismatched fins as hard as he could. His young sea turtle friend laughed and swam after him.

Squirt was visiting Nemo at his home on the reef. "This way, dude!" Squirt yelled, flinging himself through the water. "I'm catching some rad current over here!"

Nemo hesitated for just a second, watching as his friend tumbled along head over heels past some stinging coral. Squirt was so brave! Even after all that Nemo had been through – being captured by a scuba diver, then escaping from a tank to find his way home again – he still got scared sometimes.

With a deep breath, he threw himself into the current. He tumbled after Squirt, fins flying as the water carried him along. Finally, he came out the other end of the current, landing in the still ocean beside Squirt.

He giggled. "Hey, that was fun!" he cried. "Let's do it again! Squirt? Squirt, what's wrong?"

The sea turtle was staring into the distance, his eyes wide. "Hide, dude!" Squirt cried.

Before Nemo could respond, Squirt's head and legs popped into his shell and he landed on the sea floor with a flop.

Nemo started trembling. What had scared Squirt so much? He stared around, expecting to see a shark or something equally frightening. But all he could see nearby were a few pieces of coral with a lone Spanish dancer floating along above them.

He swam down and tapped on Squirt's shell. "Hey," he said. "What is it? There's nothing scary here."

"Whew!" Squirt's head popped out. He looked around, then gasped and hid again. When he spoke, his voice was muffled. "It's totally still there!"

Nemo blinked and looked around again. Again, all he saw were the coral and the Spanish dancer.

"Hey, wait a minute," he said, suddenly realizing something. "Haven't you ever seen a Spanish dancer before?"

"A – a Spanish wha-huh?" Squirt asked, still muffled.

Nemo knocked on his friend's shell again. "It's a kind of sea slug," he explained. "Don't worry, Spanish dancers are nice – you don't have to be scared. I promise."

Finally Squirt's head popped out again. He smiled sheepishly at Nemo.

"Sorry, dude," he said. "I never saw one of those before. It totally freaked me out."

"It's okay." Nemo smiled back. He already knew that new things could be scary – and now he knew he wasn't the only one who thought so. "Come on, let's go play."

# The Very Best Fisherman of All

Simba and his friends Timon and Pumbaa were hungry. They wandered through the forest until they came to an old, rotten tree. Timon knocked on the trunk.

"What's it sound like, Timon?" Pumbaa asked.

"Like our breakfast!" Timon replied.

He yanked at the bark and hundreds of grubs slithered out.

Timon handed Simba a grub.

"No, thanks." Simba sighed. "I'm tired of grubs."

"Well, the ants are tasty," said Timon. "They come in two flavours. Red and black."

Simba shook his head. "Don't you eat anything but bugs?"

"Fish!" Pumbaa declared.

"I love fish!" Simba exclaimed.

"Why didn't you say so?" said Timon. "There's a pond at the end of this trail." The three friends started off down the trail.

"What now?" asked Simba when they arrived at the pond.

"That's the problem!" said Timon. "We're not the best fishermen in the world."

"I'll teach you!" Simba said.

The lion climbed up a tree and crawled onto a branch that hung over the water. Then he snatched a fish out of the water.

"See!" Simba said, jumping to the ground nimbly. "Not a problem. Fishing's easy."

"Not for me!" Timon cried. He dangled from the branch, but his arms weren't long enough to reach the fish.

Simba laughed. "Better let Pumbaa try."

"What a joke!" cried Timon. "Pumbaa can't even climb this tree."

"Want to bet?" asked Pumbaa.

"Stay there," Timon warned. "I don't think this branch is strong enough for both of us."

With a hop, Pumbaa landed on the branch next to Timon. The limb started to bend.

"Yikes!" Timon cried as he leaped to another tree.

*Crack*! The branch broke under Pumbaa. With a squeal, he landed in the pond. The splash was enormous!

Simba, sitting on the bank, was soaked. Timon was nearly blasted from his perch. Pond water fell like rain all around them.

Simba opened his eyes and started to laugh. So did Timon.

Pumbaa was sitting in a pool of mud where the pond had been. He'd splashed so much of the water out that dozens of fish squirmed on the ground, just waiting to be gobbled up.

"Wow!" Timon cried. "I think Pumbaa is the very best fisherman of all!"

# Dressed to Scare

Cinderella worked from morning until night doing the bidding of her stepmother and stepsisters. In return, they treated her unkindly and dressed her in tattered old clothes. It wasn't a very fair deal.

Luckily, Cinderella had the friendship of the animals in the manor, including two mice named Jaq and Mary.

"Poor Cinderelly," said Jaq as he and Mary watched their dear friend scrubbing the floor. "She needs a present."

"Hmm," Mary replied. She led Jaq out to the barnyard so that Cinderella wouldn't hear them planning. "Let's make a new dress!" she suggested.

"Good idea!" Jaq replied. But he wondered what they could use for cloth. Jaq looked around, then scurried over to a sack of feed and gnawed it open with his teeth.

"Jaq, no!" Mary scolded. "You can eat later."

"No-no," Jaq explained. "This cloth is for Cinderelly's new dress. See?" He gestured toward the sack.

The other mice joined to help. They cut out the dress in no time, sewing it together with some thread they had borrowed from Cinderella's sewing kit. They stepped back to admire their work. "Too plain!" Gus announced.

"Yes," Jaq agreed in a disappointed voice.

"What should we do to fix it?"

The birds in the barn twittered excitedly. They had just the thing! In no time, they strung berries and kernels of corn, then helped the mice stitch them along the hem, sleeves and neck of the dress.

"There!" said Perla. "Much better!"

With the birds' help, the mice hung the dress on a post in the garden where Cinderella kept her straw hat. "Cinderelly's gonna love it!" Jaq proclaimed.

The mice went inside, got Cinderella, then told her to close her eyes as she walked out into the garden. "Open your eyes now, Cinderelly!" Jaq instructed.

"Surprise!" the mice shouted.

Cinderella gazed at the sackcloth dress on the post with her hat perched on top. "Oh, thank you!" she exclaimed. "I've been needing a scarecrow for the garden!"

Jaq opened his mouth wide to explain, but Mary clamped her paw over it.

"You're welcome, Cinderelly," Mary said.

After Cinderella had gone, Jaq frowned. "We sewed a bad dress."

"But we made a good scarecrow," Mary told him, trying to look on the bright side.

"Yes! And Cinderelly's happy!" Jaq agreed. And to the mice, that was the most important thing of all.

# A Prize-winning Pair

Max and his dad, Goofy, were sitting at the breakfast table. Max looked at the funny pages, while Goofy leafed through the rest of the paper. "Listen to this!" said Goofy. "Channel 10 sponsors the Father & Son of the Year Contest. The father and son who can prove that they have achieved something truly incredible together will appear on national TV on Father's Day to accept their award."

"Too bad Bigfoot ruined that video we took of him last summer," said Max. "Finding him and living to tell about it – now that was incredible!"

Max paused for a moment. "Hey, I know! Why can't we go back and find him again? And this time we'll make sure we have proof."

"Okay, Maxie. Count me in!" said Goofy. "And we can even get a little fishing in too."

Goofy and Max reached the campsite that night, pitched their tent, and went to sleep. Soon they were awakened by a loud crash.

"It's him!" cried Max. "Get the camera!" But, when they poked their heads out, they saw it wasn't Bigfoot at all, but Pete and P.J.

"I'm sorry," said P.J. "I told my dad about your trip, and now he wants *us* to win that prize. We're out here looking for Bigfoot too."

The next day, Pete set up a barbecue with several juicy steaks. "This will lure him out for sure," he told P.J. The trick worked. In a matter of minutes, Bigfoot crashed through the trees and made a beeline for the meat. "Tackle him, P.J.!" yelled Pete.

Though he was scared, P.J. did as he was told. Bigfoot threw him around like a rag doll while Pete turned on the camera. "The judges are going to love this!" cried Pete.

"Help!" P.J. begged.

Goofy and Max heard P.J.'s cries and came running from the lake. Without saying a word, Goofy jabbed the monster in the backside with a fishing lure while Max threw a fishing net over the monster's head. Howling, the monster dropped P.J. to the ground.

"You were awesome," Max told Goofy.

"Right back at you, son," Goofy replied.

"Got it!" Pete said triumphantly. "Here, P.J., take some footage of me." He struck a hero's pose in front of the captive monster.

Back at home, Pete sent the video to Channel 10. But, after viewing the tape, the judges decided it was Goofy and Max who deserved the award instead.

But on Father's Day – the day they were to appear on TV – Goofy and Max decided to go to the beach together instead. They realized they didn't need anybody to tell them what an incredible father-and-son team they were. They knew it already!

# A Good Team

"Go, Khan," Mulan whispered to the horse. "Faster!"

The horse flicked an ear towards her. But his pace didn't change.

Mulan shrugged. She was happy to have company, even if Khan didn't seem too crazy about her. She could hardly believe she was riding through the woods on her way to join the Emperor's army. But what else could she do? If she didn't take his place, her elderly father would be forced to fight.

"It will be all right," she told Khan. "This is the right thing to do."

The horse snorted. For a second Mulan thought he was answering her. Then he stopped short, almost sending Mulan tumbling.

"Hey," she said. "What are you doing?"

She kicked at his sides. But, instead of moving forward, the mighty warhorse backed up a few steps, his massive body shaking fearfully.

Mulan looked ahead. Just a few yards away, a deep, shadowy ditch crossed the path.

"Is that what you're afraid of?" Mulan asked the horse. "Don't be silly. It's just a small ditch – step over it, you big chicken."

She kicked again. Still the horse refused to go. Instead he danced nervously on the spot.

"Come on!" Mulan shouted impatiently. "You're being ridiculous!"

She kicked him. She slapped him on the neck with her hands. She even grabbed a thin branch from a nearby tree and smacked him on his hindquarters.

But the horse wouldn't take even one step forward.

Finally, Mulan didn't know what else to try. She collapsed onto Khan's neck, feeling hopeless.

"Now what?" she said.

But she didn't seem to have much choice. Sliding down from the horse's back, she walked towards the ditch. To her surprise, she heard Khan following her.

Mulan gasped. Could it be? Could the big, bold, strong warhorse really be trusting her to lead him over the scary ditch?

"Come on," she said, reaching for his bridle.

The horse allowed her to lead him forward. A few more steps, and he was standing at the edge of the ditch.

"The last step is the big one," Mulan warned.

Holding the reins, she hopped over the ditch. For a moment, she was afraid he wouldn't follow. Then he jumped. Mulan was yanked forward as Khan landed ten feet past the ditch.

"Good boy." Mulan patted the horse. "I think we might just make a good team, after all."

# The Late Shift

The shift on the Scare Floor at Monsters, Inc., had just ended when Sulley pulled Mike aside.

"Mike, our paperwork is always late," he said. "I'm worried about us getting a bad reputation."

"You're right, Sulley," Mike said earnestly. "From now on, I'm a new monster. In fact, I'm going to start getting caught up tonight. I'm going to stay at work late, just you see. Why, Celia will be so proud of me – uh-oh . . . ."

"What is it, Mike?" Sulley asked.

"Oh, nothing!" Mike grinned. "Sulley, I'll see you later. I've got lots of catching up to do. Paperwork, here I come!"

Sulley gave Mike a suspicious look but allowed himself to be pushed out the door.

But, as soon as Sulley was gone, Mike's smile faded. "What do I do?" he cried. "I have a date with Celia, and I'm already late!" Finally, Mike came to a decision. "I'll catch up tomorrow," he said to himself. "That paperwork is so late that one more day won't make a difference."

With that, Mike headed for the locker room, whistling a jaunty tune. He had just entered the quiet, empty room when he heard a noise.

"Daaaa," said a tiny voice. Mike jumped straight up in the air and gave a yelp.

"Who's there?" he asked nervously.

"Gagoooo," said the voice. That was definitely a child! Mike turned to run – but he tripped over a can of odorant someone had left on the floor and went flying across the room.

Footsteps sounded behind him. Mike looked up, expecting to see a human child. But he saw Sulley instead! "What gives?" he asked Sulley grouchily. Sulley was laughing so hard he couldn't even talk. Finally, the big blue monster calmed down enough to explain.

"I just couldn't resist!" Sulley said, helping Mike up. "After you shooed me out I ran into Celia, who told me about your date. I knew you would rather skip the paperwork than disappoint Celia."

Mike nodded, embarrassed.

"But I told her that you were really behind on your work," Sulley continued, "and I asked if it would be okay for you two to have your date tomorrow night instead."

Mike looked up, surprised. That hadn't even occurred to him. "Did she say yes?" he asked.

"She sure did," Sulley said. "And she also said that since I'm your partner and all, I should really stay here to help you catch up. So, here I am! Now, let's grab some sludgesicles and get to work."

"Okay, Sulley," said Mike. And the two monsters went off to show that paperwork what they were made of.

*Disney's* Beauty AND THE BEAST

# The Mysterious Book

"What are you looking at, Belle?" Chip asked. Belle smiled at the little teacup. "Oh, you caught me daydreaming, Chip," she said. "I was just looking up there."

She pointed to the highest shelf in the Beast's library. The only thing on the shelf was a single book.

Belle had wondered about that book almost since the day the Beast had first shown her the library. The trouble was, none of the ladders quite reached the shelf. So the book had remained a mystery.

Belle's curiosity had grown until she could hardly stop thinking about the book. What could it be about? Surely it had to be the most magical, unusual, wonderful book in the world!

She explained the problem to Chip. He went straight to his mother, Mrs Potts.

Mrs Potts called a meeting of all the enchanted objects. As soon as she told them about the book, they wanted to help Belle.

"What we need is a plan," Cogsworth said.

"Yes!" Lumiere cried. "And I've got one!"

That evening the enchanted objects gathered in the library. First the Wardrobe stood at the base of the shelves. The Stove climbed on top of her, then the Coatrack climbed up next. Soon a whole tower of enchanted objects stretched almost to the top shelf. Finally Lumiere started to climb.

When he reached the top, the book was still a few inches away. He stretched as far as he could . . .

"What are you doing?" Belle exclaimed from the doorway.

"Oh, *mademoiselle*!" Lumiere cried. "You're just in time – *voilà*!"

With that, he finally managed to reach the book, knocking it off the shelf into Belle's hands. A moment later the tower collapsed in a heap.

As soon as Belle made certain that everyone was all right, she opened the book. She couldn't wait to see what new wonders lay within its covers . . . .

"Oh!" she said when she saw the first page.

"What is it?" Chip asked breathlessly.

Belle smiled sheepishly. "I can't believe it! I've already read this one."

The enchanted objects sighed with disappointment. Had their plan been for nothing?

"But thank you anyway!" Belle said quickly. "It's so nice of you to get it for me." She hugged the book to her. "Even though I've read it before, it's one of my favourites – it's full of far-off places, magic spells . . . well, let me show you . . . ."

Soon all the enchanted objects were gathered around as Belle read the book to them. And, wouldn't you know, it became one of their favourite books too!

Walt Disney's
## Lady and the TRAMP

# In the Doghouse

"Good morning, Tramp," said Lady, with a yawn and a stretch. She rolled over on her silk cushion. "Wasn't that just the most wonderful night's sleep?"

But Tramp's night's sleep had been far from wonderful. In fact, he hadn't had much sleep at all. The past night had been Tramp's first sleeping in Lady's house . . . or in any house, come to think of it.

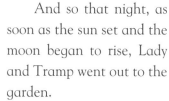

"How do you do it?" he grumbled. "That bed is so soft, I feel like I'm sinking in a feather pool. And between Jim Dear's snoring and the baby's crying, I could barely hear the crickets chirping."

"Oh, dear," Lady said, feeling truly sorry for her mate. "I know!" she exclaimed. "Jim Dear and Darling love you so – I'm sure they'd let you sleep up on their bed tonight. There's nothing in the world better than that!"

But Tramp shook his head. "I'm afraid it's the outdoors I need," he explained. "I mean, I know you grew up this way and all . . . but it's just so much fun to sleep under the stars. And the moon too. There's nothing to howl at in this bedroom."

"You can see the moon out the window," Lady told him.

But Tramp shook his head. "It's not the same. You know," he went on, "we've still got that fine doghouse in the yard. What do you say we go back out there tonight? It'll be like a honeymoon!"

"Well . . ." Lady looked at Tramp's tired eyes. "Okay."

And so that night, as soon as the sun set and the moon began to rise, Lady and Tramp went out to the garden.

Happy at last, Tramp turned three times and then plopped down. "Oh, how I love the feel of cool dirt on my belly!" he said with a dreamy smile . . . while Lady gingerly peeked into the dark and slightly damp kennel. The stars were not even out, and already she missed the comforts of Jim Dear's and Darling's room.

Tramp watched as Lady stretched out on the kennel floor, then got up and moved outside, then back in once again. It was plain to see: try as she might, Lady just could not relax on the cold, hard ground.

"Don't worry," Tramp announced, "I have an idea."

And with that, he ran into the house . . . and in seconds reappeared with Lady's cushion in his teeth. Carefully, he swept the kennel with his tail, and laid the cushion down just the way Lady liked it.

Lady smiled and lay down. And, do you know what? That night, they both had the sweetest dreams either one had ever had.

# A 'Snappy' New Ship

"My ship, my beautiful ship!" Captain Hook moaned. It had not been a good day for the pirate. Peter Pan and the Darling children had stolen his ship. And now, Hook was stranded on an island with Smee and the other pirates, their rowing boat having been chomped to bits by the crocodile.

"It's a nice island, Captain," offered Smee, trying to cheer up his boss. "And you could use a vacation. Why, look at those dark circles under your eyes."

Captain Hook turned to Smee with a furious look on his face. "Pirates don't take vacations!" Hook boomed. "Pirates seek revenge! Which is precisely what we are going to do, as soon as we have a new ship to sail in."

Smee looked around. "Where are we going to find a ship around here, Sir?" he asked.

"*We* aren't going to find one," Captain Hook answered. "You and the rest of this mangy crew are going to *build* one! And I don't mean a little one either. I mean a big, menacing, fit-for-a-magnificent-pirate-like-me one!"

For weeks, the pirates chopped trees and cut them into planks for the ship. They whittled thousands of pegs to use for nails, and crushed countless berries to use for paint. "You're not moving fast enough!" Hook complained as he sat in the shade, sipping juice out of a pineapple.

Finally, an exhausted Smee fetched Hook as he awoke from his afternoon nap.

"It's ready, Captain!" he announced.

Even Hook had to admit the ship was magnificent. Shaped like a gigantic crocodile, it was painted a reptilian shade of green. "No one will dare come near this ship. Not even that pesky crocodile. He won't want to tussle with anything this terrifying," Smee assured him.

Captain Hook was delighted. "We set sail tomorrow!" he crowed.

That night, Smee couldn't resist putting one more finishing touch on the ship. He painted a row of eyelashes on the crocodile's eyelids.

The next morning, Captain Hook and the crew climbed aboard and pushed off. The ticking crocodile soon appeared.

"Smee!" yelled a terrified Captain Hook. "I thought you said he wouldn't come near us!"

"But look how calm he is," said Smee, puzzled. "He's even smiling!"

Smee leaned over the side of the railing. "You know, it might be those eyelashes I painted. Maybe the croc thinks the ship is its mother."

Hook lunged at the roly-poly pirate. "You made my ship look like a *mother* crocodile? This vessel is supposed to be terrifying!"

"Mothers *can* be terrifying, sir," said Smee. "You should have seen mine when I told her I was going to become a pirate!"

Disney's
# BROTHER BEAR

# Sidetracked

"All right," Kenai told Koda. "No more getting sidetracked. We're heading to the place where the lights touch the earth, and I mean pronto!"

Koda gave Kenai a sideways glance. "I guess that means you're not interested in tasting the sweetest honey on the face of the earth," he said.

"What has that got to do with anything?" Kenai asked.

"Nothing," Koda said, "except for the fact that I just happen to know where to find the sweetest honey in the entire world, and it isn't far from here at all."

"Oh, no," Kenai said. "I'm not falling for that one. No more sidetracks!"

"If you say so." Koda hung his head.

Watching Koda sulk, Kenai couldn't help feeling guilty. "The sweetest-tasting honey in the world, huh?" he asked.

"That's right," Koda said.

"Prove it!" Kenai said.

"It's this way!" Koda took off running.

Koda led Kenai to a tree with a beehive hanging from it. "It's right there!" Koda pointed. "All we have to do is get it down."

Bees buzzed in and out of the hive. "That looks a little dangerous," Kenai said.

"Nothing to it," Koda said and began clawing his way up the tree. But, as he stretched out his paw to grab the hive, a swarm of bees flew towards him. Koda quickly slid down the tree. "Maybe we could use some help."

"I have an idea," said Kenai, pointing to Rutt and Tuke, who were browsing in a field not far from them. "Just don't wander too far from that tree." Kenai crouched down as low as he could and began crawling towards Rutt and Tuke.

"This is the life, eh, Tuke?" Rutt said.

"Nothing could ruin this day," Tuke replied.

Just then, Kenai jumped out at them, growling his scariest of bear growls. "Aaarrrghhh!"

"Run!" Rutt cried.

Kenai chased after them, leading them right in the direction of the tree. Rutt looked up just in time to skid to a halt, but Tuke was less fortunate. He was headed right for the tree. At the last moment, he turned so that he slammed into the tree with his shoulder and the hive came flying off right into Koda's waiting paws.

"That was pretty radical!" Rutt cried.

"I meant to do that," Tuke said confidently, and they wandered back over to their field.

"Aren't you going to have some?" Koda asked Kenai, honey smeared all over his face.

Kenai dipped his paw into the honey.

"What do you think?" Koda asked.

Kenai smacked his lips. "That's the best-tasting sidetrack I've ever had!"

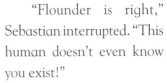

"Ahhh," Ariel sighed as she stared dreamily into space.

"Oh, no," Sebastian fretted. "A sigh like that can only mean one thing."

"What?" said Flounder.

"She's obviously writing love poetry for that human she's so obsessed with," Sebastian said.

"Oh," said Flounder.

Ariel was hard at work writing in her seaweed notebook. "How do I love thee . . ." she said out loud.

"Oh, yuck!" Flounder exclaimed.

"You're telling me," Sebastian agreed. "Terribly trite and overused."

"What would you write?" Ariel asked.

"Me? Well, this is just off the top of my head." Sebastian ceremoniously cleared his throat. "But I would write something like, 'Oh, crabby crab/ Oh, crab of my heart/ My crabbiest crab/ May our claws never part!' "

"Double yuck!" Flounder exclaimed again.

"What do you know?" Sebastian snapped.

"But he's a total stranger!" Flounder cried, turning back to Ariel.

"What's that supposed to mean?" Now Ariel looked offended.

"How can you be in love with someone you don't even know?" Sebastian said, joining in.

"I know him," Ariel protested. "Besides, haven't you ever heard of love at first sight?"

"Oh, please!" Flounder moaned.

"You're such a guppy!" cried Ariel.

"Who's being a guppy?" Flounder said defensively.

"Flounder is right," Sebastian interrupted. "This human doesn't even know you exist!"

"You don't know that!" Ariel exclaimed and went back to work on her poem.

She wrote, and wrote, and wrote some more.

Finally, when she had finished, she cleared her throat dramatically.

"How's this sound?" she asked Sebastian and Flounder, and began reading:

*"I'm always thinking of you,*
*It sets my heart a-twitter.*
*But I'm also easily distracted – ooh!*
*By things that shine and glitter.*
*Do you remember me?*
*Of me have you thunk?*
*Sorry, I've just got to go see*
*This boat that has just sunk.*
*(Now I'm back)*
*I love you more than anything,*
*Even more than my snarfblatt.*
*I wish this was a song to sing.*
*I'm really much better at that."*

"Wow – " Sebastian exclaimed.

" – that's pretty bad!" Flounder finished.

"True love, indeed!" Sebastian concluded.

# The Twilight Bark

Rolly, Patch, Lucky and the rest of the puppies were watching the end of "The Thunderbolt Adventure Hour". As the credits began to roll, Pongo turned off the TV.

"Aw, come on, Dad!" Patch complained.

"We let you stay up late to watch the whole show," Pongo said.

Lucky sat staring at the blank television screen, hoping it would magically turn itself back on.

Perdy licked his face encouragingly. "Sit down, children," she said. "Your father and I need to speak with you."

"Uh-oh," Penny said worriedly.

"Oh, it's nothing like that," Pongo assured her. "We just think it's time to tell you about the legend of the Twilight Bark."

"Sounds cool!" Pepper cheered.

"What's the Twilight Bark?" Freckles asked.

"Legend has it," Perdy began, "that there's a special way that dogs can send each other messages. It stretches from the farthest side of the city all the way to the farthest part of the countryside."

"Wow!" Penny gasped. "Why would you need to do that?"

"Sometimes," Pongo began, "you need to communicate information from one place to another quickly, and you don't have time to go

to the other place yourself."

"I don't need any Twilight Bark!" Patch said. "I can take care of myself."

"Fat chance!" Lucky said under his breath.

"What do you know?" Patch barked.

"If you ever get into any trouble," Perdy told the pups, "just go to the top of the highest hill you can find, and bark out your message, and the members of the Twilight Bark will pass it along until someone can come and help you."

"That sounds like a bunch of baloney," Patch told his parents.

"Patch!" Pongo scolded his son. "That isn't very nice."

Just then, Lucky started howling at the top of his lungs.

"What's got into you?" Perdy asked.

"I'm trying out the Twilight Bark," Lucky said. "To get us rescued from Patch."

"Lucky," Perdy scolded him, "apologize to your brother."

"That's okay," Patch said. "I don't need his apology. I was right anyway. All that howling and no word from the Twilight Bark."

Just then, the doorbell rang. All the puppies gasped and turned to look at Patch.

Perdy and Pongo smiled at each other, knowing it was actually Roger returning from the shop with milk for tomorrow's breakfast.

# Survival of the Smallest

It was the first day of summer, and Dot and the other Blueberries were getting ready for a big adventure. They were heading out for the First Annual Blueberry Wilderness Expedition. Their journey would take them to the thicket of tall grasses next to the ant colony. It was only a few yards from home – but, to a little ant, it seemed like an awfully long way.

As the group prepared to leave, some boy ants arrived to tease them.

"How do you expect to go on an expedition without supplies?" asked Jordy.

Dot put her hands on her hips. "For your information," she said in a superior tone, "the whole point is to survive using our smarts. Whatever we need, we'll make when we get there."

The Blueberries hiked a few yards from the ant colony, then Dot consulted her survival manual. "Okay," she said, "the first thing we need to do is build a shelter from the sun."

"I know!" Daisy volunteered. "We could make a hut. All we have to do is stick twigs into the dirt side by side to make the walls, then lay leaves over the top for the roof."

The rest of the Blueberries decided this was a great idea. With a lot of teamwork and determination, they completed a shelter to comfortably hold the troop.

"Now," said Dot, looking at the manual again, "it says here we need to protect our campsite."

So the girls dug a narrow trench in front of the hut, just as the manual instructed.

The girls gathered some seeds and went into their homemade hut to have some lunch. A short while later, they heard a scream. When they went to investigate, they discovered Reed, Grub and Jordy at the bottom of the trench.

It was clear to the Blueberries that the boys had been up to no good.

"Girls," said Dot, pointing to the boys, "observe one of the Blueberries' most common natural enemies – though certainly not one of the smartest."

When it was time for the Blueberries to pack up and hike home, the boys were still stuck in the trench. "Say the magic words and I'll get you out of there," said Dot.

"Okay, okay!" Reed, Grub and Jordy agreed.

"Well?" demanded Dot.

"Blueberries rock," the boys admitted.

Dot lowered down a ladder she had expertly made of sticks. "You bet we do!" she said. "'Cause if we can survive you, we can survive anything!"

# DISNEY'S
# HERCULES

## Bring a Friend

Hercules was training to be a hero, and it was a lot of work. One day, Phil, his coach, set up a practice course for Hercules and then tied his student's hands behind his back. Herc had to run the course with no hands!

Phil had put a doll at the end of the course. He said it was a "practice damsel in distress," and Hercules was supposed to rescue it. So the hero-in-training rushed into the first section of the course – a darkened cave. Herc plunged into darkness and fell headlong into stagnant water.

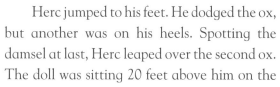

"Yech!" Hercules spat out the putrid water and scowled. He wanted to be a hero more than anything. But sometimes Phil made things a little more difficult than necessary.

Feeling his way in the darkness with his feet, Herc noticed something slithery slipping around his ankles. Snakes!

Herc shook several of the water snakes out of his sandals. He hurried towards the other end of the cave and dived into the daylight, shaking the last snake off his feet. Panting, Herc lay down on the grass to rest for a moment.

"Rest later!" Phil shouted.

Herc rolled slowly over. The doll had to be around here somewhere. Behind him Hercules heard more stamping hooves and turned around. A huge ox was thundering towards him!

Herc jumped to his feet. He dodged the ox, but another was on his heels. Spotting the damsel at last, Herc leaped over the second ox. The doll was sitting 20 feet above him on the edge of a steep cliff.

At least Phil had left him a rope. In fact, it looked as though Phil had left two. Gripping the first rope in his jaws, Herc inched steadily upward. He was about halfway up when Phil lit the end of the second rope, which was soaked with oil! The fire raced up the rope towards a stack of dry wood under Herc's damsel.

Hercules threw himself the last few feet. He tackled the damsel, rolling away from the stack of wood, which was now blazing merrily away.

Breathing hard, Hercules finally relaxed.

"And another thing . . ." Phil's gruff voice echoed up to him from the base of the cliff. Hercules held his breath, but not because he was waiting for Phil's next words. Herc was holding his breath because he had spotted a scorpion next to his foot. The insect was poised to sting!

*Crunch.* Hercules' winged horse Pegasus used his hoof to flatten the creature.

Hercules smiled at Pegasus as Phil's final words of advice reached his ears. It was the best tip yet: "Always bring a friend!"

# A Dance with the Bride

No one could remember a more glorious wedding day. The sun was shining, the church bells were ringing, and the bride was unquestionably the fairest one of all. Nearly everyone in the land had come to see the Prince take Snow White's hand in marriage, including seven rather short men sitting in the front row, soaking their handkerchiefs with tears of joy.

After the ceremony, a great ball and banquet were held at the castle. As the guests arrived in the ballroom, each was announced. "Doc, Happy, Sneezy, Bashful, Grumpy, Dopey and Sleepy!" the page cried into the great room as the Seven Dwarfs tripped over one another, dazzled by the splendour.

"Gawrsh," Bashful said, hiding behind Doc, overawed by the marble and chandeliers.

With a blast of trumpets, the bride and groom arrived. Then, as the orchestra began to play, the Prince took Snow White in his arms and they waltzed across the dance floor.

The Dwarfs sighed. They could not take their eyes off Snow White.

"Wouldn't it be wonderful to dance with Snow White?" Happy asked. That gave Doc an idea. He led the other Dwarfs into the cloakroom and borrowed a few things.

"Sneezy, stand here. Bashful, you stand on his shoulders. Dopey, do you think you can make it to the top?"

When Dopey was balanced on Bashful's shoulders, Doc wrapped a cloak around the tower of Dwarfs and buttoned it around Dopey's neck.

Wobbling, the Dwarf prince tottered towards the dance floor and Snow White.

"May we have this dance?" Bashful asked, muffled from within the cloak.

"Of course." Snow White giggled when she saw the familiar faces peeking up at her from beneath the cloak.

As the song began, Snow White and the Dwarf prince lurched and swayed precariously into the middle of the room.

"Yikes!" Sneezy squeaked. "This cloak is tickling my nose!"

Above them all, Dopey was having the time of his life, when suddenly the Dwarfs heard a sound that made their blood go cold.

"*Ah . . . ah . . . ah . . .*"

"Hang on, men!" Doc shouted.

". . . *CHOOO!*"

The cloak billowed. The Dwarf prince was knocked off balance and veered towards the banquet table.

"I got you!" The Prince caught the Dwarfs just in time. After steadying them, he turned to his bride and held out his hand. "May I cut in?" he asked.

# Walt Disney's
# Bambi

## Sweeter than Clover

"Hi, Bambi," said a soft voice.

Bambi looked up from the grass he was eating, and his friend Flower stopped searching for berries. Standing there was the pretty young fawn Bambi had met that spring.

"Hi, Faline," Bambi said. "It's nice to see you!"

"It's nice to see you too," Faline said shyly.

"Faline!" a young male deer called across the meadow. "Come over and play with me!"

Bambi's eyes narrowed. He didn't like the idea of Faline going off to play with someone else.

Faline blinked in confusion. "Do you want me to go?" she asked Bambi.

"No, don't go," said Bambi. But what could he say to make her stay? he wondered. Suddenly, Bambi had an idea.

"I want to show you something special," he told her.

"Something special?" asked Faline.

"I know where to find the sweetest clover you'll ever taste," Bambi bragged. Thumper had shown him exactly where to find it.

"Where?" asked Faline.

"Just follow me!" exclaimed Bambi.

He led Faline across the meadow to the babbling brook. Then he followed the brook all the way up a steep grassy hill. Finally they came to a big waterfall.

"The sweet clover is right here by this weeping willow tree," said Bambi.

Bambi couldn't wait to share it with Faline. But, when he got to the tree, there wasn't one single clover blossom left.

"Oh, that Thumper!" complained Bambi.

"What's the matter?" asked Faline.

Bambi shook his head. He felt very silly. He'd brought Faline all this way, and now he had nothing special to share with her!

But, just then, Bambi looked up.

"Look," he whispered. "Up in the sky."

Faline looked up and gasped.

Shimmering bands of colour had formed an arc over the waterfall.

"It's so beautiful," whispered Faline. "I've never seen anything like it."

"Neither have I," said Bambi. "But I remember hearing my mother talk about it. I think it's called a rain . . . bow."

"It's wonderful!" cried Faline.

"I'm glad you think so," said Bambi, a little relieved. "But I'm sorry you came all this way for no clover."

"Oh, Bambi," said Faline. "I came because I wanted to be with you. And, besides, a rainbow is a much sweeter surprise than some silly old clover, anyway!"

# Scare Tactics

It was still a few months until Halloween, but Jack the Pumpkin King and his crew were already busily planning for the big day.

"We've got to come up with something positively terrifying," Jack said. "The kids are getting harder and harder to scare every year."

He was right. Last year, the kids had loved Jack's screeching pumpkins – but they hadn't been afraid of them. "Cool!" one had said. "A pumpkin with a sound chip! I wonder where my mum can buy one!"

And when the children saw real ghosts swirling in the sky, they assumed they were created by some sort of projector. The vampires were especially disappointed. They lay in coffins all over town, sitting up to scare trick-or-treaters as they passed by. But, instead of shrieking and running for their lives, the kids said, "Wow! A motion-activated dummy!"

"So let's all put our heads together," Jack said. "I'm counting on you!"

The citizens of Halloweentown removed their heads and put them in a large pile.

"Oh, brother!" Jack said with a sigh. "This is going to be harder than I thought!"

A week later, the creepy creatures assembled once again and offered up their suggestions. A gaggle of witches stepped forward, cackling with excitement. "We've cooked up a horrible concoction to feed the children. It's made of worms and dirt. It's terrifying!"

"Nice try," said Jack, "but I believe there is a Halloween treat made of cookie crumbs and jelly worms that is quite similar. And the kids love it."

"What if they stuck their hands in a bowl of eyeballs?" asked a witch.

"They'll just think they're peeled grapes," Jack said with a sigh.

"We know! We know!" Lock, Shock and Barrel said in unison. "We'll steal all the candy in the trick-or-treaters' bags and put in maths homework instead. Now that's scary!"

Jack rubbed his skull. "Interesting . . . but not exactly what I had in mind."

As Jack continued to think, Sally sneaked up behind him. She put her finger to her lips, and crept closer. When she was right behind him, she screeched, "BOO!"

"Ahhhh!" Jack yelled, jumping in the air.

"Sometimes the simplest things can be the most effective, don't you think?" Sally asked.

A smile spread across the Pumpkin King's face. "Sally, that's brilliant! A well-timed 'BOO!' never fails to scare the living daylights out of people, day or night."

Jack looked at Sally with admiration. She may have been a rag doll, but her head was full of a lot more than stuffing!

June
# 26

# An Out-of-this-world Party

Every year, one of Lilo's classmates had a party to celebrate the last day of school. This year, Lilo begged Nani to let her have the party at their house. She wanted to show off her new friends Jumba and Pleakley to her classmates – and to prove to them that even though Stitch wasn't a very good dog, he was a great alien!

Lilo gave invitations to all her classmates – even Myrtle, but only because Nani said Lilo had to invite her. Myrtle didn't want to go to the party any more than Lilo wanted to have her there, but she didn't want to be left out either.

On the big afternoon, everyone went straight to Lilo's house after school.

Lilo ushered all the children to a stage in the garden. Then she pulled back the curtains to reveal Stitch in a fancy rock-and-roll costume. Stitch crooned into a microphone while swivelling his hips and strumming his guitar. All the children thought he was cool – except Myrtle. When Stitch tried to give her a kiss on the cheek during a love song, she shrieked, "Ooooh! Yuck! Dog germs!"

"Time for crafts!" Pleakley called. "Today, you are each going to make your own intergalactic communicator. You'll need to decide which planet you would like to contact so we can program your device accordingly."

A little while later, one boy shouted, "Hey, I called Jupiter!"

Another child yelled, "I'm talking to Mars!"

Myrtle stamped her foot. "This dumb thing doesn't work," she said. "All I've got is static!"

Jumba turned to Lilo and gave her a wink. "Who wants to play Pin the Smile on the Man in the Moon?" he asked.

"I do! I do!" shouted Myrtle.

Jumba hustled Myrtle into a small spaceship with no windows. Then he handed her a large, paper smile. "When you pass by the moon in a few hours," said Jumba, "try to pin the smile in the correct position. Remember that you will be travelling at several thousand miles per hour, so act quickly!" Then he shut the cockpit door.

"But the spaceship is fake," Lilo said to Jumba. "It's not moving or anything."

"Ah, but Myrtle doesn't know that," Jumba replied. "Inside the ship, it looks like she's heading to the moon. This should keep her busy for a few hours while we enjoy ourselves." He smiled. "Now, who's up for cake?"

The kids cheered, and everyone moved over to a picnic table, leaving the spaceship behind. As she followed them, Lilo heard Myrtle grumble from inside the little ship, "This is the most boring party game ever."

# Rabbit's Frightful Garden

Rabbit woke up bright and early. He had a lot of work to do in his garden. There were weeds to be pulled up. There were vines to be trimmed. And there were lots of delicious, ripe vegetables just waiting to be picked. The only problem was that Rabbit had lent all his tools to his friends – and they hadn't returned them.

In the meantime, Pooh and Piglet were enjoying breakfast at Kanga's and Roo's house when Roo bounced in with a bunch of wildflowers for his mother.

"Thank you, Roo!" Kanga exclaimed, giving him a kiss. "Let me just trim these and put them in some water." She rummaged around in a kitchen drawer, where she came across Rabbit's gardening shears. "Oh, no," Kanga said. "I never returned these to Rabbit after I borrowed them."

"That reminds me," said Piglet. "I still have Rabbit's rake. And, Pooh, I'll bet you still have Rabbit's shovel."

The friends decided the neighbourly thing to do would be to return Rabbit's tools right away. When they arrived at Rabbit's house, though, their friend was not at home. He was on his way to *their* houses to get his tools back.

"Rabbit's garden could use some work," Kanga said. "Why don't we take care of it for him as a way of saying that we're sorry for

keeping his tools for so long?"

Everyone agreed that this was a splendid plan. Pooh set about weeding while Piglet raked. Kanga snipped ripe tomatoes, peppers and cucumbers off the vines. Roo gathered them into big baskets.

When they had finished, they spotted some birds hungrily eyeing the harvest.

"This garden needs a scarecrow!" cried Roo.

The work crew sprang into action, and soon a towering scarecrow was planted right in the middle of the garden. They propped the tools against the scarecrow, placed the baskets of food in front of it, and started for home. "Won't Rabbit be surprised!" Piglet said proudly.

When Rabbit returned home a few minutes later, he couldn't quite believe his eyes. First he looked at the vegetables, all neatly picked. Then he looked at his garden tools, which had mysteriously reappeared. Finally, he looked at the strange scarecrow, which seemed to be looking right back at him! "D-d-d-did you do this?" he stammered to the straw man. Just then, a gust of wind knocked over the rake resting on the scarecrow's arm.

Convinced his garden was haunted, Rabbit turned and ran for his life. "Ahhhhhhhhh!" he screamed as he rushed past his friends.

"I *told* you he'd be surprised," said Piglet.

# Hamm's Heavy Burden

"That poor piggy bank." Bo Peep shook her head sadly. Hamm's head hung low. He hadn't moved off the shelf for days.

"He just hasn't been himself lately." Woody leaned back on Andy's pillow. "I can't understand it. He doesn't play with us any more. And Andy has been paying more attention to him than ever." Woody stood up and slid off the side of the bed. "I think the guy might need some cheering up."

Bo Peep smiled at her favourite cowboy. She was really worried about Hamm and if anyone could cheer him up, it was Woody.

"Howdy, Hamm." Woody tipped his hat. The pink piggy bank barely looked up.

"Oh. Hey, Woody," he said sadly.

"What do you say me and you take a walk down to the toy box and say hi to the Green Army Men?" Woody raised an eyebrow.

Hamm's eyes lit up, but when he looked across the room his face drooped again. "No thanks," he said with a sigh.

Woody put his arm around his friend. Something was really wrong. Hamm always liked to visit the Green Army Men. "Talk to me, Hammy. What's going on? You're not yourself."

Hamm looked at his hooves shyly. "It's just, well . . . uh . . . do I look fat?"

Woody put his hand over his mouth to keep from laughing. "Hamm, you're a pi–" Woody stopped himself when he saw Hamm's hopeful look. "A perfectly proportioned pig," he finished.

"I just feel so heavy lately." Hamm leaned against the shelf. "And, you know, I should feel great. Andy has been dropping coins in my slot almost every night! I can't remember when he paid this much attention to me. I mean, I'm not you," he concluded.

Woody nodded. He knew Andy paid a lot more attention to him than to most of the toys in the room. But he wasn't sure what to say to Hamm to make him feel better.

The next morning Woody was still worrying about Hamm when Andy raced into the room. He pulled Hamm off the shelf, took the cork out of his belly, and shook him over the bed. Coins rained out of Hamm's stomach, a huge pile of them! "Thanks," Andy said, patting the piggy bank. He gathered up his money and dashed out of the room, yelling, "Coming, Mum! I just had to get my savings."

"Wow, do I feel better." Hamm danced a little jig. "But now maybe I'm a little *too* empty."

Woody and Bo Peep beamed. "Looking lean there!" Bo Peep said, poking Hamm in the side with her staff.

"Heads up!" cried Woody, tossing Hamm a new coin.

# Laughter is the Best Medicine

"I hope Quasi is okay out there!" Laverne said fretfully.

The other two gargoyles in the bell tower, Hugo and Victor, nodded in agreement. Their friend Quasimodo had just left Notre Dame to help the young soldier Phoebus search for the Court of Miracles. It was certain to be a dangerous mission.

"The only thing we can do is stay strong, and be hopeful," Victor said solemnly.

Hugo smirked. "How can we *not* be strong?" he said. "We're made of stone, remember?"

"Good one!" Laverne giggled. "Rock solid."

"You know that's not what I meant." Victor frowned at Hugo. "And both of you – don't you have any sense of the seriousness of this situation? Our dear compatriot is out there somewhere, facing grave peril . . . ."

"*Grave* peril?" Laverne said. "Way to be optimistic, Victor – you've already got poor Quasi in his grave!"

"Hoo-hoo!" Hugo whooped. "You slay me! If I were alive, I'd be dying right now!"

As the two of them rolled around on the tower floor, chortling loudly, Victor glared at them.

"I see," he said sternly. "So you two would rather mock me and crack bad jokes than join me in my concern for poor young Quasimodo."

Laverne stood up and brushed herself off. "Why does it have to be an either-or thing, Victor?" she asked. "Just because we're laughing, it doesn't mean we're not worried too."

"But our friend could be in real danger!" Victor exclaimed.

"That's right," Laverne said. "And standing around here all stone-faced isn't going to help him any."

Hugo nodded. "If we spend all our time thinking about how terrible everything is, we'll go nuts."

Waving his arms to help make his point, he accidentally hit a bird's nest that was tucked into one of the eaves. The occupant of the nest squawked and flew upward. Laverne ducked just in time to avoid having the bird fly straight into her face, but then she tripped and fell and landed on the ground. The bird banked upwards, still squawking as it flew over Hugo.

Hugo leaped backwards – and landed on Laverne's hand. She yelled and yanked her hand out from under him. Hugo lost his footing, and landed in a heap on top of Laverne.

Victor stared at his friends, who were trying to untangle themselves.

Then he started to laugh. He laughed harder and harder, until he could hardly speak.

"You know," he said finally, "I think you just might be right. I feel much better already!"

# A Salty Surprise

**B**riar Rose picked up a large basket and stepped out of the door. It was a beautiful afternoon, and she couldn't help but sing a little song as she headed into the forest.

Rose had spent many afternoons in the forest and knew exactly where the cherry trees grew. She put her basket down by her favourite tree and began to fill it with juicy cherries. A pair of bluebirds came and landed on her shoulder while she picked. Soon the basket was heavy with fruit.

"That should be more than enough for a pie," she told the bluebirds. She was going to bake her aunts a surprise pudding. Still humming to herself, Rose carried the cherries back to the cottage.

Rose put down the basket and looked around the cozy kitchen. She felt nervous. She had never baked a pie by herself! She wasn't even sure where to find all the ingredients.

"It can't be that hard to find the butter, flour and sugar," she assured herself.

Taking a deep breath, Rose searched the cupboards. Then she set to work cutting the butter into the flour for the crust. After adding cold water, she gently patted the dough into a ball.

"And now for the tricky part," she said to the bluebirds, who had followed her home.

Rose put the dough on the worktop and began to roll it out. Soon it was a large, flat circle.

"Here we go," Rose said as she folded it in half and lifted it into the pie tin. After unfolding it, she crimped the edges. It looked perfect.

"And now for the filling," Rose said. She washed the cherries and pitted them. Then she mixed in some spice and sprinkled on spoonfuls of the coarse, white sugar.

The pie was just coming out of the oven when her aunts tumbled through the door.

"What is that delicious smell, dear?" Flora asked as she took off her pointed hat.

Rose beamed. "It's a cherry pie," she said. "I baked it myself!"

Fauna clapped her hands together. "How wonderful!"

After dinner, Rose cut four nice-sized pieces of pie. Smiling, everyone dug in. But their smiles soon turned to severe puckers.

Then Rose burst into tears. "Salt!" she cried. "I used salt instead of sugar!"

"There, there, dear," Flora consoled her. "I once made the same mistake with an entire batch of fruitcake – 20 cakes! – and it took a while before anyone would touch my cooking again! But they got over it eventually."

Rose wiped her tears as Merryweather began to giggle. "I remember that!" she said.

Rose smiled, then giggled too. After all, she had ruined only *one* pie!

# How Does Your Garden Grow?

Everything around Alice was gigantic. Flowers looked as tall as lampposts.

"The Caterpillar said one side of this mushroom will make me bigger and the other will make me smaller," Alice told a nearby dandelion, holding up two pieces of mushroom. "But I don't know which piece will do which."

"Which do you want?" asked the dandelion. "To grow bigger or smaller?"

"Bigger!" cried Alice.

"Put your roots in the ground and turn your leaves to the sun," said the dandelion. "You'll grow bigger in no time!"

"But I'm not a flower," said Alice.

"Of course she's not," said a daffodil. "She's a bug!"

Suddenly, Alice heard another voice. "Little buuuug . . ." it sang. "I can give you what you want. Just step into my petals, buglet."

Alice placed the mushroom pieces in her pocket and approached the plant. Its flower buds looked very strange – like split green kidney beans with fine hairs around the edges.

"Get in," said the plant eagerly.

Alice climbed inside one of the strange buds. Immediately, she felt the bud begin to close up tight, trapping her inside!

"What kind of plant are you?" cried Alice.

"A Venus flytrap," said the plant.

"But I'm not a fly," Alice protested.

"Doesn't matter," said the flytrap. "I eat other bugs."

"I'm not any kind of bug!" cried Alice, banging on the springy green walls. "Let me out."

The flytrap just laughed. "I can tell you're going to be a tasty treat, little bug," it mumbled.

"You know," said Alice angrily, "it's not polite to talk with your mouth full, especially when your mouth is full of me! Why, if I were my normal size, I'd – "

Normal size? she thought and suddenly remembered the pieces of mushroom in her pocket. She pulled out the two pieces. Taking a chance, she bit into one.

Alice got bigger and bigger and burst out of the flytrap and onto the ground.

Still angry, she peered down at the flytrap. It looked completely harmless now, no higher than her ankle. She gave it a glare, and then went on her way.

The flowers watched her go. "That was the biggest bug I ever saw," said the violet, in a quaking voice.

"I can't believe I let it go," the Venus flytrap said wistfully. "That bug would have been breakfast, lunch and dinner for the next 50 years!"

*Walt Disney's*

## Lady and the TRAMP

# Lost and Found

Lady stretched and rolled over. It was so cosy up on the window seat. Sunlight shone through the glass and glinted on her diamond-shaped name tag. Lady sighed contentedly. The tag was her most prized possession. Besides her owners, of course. Jim Dear and Darling were very good to her. Just last night, they had given her and Tramp steak bones to munch on. There were so many, they had not been able to eat them all.

The bones! Lady had almost forgotten them. Leaping off the window seat, she hurried to the kitchen. Luckily, they were still right next to her food bowl.

Lady began to carry the bones into the garden. It took three trips, but soon the bones were lying in a heap on the grass. Then she got to work.

Dig, dig, dig. The soil piled up behind her as Lady dug yet another hole. She carefully nosed the last bone into the hole and covered it with soil. After prancing delicately on top to pat down the soil, she collapsed in an exhausted heap. Burying bones was hard work!

Rolling over, Lady let the sun warm her belly. The garden was the perfect place for a late-afternoon nap. She was just dozing off when, suddenly, her neck itched. Sitting up, Lady gave it a scratch. But something was missing.

Lady stopped scratching and gingerly felt her neck. Her collar! It was gone!

Panicked, Lady searched the garden for the collar. It was nowhere to be found.

I must have buried it with one of my bones! Lady realized with a jolt. She looked at all the freshly dug holes. It would take her all night to dig up the bones. But she just had to find her collar!

Tramp will help, Lady thought. She ran inside to get him. He was playing with the puppies, but ran outside as soon as he heard what was wrong. Soon the two dogs were busy undoing all of Lady's hard work.

"I see something shiny!" Tramp called. Lady was by his side in an instant, but it wasn't the collar. It was just an old bottle cap. Lady dropped her head sadly.

Lady and Tramp got right back to digging. And, just as dusk was falling, Tramp unearthed a thick blue band with a golden, diamond-shaped tag. Lady's collar!

Lady let out a happy bark. Then she carried the collar into the house and sat down at Jim Dear's feet.

"Your collar came off, Lady?" Jim asked as he fastened the collar around Lady's neck. "It's a good thing you didn't accidentally bury it with your bones!"

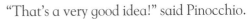

**WALT DISNEY'S**
# Pinocchio

## A Bright Idea

One day, Geppetto told Pinocchio, "I am off to deliver these puppets. I will be gone for a few hours. Stay out of trouble!" But Geppetto had not been gone for 15 minutes before Pinocchio became bored. "I have nothing to do," he said.

"You could clean the shop," said Jiminy Cricket.

"That's no fun," said Pinocchio. "I'll paint a picture instead."

"Where will you get paint?" Jiminy asked.

"From the workbench," said Pinocchio.

"You know you're not supposed to go near Geppetto's workbench," warned Jiminy. But the cricket's warning came too late.

"Oops!" Pinocchio cried.

He'd spilled red paint all over the workbench. Hurriedly, he grabbed a rag and tried to clean up the mess, but the paint just smeared. He'd made the mess even bigger!

Pinocchio looked around desperately. When he noticed Geppetto's kitten, Figaro, sleeping by the hearth, he had an idea.

"I'll say Figaro did it," Pinocchio said.

Jiminy shook his head. "That would be wrong," he said.

"What else can I do?" Pinocchio asked. "The workbench is ruined, and my father will be furious!"

"Why don't you paint it?" suggested Jiminy.

"That's a very good idea!" said Pinocchio.

So he set to work. First, he painted the bench top bright red. Then he painted the drawers green and yellow.

Figaro woke up and investigated, getting paint all over his whiskers.

Soon, the job was done.

"It looks wonderful," said Jiminy.

"Yes, it does," Pinocchio agreed. But he did not feel proud at all.

"It's a work of art!" Geppetto cried when he got home. "It's so colourful it makes the whole shop cheerful."

Then Geppetto saw the paint on Figaro's whiskers. "Did Figaro knock over the paint again?" he asked. "Is that why you painted the workbench?"

"No," Pinocchio said. "I spilled the paint. I couldn't clean it up, so I painted the whole workbench. I'm sorry."

Geppetto was quiet for a moment, and then he said, "I'm proud of you, Pinocchio."

"Because I painted the workbench?" Pinocchio asked.

"No," said Geppetto. "I'm proud of you because you told the truth and apologized instead of telling a lie. That takes courage. Now, every day, when I see my beautiful workbench, I'll remember you did the right thing, and that will make the colours seem even brighter!"

# The Fireworks Show

"It's already getting dark, and Andy hasn't played with me all day," complained Buzz.

"That's because he went out with his family," said Hamm.

"That's right!" Woody exclaimed. "I almost forgot that today is the Fourth of July!"

"What's so important about the Fourth of July?" asked Buzz, perplexed. Woody sometimes forgot that Buzz hadn't been out of the box long enough to know as much about the world as the rest of the toys. So Woody explained.

"The Fourth of July is the United States' birthday," he told Buzz. "To celebrate it, people like to go on picnics in the afternoon and watch fireworks at night. That must be where Andy and his family have gone."

"It's too bad he didn't take us with him," said Buzz. "I'd like to see fireworks myself. I'm told they look something like Space Ranger Rockets!"

"Well," said Woody thoughtfully, "last year we were able to see the fireworks from the roof. Maybe we could climb up there again tonight."

Sure enough, the toys were able to use Woody's lasso to pull themselves up on the roof, and they all climbed up in the fading light to find good seats for the fireworks display.

"Wow," said Buzz, "there sure is a lot of stuff up on this roof." He looked around and saw a football, a frisbee, a hula hoop, an old sweatshirt and a shiny red balloon.

"That's because every time Andy throws something up and it gets stuck, it stays here, since he's not allowed up on the roof," Woody explained patiently. "Look, there's that balloon he got at his friend's birthday party yesterday."

There was a flicker and a boom, and all the toys looked up as the fireworks began. Lights exploded across the sky, colours flashed and there was a deep rumbling sound.

"Why don't Andy and his mum set off their own fireworks in the backyard?" asked Buzz. "That way the fireworks wouldn't have to be so far away!"

"Fireworks are very dangerous," said one of the Green Army Men. "If one goes off near you, it makes a huge explosion and a tremendous banging noise, and you could really get hurt."

Just then, there was a tremendous banging noise – from right on the roof! All the toys gave a frightened jump. But there was no huge explosion – just Rex, looking embarrassed, with a deflated balloon hanging from the end of his tail.

"Sorry," he said, "I accidentally sat on the balloon. Did I scare everyone?"

All the toys laughed. They agreed that, for once, Rex the dinosaur had actually scared them. They also all agreed that they were glad the real fireworks were far, far away.

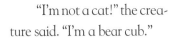

# The Storm

One summer afternoon, Jenny invited Dodger and his gang to go on a picnic with her and Oliver in Central Park.

"Good day, Miss!" said Fagin, tipping his hat. "Very nice of you to invite our scruffy gang along."

"It's my pleasure!" said Jenny. Then she set Oliver down on the Great Lawn. "Go play with your friends," she told the kitten.

As Jenny, Fagin and Winston the butler un-packed the picnic basket, they didn't notice that the animals were romping farther and farther away. Suddenly, thunder boomed and rain poured down. Then lightning struck a tree.

"I must get you home!" Winston insisted, rushing Jenny out of the park.

"Where's Oliver?" she cried.

"Don't worry," said Fagin. "Dodger will take care of him."

That night, Jenny tossed and turned. She was so worried about Oliver!

In the morning, Dodger woke up under a tree. Oliver had climbed it when the storm had started. The rest of the gang ran to find shelter, but Dodger had stayed with Oliver all night.

"Hey there, kid!" Dodger called. "You ready to go home now?"

"Yes!" said Oliver, climbing down. "And I've made a new friend. He says he's lost. Maybe Jenny will adopt him too."

"Wow," said Dodger. "I didn't know cats could grow so big!"

"I'm not a cat!" the crea-ture said. "I'm a bear cub."

"Where did you come from?" Dodger asked.

The bear started to cry. "I don't know!" he wailed. "I was scared of the storm, so I climbed a tree. Then a big wind blew me out of the tree. The next thing I knew I was out here on the lawn. So I climbed this tree and met Oliver. Can you help me find my mama?"

Oliver shook his head sadly. "I'm afraid I don't know where bears live in New York City."

The bear cub started crying again.

"Wait!" Dodger said. "I think I do." He took Oliver and the cub to a fancy entrance with a big iron gate that read CENTRAL PARK ZOO.

When the zookeeper saw the cub, he rushed over and led him back to his mother.

"Mama!" cried the bear cub. The mother bear hugged her cub close, and Dodger smiled down at Oliver. "Time to get you home too."

When Jenny saw that Oliver was safe and sound, she kissed and hugged him – and Dodger too. "Thank you, Dodger!" Jenny cried. "You're my hero!"

"Mine, too," said Oliver. "A friend like you makes even the scariest storm *bear*able!"

# RÖBIN HOOD
# The Wrong Shortcut

It was summertime in Sherwood Forest. Birds were singing, bees were buzzing and wild-flowers covered the fields.

The day was so beautiful that Robin Hood and Little John went into the woods to pick berries. Maid Marian came along, too.

"The sweetest berries can be found on the other side of the creek," Little John declared. "And I know how to get there."

A little while later, the three reached the creek. It was wide and deep. Robin frowned and shook his head when he saw the rickety old bridge over the creek.

"That bridge doesn't look so strong," Robin said.

But Marian's eyes grew wide when she saw the bushes heavy with berries on the creek's far side. "I'm sure I can make it," she said.

Little John placed his big paw on Marian's shoulder. "You heard Robin!" he declared. "The bridge is dangerous. And since I'm bigger and stronger, I should cross first."

Little John stepped onto the bridge. The wood groaned under his weight. Little John took each step carefully, but in the end it didn't matter. Halfway across the bridge, a board broke under his feet. Little John landed in the creek with a big splash!

Spluttering, he swam to the other shore.

"I made it across!" he called.

"But you weren't supposed to get wet!" called Robin. "Luckily, I'm more clever than you. I can cross the bridge and stay dry too."

"Oh, Robin, let me do it," said Marian. "I'm sure I can cross without falling into the water!"

But Robin Hood just shook his head. "It's too dangerous," he said. "Don't worry, I'm too clever to fall into the creek."

Very carefully, Robin stepped onto the bridge. He tested each plank before he put his foot on it. But, before he reached the other side, there was a loud crack. Robin broke through the bridge and plunged into the cold water. Shivering, he swam to the other side.

"The bridge is far too dangerous!" Robin called to Marian. "Don't cross. You'll only fall into the water."

But Marian just smiled. Cautiously, she tiptoed her way onto the bridge. Since she was lighter than Robin and Little John, she made it all the way to the other side – without getting a drop of water on her dress!

"How did you do that?" said Robin, scratching his soggy head.

Maid Marian smiled. "Bigger and stronger doesn't always work better," she said. "Sometimes you need a Marian to do a Merry Man's job!"

# The Flying Blueberries

Everyone in the ant colony was in a good mood. The grasshoppers had been driven off once and for all, and none of the ants had even been hurt. But Flik's amazing fake bird had taken quite a beating, and the Blueberries were determined to mend it.

"Fixing that bird is a big job," said Mr Soil, Dot's teacher, "but I know the Blueberries can do it."

The Blueberries stared at the fake bird. It was a big mess!

"I'll be back in a little while to see how you're doing," said Mr Soil before he left.

"How can we ever fix this thing?" one of the Blueberries cried.

"We can do it!" said Dot. "I bet we can make it even better this time!"

With a cheer, the Blueberries went to work. Some picked new leaves to cover the frame. Others glued those leaves into place with sticky honey.

After hours of hard work, the bird was mended.

"Let's sit in it!" Dot said.

But, just as the Blueberries crawled inside the bird, the wind began to blow. Suddenly, the breeze caught the wings. The bird took off!

It was up to Dot to save the day. She hopped into the pilot seat and took control. The Blueberries flew around Ant Island once, then twice. Soon they weren't afraid any more.

"Look!" screamed Rose. "Real birds are attacking the worker ants!" Dot jiggled the controls. The fake bird dived out of the sky and frightened the real birds away.

"Hooray!" yelled the Blueberries.

"Don't cheer yet!" Dot cried. "This contraption is out of control!"

With a bump and a crash, the bird hit the ground and skidded to a halt.

"Everybody get out!" Princess Dot commanded. One by one, the Blueberries escaped.

"It's wrecked again!" said Rose. "And here comes Mr Soil! He's going to be so mad!"

But, surprisingly, Mr Soil was smiling.

"You're heroes!" he told them. "You saved the worker ants."

"But the bird is wrecked again," said Rose.

"And you can fix it again too," Mr Soil replied.

"Yeah," said Dot, "and when it's fixed again we'll go up for another flight."

"Hooray!" the Blueberries cried.

"And here is a merit badge for you, Princess, in honour of your first flight," said Mr Soil.

Dot was confused. "I've already made my first flight," she said, fluttering her tiny wings.

"Ah, but this is a special badge," Mr Soil replied. "It is for making your first flight not using your wings, but using your head!"

# Milo's Underwater Summer

Milo Thatch loved his new life with Princess Kida in the underwater city of Atlantis. There were so many interesting and wonderful things to explore!

But, every so often, Milo found himself thinking of his old life back on the surface.

"I wonder what the weather's like today?" he mused to Kida one day as he looked at his favourite photo of himself and his grandfather. "Sometimes in the summer we'd go on these great picnics . . . ."

Kida was afraid that Milo would start missing his former home so much that he might want to leave Atlantis. She decided to help him get over his homesickness by creating a little bit of the surface world right there in Atlantis. She planned a dinner party for that very evening and invited some of their Atlantean friends.

"This is nice," Milo said in Atlantean, which he now spoke fluently.

"Goot evoning," one of the guests said in halting English. "Thanks vera much for parting."

"Party," Kida corrected quickly as Milo gave her a confused look.

"What's going on?" he asked.

Kida smiled sheepishly. "We didn't have much time to practise," she explained to Milo in Atlantean. "I thought you'd like to hear English again. To make you feel more at home."

The next morning, Milo awoke to find a bright, glaring light shining directly into his eyes.

"Ahhh!" he cried, shading his eyes against the glare.

"Sorry!" Kida cried. "Is it too bright?"

Milo squinted at her. "What is it?"

"It's a crystal," Kida said. "It's supposed to remind you of the sun. You know – to make you feel more at home."

"Why do you keep trying to make me feel more at home?" he asked.

Kida shrugged. "Because I don't want you to leave."

Milo's jaw dropped in surprise. "Leave?" he said. "Why would I leave?"

"Because you're homesick," Kida replied. "Didn't you say you missed the seasons in your old world?"

"Well, yes, I suppose I did. But that doesn't mean I want to leave!" Milo said.

"It doesn't?" Kida asked.

"Of course not!" Milo said. "Even if I get a little homesick sometimes, I would never trade my wonderful new life in Atlantis for the one I had before." He smiled. "I still have my memories of the surface world, and a few mementos. And that's okay. Because I have much more down here . . . with you."

### Walt Disney's
# 101 DALMATIANS

# One Lucky Pup

"Where are we going?" Penny asked.

"Why do we have to get in the car? We're going to miss 'Thunderbolt'!" Pepper pouted. The puppies all hated to miss their favourite dog hero TV show. They groaned in disappointment.

"This will be even more fun," Perdy said soothingly as she coaxed the puppies into the car. "I promise."

Roger and Anita got into the front seat. It didn't take long to get out of the city. Soon the car was winding down a country lane. The puppies smelled all kinds of good things. They smelled flowers and hay. Then they smelled something sweet – peaches!

"Here we are!" Anita opened the car door.

"Where's here?" Freckles asked Lucky.

"It looks like an orchard!" Lucky yipped. He loved to eat fruit.

Roger stretched. "You dogs run and play," he said. "We'll call you when it's time for our picnic."

"Don't eat too many peaches," Pongo barked, but the puppies were already running off.

All morning, the puppies romped and played in the green grass until Pongo and Perdy came to call them. "Time for lunch!" Pongo barked.

"I'm not hungry," Rolly said, rolling over in the grass.

"I hope you didn't eat too much," Perdy said.

The big dogs herded their puppies up the hill towards the spot where Roger and Anita were laying out a picnic. Perdy scanned the group. "Wait a minute," she said to Pongo. "Where's Lucky?"

The black-and-white pack stopped in its tracks. Pongo counted them. Lucky was definitely missing!

Perdy sighed and began to whimper.

"Don't worry, Mother," Pepper said sweetly. "I have an idea." He turned to his brothers and sisters. "Hey, everyone. Let's play 'Thunderbolt'!" he barked. "We have to find Lucky!"

All of the puppies yipped excitedly and tumbled over one another to find Lucky's trail. Soon every nose was sniffing the ground.

Penny sniffed around a tree and behind a patch of tall grass. She'd caught the scent! "Here he is!" Penny barked.

The rest of the dogs gathered around to see the puppy asleep in the grass. Lucky's ears covered his eyes, but there was no mistaking the horseshoe of spots on his back, or the pile of peach stones by his nose!

"Lucky is lucky we found him," Perdita said with a relieved sigh.

"And," Pepper joked, "he'll be *really* lucky if he doesn't wake up with a tummy ache!"

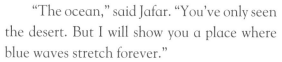

## Curses, Jafar!

"If I am to become Sultan, I must make Princess Jasmine my bride," said Jafar, pacing the Sultan's throne room.

"Well," said Iago, "you know what they say about evil magic. Use it or lose it!"

Jafar agreed. With his cobra staff in hand, he went looking for Jasmine. He found her in the palace gardens, playing with Rajah.

"Good afternoon, Princess," said Jafar.

"Go away," Jasmine told him. "You're no different from my father and Prince Ali. You all treat me like some kind of prize to be won."

Rajah growled in agreement.

"All right, I'll go," said Jafar. "I just wanted to let you know that I do understand you. You feel trapped here," he cooed. "What you really want is to see the world."

"That's true," she told him. "But I make no secret of wanting freedom, or wanting to travel. You'll have to do better than that."

"I could show you the world," promised Jafar, "*after* you marry me and I become Sultan."

Jasmine still didn't trust Jafar, and neither did her tiger. Rajah growled again.

"Don't you wish to see the world's wonders?" asked Jafar.

"Like what?" she asked.

"The ocean," said Jafar. "You've only seen the desert. But I will show you a place where blue waves stretch forever."

"Really?" said Jasmine, her eyes widening, impressed despite herself. "What else?"

"The mountains," said Jafar. "The land around Agrabah is flat and brown. But I'll show you mountains that touch the clouds."

Jasmine's eyes widened further.

"Aacch! What are you waiting for?" Iago whispered to Jafar, from his shoulder. "Her eyes can't get any wider!"

"I . . . I . . ." Jasmine said, looking into the spinning eyes of the wizard's cobra staff. She didn't realize Jafar was hypnotizing her!

With a huge growl, Rajah leaped between Jasmine and the wizard's staff. Jafar jerked back, and the eyes on the staff stopped spinning.

Jasmine shook her head and said, "I think you should go."

When Rajah growled again, the parrot cried, "Aacch! You heard the lady!"

Outraged, Jafar left.

"Don't take it too hard," Iago told his master on the way out. "There's a very good reason your trick didn't work – a 400-pound reason with long, razor-sharp teeth!"

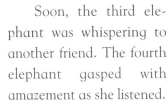

# Telephone!

"Did you hear the news, my dear?" one of the circus elephants said to another.

"What is it?" the second elephant asked.

The first elephant looked around carefully to make sure that no one was listening. "Well," she whispered in the second elephant's ear. "You know Mrs Jumbo's son, Dumbo, right?"

"Of course," the second elephant said. "The small fellow with the big ears. The one who became a . . ." she shuddered with distaste, ". . . a clown."

"That's right," the first elephant said. "Well, a little bird told me that the first show was a hit! Everyone loved the 'Building on Fire' act. Dumbo leaped off a platform 20 feet high. And they're going to raise it up much higher next time!"

"Oh, my!" the second elephant said.

"But don't tell a soul!" the first elephant warned.

But, as soon as the first elephant turned away, the second elephant turned to another of her friends. "Listen, dear," she said. "You'll never believe what I just heard!"

"What is it, dear?" the third elephant asked.

The first elephant lowered her voice to a whisper. "Oh, you'll never believe it!" she began. "It's Dumbo – 20 clowns had to hit him with a tyre to get him to leap off a platform!"

"Oh, my!" the third elephant gasped.

"That *is* big news!"

"But don't breathe a word to anyone!" the second elephant exclaimed.

"Certainly not!"

Soon, the third elephant was whispering to another friend. The fourth elephant gasped with amazement as she listened.

". . . and so Dumbo set the platform on fire, and it took 20 clowns to put out the flames," the third elephant confided.

The fourth elephant told a fifth, and a fifth told a sixth. Soon, the whole circus was buzzing with the news of Dumbo's first clown show.

A little bird was flying over the Big Top when he saw a pair of elephants chattering below.

He flew down to see what was going on, landing on one elephant's trunk. "Good day, ladies," he said. "What's the word around the circus this evening?"

"It's about Dumbo," one elephant said excitedly. "It seems he fell off a platform in the last show, and hit 20 clowns. Now they're talking about setting him on fire next time!"

The little bird didn't stick around to hear the end of the discussion. "I can't wait to spread this news!" he squawked, fluttering back up into the sky. "Wait until everyone hears – they'll never believe it's true!"

Disney · PIXAR
**FINDING**
# NEMO

# Sleep Tight, Nemo!

It was late at night at the bottom of the sea – but little Nemo was wide awake.

"Nemo," said Marlin, poking his head into the anemone, "you should be asleep!"

"But I can't sleep," said Nemo. "I need another story."

"No more stories," said Marlin. "I told you five already."

"Then maybe another snack?" said Nemo.

But Marlin rolled his eyes. "No, Nemo. You just had a plankton snack five minutes ago. What you *should* do now, young clownfish, is go to sleep!"

"Okay, Dad," said Nemo. Then he did as his dad told him and closed his eyes. But, seconds later, they popped open again.

"Dad!" Nemo called out. "Daaaad!"

"Nemo!" Marlin groaned. "I'm beginning to lose my patience!"

"But, Dad," said Nemo, "I . . . I . . . I heard a noise."

"What kind of noise?" Marlin asked.

"Um . . . a . . . a spooky noise," answered Nemo.

"*Hmph.*" Nemo could tell Marlin did not like this reason for being awake either. But still, Marlin stopped and listened . . . and listened . . . and listened.

"I don't hear anything, Nemo," he said after a moment.

So Nemo tried his best to shut his eyes really tight and get comfortable. He wiggled this way . . . then that way . . . then this way again. But nothing worked.

"Daaaaaaaaaaad!" he called out.

"Nemo," Marlin said. "For the last time, it's time to go to sleep. If you call for me again, it had better be a good one or . . . or . . . or *else*. Good night!"

Now, Nemo knew his father well, and he knew when Marlin was just a teeny, tiny, itsy, bitsy bit angry with him. But Nemo also knew that when you can't go to sleep, you can't go to sleep. And no matter how many moonfish or angelfish or sea stars you count; no matter how tightly you close your eyes; no matter how mad your dad gets – you'll never go to sleep until you're absolutely, positively, no-doubt-about-it ready. And Nemo wasn't. But why not?

Suddenly, Nemo bolted up. "Dad!" he shouted. "Dad! Oh, *Daaaaad*!"

"All right. That's it, Nemo!" Marlin said.

"But, Dad," Nemo said. "There's one more thing I really, really, truly need. Then I promise, I'll go to sleep."

And with that, he snuggled into Marlin's fins for a great big good-night hug.

"I love you, Dad," he said. "See you in the morning."

# Disney's Lilo & Stitch

## Laugh, Cobra Bubbles!

Lilo thought she was a very lucky girl. She had a lot of good friends, who she loved to laugh with. Stitch had a funny, scratchy laugh, to go with his scratchy voice. Pleakley giggled, and Jumba shouted out big guffaws. But as for Cobra Bubbles, well, the truth was, Cobra Bubbles just didn't laugh. Ever. And Lilo was just dying to find out what his laugh sounded like.

So Lilo tried to get Cobra Bubbles to laugh. She showed him the latest episode of "The World's Funniest Lobster Videos," but he didn't crack a smile, even when a lobster ate an entire jar of pickles. She made funny faces at him until her face hurt, but he just looked at her, expressionless. She even tried (at Stitch's suggestion) a whoopee cushion. But she was too busy running away to see if he laughed or not when he sat down on it.

Clearly, something had to be done. It just wasn't healthy for a person never to laugh. She explained the problem to Nani.

"Nani, Cobra Bubbles is one of my best friends. He's practically family! But he never laughs. I think I need to help him," Lilo said.

"Well," Nani said thoughtfully. "What have you tried?"

"I tried lobsters, funny faces and a whoopee cushion," said Lilo, ticking the items off on her fingers. "But none of them worked! He didn't even blink!"

"Hmm," said Nani, "I think I see the problem. Do *you* think those things are funny?"

"Well, no," Lilo admitted. "I'm scared of lobsters, my face still hurts from making funny faces, and I think whoopee cushions are silly."

"Maybe Cobra Bubbles thinks so too," said Nani. "You know, he might laugh if he is having a good time. Why don't you start out by doing something fun?"

So, the next day, Lilo enrolled Cobra Bubbles in her hula class. The music started, and the dancers came out on stage, swinging their hips and swirling their grass skirts. And there, in the middle of them, was Cobra Bubbles. He did his best to follow the complicated steps of the dance, and Lilo did her best to keep a straight face. But it was impossible. Cobra Bubbles in a grass skirt was the funniest thing she'd ever seen. The other kids in the class thought so too. Soon they were all laughing – even the hula teacher!

Then, to Lilo's surprise, Cobra Bubbles began to smile. And then he chuckled. And, soon enough, Cobra Bubbles was actually laughing! Lilo thought that Cobra Bubbles's laugh was somehow both quiet and big, and very nice. Just like him.

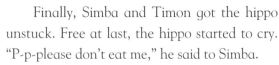

# Runaway Hippo!

One morning Simba, Timon and Pumbaa were eating breakfast.

"Mmm, crispy, crunchy bugs," said Pumbaa.

"Try the big red ones," said Timon. "They have lots of legs. They come with their own toothpicks!"

Suddenly, they heard a sad cry from the jungle.

"Sounds like somebody is in trouble," said Simba.

"The sound is coming from over here," said Pumbaa. He led them to a muddy pond full of thick vines. In the middle of the swamp was a baby hippo. He was tangled up in vines and half buried in mud.

"Help!" the hippo cried as he struggled against the vines. The more the hippo squirmed, the more tangled he became, and the deeper he sank into the mud.

When the little hippo saw Simba, he became very frightened. "Oh, no, a lion! He's going to eat me!" he cried.

"Take it easy," Simba replied. "These guys have got me on an all-bug diet."

Timon grabbed a vine and swung over to the hippo. He began digging the little hippo out of the mud.

Meanwhile Simba jumped onto the hippo's back and began tearing at the thick vines with his teeth.

That made the hippo even more afraid! "You *are* trying to eat me!" he shouted.

Finally, Simba and Timon got the hippo unstuck. Free at last, the hippo started to cry. "P-p-please don't eat me," he said to Simba.

"I'm not going to eat you, I promise," said Simba. "I just want to know how you got stuck in the mud."

"I was angry at my little brother and I bit his tail and made him cry. I was afraid my parents would be upset so I ran away from home," said the little hippo.

"I'll bet your parents *are* upset," said Simba. "Because you're gone and they're worried about you."

"They won't care," the hippo said.

"Come on," said Simba.

He led the little hippo to the edge of the river. When they got there, they could hear the other hippos calling.

"Oyo! Oyo! Oyo!"

"Listen," said the hippo. "Oyo's my name. They're calling me! They miss me!"

"Sure," said Simba. "You can't just run away without being missed. When you're part of a family, no matter what you do, you'll always belong."

"What about *your* family, Simba?" Timon asked as they watched the little hippo rejoin his family. "Do you think they miss you?"

"I didn't used to think so," Simba replied thoughtfully, "but now I wonder . . . ."

Walt Disney's
Cinderella

# Fit for a Princess

Cinderella hummed to herself as she slipped the silver needle through the colourful fabric. She had been working hard on her new quilt for weeks, and it was finally almost finished!

Though it was made of scraps of fabric from her stepsisters' old gowns and other rags, Cinderella knew the quilt would be fit for a princess. The worn fabrics were colourful and soft, and with the cotton wadding she'd found in the attic, the quilt would be wonderfully cosy. No more shivering under her threadbare blanket!

Gus agreed. He couldn't help but climb between the sewn-together quilt fabric and snuggle into the cotton filling.

"This is very cosy, Cinderelly," he called from deep inside the quilt. "I think I'd better see how it is for sleeping . . . ."

Suzy and Perla, the mice who were helping Cinderella with the sewing, giggled.

"Go and get us some more thread, sleepyhead," they called. But Gus was already dozing off. The sound of his snores drifted out from between the layers of quilt.

"Gus!" Jaq called. But the snores only got louder. "That mouse hasn't helped with this quilt one bit!" Jaq sighed and went to get the spools of thread himself.

Cinderella, the mice and the birds worked all evening. They were just sewing together the last edge when loud footsteps echoed on the attic stairs.

"Cinderella!" called an angry voice. It was Anastasia, her stepsister. A moment later she stormed into the room, carrying a fancy blue gown. "My dress was not ironed properly!" she shouted. "Can't you do anything right?" Then she spotted the quilt.

"It's beautiful!" she cried. "And it will look wonderful on my bed!"

Cinderella looked at Anastasia in shock. Would her stepsister really steal her quilt? Cinderella knew Anastasia and Drizella could be mean, but that would be very cruel!

Suddenly the quilt began to move. A moment later Gus's quivering nose poked out from between the unsewn pieces of fabric.

"A rodent!" Anastasia screamed. She dropped her dress in fright and leaped onto a small wooden chair. "Why, that quilt isn't fit for use in the stable!" she cried.

Cinderella tried not to laugh as her stepsister leaped off the chair and fled down the stairs.

Yawning, Gus climbed the rest of the way out of the quilt.

"Well, Gus," Jaq said admiringly, "I guess you did end up helping with the quilt, after all!"

Disney's
The Adventures of
**THE GREAT MOUSE DETECTIVE**

# Child's Play

"This is an outrage!" cried Basil of Baker Street, as an evil mouse named Pilfer tied him to a chair.

Pilfer and his gang of thieves had had a busy day. First they robbed the Mouse Bank of England. Then they kidnapped Basil and locked him in a shack in the middle of the woods.

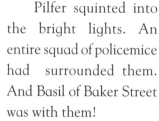

"What is the meaning of this?" demanded Basil.

"You'll be sitting here in this shack for a long time, Basil. By the time anyone finds you, our trail will be cold. So cold that even the great Basil of Baker Street won't be able to follow it," Pilfer said, rubbing his grubby paws together.

"This is an outrage!" said Basil again.

Pilfer smiled. "Bye-bye, Basil," he said. "We *won't* be seeing you." With that, Pilfer and his gang of thieving mice gathered up their loot. As they locked the door of the shack behind them, they heard Basil, tied to his chair in the shack, say once again, "What is the meaning of this?"

Pilfer and his gang carefully covered their tracks as they emerged from the woods. On the road, a car was waiting for them. They drove down to a quiet section of the waterfront. Then Pilfer raised a torch and waved it three times, signalling to a ship that was waiting in the dark harbour. The vicious gang of thieving mice was about to row out to make its final escape, when someone shouted, "Freeze!"

Suddenly floodlights blinded them from every side.

Pilfer squinted into the bright lights. An entire squad of policemice had surrounded them. And Basil of Baker Street was with them!

Soon enough, Pilfer and his gang were handcuffed. As Pilfer was led away, he passed by Basil, who was smoking his pipe and looking very pleased with himself. "I just don't understand!" Pilfer said angrily. "We left you tied up in the shack. It's like you were in two places at once! But that's . . ."

"Impossible?" said Basil. "No, just improbable. You see, I had a feeling that one day some thief would try a stunt like this. So I had toy maker Flaversham build a wind-up mouse that looked exactly like me. It could even talk, though all it could say was, 'This is an outrage!' and 'What is the meaning of this?' Granted, it wasn't the most elaborate trick. But then, you're not a very clever thief, are you?"

"Why, I –!" stuttered the astounded Pilfer.

"That's really quite brilliant, Basil," the chief inspector said admiringly.

"Nonsense," said Basil. "Thanks to the toy maker, solving this case was child's play!"

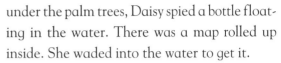

# Island Adventure

Mickey, Minnie, Donald and Daisy were on their way to their seaside holiday. As soon as they arrived, they put on their bathing costumes and ran down to the beach.

They came to a lovely cove. "I'm going to relax right here!" Minnie declared as she spread out her blanket.

"Me, too," said Daisy, opening her umbrella.

"Those waves are just perfect for surfing," said Donald.

"You boys run along," Minnie said.

"We're happy right here," said Daisy.

Mickey and Donald surfed and swam until the sun went down.

The next day was sunny too. On their way to the beach, Mickey and Donald spied a boat for rent. "Let's go fishing!" cried Donald.

But Daisy and Minnie shook their heads. "We want to relax," they said.

So Donald and Mickey went fishing alone.

On the third day, Mickey and Donald wanted to go for a long swim.

"No, thanks," said Minnie. "I want to take it easy."

"Me, too," said Daisy. "We're going to the cove to relax."

The boys went off to swim. Daisy and Minnie headed for the cove.

While she and Minnie were lounging under the palm trees, Daisy spied a bottle floating in the water. There was a map rolled up inside. She waded into the water to get it.

"It's a treasure map!" she exclaimed.

"The treasure is on an island!" cried Minnie, pointing to a big X on the map.

Minnie and Daisy decided to follow the map. They went up one hill and then down another. They crossed a stream and reached a dock with a boat tied to it.

"That's the island," said Daisy, pointing out to sea. They hopped into the boat and started to row.

They rowed and they rowed until they reached the island. Minnie and Daisy were very tired and very hungry.

"Look!" Minnie cried. "I see a fire!"

"Pirates!" exclaimed Daisy.

But there were no pirates. Just Donald and Mickey, waiting for Daisy and Minnie to arrive. A campfire was roaring, and fish sizzled on the grill.

"Looks like they found our map!" Donald exclaimed.

"*Your* map?" cried Minnie.

"It was the only way to get you two to have an adventure with us!" Mickey replied.

"Now, sit down by the fire," said Donald. "Lunch is served!"

# A Mother's Touch

**W**ork was piling up in the offices of Monsters, Inc. Celia was off with the flu, and there was no one to cover for her.

Sulley, the president of Monsters, Inc., knew he had to act fast. "Who can we get to fill in?" he asked.

"I know!" answered Mike. "I'll call my mum. She'd love to help out."

And so, later that day, in walked Mrs Wazowski. Sulley and Mike went off to discuss some new plans for the laugh factory, while Mrs W. made herself at home – *very* at home. When Sulley and Mike returned at lunchtime, they scarcely recognized the reception area. Mike's mum had hung ruffled curtains and scattered fluffy rugs everywhere. Mike gave Sulley a weak smile.

"We'll change it back when she leaves," he whispered.

Later that day, Mike rehearsed some new comedy routines. "What do monsters eat for breakfast?" asked Mike. "Anything they want!" Sulley and Mike laughed until their sides hurt.

"I couldn't help but overhear," said Mike's mum. "It might be funnier if you wore a silly hat."

Sulley shot Mike a look. "Thanks, Mum," said Mike. "That's a very helpful suggestion. Say – isn't that the phone I hear ringing?"

A little while later, Sulley and Mike summoned her over the intercom to come to the Laugh Floor. "Um, Mum, do you know anything about this?" Mike asked nervously. He pointed to the card keys, which were now filed by colour, making it impossible for anyone to know which card belonged to which door.

"I certainly do!" Mrs W. replied proudly. "I have an 'eye' for organization, if I do say so myself."

Sulley turned and spoke to Mike through gritted teeth. "She's *your* mother. Do something!"

Just before the day was over, Mike went to the front desk, sat down and took his mother's hand. He'd never fired his mother before. This wasn't going to be easy! "Mum, you know I love you. And you make a terrific receptionist, but – "

Just then, Celia walked through the front door. "Schmoopsie-Poo!" called Mike.

"Googly Bear!" Celia cried.

"What are you doing here?" Mike asked. "You're supposed to be home in bed."

"I couldn't stand being away from you one day longer," Celia gushed.

Mrs Wazowski beamed. "He *is* irresistible – isn't he? That's because he takes after my side of the family. Well, I guess my work here is done!" she said, gathering up her things.

Suddenly, Mrs W. stopped. "Oh, Mikey, what were you about to tell me?"

"Not a thing, Mum," said Mike as he gave her a kiss. "Not a thing!"

# Breakfast – O'Malley Style!

"**M**ama, I'm hungry," said little Marie. "We're hungry too," said her brothers, Toulouse and Berlioz.

"I know, my darlings," Duchess told her kittens.

The day before, they had walked for hours to reach Paris. Now, this morning, their empty stomachs were rumbling.

"I wish we were at the mansion," said Marie.

"Hey, now," said Thomas O'Malley, their alley-cat friend. "Don't you like my attic pad?"

"Yes," said Marie, "but, at the mansion, Edgar the butler brings our breakfast."

"On a golden tray," said Toulouse.

"With fine china," added Berlioz.

"Oh, I get it," said O'Malley. "Well, I can't give you the four-star treatment, but I can get you breakfast – alley-cat style."

"Well," said Marie, "I hope we're not going to root through garbage."

O'Malley laughed. "Don't worry so much, kids. Just follow me."

Duchess and her three kittens followed O'Malley into the bright Paris morning. They trotted along until they came to a little café.

"I've got a little arrangement here," O'Malley told Duchess. He led her and the kittens to the back of the café. Then he jumped onto the ledge of a window.

"Meow," he said sweetly.

A young woman in a white apron came to the window and cooed, "*Bonjour, monsieur.*"

O'Malley jumped back down and went to the back door. When it opened, the young woman put down a saucer of cream and said, "Here is your breakfast, *monsieur.*"

O'Malley called to Duchess and the kittens, "*Psssst.* Come on over."

"You've brought some friends!" the woman said.

The woman brought out two more saucers of cream – big ones. The kittens raced to the dishes and began sloppily lapping up the cream.

"Children! Children!" cried Duchess. "Where are your manners?"

The kittens looked up sheepishly, thick cream dripping from their furry chins.

"Thank you, Mr O'Malley," they said. Then Marie kissed him on the cheek!

"Aw, don't mention it," said O'Malley, embarrassed.

"I see I've made a mistake, *monsieur*," said the young woman in the doorway. "These are not your friends. They are your family!"

Wow, thought O'Malley, she certianly got that wrong! But then he stopped himself.

He did love Duchess and her kittens. And he knew they loved him too. Could it be that's what made a family, after all?

# Together Is Better

The Beast paced up and down his castle's long hallway. *Click, click, click* went his claws against the marble floor.

"It's been hours," he grumbled. "What do you suppose she's doing in there?" the Beast asked Lumiere.

"Reading," Lumiere replied. "After all, *monsieur*, it *is* the library."

"I know it's the library!" bellowed the Beast. "I know my own castle!"

Suddenly, the library doors burst open. Belle stormed out. She looked around the hallway.

"What is going on?" she asked. "There's a terrible ruckus out here."

"It's the servants," complained the Beast. "They make too much noise."

"Don't blame them," said Belle. "*You're* the one who's been clicking your claws for hours."

"I have not," said the Beast, embarrassed.

"You have so!" insisted Belle. "It's been driving me crazy!"

"You were hearing things," said the Beast.

"And then you started bellowing," said Belle.

"So what if I was?" roared the Beast. "It's my castle!"

Suddenly, Mrs Potts rolled up on a serving cart. "Anyone care for tea?" she asked.

"Not me," huffed Belle.

"Me, neither," huffed the Beast.

"Oh, come now. Just a spot?" asked Mrs Potts, pouring two cups anyway. Humming merrily, she rolled her cart into the library.

Belle and the Beast followed her in and sat down.

"So why were you so angry?" asked Belle, sipping her tea.

"I was bored," said the Beast. "I guess I . . . missed you."

"Why didn't you just say so?" Belle wondered.

"Because . . . I didn't think you missed me," said the Beast.

"I've been reading," said Belle. "I just love to read."

"I know," said the Beast.

Belle thought for a moment. "I have an idea," she said. "How about we read together?"

Belle picked out a book about a princess and a dragon. First Belle read aloud to the Beast. And then the Beast read aloud to Belle.

"That was fun," said the Beast.

"Yes," said Belle. "Let's do it again tomorrow night."

"Tomorrow," he said, "and every night after."

In the hallway, Lumiere sighed with relief.

"Maybe now we'll get some peace!" he said to himself.

*Walt Disney's*
## Lady and the TRAMP

# A Tramp Tale

It was a warm, spring evening, just about the time the first star comes out to shine, and *long* past the time for Lady's and Tramp's puppies to go to sleep.

"Just one more story, Dad," begged Scamp.

Tramp rolled his eyes.

"Well . . ." he said, "okay, but just one."

Happily, the puppies snuggled down onto their cushion. Tramp stretched out beside them.

"Did I ever tell you kids about the time I stole my very first sausage?" he asked.

"*Tramp!*" Lady warned him from her seat across the parlour. "That hardly sounds like a proper story for the children."

"Oh, tell it, Dad!" Scamp urged him.

"Well, maybe 'stole' isn't exactly the right word," Tramp reassured his wife. "And besides, it's got a great moral!" And with that, he began his tale:

"Now this all happened way back when I was just a little pup, already living on my own in the big city. I hope you puppies know just how good you have it living here in this nice house, with Junior and Jim Dear and Darling. Your old dad, though, was not so lucky. Oh, I had a lot of friends. And I had a lot of fun. But I'd be lying if I said I wasn't hungry – just a little – nearly every day.

"Well, one day I was especially hungry, and my nose was picking up all sorts of savoury scents. If there was bacon frying a mile away, I could have told you how many strips. So you can imagine the interest I developed in a certain, spicy smell coming from the butcher shop. Well, I followed my trusty nose, which has still never let me down and, sure enough, there was a heaping tray of steaming sausages. Can you believe it?"

"So you jumped up and gobbled them all up! Right?" Scamp broke in.

"That's my boy!" Tramp laughed. "But no. Don't forget, I was just a little guy. Couldn't reach the tray. All I could do was think about how to get that sausage . . . when up walked a lady with a kid in a carriage. Well, at first I was irate. Competition! But then I noticed the crumbs all over the carriage. Hey! I thought to myself. This might be the ticket – this kid obviously can't hang on to anything. Sure enough, when the lady handed the kid a piece of sausage, the kid dropped it, and down it fell into my waiting mouth! Delicious!

"See, Lady," Tramp added with a grin, "no stealing!"

"And what exactly is the moral of that story?" Lady asked.

Tramp laughed. "Why, good things come to those who wait, of course!"

THE EMPEROR'S
### New Groove

# Leaping Llamas!

"So Yzma and Kronk were out to get me the whole time! Some friends *they* were," Kuzco muttered as he trotted through the forest. Things had not been going very well for the Emperor-turned-llama. First, well, he had been turned into a llama. Then, while trying to get back to his palace, he had learned that his trusted adviser, Yzma, had actually been trying to kill him!

No, Yzma was no friend of his. Kuzco paused to scratch his ear with a hind hoof. And now he was all alone, without a friend in the world – not even that grubby peasant, Pacha. Actually, Pacha had probably been the closest thing Kuzco *had* to a friend. But now he was gone too.

Kuzco sighed. His best bet was still to get back to the palace. The problem was, Kuzco had spent his whole life having things done for him. Now that it was time to actually do things for himself, he wasn't sure if he could.

"Why me?" the llama whined to himself, as he wove in and out of vines and bushes. He was pretty sure he was headed in the right direction, but the forest was so dense and dark. Why, there could be *anything* hiding in that tree . . . under that fern . . . behind that rock . . . .

Behind that rock! Kuzco quickly leaped back as a panther lunged at him from behind a large rock. The panther's hungry jaws clicked shut just inches from Kuzco's snout.

"Heeeelp!" the llama bleated. Kuzco ran as fast as he could, but the panther was still gaining on him. This is it, thought Kuzco. I'm doomed!

Up ahead of him, Kuzco spotted a deep ravine. It was only about ten feet wide. "Okay," Kuzco said to himself. "Here's your chance. Llamas are nimble. Llamas are quick. Llamas can jump . . . really . . .

"Faaaaaar!"

*Thump.*

Kuzco shook his head and looked around him. He had leaped across the ravine! And, back on the other side, snarling and pacing back and forth, was the angry panther.

Kuzco stuck his tongue out at the panther and trotted on his way. He had done it! He had escaped a panther, all by himself! "But I know," he said thoughtfully, "that I could do even better with a friend at my side. I wonder where Pacha went, anyway."

Just then, the forest opened up into a broad, sunny field. Kuzco heard a faint bleat. Llamas! There were llamas here, and Pacha was a llama herder. A broad smile appeared on Kuzco's furry face. He headed towards the herd, and, sure enough, there was Pacha. For the first time since the day he had woken up as a llama, far from home, Kuzco began to feel like he might really stand a chance. It was good to have friends.

Walt Disney's
# Peter Pan

# A Feather in His Cap

Peter Pan and Tinker Bell were off on an adventure and the Lost Boys were bored.

"Never Land is a dull place without Peter Pan," Slightly complained.

Then Rabbit spoke up. "We can play Pirates! That's always fun."

"Can't," said Slightly. "I lost the feather off my pirate hat."

"We could find another feather," Tootles suggested.

"An extraordinary feather," Cubby said. "Like Captain Hook's."

"That it!" Slightly cried. "I'll steal Captain Hook's feather!"

A short time later, the Lost Boys were sneaking aboard Hook's pirate ship. Luckily for them, the pirates were taking a nap!

There, hanging from a peg on the mast, was Captain Hook's hat.

"There it is," whispered Tootles. "Get it!"

"M-m-m-me?" stammered Slightly.

Smee, Hook's first mate, awoke with a start. He thought someone had said his name. "Smee you say! That be me. But who be calling Smee?"

He opened his eyes and spied the Lost Boys. "Ahoy!" he cried, waking up the others. Quick as a flash, the Lost Boys were caught.

Captain Hook burst from his cabin. "Lash them to the mast!" he commanded. "We'll catch Peter Pan when he comes to save his friends."

Floating high on a cloud, Peter Pan and Tinker Bell saw their friends being captured.

They flew down to Pirates' Cove and landed on the ship's mast. Peter cupped his hands around his mouth and made a most peculiar sound.

"Tick tock," Peter went. "Tick tock!"

Down on deck, Captain Hook became very frightened. "It's that crocodile!" he cried. "The one that ate my clock and my hand! Now he's come back to eat me!"

"Tick tock…tick tock," went Peter.

"Man the cannons!" Hook cried. "Shoot that crocodile!"

The Lost Boys, tied to the mast, were forgotten. As the pirates ran in circles, Tinker Bell began to flap her wings. Fairy dust sprinkled down onto the Lost Boys. Soon they floated right out of the ropes and up into the clouds. On the way, Slightly snatched the feather from Hook's hat and stuck it in his own.

Peter Pan, Tinker Bell and the Lost Boys met on a drifting cloud.

"Thanks for saving us!" exclaimed Tootles.

"You helped me scare old Hook!" Peter Pan cried. "That's a feather in all your caps."

"But the best feather of them all is in mine," Slightly said, as he showed off Captain Hook's prized feather!

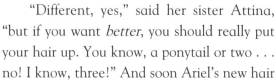

# A Hair-raising Experience

Ariel looked at her hair in the mirror and sighed. *Ugh!* It was so straight . . . and red . . . and boring! Ordinarily, it wasn't such a big deal. She'd run a dinglehopper through it, and that would be that. She had more important things to think about, you know. But today, for some reason, she felt like a change.

Ariel was still staring in the mirror when her six mermaid sisters arrived.

"Hi, Ariel, what are you doing?" the oldest, Aquata, asked.

"Oh, nothing," said Ariel. "Just trying to figure out something new to do with my hair."

"Just parting it on the other side can make a big difference," said Aquata. "Shall I try?"

"Sure!" said Ariel.

But, when Aquata had done it, Ariel's sister Andrina shook her head. "Not enough," she declared. "What you need, Ariel, are some curls."

"Okay." Ariel shrugged. She sat patiently as Andrina rolled her hair in curlers and took them out a half hour later.

"Oh, my," said Ariel, gazing into the mirror.

"Still not enough," said another sister, Arista. "Imagine how great your hair would look if we coloured it black with squid ink!" And, just to prove her point, that's exactly what she did.

"Well it certainly is different," said Ariel, looking at her new inky-black hair.

"Different, yes," said her sister Attina, "but if you want *better*, you should really put your hair up. You know, a ponytail or two . . . no! I know, three!" And soon Ariel's new hair was in not one, not two, but three curly black ponytails – all sticking straight up from her head.

"You know what you need?" said her sister Adella, looking at the finished product. "Braids! Definitely braids! Girls, come and help me." And, before she knew it, Ariel's ponytails had been divided into 99 tight, twisty plaits.

Ariel looked in the mirror . . . and then looked away twice as fast!

"What if we just cut it all off?" said her sister Alana.

"Hold it!" said Ariel, suddenly jumping up. "You're *not* cutting off my hair! I wanted a change – not a total reconstruction!" She reached up and began to unbraid her hair.

"Suit yourself," said her sisters. They helped her undo their hard work. Soon Ariel was back to normal, to her great relief. Still, she thought, it had been an interesting experiment. Changing her hair hadn't worked out so well, but what about changing something else? She shook her head and sighed. She was a red-headed mermaid princess, and that was that.

Or was it?

July
# 25

# The Ups and Downs of Babysitting

"Roo, I have to go out tomorrow evening," said Kanga. "So you'll need a babysitter. Who would you like?"

"Tigger!" shouted Roo.

Kanga was not surprised. Tigger was the only animal she knew who liked to bounce more than a baby kangaroo!

The next day, Tigger came over to Kanga's house.

"Now, Tigger, I know you and Roo like to bounce," said Kanga. "But a good babysitter must know when to put the bouncer to bed."

"Don't worry, Kanga!" said Tigger.

For hours, Tigger and Roo had a fine old time bouncing around. Then Tigger looked at the clock and said, "Time for bed!"

Roo hopped right into his room.

"That was easy," Tigger said to himself. "Now I'll just tuck you in and – hey! I said bounce *into* bed. Not *on* it!" cried Tigger. But Roo wouldn't stop. So Tigger gave up and started bouncing too.

Then Tigger remembered Kanga. "Wait a minute! I'm the babysitter!" said Tigger. "I'm supposed to be tucking you in!"

"I don't want to be tucked in!" said Roo.

"What if I read you a story?" asked Tigger.

"No," said Roo. "I'm not even sleepy. I could bounce all the way to Pooh's house!"

"But it's time for *bed*, not bouncing," said Tigger. "I'll get you some milk. That will make you sleepy."

But when Tigger came back to Roo's bedroom, Roo was gone!

"Uh-oh!" said Tigger. He rushed to Pooh's house.

"I'm sorry, Tigger," said Pooh, "but Roo isn't here."

Then Tigger rushed to Piglet's house. But Roo wasn't there either. And he wasn't at Owl's or Rabbit's.

Finally, Tigger returned to Kanga's house. Where could Roo be? Just then, Tigger passed Roo's room – and saw Roo in his bed!

"Where were you, Tigger?" asked Roo.

"Where was I?" said Tigger. "Where were *you*?"

Roo explained that when Tigger had gone to get the milk, Roo had decided he did want to hear a story. But his favourite book was under the bed.

"You were *under* the bed?" cried Tigger.

"I'm home!" called Kanga at the front door.

Tigger sighed with relief.

"How did it go?" she asked Tigger.

"Kanga," said Tigger, "the wonderful thing about Tiggers is bouncing – and from now on I'm sticking with that. Babysitting just has too many ups and downs!"

HUNNY

Disney's *Aladdin*

# A New View of the World

"It's beautiful," said Jasmine, as she and Aladdin, who was disguised as Prince Ali, soared above the desert on Aladdin's magic carpet. "I have never done anything so exciting!"

"I'm very glad you're enjoying it, Princess," said Aladdin.

"Well, I'm hardly ever allowed out of the palace," she replied ruefully. "And when I am, it's always in a procession, where my view of the world is from high up on an elephant's back."

"Come on, I'll show you the world," said Aladdin. The carpet zoomed across the desert, which was lit by the stars and the moon. They approached a huge mountain range and hovered above a silvery waterfall.

Next, they sailed past the mountains. Finally, they reached the sea. It glittered like glass in the moonlight, and Jasmine spied a pod of dolphins leaping out of the waves.

They flew away from the sea and over a meadow filled with beautiful golden flowers. A breeze blew, and Jasmine smelled their delicious fragrance. Aladdin steered the carpet downwards so that they flew just above the flowers. He swept up a handful and presented Jasmine with a beautiful bouquet. As they rose back into the air, a flock of white birds flew by, and Aladdin's carpet swooped and danced so close to them that Jasmine could nearly feel the wind from their beating wings.

Jasmine stole a look at the mysterious Prince. He seemed so familiar, though she was sure she had never met him before. He reminded her of someone she had once met . . . . But then she shrugged. They couldn't possibly be the same person!

Aladdin stole a look at the beautiful Princess. How long could he make her believe that he was a prince, and not just a street boy in disguise? Thanks to the Genie, Aladdin's wish to look like a prince in order to impress Jasmine had come true. But what if she remembered that they had once met at the marketplace? If she recognized him as the street boy who had spoken to her that day, all would be lost.

The sun was just rising over the east as Aladdin brought Jasmine back to the palace and said goodbye to her. After he left, Jasmine went inside and threw herself onto her bed, a dreamy look on her face. Rajah, her pet tiger, came over to greet her, and she absently stroked his silky head.

"Oh, Rajah," she said. "I saw the world tonight, and it was beautiful. I think I may have met someone interesting. It's all so wonderful and confusing!" She sat up and looked at Rajah. "I think," she said softly, "I just might be starting to fall in love."

# A Purr-fect Night for a Stroll

Bernard was sweeping the floor of the Rescue Aid Society when Miss Bianca appeared.

"I'm going for a stroll," she said. "Would you like to join me?"

"Gosh, I don't know," Bernard said. "It's dark out. And it's raining too!"

"Yes," Miss Bianca said, smiling. "It's the *perfect* night for a stroll!"

Outside, Miss Bianca pulled her collar tight. Bernard opened a big umbrella.

"Let's walk to Central Park," said Miss Bianca.

Bernard choked. "But that's *thirteen* blocks away. Thirteen is unlucky!"

"Don't be silly," Miss Bianca said.

As they walked, it rained harder.

Suddenly, Bernard stopped. "Listen!" he cried.

"Meow!"

"It's a kitten," said Miss Bianca. "He's in trouble."

"Stay back!" Bernard warned. "Cats are dangerous. They eat mice like us!"

"Over there!" cried Miss Bianca, pointing.

Under a mailbox, a little orange kitten cowered from the rain. His fur was wet and he looked very sad.

"We've got to help!" Miss Bianca said.

"Let me go first!" Bernard insisted. He crept up to the kitten. "Er . . . hello," he stammered. "Are you lost?"

"I'm lost and very hungry!" the cat cried.

"I was afraid of that," said Bernard, eyeing the kitten's sharp teeth and claws nervously.

"Where are your parents?" Miss Bianca asked.

"I'm an orphan," the kitten replied.

"We must help him!" said Miss Bianca.

"I have an idea," said Bernard. "Follow us!" Bernard took Miss Bianca's arm and they walked to Morningside Orphanage. They knocked, and old Rufus the cat answered.

"Nice to see you two again," Rufus said. "Who's your friend?" he asked.

"He's Young Mister Kitten, and he's an orphan," Miss Bianca replied.

"He's hungry," said Bernard nervously.

"Here's a nice bowl of milk," said Rufus. The kitten lapped it up.

"You know," Rufus said. "I could use a helper around here. Would you like to be adopted?"

The kitten threw his paws around Rufus's neck and purred with joy.

It was late, so Miss Bianca and Bernard said good night. Out on the street, Bianca took Bernard's arm.

"See," she said. "I told you it was the purr-fect night for a stroll!"

# A Relaxing Picnic

"What a lovely day for a picnic!" Snow White cried as she arrived at the Dwarfs' cottage for a visit one spring morning.

"We can't have a picnic," Grumpy said. "We have to work."

"But we've been working so hard in the diamond mine." Sleepy yawned. "Can't we take a day off?"

The other Dwarfs cheered – all except for Grumpy. He just folded his arms and frowned.

"Please don't worry, Grumpy," said Snow White. "A relaxing picnic will cheer you up."

"I doubt it," he grumbled.

"Now, what shall we rake – I mean take – on our picnic?" Doc asked.

"How about some porridge?" suggested Sleepy with a yawn.

"That is not a very good picnic food," said Snow White. "It's much more fun to pack food you can eat without spoons or forks."

"Gosh, like s-s-sandwiches?" stammered Bashful shyly.

"Exactly!" cried Snow White.

"How about fruit?" asked Doc.

"And cookies!" suggested Happy.

"And hard-boiled eggs," added Sneezy.

"Wonderful!" exclaimed Snow White. The Dwarfs helped Snow White pack.

"After lunch, we'll want to play," said Snow White. "So you should pack up some things to play with."

They did, and then they were off, hiking through the forest. When they came to a clearing with a babbling brook, Snow White spread a blanket on the grass, and they all sat down to eat.

After lunch, Doc and Happy played draughts, Bashful and Sneezy tossed a ball back and forth, Sleepy took a nap and Dopey launched an enormous blue kite.

Snow White watched Dopey as he ran through the meadow. She clapped when the wind took the kite up in the air. Then the kite lifted Dopey off the ground too!

"Oh, my!" cried Snow White. "Someone help! Dopey is flying away!"

Grumpy, who had been pouting by the brook, jumped to his feet. He raced after Dopey. Huffing and puffing, he followed the kite up one hill and down another.

Finally, Grumpy climbed all the way up a tall oak tree and grabbed Dopey as he flew by. Snow White cheered.

Still huffing and puffing, Grumpy collapsed on the blanket.

"Jiminy Crickets!" he cried. "I can't wait to get back to the diamond mine tomorrow. Relaxing picnics are way too much work!"

# Disney's POCAHONTAS

## Fishing Hole

"Come on, slowpoke," Pocahontas teased. "It's just ahead."

John Smith followed her across a grassy meadow and up a hill. Pocahontas moved as quickly and quietly as a deer. Sometimes it was difficult for John to keep up.

Pocahontas waited at the top of the hill. Below, a river wound its way through a wide canyon.

She pointed. "The fishing hole is down there."

She raced down the other side of the hill towards the water. John hurried after her. Soon they were at the water's edge.

Pocahontas leaned forwards slowly and peered into the water. Then she raised her spear and – *splash!* – thrust it into the water. But, when she lifted it out, the spear was empty.

"We prefer to use fishing rods," John said with a laugh. He baited his hook, cast it into the water and waited. But the water was moving so quickly, the line was soon unwinding with remarkable speed.

"I see," Pocahontas said.

John reeled his line in and got ready to cast again. But then a low growl startled him.

"Hold still," Pocahontas instructed.

John turned his head slowly and saw a large grizzly bear above them on the boulders.

"Grrrr!" The great animal rose up on its hind legs.

In an instant, John had dropped his fishing rod and was raising his rifle.

"No, John," Pocahontas said. "Follow me." Keeping her eyes on the bear she began to move, very slowly and carefully, away from it.

"Grrrr!" the bear growled. John's hand instinctively lifted his rifle a second time.

"He's just telling us that this is his territory," Pocahontas whispered calmly. "He doesn't want to hurt us. He just wants to fish."

John wasn't so sure, but he knew that he didn't want to shoot the grizzly. They were very big and hard to kill. And a wounded grizzly would be dangerous.

Pocahontas kept moving along the river's edge, away from the bear. When they were about 100 feet away, the grizzly leaped off the boulder, landing in the exact spot where John and Pocahontas had been fishing a few minutes before.

"Grrrr!" the bear rumbled a third time, before beginning to fish.

While Pocahontas and John watched, the grizzly caught salmon after salmon with its giant claws.

Pocahontas laughed. "I guess the bear's method is best!"

John had to agree.

*Walt Disney's*

# Bambi

# A Manner of Speaking

**B**ambi and his mother were out for a summer's walk. As always, they stopped by the rabbit den where Thumper lived.

"And how are you today, Thumper?" asked Bambi's mother.

"I'd be better if my mum didn't just give me a dumb old bath," he said.

"Thumper! Mind your manners!" his mother scolded.

"I'm sorry, Mama," Thumper said. He looked back at the doe. "I'm fine, thank you," he replied.

Bambi and Thumper were given permission to play, and they headed off into the woods. "So, what do you want to play?" the fawn asked his friend.

"How about hide-and-seek?" Thumper suggested. "I'll hide first, okay?"

Bambi turned his back to Thumper, closed his eyes, and started to count. "One . . . two . . . three . . . four . . . five . . ."

"Save me! Help! Bambi, save me!" Thumper cried. Bambi whirled around to see Thumper hopping towards him with a terrified look on his face. A moment later, a mother bear emerged from a nearby cave with three small cubs toddling behind her.

Though he was terrified, Thumper *still* managed to make a rude comment. "That's the ugliest, meanest-looking creature I ever saw!"

"I beg your pardon?" the mother bear said.

"First, you come into my home and disturb my children while they're sleeping. And then you have the nerve to call me ugly and mean? I think you owe me an apology!"

"Do it!" whispered Bambi. "Apologize."

"I'm s-s-sorry you're ugly and mean," Thumper stammered.

"Thumper!" Bambi cried. "That isn't funny."

Thumper looked confused. "I wasn't trying to be funny," he said.

"Try again!" the bear boomed.

"Um, ma'am," Thumper tried again. "I'm, um, sorry I disturbed your cubs . . . and, um, you look just like a bear mum should look . . . which is big. And nice. Yup, you sure look nice."

Before the mother bear let Thumper and Bambi go, she said, "Like I always tell my children: manners are important. Today, young man, they saved your life!"

Bambi and Thumper ran home as quickly as they could. When they arrived at Thumper's, his mother said, "Just in time for a nice lunch of greens." Thumper was about to tell his mum how awful he thought the greens tasted, then changed his mind. "Thank you, Mama. That sounds wonderful," he said.

Thumper's mother beamed. "What lovely manners! I guess you have been listening to me, after all!" she said, pleased as could be.

# The Game

"Hey, guys!" said Woody as he gazed out Andy's window on a warm, summer day. "Check this out."

Down below, in Andy's garden, Andy and his friends were playing a game of American football.

"So *that's* what this thing's for," said Rex, picking up a small blue football.

"I have an idea," said Woody. "Why don't we play?"

Happily, all the toys agreed. Andy's bed would be the field – and Woody and Buzz would each be captains. Woody was pretty pleased with his team – Rex, Hamm, Slinky Dog and Bo Peep. As for Buzz, he ended up with Sarge, Jessie and Bullseye. But who else would he pick? He looked around Andy's room at all the eager toys . . . and then he saw it! That bobble-head football guy Andy had brought in just the other day. A real football player, with a helmet and everything!

"I pick him!" Buzz declared. "C'mon, Number Three. You're gonna win me a football game!

"Okay, team," said Buzz as they gathered in their huddle. He pointed to a game plan drawn out on Etch-A-Sketch. "Jessie and Bullseye, you'll guard me here. Then, Sarge, I'll fake to you. Number Three . . . could you stop nodding for one second? You run straight and watch for me to throw you the ball. Got it?"

The football player nodded eagerly.

But no sooner did Buzz fire his pass than he realized Number Three was never going to catch it. His head was bobbing so much, he couldn't see the ball – much less the players. Before Buzz could stop him, he'd tripped over Rex's tail. Bo Peep snatched the ball and brought it back for a touchdown.

"Hooray!" Woody's team cheered.

"Okay, team," said Buzz as they huddled once again, "this time let's really show 'em what we're made of. Sarge, you block Rex and Hamm. Jessie and Bullseye, you block Bo Peep and Slinky Dog. Don't worry about Woody. I'll take care of him. Then, Number Three, I'll hand the ball off to you. All you've got to do is run."

Again, the football guy nodded like crazy.

"Okay!" Buzz pumped his fist. "Let's go!"

But instead of taking the ball when Buzz tried to hand it to him, all the bobble-head football player did was nod . . . and nod . . . and nod. And he probably would have kept nodding all day if Slinky Dog hadn't run up and accidentally knocked him over on his face.

Buzz looked down at his disappointing team mate and said with a sigh, "Anybody up for a game of checkers?"

# Walt Disney's Sleeping Beauty

# Woodland Washing

"La, la, la, la, la," Briar Rose sang as she hung the sheets on the washing line. She could feel the sunshine on her back and it felt good. It had been raining for days, and the change in the weather was a welcome surprise. She could catch up on the washing and spend some time outdoors.

"Doesn't the sunshine make you want to sing?" she asked a bluebird who was chirping along with her. The bird chirped a new song in response, and Briar Rose laughed as she pulled her Aunt Flora's red dress out of the basket of clean laundry. Once she was finished, she could take a nice walk through the forest.

Aunt Merryweather's blue dress was next. Briar Rose was just pegging the shoulder to the washing line when suddenly a pair of cheeky chipmunks leaped onto the line from a tree branch and raced down the length of it, covering the dresses and the sheets with muddy footprints.

"Look what you've done, you naughty chipmunks!" Briar Rose scolded, shaking a finger at the wayward creatures. "It took me two hours to get those dresses and sheets clean!"

The chipmunks leaped up to a tree branch and twittered guiltily at her in response. Then they turned and scampered off into the forest, their striped tails waggling.

Sighing with frustration, Briar Rose unpegged the sheets from the line and pulled a fresh bucket of water up from the well. Then, taking the washboard and the bar of laundry soap, she began to scrub out the muddy prints. It looked as if she wouldn't get a walk in today after all.

Suddenly, a chattering noise caught her attention. Looking up, she saw the chipmunks hurrying out of the forest with several other forest animals at their heels! There were two rabbits, four chipmunks, three bluebirds, a deer, a skunk and an owl.

Briar Rose laughed. "Why, you've brought all your friends!"

The chipmunks chattered excitedly while everyone got to work. The bluebirds lifted the sheet into the air so the edges wouldn't get dirty while Briar Rose scrubbed. The deer, the skunk and the rabbits brought fresh water from the well. And the chipmunks scampered across the laundry soap to get their feet all soapy, then walked across the muddy parts of the sheets until they were clean. Then everyone helped hang the newly washed laundry on the line for a second time.

Briar Rose smiled at her animal friends and gave the chipmunks a little pat. "Finished at last," she said. "Now we can all take a walk in the forest . . . together!"

# Alice's Mad Manners

"Clean cup! Clean cup! Move down!" the Mad Hatter shoved Alice aside, nearly spilling her tea. Poor Alice had been at the tea party for some time and had not even had a sip. It was a most unusual tea party.

Alice took a new spot and waited patiently while the Hatter and the March Hare poured a fresh round of tea. Folding her hands in her lap, Alice tried to recall what her mother and sister usually did at tea parties. It seemed to her that they just sat around and chatted. Perhaps, thought Alice, that is what I ought to do too.

"Pardon me," Alice addressed the March Hare because the Mad Hatter seemed quite busy buttering his saucer. "Our neighbours got a new dog. He's a – "

"A dog? *A dog?*" the March Hare shouted. "Where?" He hopped up onto the table, upsetting a plate of toast.

"Oh, I'm terribly sorry." Alice stood and tried to calm the poor hare. "I should have known you wouldn't like dogs. Dinah hates them too, you know." The March Hare was hopping all around the table and Alice had to jog in circles beside him to keep up the conversation. "When Dinah sees a dog, she practically climbs the curtains."

"Very sensible!" the Hatter said, waving his butter knife. "Just who is this clever 'Dinah'?"

"Oh, she's my – " Alice stopped herself. She had got into trouble for mentioning her cat before. The Dormouse had run off in a panic, and the Hatter and March Hare had given chase. She would not make that mistake again. She whispered in the Hatter's ear. "She's my kitten."

"But that's a baby cat!" the Hatter cried.

Just as Alice feared, the Dormouse bolted. The March Hare started hopping about just as soon as the word 'cat' was out of the Hatter's mouth. The Hatter chased the Dormouse round and round the garden. Finally, the Hatter tossed his hat over the little creature. Alice caught him in the teapot and closed the lid.

"Really, my dear. It is most rude to threaten us on our unbirthdays!" the Hatter cried.

"I'm really very sorry," Alice sighed, sinking back into a chair. She was only trying to be polite. Perhaps, Alice thought to herself, in this place it is better to say what you think you oughtn't instead of what you think you ought.

Turning to the Hatter, she said, "This party isn't very fun, and you aren't very nice!"

The Hatter grinned. "Thank you ever so much, my dear young lady. Tea?" he asked.

"Thank *you* ever so much," said Alice. She was beginning to get the hang of this!

**Walt Disney's**
**THE JUNGLE BOOK**

# Monkey Trouble

"Hey, let me go!" Mowgli cried. "Baloo!" But the big bear couldn't help him. Mowgli was being carried off through the treetops by a band of wild monkeys!

The monkeys laughed and chattered as they swung Mowgli from one tree to another. One monkey dropped him, and Mowgli yelled. But another monkey caught him by the ankles just in time. Then a third monkey pulled him away by one arm, swinging over to another tree on a large vine, where more monkeys grabbed at him.

Soon Mowgli was out of breath and confused. "Hey!" he yelled. "Quit it! I want to go back to Baloo! Let me go!"

The monkeys laughed. "Sorry, Man-cub!" one shouted. "We can't let you go. You might as well forget about that bear!"

"Yeah!" another monkey said, catching Mowgli by the arm. "You're with us monkeys now. We're better than any old bear! You'll flip for us monkeys."

He tossed Mowgli straight up. Mowgli felt himself flipping head over heels.

A second later a pair of monkeys caught him by the legs. "See, Man-cub?" one of them said. "Monkeys know how to have fun!"

Mowgli laughed, feeling dizzy. "That was kind of fun!" he cried. "Do it again!"

The monkeys howled with laughter. They tossed Mowgli up, over and over. Mowgli somersaulted through the treetops until he couldn't tell up from down any more. After that, the monkeys taught him how to swing from branch to branch and vine to vine. They even showed him how to shake the trees to make bananas fall into his hands.

"Being a monkey is fun!" Mowgli exclaimed through a mouthful of banana.

Maybe it was good that the monkeys had found him, Mowgli thought. Being a monkey might even be more fun than being a wolf or a bear. And it was definitely more fun than going to the Man-village.

Mowgli swallowed the banana and looked around at his new friends. "What are we going to do next?"

A monkey giggled. "We're going to see King Louie."

"Yeah!" another monkey said gleefully, clapping his hands. "He's the most fun of all!"

"King Louie?" Mowgli said suspiciously. He didn't like the way the monkeys were grinning at him. "Who's that?"

"You'll see, Man-cub!" the monkeys cried, swinging through the treetops.

Mowgli shrugged. How bad could this King Louie be?

# Late for Supper

Widow Tweed filled the large baking pan with meat and vegetables, then rolled out a flaky crust and set it on top. After crimping the pie's edges, she slipped the pan into the oven. "Chicken pie," she said. "Tod's favourite!"

Humming to herself, she washed the dishes in the sink and tidied up the cottage. Then, she set the table with her best tablecloth and dishes. She added a special milk saucer for Tod.

Widow Tweed looked out of the window and noticed that the sun was setting. "I wonder where that clever little devil has got to," she said.

She watched the sun sink behind the rolling forest hills, then sat down and picked up her knitting. She had a project to finish. Besides, the pie should be ready soon, and Tod was never late for supper.

"Knit one, purl two, knit one, purl two," the Widow said quietly as she put the finishing touches on a soft blanket she was knitting for Tod's bed. She knew the little fox had a fur coat of his own, but everybody liked something cosy to lie on when they curled up to go to sleep.

The smell of chicken pie drifted past her nose, and the Widow got up to take it out of the oven. The crust was golden brown, and the creamy sauce was bubbling around the edges.

She set it on the counter just as she heard a scratching at the door.

"Right on time, as usual," she said as she opened the door. "Dinner's ready, Tod."

But Tod wasn't there. The scratching had just been a small twig blown against the door by the wind. "Tod?" the Widow called, peering into the darkness. "No playing tricks now." But the little red fox did not appear.

The sky was dark now. A few clouds drifted across the moon. The Widow shivered. "Oh, Tod," she said. "Where are you?"

Stepping back into the house, she pulled on her shoes and a sweater. She'd just have to go out to look for him. After lighting an old kerosene lantern, she opened the door for a second time – and nearly tripped over the red fox on her front porch. He sat there quietly, a colourful bouquet of wildflowers at his feet.

"Oh, Tod!" she cried. She picked up the bouquet and scooped him into her arms. "You sweetie pie."

Tod nuzzled the Widow's neck as she carried him into the house and deposited him on his chair at the kitchen table. Soon, the two were sharing a delicious feast of chicken pie. And, after supper, the Widow admired her bouquet above the mantel while Tod curled up in his bed with his cosy new blanket.

# Lilo's Riches

Stitch stretched his blue arms and folded them behind his head, soaking up the rays on the wide Hawaiian beach.

*Flash*! Lilo snapped his photo. *Flash*! Lilo turned and snapped a picture of Nani and David riding their surfboards.

Suddenly Stitch stood up. He grabbed Lilo's camera. Lilo struck a hula pose and – *Flash*! – Stitch caught it on film.

"Let's take some more!" Lilo giggled, running toward the shoreline. Stitch was right behind her, snapping picture after picture. *Flash*! He got two kids splashing. He turned quickly and – *Flash*! – he momentarily blinded a bald man holding an ice-cream cone.

The man looked at Stitch, dazed. Lilo had seen that look before. Most people didn't know what to make of Stitch. Then, as the man stared, his mint-chocolate-chip ice cream rolled off his cone and splatted in the sand.

"Sorry," Lilo muttered. She grabbed Stitch's arm and tried to lead him away, but Stitch strained against her, pulling her closer to the melting green blob.

With one swipe of his tongue, Stitch lapped the mess up. "Ptooey!" He spat it out, all over the man's feet. It was too sandy. "Ptooey! Ptooey!" Stitch continued spitting out sand as Lilo dragged him away.

As soon as he stopped spitting, Stitch pointed at the snack shack.

"Sorry, Stitch. I don't have any money for ice cream," Lilo explained. "How about if we play a few songs instead? Here, you play," Lilo tossed Stitch the ukulele. "I'll dance."

At first, Stitch just plucked a few sour notes. But soon the rhythm got him and he was playing like a real-life rock star.

Lilo was enjoying dancing so much, she didn't even notice that the tourists had begun to toss coins to them.

Stitch hammed it up, tossing his head and wiggling his hips. Lilo waved her arms and smiled her most winning smile. When the song ended, the two took a bow. Quickly, Lilo gathered the coins.

"We've got enough! Come on!" Lilo went running towards the snack shack.

"Three mint-chocolate-chip cones, please," Lilo said.

Lilo handed one cone to Stitch. She took a quick lick of the second one as she scanned the beach. Spotting the bald man, she hurried over and thrust the third cone towards him. "Here," she said. "Sorry about before."

The man smiled and he took the cone. Then Lilo handed him her camera. He snapped a picture – *Flash*! – of Lilo and Stitch eating ice cream.

**WALT DISNEY'S**
# Pinocchio

## In a Tangle

One night, while Pinocchio was sleeping, a loud crash woke him. He jumped up and raced downstairs to Geppetto's workshop.

"Is anybody here?" Pinocchio called nervously.

"Meow!" came the reply. It was Geppetto's little kitten, Figaro.

"I hear you, but I can't see you!" called Pinocchio.

Suddenly, the puppets above Geppetto's workbench began to move.

"Yikes!" cried Pinocchio, startled.

Pinocchio looked up to see Figaro tangled in the puppets' strings. Pinocchio began to laugh.

"That's funny!" he said.

"Meow!" cried Figaro. He didn't think it was funny! The kitten struggled to get free, but he only became more tangled in the strings.

Pinocchio just laughed harder.

Jiminy Cricket hopped down from the hearth. He rubbed his tired eyes. "What's going on?" he asked.

Pinocchio pointed to the little kitten.

"Pinocchio, maybe you should help poor Figaro instead of laughing at him," Jiminy said.

"Maybe I should leave him there," replied Pinocchio. "Then Geppetto can see how naughty he's been."

"Meow!" poor Figaro wailed.

"That's not very nice," said Jiminy. "How would you feel if you were all tangled up?"

Pinocchio sighed. "I guess I wouldn't like it very much."

He was about to free the kitten, when he suddenly exclaimed, "Hey, Jiminy, look at that!"

Figaro's paws were now wrapped around the strings in such a way that when his paws moved, the puppets began to dance!

"That's a neat trick," said Pinocchio. "Figaro can work the puppets!"

The kitten moved his paws some more, and all the puppets danced on their strings.

"I have an idea," said Jiminy Cricket. "Do you want to hear it?"

Pinocchio and Figaro both nodded.

The next morning when Geppetto awoke, he got a surprise.

"Look, Father!" Pinocchio said. "Figaro can make the puppets dance!"

Pinocchio winked at Figaro, and the cat leaped onto the puppet strings again.

"Amazing!" Geppetto cried, watching the show. "We can put on a puppet show for all the children of the town!"

Pinocchio was thrilled to see Geppetto so happy.

"But when did you discover Figaro's talent?" asked Geppetto.

"Just last night," said Pinocchio, "when I found him in your workshop . . . uh, hanging around."

**WALT DISNEY PICTURES PRESENTS**
# DINOSAUR

# Things Go Better With Friends

Not long after the dinosaurs reached the Nesting Grounds, new dinosaur babies were born. Among the happy parents were Aladar and Neera.

Zini wanted to give them a special gift. He decided to go to the farthest reaches of the Nesting Grounds where the melon vines grew, and pick them a juicy melon. When Zini told the others of his plan, everyone wanted to help.

"No way!" Zini cried. "It's my idea and I'm going to pick the fruit myself!"

Yar, chief of the lemurs, told Zini, "You will need help for such a big job."

But Zini laughed. "Any lemur can pick melons," he said.

But the walk to the melon vines was long. When he finally reached them, Zini was almost too tired to lift up the huge leaves of the melon vines. But lift he did, because every lemur knows that the best melons grow under the biggest leaves on the vine.

To make matters worse, the leaves were also slippery! Zini would get a leaf lifted *almost* high enough but, when he let go to grab the melon underneath, the leaf would slip right back down again!

"What am I going to do?" Zini said.

Suddenly, Zini spotted a dinosaur coming towards him. She was a big dinosaur – the biggest of them all – Baylene! And spiky old Eema was not far behind.

"Are you having trouble?" Baylene asked, her long neck bent low.

"I can't lift the leaves high enough to pick fruit for Aladar and Neera," Zini complained. "And even if I could pick melons, I don't think I'm strong enough to carry even one of them home."

"That's why Yar sent us," Baylene explained. "He said you were too stubborn to ask for help, but you needed it anyway."

"Will you help me?" Zini asked.

"What are friends for?" Baylene replied. She took the edge of a leaf in her teeth and lifted it off a huge, ripe melon.

"This is easy! And fun too," said Zini as he scampered under the leaf and rolled the melon out from under it.

"I'll carry that, Zini," said Eema. "I might be slow, but I'm not too old to handle one melon – even a melon as big and ripe as this one!"

Before sunset, the three friends had returned to the Nesting Grounds with their prize.

"So you got it on your own?" Yar asked when he saw the melon.

"I had help," said Zini. "And I figured something out. Things go better when you have friends!"

DISNEP's
ROBIN
HOOD

# Robin Lends a Hand

It was a hot day in Sherwood Forest – a very hot day! So hot that the Sheriff of Nottingham had decided not to collect taxes, for fear the coins would burn his greedy hands!

As for himself, Robin Hood was trying to keep cool in the shade of Sherwood's oaks. Taking off his hat, he stretched out under the tallest, broadest tree, closed his eyes, and waited for a breeze.

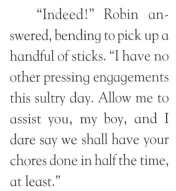

"Halt! Who goes there?" he shouted suddenly. "Oh!" His eyes rested on a startled little bunny with a load of twigs scattered about his feet. "Skippy, my good man. Forgive me. I didn't mean to scare you."

Quickly, Robin helped to load up Skippy's arms once again. "Now, then," he said, patting the bunny on the shoulder. "That's better." But Skippy didn't seem to agree. Robin didn't think he had ever seen him look so unhappy.

"Why so glum, old chum?" Robin couldn't help but ask.

"Oh, Robin," Skippy sighed. "It's so very hot, and all the other children have gone to the swimming hole. But Mother has so many chores for me to do, I don't think I'll ever be able to join them."

"I see," said Robin, nodding. "That could get a fellow down, now, couldn't it?"

"I'll say," said Skippy.

"Unless . . ." Robin went on with a big grin, ". . . a fellow had a friend to help him out!"

Skippy's sorrowful face grew brighter. "Do you mean . . . ?"

"Indeed!" Robin answered, bending to pick up a handful of sticks. "I have no other pressing engagements this sultry day. Allow me to assist you, my boy, and I dare say we shall have your chores done in half the time, at least."

"Hooray for Robin Hood!" Skippy cheered, nearly dropping his sticks once again. "Hip, hip, hooray!"

And so, working together, Robin Hood and Skippy gathered firewood. They wrung out the laundry and hung it out to dry. They picked some juicy plums and a basketful of lettuce, weeded the garden and built a scarecrow. By lunchtime, in fact, not only was every one of Skippy's chores done, but he and Robin had washed all the windows and swept Skippy's cottage floor.

"Robin Hood, how can I ever thank you? I'd still be hard at work if it wasn't for you!" Skippy asked when they were through.

Robin scratched his head and thought for a moment. "I have it!" he declared at last. "Take me swimming with you!"

"You betcha!" Skippy said happily. "C'mon, let's go! Last one in is a rotten sheriff!"

# Dot Rules!

Atta was exhausted! Ever since she had taken over as Queen, she had not had a moment's peace. There were decisions to make, disagreements to settle and speeches to compose. Princess Dot didn't like her big sister being so tired and cranky all the time. "Why don't you just take a day off?" Dot asked.

"But who will run the colony?" Atta said irritably.

"I will. I am a princess, you know," Dot said.

"Okay. Tomorrow you can be in charge," Atta said jokingly.

"Really? You mean it?" Dot asked.

Atta smiled. She was sure that after a few hours, Dot would realize just how difficult being in charge could be.

The next day, Dot began her one-day reign. The first problem arose when their mother's pet, Aphie, ate some leaves that were going to be used to build a rain shelter.

"You need a time-out!" scolded Dot. She put Aphie in a pen for ten minutes. When he came back out, he was a model aphid.

Later, she found Thorny and Cornelius disagreeing over the best way to transport seeds.

"I want you both to cooperate and come up with a solution," Dot said. A short time later, Thorny and Cornelius reached a compromise. It turned out they were *both* right!

Flik was the next ant to receive Dot's help. "I can't seem to get this new ant mover to work," he complained.

"How long have you been working on it?" Dot asked.

Flik thought for a moment. "Ever since I woke up," he answered. "I worked right through breakfast and lunch – although I did snack on a few seed crumbs."

"Flik," Dot said, "you can't think properly if your body doesn't have fuel. You need to stop and eat something – and I don't mean a few seed crumbs. And why don't you take a nap while you're at it?"

Dot had a lot of advice to share with her royal subjects that day. She reminded Mr Soil's conservation class that everyone should have a turn to speak. She insisted that the ant boys pick their toys up off the ground. And she firmly told her mother that there was no whining allowed – even if she was upset about Aphie getting a time-out.

By the end of the day, both Atta and her mother had to admit the colony had run smoothly with Dot in charge. "What's your secret?" asked Atta.

"It was easy," Dot explained. "Time-outs, cooperating, taking naps and taking turns – I learned it all in my Blueberry troop!"

Walt Disney's
# Peter Pan

# Tiger Lily

It was a hot summer night in Never Land – so hot, in fact, that the poor Lost Boys couldn't sleep. And so it was decided that instead of trying to stay in their hideout in Hangman's Tree, Peter Pan and the Lost Boys would camp out for the night in the wild, wild wilderness.

Certainly, they thought, the woods would be cool and shady, and the tall trees would catch any breeze kind enough to blow through. But little did they know how mysterious – and downright spooky – a forest could become once the sun went down.

"It's dark out here," said Cubby.

"And awful quiet," said Tootles.

"Won't you tell us a story, please, Peter?" asked Slightly, who was shivering in his fox suit despite the sticky heat.

"Very well," agreed Peter. "If it will make you all be quiet! I will tell you the story of the very first time I ever camped out in the wilderness – which, by the way, was the first time I met Tiger Lily . . .

"I had made myself a fire, a great big one, 'cause it was fall and the nights were getting cool. I'd just laid my head down on a patch of nice, soft moss, when all of a sudden I heard a rustling in the shadows."

"*Indians?*" the Lost Boys gasped.

But Peter shook his head. "Not Indians," he told them. "That's what I thought at first too. No, this was something bigger. It was a *bear*! It jumped out of the trees, growling and snarling and waving its big, fat paws in the air like Captain Hook swattin' blue flies. I've never seen such a mean, angry beast, before or since!"

"So wha-wha-what did you do?" asked the Lost Boys.

"Told him to get lost, of course. To *scram*! Apparently, he didn't understand English, however, 'cause he just kept charging. Well, I'm not going to lie to you; I started to get nervous. And then, there she was – Tiger Lily – as quiet as a mouse. Without a 'hi' or 'how do you do', she grabbed a stick from my fire and waved it at the bear. And the next thing I knew, the bear had turned around and was running off crying! I suppose Tiger Lily saved my life that night," said Peter. "And it wasn't the last time either. The end. Good night."

"Um . . . Peter," said Cubby, peering out into the darkness, "do you know what ever happened to that bear?"

Peter thought for a moment. "Nope," he said and shrugged. "Probably still out there, wandering around, I guess." He yawned a big, mischievous yawn. "Now stop yer yammerin' and close your eyes and go to sleep!"

# Doctor Doppler, Daredevil

Dr Delbert Doppler didn't know how he had got himself into this mess. There he was, standing on top of a cliff on a solar surfer with 15-year-old Jim Hawkins, who was about to launch them into the etherium on a narrow plank of metal powered by energy-panel sails.

"Hold on, Doctor," said Jim. "Here we go!" Jim launched the surfer off the cliff. In a flash, they were sailing through the etherium, and Dr Doppler was regretting his decision to be a daredevil. Ever since they had both returned from their amazing adventure on Treasure Planet, the two had become quite close. Doppler had thought solar surfing would be a great bonding experience. But now he wasn't so sure.

The unadventurous doctor hadn't expected to get roped into solar surfing. He stifled a scream as the solar surfer rode currents of air and floated towards the port of Benbow far below them. Jim, an expert solar surfer, was in complete control. In fact, he was going easy on Dr Doppler. If Jim had been surfing on his own, he would have been free-falling, rolling and twirling through the air. But he didn't want to scare his passenger.

Nevertheless, Dr Doppler was having a hard time keeping it together. His hands gripped the crossbar so tightly that his knuckles turned white, and Jim could feel the surfer trembling beneath his feet – a result of the doctor's knocking knees. But Dr Doppler wanted to put on a brave face. "Wow, Jim," he said through clenched teeth. "This is awful . . . er . . . *awesome!*"

"Really? You like it?" Jim replied. "Well, then, maybe we should try some more advanced moves. Like maybe a barrel roll?"

"No, no, no, no!" Dr Doppler cried out anxiously. "I mean . . . m-maybe not today. Perhaps never . . . er . . . *next* time."

"Okay," Jim said with a shrug. He steered the solar surfer cautiously down towards the Benbow Inn, where Jim lived with his mum. Five minutes later, he landed the surfer smoothly on a level patch of ground out behind the inn.

For Dr Doppler it was none too soon. He leaped off the surfer and stooped to kiss the solid ground. Then, realizing that Jim was looking at him, he straightened up and cleared his throat.

"Thank you, Jim," he said, a slight quiver creeping into his voice. "That was really intimidating . . . I mean, *exhilarating!*"

Jim smiled. "So maybe I'll take you solar surfing again sometime?"

Dr Doppler flushed, unprepared for the question. "Uh . . . er . . . that sounds terrifying . . . er . . . terrible . . . I mean, *terrific!*"

*Disney's* Aladdin

# Around the World

"**I** can't believe it!" the Genie shouted as he sped away from Agrabah. "I'm *freeeeeeee*!"

He didn't have to hang around in his lamp any more, waiting for yet another master to demand wishes from him. It felt great!

Now the Genie could hardly wait to see the world. He still had some of his magic genie powers, so he sent himself straight to the Great Wall of China.

"Ah!" he exclaimed as he looked over the view of the Chinese countryside. "Now, *this* is what I call a wall! Eh, Al?"

He looked around, then laughed at himself. Aladdin couldn't answer. He was back in Agrabah.

"Oh, well." The Genie scratched his head. "Now what? I know . . ."

A second later, he was in India, staring at a magnificent palace. It was big. It was white. It was an awful lot like the Sultan's palace back in Agrabah.

He shrugged. Not every place could be totally new and different. But for his next destination, he wanted a real change of pace.

"Next stop," he exclaimed, "the Amazon!"

After visiting the Amazon rainforest, he went to the Sahara desert. After that, he paid a visit to the Pyramids, the Rio Grande, the Hanging Gardens of Babylon, the Colossus of Rhodes, Mount Olympus – the list went on.

But, as the Genie leaned against a column of the Parthenon at the Acropolis, he couldn't help thinking that his travels weren't quite as satisfying as he'd expected.

"It's like there's something missing, you know?" he commented to a passing eagle. "Could it be that being free isn't all it's cracked up to be?"

The eagle soared up into the sky, not seeming to have any answers.

The Genie sighed. What was wrong with him? Why wasn't he having more fun?

"Al would probably know," he muttered. "He always had a knack for figuring things out. He and that crazy little monkey, Abu. And, of course, Princess Jasmine – now she's a smart cookie. . . ." He gasped, suddenly realizing the answer was right there in front of him. "That's it!" he cried. "That's what's missing – friends!"

Of course! Being free and travelling was fun. But all the interesting and exotic sights in the world couldn't offer the one thing that Agrabah had – the Genie's best friends.

He laughed out loud. Now that he was free to do anything he wished, he knew exactly what he wanted to do next. Gathering his suitcase, he sped towards the horizon.

"Next stop, Agrabah!" he cried.

# An Uncle Mickey Day

Morty and Ferdie Mouse were oh-so-very excited. Today was their number one favourite kind of day. An Uncle Mickey day! That meant their Uncle Mickey was going to take them out to do all kinds of special, surprising things.

"Uncle Mickey!" the twins shouted when he came to pick them up. "What are we doing today?"

"What *aren't* we doing today, you mean," said Mickey. "I thought we'd start with bowling."

"Hooray!" cheered Morty and Ferdie.

At the bowling alley, Morty and Ferdie discovered that if they rolled the bowling ball together, they could knock at least four or five pins down every time.

Then it was off to the park for some hide-and-seek and a game of catch. Uncle Mickey didn't mind being the finder in hide-and-seek every time. And he didn't mind chasing the balls that Ferdie sometimes threw way, way over his head.

"I'm hungry," said Morty when at last they stopped to rest.

"Me, too," said Ferdie.

"How about some pizza?" suggested Mickey.

"Okay!" the twins shouted together.

At the pizza parlour, Mickey let Morty and Ferdie choose their favourite toppings. Morty picked pepperoni. Ferdie picked black olives. Mickey, meanwhile, had his usual: extra cheese!

"All finished?" asked Mickey. "We'll have to hurry if we're going to go to the carnival."

"All right!" the boys shouted.

After the carnival, where they each won a prize, the boys told Mickey what a great day it had been.

"Well, it's not over yet," Mickey told them.

"Really?" said Morty.

"What's next?" asked Ferdie.

That's when Mickey held up three tickets – and a mitt. A baseball game! Oh, wow!

There was nothing in the whole, wide world that Mickey's nephews liked better than baseball games . . . and popcorn . . . and peanuts . . . and ice cream. And to make things even better, Uncle Mickey caught a foul ball, and their favourite team won. They even watched fireworks at the end of the game.

"Wow, Uncle Mickey! Thank you so much!" said the twins when they finally returned home, tired and full and very, very happy. "This has been one of the best Uncle Mickey days ever!"

"Oh, this was nothing," said Uncle Mickey. "Just wait until next time!"

# Looks Can Be Deceiving

Yao, Ling and Chien-Po missed Mulan. They had become friends in the army – even though when they had first met her, Mulan was disguised as a young man. They forgave her for tricking them, because Mulan went on to bravely save China from Shan-Yu and the rest of the Huns. Mulan was famous; even the Emperor himself had bowed to her!

Now, her three friends decided they would journey to her village and follow Mulan in whatever adventure she might embark on next.

"But what if Shan-Yu is seeking revenge?" Ling said. "He might be looking for us. After all, we did help Mulan defeat him."

Yao thought they should disguise themselves. So the friends donned kimonos, wigs and makeup, and set out for Mulan's village, looking like a trio of women.

When they arrived, the Matchmaker instantly approached them. "And who would you lovely ladies be?" she asked. The Matchmaker was desperate. There weren't many single women in the village, and she had a list of bachelors a mile long to marry off!

"Visitors from far away," said Chien-Po, speaking in a high voice.

"And are you unmarried ladies?" the Matchmaker asked.

Ling said, "We're unmarried, all right!"

"Well, let me be the first to welcome you to our village," the Matchmaker said, ushering them into her house. "Would you like some tea?"

The three men were hungry and thirsty after their long journey. They didn't realize the Matchmaker wanted to see if they would make suitable wives.

"Perhaps you would like to pour?" she asked Yao. He tried to remember the way his mother served tea at home. Yao set out the cups and poured as daintily as he could.

"Cookie?" the pleased Matchmaker asked Chien-Po, holding out a plate.

Chien-Po resisted the urge to grab a fistful of cookies. Instead, he chose one, stuck out his little finger, and took small bites.

Perfect! The Matchmaker was delighted.

Next she asked Ling what his favourite pastime was. "Wrestling," he answered.

Then, seeing the shocked look on the Matchmaker's face, he added quickly, "Yes, I find that *resting* keeps my complexion lovely." He batted his eyelashes.

The Matchmaker led the three back outside, just as Mulan was riding into the village. "Stop! You can't marry them off!" Mulan cried, seeing her friends with the woman.

"I certainly can," said the Matchmaker. "Unlike you, Mulan, these three are real ladies!"

Walt Disney's

# DUMBO

# Lend Me Your Ears

"I think I can, I think I can, I think I can," chugged Casey Jr, the circus train. The train moved slowly around a bend. "I think I can. I think I . . . *Ah-choo!*" he sneezed. Suddenly, he came to a halt. "I know I can't," he admitted finally. The animals and the performers poked their heads out, wondering what was wrong.

"Well?" asked the Ringmaster.

"Casey Jr here has a cold," the engineer replied. "He's going to need some rest before he can take us any further."

The Ringmaster frowned. "But we're due at the fairground in a few hours. What will we do? After all, the show must go on!"

The engineer just shrugged and turned his attention back to the sneezing, coughing and spluttering little engine.

The Ringmaster went down the train, swinging open the doors to all the cages and cars. "Come on, everyone," he said. "Might as well stretch your legs."

The animals lumbered, scampered and pranced onto the wide open field. Next, the clowns and acrobats and animal trainers sauntered out. Some set up crates in the grass and played cards, others rehearsed and a few pulled out packed lunches and sprawled on the ground.

Dumbo the elephant and his mother, Mrs Jumbo, took a drink from the bucket of water the Ringmaster had set out.

Mrs Jumbo gazed around. "Looks like we're in the middle of nowhere," she said. "I do hope poor Casey Jr is feeling better soon."

"Me too," Dumbo's friend Timothy Q. Mouse said hopefully.

Just then a clap of thunder sounded. Raindrops began to fall from the sky. The animals and performers ran for the shelter of the circus wagons. Dumbo held on to his mother's tail, but just as they were about to board, the wind picked up. The gust caught Dumbo's huge ears and sent him flying backwards.

"That's it!" yelled the Ringmaster over the howling wind. "Dumbo, come with me!" He led Dumbo over to the train, climbed onto the front wagon, and motioned for the little elephant to join him.

"Now spread out those great ears of yours!" the Ringmaster said. Dumbo's ears billowed out, catching the wind like giant sails and pushing Casey Jr along the tracks. "The show will go on!" the Ringmaster shouted happily.

"I know I can. I know I can. I know I can," chanted Casey Jr. And then he added, "Thanks to Dumbo!"

# Nemo's Best Shot

"Come on, Dad! We're going to be late!" cried Nemo.

Nemo and Marlin were hurrying through the busy swimming lanes of the colourful Great Barrier Reef.

"Are you sure you want to play pearl volleyball?" Marlin asked nervously. "There are lots of other things you can do. Sponge jumping, for example. Or maybe reef dancing."

"Reef dancing!" cried Nemo, horrified. "No way! That's for babies! I want to play pearl volleyball!"

After they arrived at Sea Urchin Stadium, Mr Ray gave the opening announcements. "Hello and welcome, everyone! Before we get started, let's give a big thank you to Ms Esther Clam for donating today's ball."

Everyone applauded as Esther opened her shell and spat out the pearl.

"Let's play pearl volleyball!" cried Mr Ray.

"Good luck, son," said Marlin. "Just remember what I told you – "

"I know! I know!" said Nemo, rolling his eyes. "When you give it your best shot, even if you lose, you win."

The players lined up on either side of the sea fan net. Ray's Raiders were on one side, and Nemo's team, the Fighting Planktons, were on the other.

Marlin watched anxiously. He was sure that Nemo wouldn't be able to play as well as the other fish because of his small fin.

Marlin wasn't the only one who had doubts. Turbot Trout sidled up to Nemo on the court.

"Coach may be letting you play today," Turbot snapped, "but you better not mess up the Planktons' winning streak."

Nemo narrowed his eyes. Turbot didn't know that Nemo had spent many hours smacking around pebbles in a dentist's office aquarium.

"Just watch and learn," murmured Nemo.

Suddenly, the pearl came right to Nemo. *Smack!*

Using his good left fin, Nemo sent the pearl flying right over the net. The pearl flew so fast, the other team couldn't return it. Nemo scored his first point for the Planktons!

Nemo played like a pro. He scored again with his good fin, then with his tail. And, just to show his father and Turbot Trout, he scored the winning point with his little fin.

"Go, short fin!" cried Turbot Trout. "With a player like you, we're going to go all the way to the Lobster Bowl Clam-pionship!"

"Wow, Nemo," said Marlin after the game. "That was amazing."

"Thanks, Dad," said Nemo. "I gave it my best shot, like you said. And we actually won too!"

# The Hic-hic-hiccups

"What a day!" Pumbaa said as he led Simba and Timon through the forest.

"What a day, indeed," Timon agreed.

"*Hic!*" said Simba.

"What was that?" Timon cried.

"Don't be scared. It's just that I have the – *hic!* I have the hiccups," Simba explained.

"I'll tell you what to do," Timon said. "Forget about it! They'll go away – eventually."

"Forget about it? *Hic!* But I can't roar," Simba explained. And to demonstrate, he opened his mouth really wide. But, just as he was about to roar, he hiccupped! "See?" he said sadly.

"Have you tried licking tree bark?" Pumbaa asked.

"Licking tree bark?" said Simba.

"It always works for me," Pumbaa explained. "That or closing your eyes, holding your nose and jumping on one foot while saying your name five times fast – backwards."

Timon watched Simba hop around on one foot, holding his nose with his eyes closed. "Abmis, Abmis, Abmis – *hic!* It's not working!" Simba cried.

"Maybe there's something caught in his throat," Timon offered.

"There's nothing caught in his throat," Pumbaa said.

"How do you know?" Timon asked.

"I just know about these things," Pumbaa answered.

Suddenly, right on cue, Simba interrupted their argument with the biggest hiccup of all.

"*HIC!*"

And, wouldn't you know, just then the biggest fly you've ever seen came soaring out of Simba's mouth. It flew right into a tree and crashed to the ground. The fly stood up groggily and shook itself off.

"It's about time, buddy!" the fly said to Simba.

Simba was about to reply, but he was interrupted by two voices, shouting in unison –

# "DINNER!"

The fly gave a frightened squeak and flew off, as Timon and Pumbaa both pounced on the spot where it had been just a moment earlier.

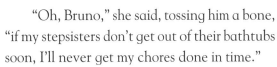

# Lucifer's Bath

Cinderella's stepsisters didn't like the idea of Cinderella going to the Prince's ball.

"But Stepmother told me I could," said Cinderella.

"*Only* if you finish your chores," pointed out Drizella. "Which includes giving our cat, Lucifer, his bath."

"And that reminds me," said Anastasia. "I'll be needing a bath myself."

"Me, too," said Drizella.

"You heard my girls, Cinderella," her stepmother said. "Get their baths ready at once!"

Cinderella already had far too many jobs to do. But she didn't argue.

Once Anastasia and Drizella were soaking in their bubble baths, all Cinderella had to do was mend their clothes, clean the house, wash the curtains and give Lucifer his bath – then she could get ready for the ball.

Unfortunately, her stepsisters wouldn't leave her alone.

"Cinderella! Bring my face cream!" cried Drizella.

"Cinderella! My bath salts!" cried Anastasia.

Each time her stepsisters called, Cinderella had to stop whatever she was doing and take care of them.

When Drizella called for tea, Cinderella went down to the kitchen and put the kettle on. Then she let Bruno the dog in for a snack.

"Oh, Bruno," she said, tossing him a bone, "if my stepsisters don't get out of their bathtubs soon, I'll never get my chores done in time."

Bruno narrowed his eyes. Those stepsisters were the most selfish, lazy, nasty girls he'd ever known – and their cat was just like them. He wanted to help Cinderella. So, when the tea was ready, Bruno followed her up the stairs and down the long hallway.

Just as Cinderella walked up to Drizella's bathroom door, Bruno noticed Lucifer sleeping nearby.

"Woof, woof!" Bruno barked.

With a screeching yowl, Lucifer ran into Drizella's bathroom.

*Splash!* Bruno chased the cat right into Drizella's tub! Then Bruno jumped in himself!

Drizella screamed. Lucifer jumped out. And Bruno chased the cat down the hall and into Anastasia's bathroom.

*Splash!* Lucifer was now in Anastasia's tub. And Bruno jumped right in after him!

"Get out of your tubs this instant!" Cinderella's stepmother cried. "You don't want to smell like that dog, do you?"

Cinderella sighed in relief. Although she still had many jobs to finish before the ball, at least one job was now done. Thanks to Bruno, Lucifer had had his bath!

Disney's
BROTHER
BEAR

# Stay Loose, Moose!

Two moose named Rutt and Tuke were grazing on some grass on a plateau when Rutt lifted his head and moved it from side to side, stretching his neck.

"Tuke," he said to his brother, "you gotta try some of these new stretches I learned. They're just the thing to get your mind, body and spirit back into balance, eh."

"Take off, eh," Tuke replied, his mouth full of grass. "My balance is fine the way it is."

"Aw, come on," said Rutt. "We've been on our hooves all day. Don't tell me you're not feeling a tweak in your back."

Tuke didn't reply right away. "Well . . ."

"Aha! I knew it," said Rutt. "I promise these stretches will fix you right up."

Tuke hesitated, but finally agreed. "Oh, all right," he said. "But nothing too strenuous."

"Excellent!" Rutt exclaimed. He proceeded to demonstrate the first posture. "Try this one: the Cat-Cow," he said. "Arch your back like a cat. And breathe in. Now drop your back, letting it curve the other way. And exhale."

Tuke followed along. He felt silly at first, but after a few rounds of the Cat-Cow, he was really getting into it. "Hey," he said, "this isn't bad."

"You're doing great, eh," Rutt replied. "Now let's try the Downward-facing Dog."

Rutt moved his front and back hooves closer together and raised his rear end high into the air. Tuke did the same.

"How does that feel?" Rutt asked as he held the pose.

"Good," Tuke replied. "Really good."

Rutt smiled. "Tuke, you're a natural, eh!"

Tuke couldn't help smiling himself. "I think you're right, eh."

"Let's try something more advanced," Rutt suggested. "This one's called the Resting Lizard."

Rutt crossed his right back leg over his left back leg, much like a pretzel. He then placed his two front hooves together. He closed his eyes so he could really concentrate and breathed in and out deeply.

Tuke did the same. He was doing fine for the first few seconds. Then he lost his balance. Tuke fell over onto his side and rolled onto his back, coming to rest with his legs pointed straight up into the air.

Rutt was concentrating so hard on his Resting Lizard pose that he didn't notice what happened – until he opened his eyes.

"Hey, all right." Rutt smiled. "You're already getting creative and coming up with your own poses, eh? What do you call that one?"

Tuke scowled. "I call it the Mad Moose," he replied sarcastically. "Now help me up!"

DISNEY·PIXAR
**MONSTERS, INC.**

# Monster Day Care

**M**ike always arrived at Monsters, Inc. at half past eight, put his lunch box in his locker and promptly reported to his station on the Laugh Floor. But one morning, as he came out of the locker room, there was Celia. "We have a little problem, Mike," she said. "The day care teacher is sick today, so we need a sub. And seeing as how you've already met your laugh quota for the month, I thought maybe *you* – "

"Day care!" cried Mike. "Wait just a – "

Just then Sulley stepped in. "Happy to do it, Celia," he interrupted. "Day care, here we come."

"Are you crazy?" Mike grumbled.

"What's the big deal?" Sulley shrugged. "We handled Boo, didn't we? What's a few more kids? We'll eat a few snacks. Watch a few videos. Play a little peekaboo. It's like having a paid vacation, Mike, my man!"

But the minute they opened the day care room door, they both knew Sulley was wrong. . . .

There were monster children everywhere! Swinging from the ceiling. Slithering up the walls. Bouncing from corner to corner. Mike's and Sulley's jaws dropped open. What were they going to do?

Sulley took a deep breath. "We just have to let them know who's in charge, is all," he told Mike. "Okay, kids!" he announced. "Uncles Sulley and Mike are here. It's time to settle down."

But, instead of settling down, the little monsters dived for Sulley and Mike, yelling, "Horsey rides! Yeah!" and "Play ball!"

"I think they know who's in charge," Mike said as an oversized, six-handed monster child scooped him up and tossed him to his twin. *"Help!"*

Sulley quickly intercepted Mike and set him back down on his feet.

"'Paid vacation,' my eye," muttered Mike.

"All we need to do," said Sulley calmly, "is get their attention. Let's see . . . a video?" But the TV was too covered with monster slime and finger paint for anyone to watch it.

A snack? No. Every cracker and fright roll-up had been gobbled up long before.

A story? Of course! Except a four-eyed toddler seemed to be happily tearing the pages out of each and every book.

"How about a song?" said Mike finally.

"Great idea!" said Sulley. And do you know what? It was! They sang "The Huge Gigantic Spider" and "The Wheels on the Monster Bus". Before long even Mike was having fun.

"What did I say, Sulley? I said it'd be like paid vacation, and it is! I don't understand why you were so reluctant," Mike said.

Sulley rolled his eyes. "Whatever you say, Mike."

# The Case of the Missing Vegetables

Of all the things Belle loved about the Beast's castle, the thing she loved the best was the garden at the back. She had read every one of the Beast's books about gardening, and every season she experimented with something new. This summer, she'd decided to try growing vegetables. And now they were ready to be picked.

"Don't tell the Beast," she whispered to Mrs Potts, "but today for lunch I'm going to make him a salad."

"Oh, really," said Mrs Potts.

"Mmm-hmm." Belle nodded proudly. "Yesterday, I saw so many things ready to be harvested. Lettuce, carrots, cucumbers, peas . . . even tomatoes! Can you believe it? The Beast is going to be so surprised!"

"Indeed," Mrs Potts smiled. "Lunch is definitely going to be a surprise."

Belle slipped on her gardening gloves and her sun hat, grabbed her biggest basket, and happily skipped out into the garden.

"First," she said out loud, to no one in particular, "let's get some lettuce!"

But, when she bent down where the lettuce should have been, she found a bed of empty soil.

"My lettuce!" she cried. "Where did it go?"

Rabbits? Deer? Bewildered, Belle moved on to where her tender, sweet, young carrots had been growing.

"Oh, dear!" she cried. "There's nothing here now either!"

There wasn't a single pea to be found. "I don't understand," she said.

But facts were facts. The garden was empty and there was nothing she could do . . . but go back to the castle and look for a book about building fences for next summer's garden!

As she walked inside, empty-handed and disappointed, Belle passed Mrs Potts and Chip.

"What's the matter?" asked Mrs Potts.

"Oh, everything!" Belle sighed. "My whole garden has been robbed." Then she shrugged. "So much for my salad idea."

"Don't feel sad, Belle," Chip said. "Come and have some lunch."

"I'm not hungry," Belle replied, smiling sadly.

"Oh, I don't know," said Mrs Potts, steering her into the dining room. "You might be . . ."

"SURPRISE!" called the Beast.

"What?" Belle gasped. There, laid out upon the table, was what looked like every possible vegetable from her garden, washed and sliced and arranged, just so, on fancy dishes.

"You've worked so hard in the garden," the Beast explained, "I thought it would be nice if I did something for you. I hope you like it."

Belle smiled. What a treat!

August
22

# Eeyore Beats the Heat

One day, when it seemed the sun was shining even more sunnily than ever over the Hundred-Acre Wood, Eeyore sighed and wished that autumn – if it wouldn't be too much trouble – would hurry itself up and get there.

"Something the matter, Eeyore?" asked Roo.

"Oh, it's just that it's so terribly hot," replied Eeyore. "If I weren't stuffed with saw-dust, I think I would melt."

"Well, come with me!" squeaked Roo. "I'm going to the swimming hole to cool off."

But Eeyore shook his head. "Can't do, Roo," he said. "Not with my sawdust and all . . . I'd probably just sink. And that's if I'm lucky."

And so Roo, who felt sorry for Eeyore, but who was also eager to swim, continued on his way.

Soon, another friend came along. And this friend was Winnie the Pooh.

"You're looking a little warmish, Eeyore," Pooh said.

"Same to you," said Eeyore with a sigh. "Same to you."

"Ah," said Pooh, "but I am off to catch a breeze – and pay a call on some bees – with my trusty balloon here. Care to join me?"

"No, thanks, Pooh," said Eeyore. "I never did like feeling like the ground was missing. And . . . I expect that with my luck, the balloon would probably pop."

"Well, Eeyore, I understand completely. Wish me luck, then, won't you?" Pooh replied.

"Good luck, Pooh," said Eeyore. "As if anything I ever wish comes true . . ."

The next friend to come upon Eeyore was little Piglet.

"Hello, there, Eeyore," said Piglet. "Whoo! Are you as uncomfortably hot as I am?"

"Oh, no," said Eeyore. "I'm sweltering. Parched. Smouldering. Torrid. Yes – 'uncomfortably hot' would be an understatement."

"Poor Eeyore," said Piglet. "Why don't you come play in the cool mud with me?"

But once again, Eeyore shook his head. "Afraid mud is not an option, Piglet," he explained. "Once I get dirty, I'll never get clean. No. Go enjoy yourself on this hot day like everyone else. All except me. As usual. I'll just suffer."

And suffer poor Eeyore did . . . until not too terribly much later when his friends all returned with something sure to cool even Eeyore off on this sultry day.

"Guess what we've brought you, Eeyore!" Roo squealed with delight.

"It's ice cream," whispered Pooh.

"Ice cream, huh?" Eeyore sighed. "I suppose I'll have to eat it all before it melts."

And do you know what? He did!

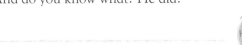

August
23

# A Not-so-relaxing Holiday

No doubt about it: Hercules badly needed a holiday!

"But what about your training!" argued Phil. "You can't stop now! If you're ever gonna be a god, you've got to train like one!"

"If I don't take a break," said Hercules, "I'm never going to become a god, because I'll be so burned out. Sorry, Phil, but I've got to go."

And, with that, he put away his dumbbells and his javelins, cancelled his Herculaid Sports Drink infomercial, and rounded up Pegasus.

"We're off to the Greek Islands, my friend," he told the winged horse. "Sand castles, beach blankets, umbrella drinks . . . here we come!"

And, before you can say 'Mount Vesuvius', there they were, at the finest resort in the ancient world, soaking up the sun and doing absolutely nothing.

"A hero could get used to this," said Hercules as he bobbed in the water, sipping a smoothie and adjusting his sunglasses.

Suddenly, a cry rang out from the beach. "Shark! Shark!"

"Shark?" said Hercules. "In the Aegean Sea?"

But sure enough, a big, grey dorsal fin was speeding towards the crowded shore!

"Help!" cried the people in the water.

"Help!" cried Hercules . . . until he realized he was the one who could save them.

He swam up to the shark, grabbed it by the tail and tossed it up into the sky, all the way to the Atlantic.

"Whew," said Hercules, as the people clapped and cheered.

But not five minutes later, another frightened scream rang out – this time from the hills.

"Volcano!"

From the island's mountain centre rose a plume of thick, black smoke and fiery bursts of molten lava.

"Help!" cried the people.

Hercules knew what he had to do. He raced around the island until he found the biggest boulder. He rolled it all the way to the mountain top, then with one great push, he tipped it over the edge and into the bubbling mouth of the volcano. A perfect fit. The volcano was stopped.

"Hooray!" cheered the people.

Before any more natural disasters could occur, Hercules decided it was time to pack up and head back home.

"Back so soon, Herc?" asked Phil, pleasantly surprised.

Hercules shrugged. "Let's just say that for a hero, work can sometimes be easier than vacation!"

*Walt Disney's*
**Lady and the TRAMP**

# Trusting Trusty

"Tramp!" cried Lady one morning. "One of our puppies is missing!"

"Don't worry," said Tramp with a yawn. "Scamp is always getting into mischief."

"Its not Scamp," said Lady. "It's little Fluffy! She never gets into trouble. Tramp, what should we do?"

"You look inside. I'll look outside," said Tramp worriedly.

Tramp searched their back garden. Then he went to the next garden, and the next.

From a neighbour's porch, Trusty the bloodhound called, "Howdy! Whatcha looking for?"

"My daughter, Fluffy! She's missing," said Tramp.

Trusty's long floppy ears pricked up. "A missing puppy – now that's serious! And I should know. I used to help my grandpa track down missing persons through the swamps!"

"I know," said Tramp. He'd heard Trusty tell that story 100 times.

"Have you found a trail yet?" asked Trusty. Tramp shook his head.

"Well, let me at it!" Trusty loped back to Tramp's garden. He put his big nose to the ground. *Sniff, sniff, sniff . . . .*

"Tramp, have you found Fluffy?" Lady called from the dog door.

Tramp ran over. "No," he replied. "But Trusty offered his . . . uh . . . services."

"He can't smell any more," Lady whispered. "I know he tracked that dogcatcher's wagon and saved you – but he hasn't tracked anything since."

"He helped us once," said Tramp. "I think we should trust him again."

Just then, Trusty shouted, "Look at this!"

He had spotted a bluebird's feather below a window. "That's the window the puppies look out," said Lady.

"Look! A bit of puppy fur," said Trusty. "And footprints!" Trusty followed the trail of footprints to the back of a shed.

And that's where Trusty found the missing puppy! Fluffy was fast asleep under a big tree.

"Fluffy! What happened?" Lady cried.

"I woke up and saw a bluebird," said Fluffy with a yawn. "And I didn't want Scamp to bark and scare it away, like he always does. So I didn't wake anyone. I followed the bird all the way to this tree. Then I guess I got sleepy."

Lady walked over and gave Trusty a kiss.

"Thank you," she told the bloodhound.

"Aw, shucks," said Trusty, blushing. "It weren't nothin'."

As the bloodhound trotted home, Tramp turned to Lady. "See that," he said with a grin, "I told you we should trust Trusty!"

WET CEMENT

# Where's Tink?

Peter Pan was in a hurry to meet Tinker Bell. (Because you know how Tinker Bell gets if you keep her waiting.) Today they had a date for a game of tag.

"Tink!" he called as he arrived at his hideout. He took off his hat and placed it on the table. "I'm home!"

But there was no reply.

How strange, thought Peter. Tinker Bell was never late. He called her name again as loudly as he could. But still no answer. He started to worry.

"Wake up! Wake up!" he shouted to the Lost Boys, who were napping in hammocks. "Tinker Bell is missing!"

"Tinker Bell?" Cubby yawned. "I know I saw her flying around here this morning."

"Yeah," said Rabbit. "She helped me fix my slingshot."

"Well, she's not here now," said Peter.

"Where would she go?" asked Tootles.

Peter thought for a moment. He knew that Tinker Bell liked to fly around Never Land. And she especially liked paying visits to other fairies. But not when she had a game of tag to play with Peter. No, that was not like Tinker Bell at all.

"The question," Peter Pan finally declared, "is not where would she go, but who could have taken her!"

"Oooh . . ." the Lost Boys shuddered.

"Do you mean . . ." the Raccoon Twins began.

"Indians?" finished Peter. "I certainly do. I can see it right now. While you were sleeping, a whole band crept in and stole our Tinker Bell away."

Then Slightly spoke up. "Or what if it was . . ."

"Pirates!" cried Peter. "Of course! Those dirty, rotten scoundrels! It would be just like them to lure Tinker Bell outside, ambush her and kidnap her and hold her for ransom! They probably have her chained up in the deep, dark hold of their ship at this very moment!

"Men!" Peter cried. "We can't just stand here while Tinker Bell suffers in the grimy hands of bloodthirsty pirates – in mortal danger! I hereby declare that a rescue mission be formed at once. Are you with me?"

"Hoorah! Hoorah!" the boys cheered.

"Then let's go!" said Peter. And with that, he grabbed his hat and–

*Ring-a-ling! Ring! Ring! Rrrring!*

"Tink!" Peter exclaimed as his missing (and furious!) friend shot up into the air. "Where have you been? You had me worried sick!"

Tinker Bell just jingled angrily at Peter. She hadn't been kidnapped. She'd been trapped under Peter's hat the whole time!

# A Visit from Jack Skellington

'Twas a hot night in August in Halloweentown
and good old Jack Skellington could not help
but frown.
He knew Halloween was
but two months away,
and his scaring really
should come before play,
and yet, within him restless
feelings did stir . . .
all the ghosts in the town
were beginning to blur.
"I think," Jack declared,
full of determination.
"It's high time that I took
a summer vacation!"
But where in the world does a skeleton go
When he needs to unwind from the grind?
Do you know?
"I have it!" cried Jack, without even a pause.
"I'll call my old buddy, my pal, Santa Claus!"
So he rang up his friend in the chilly
North Pole
and asked the advice of the Jolly Old Soul.
"Jack!" Santa said, with a warm "Ho-ho-ho!"
"I surely can tell you where you should go!
My beach house!" said Santa, "in Summertown.
I'm just back myself, and, boy, am I brown!"
"Sounds perfect," said Jack, "if you're sure you
don't mind."
"Of course not," said Santa. "Now go and
unwind!"
So Jack packed his suitcase and posted a note.
"Gone on vacation!" is all that he wrote.

And what a vacation it was for old Jack:
With the sun and the surf and the sand on
his back;
The feel of the waves on his cold bony toes;
The itchy red sunburn he got
on his nose.
In fact, as he lay there,
applying sunscreen,
Jack almost forgot all about
Halloween.
Every day he was up at the
first crack of dawn
To get in a game of croquet
on the lawn.
Each evening he wished on
the first evening star,
Then hunted for fireflies to catch in
a jar.
And sometimes he'd call up a new friend
or two
And graciously host a backyard barbecue.
But everyone knows that all good things
must end.
And after a while, Jack missed his old friends.
He missed the old graveyard and spooky,
cool nights.
He missed the big monsters and all of their
frights.
No longer did Halloween make old Jack sick . . .
His summer vacation had sure done the trick!
And so, engines recharged and his frown
upside-down,
Jack smiled all the way back to
Halloweentown.

# A Working Holiday

Sebastian the crab loved his busy job as court composer to King Triton. He wrote songs, ran rehearsals, consulted with the King – and he even watched out for Ariel to make sure she stayed out of trouble.

One day, King Triton burst into the rehearsal hall and announced, "Sebastian! You need a vacation! I want you to relax and forget about work for a few days. And that's an order."

"Yes, sire," said Sebastian without enthusiasm. Sebastian wasn't very good at relaxing.

After Sebastian had gone, King Triton assembled his daughters and the court musicians. "Sebastian has been my court composer for many years," he announced, "and I've been wanting to honour him with a grand concert. Now that he's away, we can finally prepare a wonderful surprise for him." Triton smiled. "I can't wait to see the look on Sebastian's face when the big night arrives!"

Meanwhile, Sebastian was at the Coral Reef Resort. "Well, here I am at the most beautiful spot in the sea," he said to himself. "But I am bored out of my mind!"

When he couldn't sit still any longer, Sebastian decided that he would sneak back to the palace for a few minutes just to see how everything was going. He wandered into the concert hall, where he found the orchestra and Triton's daughters about to rehearse. "Sebastian!" cried Ariel. "What are you doing here?"

"Oh, nothing," he said. "I forgot my conducting baton. I never go on a vacation without it." He looked at Ariel. "And what are *you* doing here?"

Thinking quickly, Ariel told Sebastian that they were preparing a last-minute concert for her father. That was all Sebastian had to hear! He immediately set to work rehearsing the musicians. He worked harder than he had in weeks. And he loved every minute of it.

After the three days were up, Sebastian made a big show of returning to the palace. "I feel so refreshed!" he announced to the King. "Thank you, sire, that was just what I needed."

"That's grand, Sebastian!" replied the King. "Now follow me."

Triton led Sebastian to the concert hall, where the King gave a glowing speech about the crab's many contributions throughout the years. Then the elaborate programme of music began. The orchestra played beautifully, Ariel and her sisters sang exquisitely, and the King beamed proudly.

"What do you think?" Triton asked.

"It's perfect!" said Sebastian. "I couldn't have done a better job myself!"

# A Ropin' and a Ridin'

"Yippee-ki-yay!" whooped Jessie as she twirled her lasso. "I'm going to show Woody that he's not the only cowpoke who can do fancy rope tricks! All I need is something to rope."

Bullseye walked over to Andy's open window and stomped his hoof.

"Good idea, pardner!" said Jessie. "I'll lasso some acorns on that tree."

Jessie stood on the edge of the bedroom window. She spied a lone acorn hanging on a nearby branch.

"Next time Woody shows off, we'll just see who's better with the lasso!" cried Jessie as she twirled the lasso over her head.

Up went the rope – just as a hungry squirrel reached for the acorn.

"Oops!" Jessie cried. She had lassoed the squirrel instead of the acorn!

With a squeak the squirrel ran away, dragging Jessie along with him!

"Yow!" yelled Jessie. "I lassoed the wrong nut!"

As the squirrel raced up the tree, Jessie held on tight. When the squirrel hopped from the tree to the roof, Jessie found herself being pulled across the tiles.

"Now that's just about enough!" she cried.

Pulling herself to her feet, she planted one foot against the edge of a roof tile and tugged hard.

"Whoa," commanded the cowgirl.

The squirrel jerked to a stop. But he still wanted to get away. He was about to take off again, when Jessie made her move.

"Sorry, Mr Squirrel, but I don't want to lose a good rope!" And, in a flash, she was sitting on his back.

"Time to break this bronc!" she cried.

The squirrel bucked up and down. "Yee-hah!" Jessie whooped. Finally, the squirrel got tired and sat down to catch his breath.

Jessie hopped off the creature's back and slipped the lasso off his neck.

"Okey-doke," said Jessie. "Now that I've got my rope back, can you give me a ride back to Andy's room?"

But the squirrel just chattered angrily at her. Free of the rope, he raced away.

"Shoot!" Jessie said. The roof was too steep, and her rope was too short. She was stuck! What she needed was a sure-footed creature to help her out. She thought for a moment, then whistled loudly.

A few minutes later, Bullseye burst out of the attic window and trotted to her side.

"Good horse," said Jessie as she climbed into the saddle. "I just did some fine bronco bustin'."

Bullseye whinnied.

"That's right, Bullseye," Jessie said with a chuckle. "Woody can brag about his lasso tricks, but I'll bet he never won a squirrel rodeo!"

DISNEY'S
THE HUNCHBACK
OF NOTRE DAME

# A Major Mess

High in the bell tower of Notre Dame cathdral, the gargoyles, Victor, Hugo and Laverne, began their 45th game of hide-and-seek that day.

"Ready or not, here I come!" called Victor. "And no one better be hiding in Quasimodo's underwear drawer! It's neither funny nor proper." And with that, he leaped over a pile of rumpled clothes and began searching among stacks of books and games and other scattered objects.

The tower, you see, was a mess! Quasimodo had only been away for a few days and still the tower looked like a hurricane had hit it. And why was that? Simply because the gargoyles were slobs!

Quasi had asked them to look after his things – particularly his carvings and precious bells – while he was away. "And of course," Quasi told them, "feel free to make yourselves at home." And, well, they had!

They had tried on his clothes and left them scattered all over the floor. They had leafed through his books and played all his games, without ever putting a single thing back. And they had even used his pillows for pillow fights!

And so it was with some shock and horror that Victor suddenly stopped their game and shrieked, "Do you know what day it is?"

"Excuse me?" said Hugo, peeking out from behind a pillar.

"It's Friday!" said Victor. "The day that Quasi returns home!"

"Oh!" Hugo gulped, gazing at the mess. "He's not going to be happy with us, is he?"

"Oh, but he is," said Victor, "because we're going to clean all this up. If we don't, he'll never trust us again."

"Maybe he shouldn't," muttered Hugo.

"Where is Laverne? Laverne!" Victor called. "Come out, come out, wherever you are. We have work to do!"

And work they did. They folded the clothes. They made the bed. They put the books back on the shelf. They washed the dishes and scrubbed the floor. They dusted Quasi's hand-carved models and carefully put them back. And they polished every one of Quasi's bells.

"You missed a spot on Big Marie!" Victor called to Hugo . . . just as Quasimodo arrived.

"Guys! I'm home!" he shouted.

"Quasi! We missed you! How was your vacation?" the gargoyles asked.

"Great!" said Quasimodo. "You should try it sometime!"

And, after all the work the gargoyles had just done, a holiday is exactly what they needed!

# The Good Old Summertime

The Seven Dwarfs were on their way back home after a long day at the diamond mine. Each swung a shovel in one hand and a bucket in the other.

As they marched through the forest, Happy enjoyed the sounds of the birds singing and the warmth of the summer sun on his face. "Summer is such a wonderful time of year!" he exclaimed.

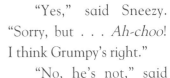

"Oh, yeah?" snapped Grumpy. "What's so wonderful about it?"

"Well . . . the days are longer," said Happy.

"The days are hotter," complained Grumpy.

Doc spoke up. "I like the summertime too. It's a very healthy season."

"Healthy?" said Grumpy. "This heat?"

"Look at all the fresh vegetables and fruit you can eat all summer long," said Doc.

"Like what?" asked Grumpy.

"Like peaches," Sleepy said with a yawn. "I like them with cream before I go to bed."

"And just look at the melons on those vines," said Doc. "They're as big as Dopey's head!"

Dopey grinned and nodded.

Grumpy rolled his eyes and said, "Dopey's a melon head, all right!"

"Don't be such a grump!" scolded Doc.

"Yes, cheer up! Summer's a great season,"

Happy said with a grin.

"It's too hot, I say," Grumpy insisted. "And all those blooming plants make Sneezy sneeze even more!"

"Yes," said Sneezy. "Sorry, but . . . *Ah-choo!* I think Grumpy's right."

"No, he's not," said Happy. "Summer's the very best time of year."

"It's too hot, I say!" repeated Grumpy.

By this time, the Seven Dwarfs had reached a small bridge running over a brook.

"Well, if it's too hot for you, Grumpy, then I have a special warm-weather remedy," said Doc, stopping in the middle of the bridge.

"Yeah?" snapped Grumpy. "What is it?"

Doc motioned for the other Dwarfs to gather around him. They blocked Doc from Grumpy's view as he leaned over and filled his bucket with cool water from the stream.

"Well?" said Grumpy. "Are you going to give me your special remedy?"

"Of course," said Doc.

With a big "Heave-ho!" Doc dumped his bucket of water over Grumpy's head.

*Splash!*

"That should cool you off," said Happy.

Grumpy sputtered with surprise. But he had to admit, the soaking actually did cool him off!

WALT DISNEY'S
# Bambi

## Flower's Power

It was a warm summer afternoon in the forest, and a shy little skunk named Flower was playing a game of hide-and-seek, searching for his friend Thumper. He had been looking for quite a while.

"Come out, come out, wherever you are!" Flower called. "I give up."

"*Surprise!*" shouted Thumper, bursting out of a thicket. "Here I am! *Ugh!*" Thumper wrinkled his nose. "What's that *smell?*"

Flower blushed bright pink. "Sorry," he said miserably. "I sprayed. It happens when I get scared."

"*Whew!*" Thumper waved his paw in front of his face. "You should warn us before you let out that kind of stink!"

"Well *you* should warn *me* before you jump out like that," Flower said. "Anyway, it'll go away . . . in a day or two."

But a day or two was too long for his friends to wait. The smell was just too strong!

"Sorry," Bambi told Flower. "I, uh, think my mother's calling me," he said.

"Me, uh, too," Faline gasped. "See you later, Flower . . . in a day or two."

"Or three!" Thumper added, giggling.

And the next thing he knew, Flower was all alone.

Poor Flower. If only he weren't a skunk, he thought. If only he didn't *stink* so much

whenever he got scared. What was the point? It only drove his friends away. But now it seemed he couldn't even play hide-and-seek! No matter what his mother and father said, as far as Flower was concerned, being a skunk stunk!

And that's why Flower wouldn't have been very surprised if, two days later, his friends had still stayed away. But, to his bashful pleasure, there, bright and early, were Bambi and Faline – with Thumper hopping close behind.

"Want to play?" Bambi asked Flower cheerfully.

"Anything but hide-and-seek!" said Flower.

"How about tag?" said Thumper. "Ready or not, you're It!"

But before the game could begin, a soft *crunch, crunch* of leaves made the friends turn.

"Wha-wha-what's that?" Bambi said, staring straight into a hungry-looking, red face.

"That's a fox!" said Thumper.

"A fox?" shrieked Flower. "Oh no!" He span around and lifted his tail and buried his head in fear . . . and the next thing the friends knew, the hungry fox was running away, whimpering and rubbing his nose.

"Sorry," Flower sighed, blushing.

"Don't be!" said Bambi and Thumper.

And do you know what? Flower wasn't!

Walt Disney's

101 DALMATIANS

# Patch's Plan

"Whoa!" Patch said, "Look at all these other puppies!"

His brothers and sisters were still whimpering with fear. They had just been dognapped and, after a long, bumpy ride in a car, they had arrived at a big, draughty house. But Patch was already trying to work out a way to get back home. He looked around the large shabby room. "Hey," he asked the closest stranger. "Where are we?"

The spotted puppy smiled at him. "Oh, you must be new!" he said. "Which pet shop did you come from?"

Patch scowled at the strange new puppy. "We're not from a pet shop – we were stolen from our house."

Several other puppies heard him and moved closer. "Stolen? Really?" they exclaimed.

The first puppy shrugged. "Well, bought or stolen, we're all stuck here now."

"Maybe *you're* stuck here," Patch said boldly. "Our parents and their human pets will be here soon to rescue us, just see if they don't!"

"I hope so," Patch's sister Pepper said. "I wonder why someone would want to steal us, anyway?"

Patch didn't know. But he was sure that their parents would find them soon. In the meantime, he wanted to make sure he and his siblings stayed well away from all the pet-shop puppies, so there wasn't any confusion.

"We don't know why there are so many of us," the strange puppy told Pepper. "I guess Cruella just really likes puppies."

Patch gasped aloud. "Cruella?" he cried. "Do you mean Cruella De Vil?"

His brothers and sisters shuddered. Their parents had told them scary stories about that nasty woman. Could it be true?

"Yes, she's the one who bought us," several of the other puppies spoke up, while others nodded their heads.

This changed everything! "We have to get away," Patch declared.

Rolly sighed. "We know," he said. "Mum and Dad will be here soon. I just hope we get home in time for breakfast . . . ."

"No, you don't understand!" Patch shook his head. "Cruella is bad news – that's what Dad always says. We have to get away from her now – all of us!" He gestured to the entire group of puppies, bought and stolen. It didn't matter where they'd come from. What mattered was they were in this mess together. "We have to work as a team."

The first puppy smiled at him. "I'm with you!" he exclaimed. "When we're done with her, Cruella will be seeing spots!"

# First Day of School

It was the first day of a brand-new school year for Nemo and his friends.

"Hey, Tad! Hey, Pearl!" called Nemo as he swam into the playground. "Isn't it great to be back at school?"

"Well," said Tad, "I wouldn't go *that* far."

"What do you mean?" asked Nemo. "It's gonna be awesome! I heard this year we get to learn how to sub-tract and speak Prawn."

"Sure," said Tad, "but did you also hear who's gonna be teaching us all that?"

"No," said Nemo. "Who?"

Just then, up swam Sheldon, Jimmy and Jib.

"Hey, Sheldon," Tad called out. "Why don't you tell Nemo here about our new teacher, Mrs Lobster?"

"Mrs Lobster?" said Nemo.

"Yeah," said Sheldon. "Ooooh, they say she's the worst!"

"Who says she's the worst?" asked Nemo.

"Well, Sandy Plankton, for one. He says his cousin, Krill, had her last year – and that she was so mean, he'll never go to school again!"

"And you know what I heard from Sandy," said Tad. "I heard she has these great big claws, and that she uses them to grab students real hard when they give the wrong answer!"

"Oh!" said Pearl. "Don't say that. You're going to make me ink!"

"Yeah," said Nemo. "That sounds awful!"

"I know," said Jimmy. "Sandy says Mrs Lobster never goes on field trips like Mr Ray did. And she sends you home with tons of homework, and makes you stay after school if you forget to bring it in the next day!"

Oh, no! Nemo shud-dered. All summer long he'd been looking forward to this day. And now school hadn't even started yet and already he wished it would end!

"Don't look now," Sheldon whispered, "but I think she's coming!"

"I'm gonna ink!" whimpered Pearl.

Nemo shut his eyes and wished with all his might for his dad to come and take him back home . . . .

"Hello there," said a warm voice. "You must be my new pupils! I'm Mrs Lobster."

Huh? thought Nemo. Surely, this wasn't the Mrs Lobster the kids had been talking about. And yet, when he opened his eyes, there she was, taking the register.

"Jib, Jimmy, Nemo, Pearl, Sheldon, Tad . . . my, what a smart-looking class. I do hope you kids are ready to have fun."

Nemo sighed. That silly Sandy Plankton – they should know by now not to believe every-thing he said. Because now Nemo was pretty sure: this was going to be a great year, after all!

Walt Disney's
# Sleeping Beauty

# Ask Nicely

"Steady, Samson," Prince Phillip said absentmindedly, tightening the horse's reins. "No need to hurry. We'll get there soon enough – and I need some time to think."

Phillip had a lot to think about. He was riding through the forest towards the castle of King Stefan and Queen Leah. Phillip's father, King Hubert, would be meeting him there. So would the girl Phillip was destined to marry.

Princess Aurora. Phillip had heard her name since her birth exactly 16 years earlier. Their parents had long planned their marriage. But Aurora had been cursed by the evil Maleficent at birth, and had been forced to go into hiding until her 16th birthday, when the curse would end.

That meant Phillip had never set eyes on his bride-to-be, nor spoken with her. He had always wondered what she might be like.

"I hope I like her," he murmured to his horse. Then another thought occurred to him. "I hope she likes me!" he added. "I'd better make sure I impress her." But how? he wondered

"I know!" he exclaimed. "I'll make a dramatic entrance. We'll gallop in and slide to a stop right in front of her. That will impress her for sure!" He whistled and gave Samson a little kick. "Come on, Samson! We've got to practise."

The startled horse snorted and gave Phillip a dirty look. He planted his hooves and stood stock-still.

Phillip frowned impatiently. "Come on!" he urged his horse. "Go, Samson!"

But Samson refused to budge.

"It's like you don't even *want* to help me," he muttered. Suddenly, Phillip blinked. "Wait a minute," he said. "Why should you want to help me when all I do is yell at you?" He patted the horse's shoulder. "Sorry, old boy."

He reached into his pocket for a carrot. He fed it to the horse, still patting him.

Samson finished the carrot and snorted. Suddenly, he galloped forward, then leaped up and kicked out his heels. Phillip hung on tightly, gasping with surprise as the horse skidded to a halt.

Phillip laughed. "Wow!" he exclaimed. "Thanks, Samson. That was perfect – I guess all I had to do was ask you nicely! Now if we can just repeat that for the princess–"

Suddenly, he stopped short. He heard the faint sound of beautiful singing. He listened carefully. Who would be out in the forest singing like that?

"Come on, Samson," he said. "Let's go see – if you don't mind, of course!"

Disney's
OLIVER
&
Company

# The Sleepover

Oliver couldn't wait. "Are we there yet?" he wondered as he peered out of the limousine window.

"Don't worry, Oliver," Jenny told him. "We'll be there soon."

At last, Jenny's limo pulled up to the docks. Even before the chauffeur could open the door, Oliver leaped out of the window and began racing towards the barge. Then, remembering Jenny, he stopped, turned around and waved his paw in her direction.

"Goodbye, Oliver!" she called. "Have a fun sleepover!"

Don't worry! thought Oliver. I will!

This was the first time, you see, that Oliver had been back to the barge since he'd gone to live in Jenny's mansion. And, though he loved Jenny dearly, boy, did he miss his friends!

"Tito! Einstein! Francis! Rita!" Oliver called as he ran in to find his four-footed friends waiting for him.

"Hey! What about me?" barked a voice from the back of the barge.

"Dodger!" yelled Oliver. He leaped up on the shaggy dog and gave him a friendly face-rub. "It's so good to see you!"

"So how's life in the mansion?" Dodger asked.

"I can't complain," said Oliver. He told his friends about his latest cruise on Jenny's yacht.

"All those fish!" he said dreamily. Then he told them about her house in the country. "The best part is just lying out in the sun! You've got to come with us someday!"

"Hey," said Dodger, "check out what good ol' Einstein found for our viewing pleasure this evening." He pulled out a scruffy blue backpack and shook it until a video fell out.

"It's *The Aristocats*!" Oliver cried. "My favourite!"

Just then, Fagin walked in carrying a great big tray. "Oliver, my good friend! Welcome back! I do hope you're hungry!"

Oliver's eyes grew wide as he took in the piles of hot dogs, chicken drumsticks and fish fingers (his favourite!).

Oliver and the dogs tucked in and ate . . . and ate . . . until they could not eat another bite. Then it was time for games!

Fagin dealt the playing cards.

"I'm gonna stay up all night!" Oliver cried.

"Whatever you say, little buddy," Dodger said. "It's your night."

So they played a little Go Fish, then some Duck, Duck, Goose. Then Fagin told them some of Oliver's favourite spooky stories.

When he had finished, Dodger turned to Oliver. "So, what's next, little buddy?" he asked.

But Oliver didn't answer . . . he was fast asleep!

Walt Disney's
**ALICE**
in
**WONDERLAND**

# Variety is Best

"What in the world is *that*?" The Red Queen stopped short. It was a crisp autumn day, and she was taking a stroll in the royal gardens.

"What? What is it, Your Majesty?" several of the Queen's servants cried.

The Queen pointed to a tree. "Look!" she commanded. "That leaf. It's – *red*! Who ever heard of such a thing? Leaves are supposed to be green!"

"Yes, my dear," the King said calmly. "But, you see, it's autumn, when many leaves change colour."

The servants quivered, waiting for the Queen's usual cry: OFF WITH THEIR HEADS!

But instead, the Queen . . . smiled!

"Red," she murmured. She looked down at her own red outfit. "Yes, perhaps this tree is on to something. Red is a fine colour for just about anything." She cleared her throat. "From now on, I want *everything* to be red!"

"Yes, Your Majesty! Right away, Your Majesty!" The servants ran off in a tizzy. Soon everyone was busy painting things red.

Later, the Red Queen went for another stroll with the King. "Look, my dear," the King said. "Everything is red, just as you wished."

The Queen looked around. The leaves were red. The trunks of the trees were red. The grass was red. Even the castle was red!

The Queen frowned. Somehow, all the red didn't look quite as wonderful as she'd expected. "Hmmph," she said. "I don't like it. TOO MUCH RED!"

She glared at the servants still holding their red paintbrushes. "Yellow!" she bellowed. "I want everything *yellow* instead!"

The servants ran about. "Yellow paint!" one yelled frantically. "Find the yellow paint!" The yellow paint was found, and soon everyone was busy painting again.

"*Wait!*" the Queen shouted. "I changed my mind. GREEN! No more yellow, GREEN!" Out came the green paint. "No, PURPLE!" Out came the purple paint. "No, ORANGE! No, BROWN! No, PUCE! MAGENTA! LAVENDER! NAVY! LIME! PINK! SKY BLUE! TAN! CARNELION! CYAN! BLACK! GOLD! CREAM! OLIVE! WHITE! BLUUUUUUUE!"

The Queen stopped to catch her breath. She looked around.

"Now that's more like it," she said to the King. "Plenty of variety, just as it should be."

The King blinked. He stared at the purple leaves, the yellow tree trunks and the pink grass.

"Of course, my dear," he said. "Just as it should be."

**WALT DISNEY'S**
**THE JUNGLE BOOK**

# Mowgli's Nap

**M**owgli leaned forward for a better look. When Baloo yawned, you could almost see his tonsils. The big bear closed his gaping mouth and blinked sleepily.

"Am I ever sleepy." Baloo stretched, leaned against a tree trunk and scratched his back as he slid to the ground. "I think it must be time for an afternoon snooze."

"Good thinking, my friend." High above them, stretched out on a branch, Bagheera the panther dangled a limp paw. His golden eyes were half closed in the heat of the day.

"A nap? Not for me!" Mowgli shook his mop of dark hair. "I'm not tired."

"Now, hold on a second there," Baloo said. "Don't you want to go hunting with us after it cools off? You're going to need energy."

"I have plenty of energy," Mowgli insisted. "I have energy right now!" He started to walk away from the bear, but Baloo stretched out a paw and grabbed the boy's ankle.

"Not so fast," Baloo said.

"You may have energy but, if you use it now, you will not have it to use later," Bagheera said wisely.

"Listen to the cat." Baloo yawned. "He knows what he's talking about." And with that, Baloo pulled Mowgli onto a pile of leaves and held him down with one great paw.

"I have energy for now *and* later," Mowgli grumbled. He struggled to get out from under Baloo's big arm. But he couldn't move the bear.

"Good nap, Man-cub," Bagheera purred at the scowling Mowgli.

A moment later, the panther and the bear were sleeping soundly. As soon as Mowgli heard their snores he hoisted up the arm that was pinning him down.

"Good nap, yourself," Mowgli whispered. And he tiptoed off to swing in the trees and drop sticks on the animals below.

Baloo's snores shook the jungle for an hour, perhaps two, before Mowgli returned to the shady napping spot again. He'd had a grand time in the treetops, but the sun and the swinging had tired him. The great grey bear looked so soft and peaceful lying against the tree that Mowgli could not help himself. He curled up against his friend and closed his eyes.

Not two minutes later, Bagheera awoke and stretched his inky paws. The panther flicked his tail under Baloo's nose.

"I'm up. I'm up and ready to go!" Baloo sat upright. Then, spying Mowgli, the bear gave the boy a good shake. "How about you, Man-cub? You awake?"

But the only sound that came from Mowgli's mouth was a loud snore.

Disney's
# ATLANTIS
### THE LOST EMPIRE

# The Power of Reading

Princess Kida and Milo were helping the fishermen pull their nets to shore after a long day of fishing for tuyeb.

"This is hard work," Milo declared.

"But worth the effort," Kida replied. "Tuyeb is an Atlantean delicacy."

Milo's net was filled with strange-looking creatures with long, slimy tentacles and a tail like a lobster.

"You actually eat these ugly things?" asked Milo.

"They are very delicious!" the princess insisted. "The meat is sweet, and the tentacles are excellent when fried. We will have some for dinner tonight."

"I think I'll stick to tuna!" said Milo.

Milo and the princess went back to work. It took a long time to drag in the nets to shore – so long that most of the tuyeb slipped through the nets and swam away.

"There has to be a better way." Milo sighed, wiping the sweat from his brow.

"If there is, we have not found it," Kida said.

When they reached the shore, Milo yawned. "I'm tired. Let's take a break."

They sat down next to a great big statue of a tuyeb with long, metal tentacles.

"What's this thing for?" Milo asked.

"I do not know," Kida replied. "There are many of these statues along the shore, but no one knows why they are here because no one can read the words written on the statues."

"I'll bet I can," Milo declared.

He adjusted his glasses and began to read the ancient words.

"This is amazing!" Milo cried. "This thing is a machine."

"But what does it do?" Kida asked.

"You'll see!" said Milo. "But first you have to power it up with your crystal."

Kida plugged her crystal into a slot in the statue's head.

"Now, watch!" said Milo. He pressed a few buttons and the statue began to hum.

"It's moving!" Kida cried.

"Look out!" Milo warned.

Fishermen on the beach scattered as the mechanical tentacles shot out over their heads, grabbed nets full of squirming tuyeb, and dragged them to the beach.

"It is incredible!" Kida cried, clapping her hands. "This machine will make catching tuyeb much easier!"

To Milo's surprise, the princess gave him a big hug. "You have given us a wonderful gift. Thank you," she said.

"It was nothing," Milo replied, blushing. "All I did was read the instructions. That's the power of reading – if you can read, you can learn anything!"

# Playing School

Now, it just so happened that when the wind changed ever so slightly, and the leaves began to turn scarlet or golden, depending on their preference, and the days grew ever so much more eager to be over and done, this was also the time that Christopher Robin returned to school, as well as the time, not so surprisingly, when his friends in the Wood felt as if they should really do the same.

But *playing* school, as you might suspect, is not as similar to real school as perhaps it should be. First of all, there's no teacher to tell you what to do. And, after sitting at their desks for what seemed like a good three and a quarter hours (but was really just five or so minutes), Winnie the Pooh and his friends came to the conclusion that something rather important in their game of school was missing.

"Perhaps it's time we had a snack," suggested Pooh.

"I don't think that's it, Pooh," said Piglet.

"Our problem," announced Owl, "is that we do not have a teacher. No classroom is complete – and this is a well-known fact – without a teacher. Which is why I'm quite happy to offer my considerable expertise."

"Just a minute, Owl," Rabbit broke in. "And why is it, exactly, that we should let you be the teacher? Some might say – myself included – that I'm better suited to the job."

"You?" Owl scowled.

"Perhaps we should have a vote," said Piglet. "I'd like to nominate Pooh."

"Me?" Pooh said. "Why, thank you, Piglet. I gladly accept. Now . . . what's a 'teacher' again?"

"Really!" said Owl, with no small amount of scorn. "A 'teacher,' my dear Pooh, is the someone who stands before the class."

"To give out snacks?" asked Pooh hopefully.

"No," said Owl. "To give out knowledge."

"Oh," said Pooh. "I don't think I'd enjoy that nearly so much."

"Well, if it's all the same to you, and if anyone cares, I'll be the teacher," Eeyore said glumly. "I probably wouldn't have made a good student anyway."

"That will never do!" exclaimed Rabbit.

"Hi-ho!" said Christopher Robin, returning from a thoroughly enjoyable, and very well-taught, day at school. "Whatever are you up to?"

"Playing school . . . I think," said Pooh.

"Only we don't have a teacher," Piglet explained.

"I could teach you. I learned ever so many things today," said Christopher Robin.

"Hooray!" cheered Roo. "Let's start right away!"

DISNEY's
## Lilo & Stitch

# Homework Helper

Stitch didn't care for weekdays much now that Lilo was back in school. To Stitch they were the longest and most boring days of the week, spent waiting . . . and waiting for Lilo to come home.

And so you can imagine Stitch's excitement when three o'clock finally rolled around and Lilo's school bus dropped her off.

"Lilo!" Stitch would shriek, racing down to meet her. "Play time! Play time! Lilo and Stitch play time!" And, usually, Lilo would toss her backpack onto the porch and they would hop on her trike.

But then, one day, Lilo didn't drop her backpack. And she didn't run after Stitch. "Sorry, Stitch," was all she said. "My teacher says if I don't start doing my homework, she's going to have a talk with Nani!" And Lilo certainly didn't want that to happen! Her sister had enough to worry about – and so did Lilo.

And so, with that, Lilo went inside her house, took out her schoolbooks, and sat down at the dining-room table to study.

Stitch didn't understand. "Homework?" he said, peeking into Lilo's backpack. "What's that?"

"Homework," said Lilo, "is maths problems and a book report and a week's worth of spelling words that I have one day to learn! Now please, Stitch, be a good alien and shoo."

But Stitch wasn't about to give up so soon.

He was back in less than a minute with a basket full of Lilo's favourite action figures.

"You've got to be kidding," said Lilo. "I am not playing superheroes. Can't you see I'm busy?!"

"Noogy Bay!" muttered Stitch. This was very frustrating! But Stitch loved a challenge. Off he ran again. And this time he came back wearing a catcher's mask and vest, carrying a baseball, a bat and Lilo's glove.

"Play ball!" Stitch shouted.

And, for a second there, Lilo almost got up. Then she shook her head. "No, Stitch," she sighed. "If I don't start these spelling words now, I'll never finish them tonight."

Stitch thought for a second, then dashed off once again. Lilo could hear all sorts of banging and slamming coming from her room. It sounded as though Stitch was turning it upside down! Oh, great, she thought to herself. But at least he's leaving me alone . . . .

Then, to Lilo's surprise, Stitch once more appeared before her, carrying a book of crossword puzzles under his arm.

"Lilo play *and* spell words!" Stitch cheerfully told her.

"Why didn't I think of that!" said Lilo. "Stitch, you can help me with my homework any time!"

# WALT DISNEY'S
# Pinocchio

# Boy's Best Friend

Like all little boys, Pinocchio wanted a puppy. And, like all little boys, he promised to feed it and walk it and do everything and anything required to care for it.

"Puppies are a lot of work," Geppetto told his son. "And puppies like to chew things, like slippers – and wood." The toy maker glanced over at the rows and rows of wooden toys on his workbench. "No, I don't think a dog is a good idea," he said finally.

That afternoon, when Pinocchio returned from school, Geppetto had a present waiting. The boy wasted no time in opening the box. "It's a dog," Pinocchio said, trying to hide his disappointment. "A wooden dog." Not wanting to hurt Geppetto's feelings, Pinocchio thanked his father and placed the toy on his bed.

A few days later, as Pinocchio was walking home from school, he heard a puppy whimpering in an alleyway. With a little coaxing, the puppy emerged. "Why, you look just like the wooden dog my father carved for me," Pinocchio said.

Pinocchio wondered what to do. "Well, I can't leave you here all by yourself," he decided. The boy went home and tied the dog to a tree a few doors up the street. Then he sneaked the puppy a bowl of food and went back inside.

After Geppetto had fallen asleep,

Pinocchio slipped outside and scooped up the dog. "Now, you're going to have to be very quiet," he warned.

Once inside, the puppy sprang from Pinocchio's arms and made a dash for Figaro. As the dog bounded after the fleeing cat, they upset chairs and knocked over crockery. "Look out!" cried Pinocchio. Geppetto soon appeared in his night clothes. "What's going on here?" he asked.

"Well," Pinocchio began. Suddenly, the puppy sprang onto Pinocchio's bed, knocking the wooden dog beneath it. Geppetto blinked. The puppy looked just like the toy he had made for his son!

"Could it be?" the toy maker asked. "Pinocchio! You wanted a puppy so much that the Blue Fairy must have turned your toy dog into a real one!"

Pinocchio just picked up the pup and brought it over to meet Geppetto. A day later, when Pinocchio finally found the courage to tell Geppetto the truth, the little puppy was in no danger of becoming an orphan again. "Well," Geppetto said affectionately when he found the pup carrying the wooden dog around the house, "I suppose we have room for two dogs here – especially if one of them walks the other!"

# Disney's ROBIN HOOD

# School Days

Robin Hood was looking forward to a jolly day of giving to the poor (and possibly stealing from the rich), when whom should he run into but a troop of happy children.

"Cheerio, kids!" he called.

"Come play with us!" shouted the children.

"Ah, I wish I could," said Robin. "But, alas, my work is never done. Enjoy yourselves, though. That's what childhood is all . . . hey now! Just a minute. Shouldn't you scallywags be in school?"

"School!" exclaimed Skippy. "We haven't been to school in ages!"

"And why not?" asked Robin.

"No teacher will come to Sherwood Forest. They fear Prince John will jail them for not paying taxes!" said Sis.

"Well!" huffed Robin. "We'll just see about that. The children of Sherwood Forest shall have a teacher, or my name isn't Robin Hood!"

"Will *you* teach us?" asked Skippy.

"Ah . . . well . . . I think not," said Robin. For while Robin Hood knew his sums and spellings backwards and forwards, his science and history had grown a little rusty.

"Then, who?" asked Sis.

"Never fear," said Robin. "A teacher I will find." But where? he silently wondered . . . .

First, Robin went to the village. "I'm looking for a teacher," he announced.

"You know any one of us would if we could," said the miller. "But we already work day and night just to pay Prince John's taxes."

So Robin Hood went back to the forest to seek out his Merry Men.

"Little John!" he called. "The children need a teacher, and I think you're just the man!"

"Why, thank you, Robin," said Little John. "But I don't think I can do it. I've already promised my help to the baker and the blacksmith."

In fact, not one of his Merry Men could help Robin Hood. They were all too busy.

"Is there no one with time to help the children?" Robin sighed, when suddenly he spied Friar Tuck dozing, as usual, in a mossy glade.

"Wake up, Friar!" said Robin, giving him a shake. "Do I have a job for you!"

Robin explained, and Friar Tuck accepted happily. Then Robin headed off the other way. There was one more thing he had to do.

Later that day, just as Friar Tuck was finishing his alphabet lesson, Robin Hood appeared, carrying a heavy sack.

"What's that?" enquired the children.

"Books!" Robin replied. "Courtesy of Prince John's library! Although," he said with a wink, "he doesn't know it yet."

# Happy Campers

It was a warm, sunny day on Ant Island – the perfect day for Princess Dot and her fellow Blueberries to go on a camping expedition! Flik volunteered to be their leader.

"Single file! Forward march!" called Flik. "Follow me, Blueberries. Watch out for those twigs!"

"This is gonna be so much fun, Flik!" said Dot, marching behind him. "Pitching our tents! Making a campfire! Telling ghost stories all night long!"

"Well, we've got to get to our campsite first," Flik reminded her. "The perfect campsite for the perfect campout!"

"Where's that?" asked Dot.

"I'm not exactly sure," said Flik. "But don't worry! I'll know it when I see it."

So on they hiked, until they came to some soft moss beside a quiet stream.

"Is this it?" asked Daisy excitedly.

Flik shook his head. "Definitely not," he said. "Too out in the open."

"We're getting tired," Dot said.

"Chins up, Blueberries," said Flik. "We'll find the perfect campsite soon. I'll bet it's just across that stream."

Flik guided the Blueberries onto a broad leaf. Together they rowed across the water. But the other side of the stream was not quite perfect enough for Flik either.

"No worries," Flik said. "See that hill over there? I'll betcha the perfect campsite is just beyond it."

The Blueberries followed him up the grassy hill and down the other side.

"We made it!" the Blueberries cheered.

"Not so fast," said Flik, frowning. "The ground is too damp here. We'll have to keep looking."

"But Flik! We can't go any further," they complained.

"Nonsense!" said Flik, tightening his backpack. "You're Blueberries! C'mon!"

And so, with the Blueberries dragging their poor, tired feet, Flik hiked on. He looked behind a big rock, but it was too dusty. He looked near a hollow log, but a troop of boy beetles was already there. He even looked inside an old, discarded shoe, which might have actually worked . . . if it hadn't been so stinky.

Just when the Blueberries thought they couldn't walk another inch, Flik suddenly froze in his tracks. "The perfect campsite! We've found it! Let's pitch those tents, Blueberries, and get a fire started!"

But instead of cheers, Flik heard only silence. He turned around and saw that those poor Blueberries, still wearing their backpacks, were already fast asleep!

# Disney's MULAN

## Invincible Mushu

After helping Mulan defeat the Huns and restore the Fa family honour, Mushu had been given back his old job as family guardian. He was supposed to help guard the temple of the Fa ancestors.

One day Mushu was sunning himself on the temple roof, when a big lizard waddled up. He seemed to be staring right at Mushu.

Mushu frowned. "Who you lookin' at?" he said to the lizard.

The lizard flicked out his tongue.

Mushu was offended. "Oh, yeah?" he said. "Stick your tongue out at me, will you? Well, get a load of this!" Puffing out his tiny chest, Mushu spat out a miniature burst of fire, no bigger than the flame of a match.

The lizard just blinked.

"Not good enough for you, eh?" Mushu said. "All right, tough guy. Try this on for size!" Mushu cleared his throat dramatically. Taking a deep breath, he opened his mouth and spat a bigger flame at the lizard.

The lizard crouched, lowering his chest to the ground. Then he straightened his legs. Then he crouched again. The lizard was doing push-ups, as lizards will do.

"Oh-ho!" Mushu shouted. "Think you're tough, do you? Well, Scales for Brains, I didn't spend time in the Imperial Army for nothing!" And with that Mushu crouched down on all four legs and began to do push-ups, too.

". . . Ninety-eight . . . ninety-nine . . . one hundred!" Mushu counted, panting. He leaped to his feet and began to run circles around the lizard. "Just ask anyone," he told the lizard. "I'm the dragon that defeated hundreds of Huns. I could eat you for lunch, small fry."

The lizard just sat there.

Huffing and puffing, Mushu stopped in front of the motionless reptile. He began to box at the air, bouncing around on his hind feet. "Think you can take me on, do you? Well, watch out. I'm a three-time champion in the featherweight division. 'Float like a dragonfly, sting like a bee,' that's me all ri –"

Suddenly – *snap!* – the lizard snatched up a fly that landed on Mushu's nose.

"Ahhhh!" Mushu screamed. He was so startled, he leaped backwards . . . and fell off the roof. He landed on the ground in a puff of dust.

"Ha-ha-ha-ha-ha-ha-ha!" The air filled with the sound of roaring laughter. The ancestors had seen everything.

"Cheer up, Mushu," one ancestor said. "It looks like you have a new friend."

Sure enough, the lizard had followed Mushu down from the roof. "Well," Mushu said, "I always did want a pet."

Walt Disney's
# 101 DALMATIANS

# Cruella Sees Spots

Cruella looked around the living room of the old De Vil mansion and rubbed her hands together. The room was full of Dalmatian puppies. Everywhere Cruella looked she saw spots, spots, spots! At last, her dream was coming true! Cackling with glee, Cruella thought back to the day this had all started . . . .

It had begun as a perfectly miserable day. Cruella had been shopping for fur coats all morning and she hadn't found a single thing she liked.

"Too long! Too short! Too black! Too white!" she screeched, knocking an armload of coats out of the shop assistant's hands. "I want something unusual! I want a coat that has never been seen before!"

Cruella stormed out of the shop, slamming the door so hard that the glass cracked. She needed something to cheer her up. Just then she remembered that her old school friend, Anita, lived nearby.

Soon Cruella stood at the door, ringing the buzzer impatiently. She could hear cheerful piano music coming from an open window.

Just then, a pretty brown-haired woman answered the door. Her eyes opened wide when she saw the skinny woman covered in fur standing on her doorstep. "Oh, Cruella!" she cried. "What a surprise!"

"Hello, Anita, darling," Cruella said, walking into the sitting room. At that moment, a tall, thin man strolled down the stairs, smoking a pipe. But, when he caught sight of Cruella, he leaped back in fright!

"Ah, prince charming," Cruella said, smirking at Anita's new husband. Roger scowled. Suddenly something else caught Cruella's eye. Two black-and-white spotted dogs were sitting in the corner of the room.

"And what have we here?" Cruella asked.

"Oh, that's Pongo and Perdita," Anita explained. "They're wonderful pets." But Cruella wasn't looking at the dogs. She was looking at their coats. Their glossy fur wasn't too long or too short. It wasn't too black or too white. Cruella had never seen anything like it before. It was perfect.

"And soon we'll be even happier," Anita went on. "Perdita is going to have puppies!"

"Puppies!" Cruella shrieked. Suddenly she had an idea that made her smile an evil smile.

"Oh, Anita, you have positively made my day. Now, you must call me just as soon as the puppies arrive. I think they are *just* what I have been looking for."

Pongo snarled, but Cruella didn't notice.

"What a perfectly *marvellous* day," Cruella said to herself as she strode out of the door.

. . . And *that* was how it all started.

# Disney's Aladdin

## Market Day

"What's wrong, Abu?" asked Aladdin. The normally lively little monkey hadn't been himself lately. Abu sat at the window gazing longingly towards the village. "You're right," Aladdin said. "A trip to the marketplace is exactly what we need. Let's go right now!"

The pair had a wonderful afternoon visiting old friends. Abu played with Salim the goat, joked with Kahlil the ox and teased Gamal the camel. He and Aladdin stopped at each vendor's stall to say "hello." Aladdin saw how happy Abu was in the hustle and bustle of the marketplace.

"You know, Abu," said Aladdin that night, "you can invite your friends from the marketplace to the palace anytime you'd like." The monkey jumped up and down, hugging Aladdin and knocking off his hat. "Okay! Okay! You're welcome!" Aladdin laughed.

The next day, Abu disappeared first thing in the morning. When he returned, Salim and Kahlil were with him. "Welcome," said Jasmine. "Please make yourselves at home." But they already had. The goat was chewing on the curtains, and the ox was wandering in the garden, eating the tops off the flowers.

"We can always buy new curtains or plant new flowers. The important thing is that Abu is happy again," Aladdin said to Jasmine, who sighed and agreed reluctantly.

The following day, Gamal and several other camels arrived. Jasmine was not pleased when they spat on the new carpet. "Think of Abu," Aladdin told her.

The day after that, the fruit seller rolled through the palace with his cart. Another vendor came with a pile of smelly fish. Next came the lady who sold dates, and the man who sold pottery.

"Isn't it wonderful that Abu has so many friends?" said Aladdin.

"It is," Jasmine agreed. "But have you noticed that we only see his friends coming and not going?"

"Now that you mention it, I have," Aladdin replied. "Let's find out what's going on." The couple followed Abu as he led his guests out to the garden. What they saw made them gasp. There was the entire marketplace! Aladdin burst out laughing. "I guess the next time Abu is feeling homesick, he doesn't need to go any farther than his own backyard!"

Jasmine sighed. "Aladdin, these people can't stay here." But, when Jasmine saw the sad look on Aladdin's face, she added, ". . . Well, maybe they could come back next month."

And so began a new tradition – "Palace Market Day," which happened once a month. And *that* made little Abu *very* happy!

# Dumbo's Parade Pals

When Dumbo's circus came to town, the animals and circus folk marched in a big parade. The crowd loved seeing all the circus animals marching down the street.

Well, it may have been fun for the crowd, but it was no fun for Dumbo. His feet hurt, and he was *hungry*.

Then Dumbo noticed a peanut on the ground. He picked up the peanut with his trunk and ate it. Then Dumbo saw another peanut, and another. Leaving the parade, Dumbo followed the trail of peanuts all the way to a playground.

"See, the peanuts worked!" exclaimed a little girl with pigtails. "Now we have our own elephant to play with."

The girl and her friends surrounded Dumbo, patting his head. They marvelled at his long trunk and big ears. "What a wonderful little elephant!" they cried.

"Let's have our own circus," said a boy.

"I'll be the ringmaster!" cried the little girl. She led Dumbo to the middle of the playground. "Ladies and gentlemen! Presenting our star attraction – The Little Elephant!"

Dumbo knew just what to do. He stood up on his two back legs. Then he juggled some balls with his trunk. The children cheered.

Suddenly, Timothy Q. Mouse appeared. "Here you are!" he said to Dumbo. "We have to get back to the circus camp and get ready for the show!"

Dumbo nodded, and waved goodbye to his new friends. The children watched him go, looking terribly disappointed.

"I wish I could go see him in the circus tonight," one of them said. "But I don't have enough money for a ticket."

"Me neither," said the other children.

Dumbo was sorry that the nice children he had met would not be able to go to the circus. That night, he felt very blue as he put on his stage makeup and warmed up his ears. Finally, he tucked Timothy into the brim of his hat, then climbed onto a tall platform.

"Ladies and gentlemen!" the ringmaster cried. "I give you *Dumbo, the Flying Elephant!*"

Dumbo leaped off the platform, and his giant ears unfurled. The crowd cheered as Dumbo flew around the tent.

Suddenly, Dumbo spotted his playground friends. They were sitting in the first row! He swept by them, patting each child on the head with his trunk. The girl with pigtails waved at Dumbo. "Your mouse friend gave us free tickets!" she cried.

Dumbo smiled and reached his trunk up to the brim of his hat, where Timothy was riding. He gave Timothy a pat on the head too. He was the luckiest elephant in the world to have such wonderful friends!

# What a Crab!

Nemo was having trouble at school – and its name was Ruddy. The big crab was mean to Nemo and the other kids whenever he got the chance. The trouble was, he was crafty and he never did it when the teachers were looking.

One day, he shoved Nemo into a tide pool and made him late for their coral lesson. Another time, he taunted Nemo by saying, "My dad's bigger and stronger than your dad!"

"Ignore him," Marlin told his son. "And just so you know, his dad *may* be bigger and stronger than I am, but he's certainly not as smart or good-looking."

"My friends and I have tried everything," Nemo complained to his shark friends, Bruce, Chum and Anchor. "But he won't leave us alone. What do *you* think we should do?"

"Just leave it to us!" said Bruce. "We're experts in behaviour modification."

The next day, three huge shadows fell over Nemo's classmates as they played in the school playground.

"Hello," Bruce said, putting a fin around the crab. "You must be Nemo's new little friend."

While Ruddy trembled, Bruce snarled, "We just wanted you to know that any friend of Nemo's is a friend of ours. You are a *friend* of Nemo's, aren't you?"

Everyone looked at Ruddy. "Oh, yeah!" he managed to splutter, throwing a claw around Nemo. "You bet! Nemo and I are buddies. Yessiree!"

"Good!" Anchor said. "Because you don't want to know what happens to anyone who's not nice to our little pal here."

Chum cleaned a piece of seaweed from between his razor-sharp teeth with a spiny urchin. "You should stop by for lunch some-time," he said to Ruddy with a wink.

When Mrs Lobster arrived to pick up the class, the sharks said goodbye and swam away.

Ruddy sidled up to Nemo. "You're friends with three sharks?" he said. "Wow! That's pretty cool! I wish I had friends like that. In fact, I wish I had any friends at all."

"How do you expect to have friends when you're so, well, *crabby* all the time?" Nemo said.

Ruddy admitted that he hated being the new kid. He had decided to pick on everyone else before they had a chance to pick on him.

"If you promise to stop acting mean, I promise to be your friend," Nemo said.

"Deal," Ruddy agreed. "Besides, I guess I'd better be your friend if I don't want your shark pals to eat me."

Nemo didn't say a word. Bruce, Chum and Anchor were vegetarians, but Ruddy didn't need to know that – at least not today!

# A Wonderful/Terrible Day

"What a wonderful day!" Mickey Mouse said to himself. He hummed as he strolled through the outdoor market. The air was crisp. The leaves were pretty shades of red, yellow and orange. And the perfect hunk of cheese was right in front of him.

"I'll take that cheese and a loaf of bread," he told the market seller.

"You're just in time," the seller replied. "I'm about to close up shop."

Meanwhile, Donald Duck was just leaving his house. "What a terrible day!" he said in a huff. He had overslept and woken up with a crick in his neck. He hurried to cross the street, but had to stop for a red light.

When the light turned green, he stepped into the street.

*H-o-n-n-k-k!* A big truck roared past, just missing Donald.

"Watch where you're going!" Donald shouted. He raced ahead to the market.

"I'll take a loaf of bread," he told the seller.

"Sorry," the seller replied. "I'm sold out."

"Sold out?" Donald's eyes bulged in his head. "Sold out?"

Down the block, Mickey Mouse was having a friendly chat with Goofy. "How have you been, Goofy?" he asked.

"Fine," Goofy said as he peeled a banana. He ate the whole thing in one bite and dropped the peel on the ground.

In the market, Donald sulked. He was hungry!

"This is so unfair!" he said. Slumping his shoulders, he started off towards the park at the end of the street. But a second later he slipped on a banana peel.

"*Ooof!*" Donald fell to the ground with a thud. Scowling, he got to his feet.

Not far away, Mickey was spreading out his picnic blanket in the park. All around him, children were laughing and playing.

"Hey, kids!" he called with a friendly wave. He took a big bite of his cheese sandwich and chewed happily. "What a wonderful day," he said again.

Donald kicked a pebble on the sidewalk while his tummy growled. And then, all of a sudden – *thunk*! – a ball hit him on the head.

"Watch it, kids!" Donald shouted. He rubbed his sore head. "What a terrible day."

Just then, Donald heard a familiar voice call out, "Hey, Donald! Come have a cheese sandwich with me!"

Donald saw Mickey waving to him from under a tree. Donald wanted to stay mad. But the truth is that no duck can resist a cheese sandwich. He smiled and ambled over. Maybe it wasn't such a bad day after all!

# Basil's Blunder

I was just settling down in front of the fire at 221B Baker Street when I heard a sharp rap at the door.

"Who on earth could that be, Dawson?" Basil barked at me as he set down his microscope.

The famous detective, Basil of Baker Street, hates to be interrupted when he's working. I stood up to answer the door, but Basil marched to the door ahead of me.

"Yes, yes. What is it?" he asked, peering outside.

There on the doorstep stood a very young, very wet and very bedraggled-looking mouse. Water dripped from his whiskers. He had no hat or umbrella to shelter him from the London rain. He wore a large bag over one shoulder, and in his hands was a damp package. "I'm looking for–"

"No. No. Don't tell me," Basil said. "Let me guess." He started pacing about the room. It is a habit I have observed before. He does it when he is deep in deductive thought. Basil hates interruptions, but he loves mysteries.

"Come in, dear boy," I said, ushering him into the room and taking his worn coat, package and bag. "Have a seat by the fire."

"Thank you, er . . ." The boy offered me his hand.

"That is Dr Dawson!" Basil said. "And you," he said, "are a university student!"

"Y-yes," the boy stammered. "Are you – "

"I'd say you are a struggling student by the looks of things. You appear to be tired from too much studying. But what are you looking for?" Basil's eyes narrowed.

"I was looking for a – "

Basil put his hand up. "You've lost a parent?" he said. "No! An instructor? Perhaps. But wait. You arrived on my doorstep with something in your hand." Basil whirled and pointed at the damp package. "Aha!"

"Yes, sir. It's for – "

"Please don't tell me!" Basil cried.

"Really, Basil, if you would just let the boy speak." I sat down. Sometimes the great detective's reasoning wore me out.

"It is for . . . why, the address has washed completely away!" Basil exclaimed as he turned the box over in his hands. "It's a mystery!"

I leaned towards the shivering student and whispered something in his ear. Basil was so busy pacing he did not even notice when the dear lad whispered back his reply.

"I have solved the mystery, Basil," I announced. "The package is for you!"

Basil looked at me, dumbfounded. "How do you know?" he gasped.

"It's elementary, dear Basil," I replied. "This student has taken on a job as a delivery boy to pay his school bills. And . . . I asked."

# Timon and Pumbaa Tell It All

It was a very hot day on the savannah, Simba, Timon and Pumbaa were lying in the shade, barely moving. It was too hot for the three friends to do anything except talk. Pumbaa had just finished telling a story about the biggest insect he had ever eaten (to hear him tell it, it was the size of an ostrich) and a silence fell over the little group.

"I know," said Simba. "Hey, Timon, why don't you tell me the story of how you and Pumbaa met each other?"

Timon looked at Pumbaa. "Do you think he's ready for it?" he asked.

"Knock him dead," said Pumbaa.

"It all started in a little meerkat village far, far away," began Timon.

"No," interrupted Pumbaa. "You've got it all wrong. It all started near a little warthog watering hole far, far away."

"If I recall correctly, Simba asked *me* to tell the story," said Timon. "And this is the story as told from *my* point of view."

"All right," said Pumbaa sulkily.

"And in that little meerkat village there was one meerkat who didn't fit in with the rest. All the others were content to dig, dig, dig all day long," said Timon. "*I* was that isolated meerkat. How I hated to dig! I knew I needed to go elsewhere, to find a home of my own, a place where I fitted in. So I left. Along the way I ran into a wise old baboon who told me what I was seeking – *hakuna matata* – and pointed me in the direction of Pride Rock. So I boldly set off towards this rock of which he spoke. And on my way there, I . . ."

"Met me!" Pumbaa interrupted.

Timon gave him a dirty look and continued. "I heard a strange rustling in the bushes. I was scared. What could it be? A hyena? A lion? And then I found myself face to face with a big, ugly warthog!"

"Hey!" said Pumbaa, looking insulted.

"We soon realized we had a lot in common – our love for bugs, our search for a home to call our own. So we set out for Pride Rock together. A lot of bad things happened along the way – hyenas, stampedes, you name it. But before long we managed to find the perfect place to live. And then we met you, Simba!"

"That's a nice story," Simba said with a yawn. "Now I think I'm going to take a nap . . . ."

Pumbaa cleared his throat. "It all started near a little warthog watering hole far, far away," he began.

"You always have to get the last word, don't you?" said Timon.

"Not always," said Pumbaa. And then he continued with *his* side of the story.

*Walt Disney's*
# Cinderella

## The Prince's Dream

The Grand Duke was a little worried about Prince Charming. At tonight's ball, the Prince had finally met the girl of his dreams. But, at the stroke of midnight, she'd run away. And now it was impossible to reason with the Prince.

"You must bring her back!" the Prince told the Grand Duke.

"Of course, Your Highness!" said the Duke. "I've already sent the royal guards after her carriage . . . as I told you four times already!" he added under his breath.

But the guards returned without her. The captain bowed to the Prince. "I'm very sorry, Your Highness," he said. "I don't understand what happened. I could see her carriage ahead of us – and an extraordinary carriage it was. It actually seemed to shimmer."

The Prince remembered how the girl's gown and tiara had shimmered too. The Duke sighed as he watched Prince Charming's eyes glaze over. The Prince would clearly be distracted until they found this mystery girl.

"Then what happened?" asked the Duke.

"We turned a corner and the carriage simply . . . vanished," said the captain.

"I don't even know her name," said the Prince, in a daze.

"Well, for now, you must try to focus on your duties as the host of the ball," the Duke advised the Prince. "The ballroom is still filled with eligible maidens."

The Prince shook his head. "There is no other maiden. Not for me. If only she had left some clue!" he cried despairingly. "Some token to remember her by!"

The Duke rolled his eyes. "Your Highness might try investigating your right jacket pocket, then."

Startled, the Prince stuck his hand into his pocket and withdrew a glass slipper! He had been so distracted by his new-found love for the mystery girl that he had completely forgotten about the tiny glass slipper she had left behind on the stairs. He looked at the slipper, then at the Duke.

"I . . . I . . ." the Prince stammered.

"I suggest you allow me to see to the arrangements," the Duke said kindly, taking the slipper. "We'll find your mystery lass, Your Highness."

The Prince nodded gratefully, then turned towards the window and gazed out into the night. Somewhere out there, his princess was waiting for him. "Dreams can come true," he murmured. "After tonight, I'm sure of it."

Little did he know that on the other side of his kingdom, Cinderella was standing by her own window, holding the other glass slipper – and saying the very same thing!

# Celia's Bad-hair Day

"Some encrusted evening," Mike sang to himself as he danced around the bathroom getting ready for his date. He could not wait to see his girlfriend, Celia. The round green monster was in the mood for love.

Pulling his car into the restaurant car park, Mike hopped out and hurried inside. "Here I come, my little Schmoopsie-Poo," he murmured.

When Mike caught sight of his snake-haired sweetie, his heart skipped a beat. The stunning cyclops was sitting alone at a table for two. Her green scales glowed in the candlelight. She was monstrously beautiful.

But, as Celia turned towards Mike, he noticed something. Rather than rustling happily, her hair-snakes were writhing angrily!

"How's my little Schmoopsie Woopsie?" Mike decided to ignore the grumpy-looking snakes. He leaned in to kiss Celia on the cheek, but the closest snake lashed out at him.

"Yowch," Mike exclaimed, jumping back. "Bad-hair day, snookums?"

"Oh, Googly Bear." Celia sighed, running her hand through her serpentine tresses. "It's just awful. I'm out of conditioner, my shower went cold on me, and I've been in an awful tangle ever since. Are they terrible?"

Choosing a seat far enough away from his sweetie to avoid being bitten, Mike looked closer. Celia's snakes glared at him, their fangs bared. Mike tried not to flinch when they hissed at him. But, he had to admit, they were a little knotted, and they did not have their usual body or lustre.

"They're not so bad," Mike fibbed. He blew Celia a kiss from across the table and tried to smile. This was not the romantic evening he'd been looking forward to.

At the next table a pair of many-armed monsters held hands and hands and hands. They rubbed their warty noses together and whispered sweet nothings into each other's many ears. Mike sighed. They looked so cosy. Then he had an idea.

"Excuse me, my sweet." Mike stood up and approached the couple. When he came back to the table, he was holding a large purple hat. "Amelia, Ophelia, Octelia, Bobelia and Madge," Mike addressed Celia's snakes. "How would you like to cosy up in this until we can get you untangled?" Celia's snakes cooed in delight.

"Oh, Googly Bear!" Celia cried. She wound her hair-snakes and stuffed them into the hat. "You even know how to fix a bad-hair day!"

With her hair contained, Celia gave Mike a big hug and a well-deserved smooch.

# How to Win at Hide-and-seek

"Belle," Mrs Potts called. "Oh, Belle!" Belle was sitting in the library, surrounded by a pile of books.

"There you are!" Mrs Potts cried.

"Hi, Belle," Mrs Potts's son, Chip, chimed in.

"Hello to both of you. Were you looking for me?" Belle asked Mrs Potts.

"As a matter of fact, I was," Mrs Potts told her. "I was just stopping by to enquire as to whether or not you would like some tea."

"Thank you," Belle said. "I would love some."

Mrs Potts poured Belle a piping hot cup of tea. Belle drank it, and thanked her.

"You're welcome, Belle," Mrs Potts said. "Come along, now," she called to Chip.

"But, Mama," Chip whined. "I want to stay here with Belle!"

"Belle is busy," Mrs Potts explained. "You'll just get in the way."

"That's all right," Belle said. "I was just about done for today. I'd love to spend some time with Chip."

"All right," Mrs Potts said. "But Chip, you come right back to the kitchen when Belle tells you to."

"Okay, I promise," Chip said.

"So," Belle began when Mrs Potts had left, "how about a game of hide-and-seek?"

"How do you play that?" Chip asked.

"It's simple," Belle said. "One person hides, and the other person tries to find him."

"I can do that!" Chip said.

"Of course you can," Belle told him. "So, do you want to be the hider or the seeker?"

"I want to be the hider," Chip told her.

"Okay," Belle said. "I'll close my eyes and count to ten. One, two, three . . . ."

Chip took off, darting behind the velvet curtains just as Belle called, "Ten! Ready or not, here I come! Hmm, now where could he be?" she wondered aloud.

Belle looked under the table. "He isn't there," she said. Then she looked in the corner. "He isn't there, either," Belle continued. She looked high. She looked low. But she just couldn't seem to find Chip anywhere. "I give up," Belle said. "Come out, come out, wherever you are!"

Chip silently giggled from behind the curtain, but he was careful not to make too much noise. He was having fun!

"It seems that Chip doesn't want to come out from his hiding place," Belle said. "I guess that means I'll have to eat a slice of Mrs Potts's chocolate cake all by myself."

And, upon hearing that, Chip jumped out from his hiding place and called after Belle, "Here I am! Wait for me!"

# Street Cats

"Oh, Mama!" said Marie dreamily. "Paris is so pretty in the morning! May we please go explore just a bit?" The kittens and their mother had spent the previous night in Mr O'Malley's swinging bachelor flat, and were now making their way through the streets of Paris back to Madame's house.

"All right, darlings," their mother replied. "But just for a few minutes. Madame must be missing us terribly. Be sure to stick together!"

They passed a doorway to a jazz hall, where the previous night's party appeared to be still in full swing. "Oh, yeah!" said Toulouse as he danced in the doorway to the swinging beat.

"Come on, Toulouse," said Berlioz crossly. "I'm hungry!"

A few steps down the block, a fishmonger was just setting out his wares in the window of his shop. The three kittens put their paws on the windowsill, licking their lips as they watched him lay out the gleaming fish. The fishmonger smiled at them through the window, then came out of his shop and tossed them each a sardine. "Here you are, my pretty cats!" he said to them.

Yum! Sardines! The three meowed back a thank you and gobbled up the tasty treat.

"The streets of Paris are the coolest place

on Earth!" said Berlioz as they continued walking. "I don't want to go back to Madame's house!"

"Berlioz! You mustn't speak like that!" said Marie. "You know how much Madame needs us . . . ." Suddenly, she broke off. Her brothers followed her gaze, which was directed at the window of a fancy pet shop. "Oh, my!" she cried out delightedly. "Look at those!" In the window of the shop were several jewelled cat collars, all in different shades of the finest leather. Marie thought they were simply beautiful – especially the pink one. "I must say, the streets of Paris are a wonderful place!" Marie said dreamily.

Just then, they heard a deep barking. A moment later, a huge dog came bounding around the corner. The kittens froze in fear for a moment. Then all three of them turned and scampered back down the street in the direction of their mother and Mr O'Malley, with the dog hot on their heels.

"Paris is a fine city," said Berlioz, panting, as he raced down an alleyway. Darting behind some dustbins, the kittens were able to lose the snarling dog.

"Yes," replied Marie. "But I'm not sure how I feel about the Parisians – particularly the canine kind!"

# Disney's
# Lilo & Stitch

# Travelling at the Speed of Stitch

Stitch was bored. Everyone seemed to have somewhere to go and something to do during the day but him. Lilo went to school. Nani went to work. And Jumba and Pleakley headed off to serve beach-goers at their new snack stand, the Galactic Burger.

So Stitch decided he needed a job. He and Lilo looked through the news-paper, searching for a job just right for a small, blue alien with a huge love of adventure. "Listen," said Lilo, pointing to an advert. "'Wanted: tour guide. Must have an outgoing personality and lots of energy.' That's you!"

So, the next morning, Stitch arrived at the tour agency, wearing his best Hawaiian shirt and a big smile. The woman doing the inter-view thought he was pretty scary-looking, but a group of tourists was arriving from the airport any minute and no one else had turned up to apply for the job. "You're hired!" she said.

"Aloha!" Stitch exclaimed when the holidaymakers arrived. He stacked leis on them up to their eyeballs and shook their hands enthusiastically. "Welcome onto the Hawaiian galaxy!" He showed them to a tour bus and pressed down on the accelerator as far as it would go. "Palm trees!" he yelled as the scenery passed by in a blur. "Pineapples!" he shouted as they drove through a fruit stand. Finally, the bus screeched to a stop at the beach.

"Surfing!" Stitch announced, hurling his group onto surfboards and pushing them out to sea. After being battered by the waves, the tourists were eventually tossed onto the beach.

Stitch herded them over to a barbecue. "Luau!" he explained.

"Now, that's more like it!" an elderly woman said, collapsing onto a bench.

"I'm starving," admit-ted a man with a lobster still hanging on to his Bermuda shorts.

But, instead of food, Stitch returned with several flaming torches. Nani's friend, David, had taught Stitch how to juggle fire. The little alien was sure the tourists would want to learn too. Thank goodness Stitch just happened to bring along a fire extinguisher!

The last stop on Stitch's tour was the 24-hour Hula Marathon. He gave his guests grass skirts and insisted they dance until they dropped as he played the ukulele.

When the holidaymakers returned to the tour agency that night, they emerged from the bus exhausted, battered, bruised and confused. The first thing they saw was the sign on the front of the tour agency: HAWAII: THE MOST RELAXING PLACE ON EARTH. Unless, of course, your tour guide happens to be from the planet Turo!

# The Hottest Thrill Ride Ever

Scout Leader Kronk wanted to reward his pupils for learning to speak Squirrel. He decided to fix the roller coaster hidden inside Kuzco's castle, so they could have a ride after they took their Squirrel 101 final exam. Kronk headed into the entrance chamber. He jumped when a small shadow slid across the floor in front of him. It was Yzma – still as bad-tempered a cat as Kronk had ever met.

"Do you know where you are standing?" Yzma asked Kronk, with a smug purr.

"Over the trapdoor that leads to the roller coaster," replied Kronk.

"Isn't that dangerous?" said Yzma, curling her tail around his leg.

"It's safe as long as no one pulls the lever," Kronk replied.

"What lever?" Yzma asked slyly.

"This one," said Kronk. "Oops!"

Down they went, right through the trapdoor.

"Ouch!" Kronk cried when he landed in the roller-coaster car. To Yzma's surprise, she landed right next to him.

The out-of-control coaster car headed into a dark tunnel.

"Hold on. It's going to be a bumpy ride," said Kronk.

"You don't know the half of it, you dolt!" Yzma cried. "The brakes don't work and the tracks are broken!"

"Then you *really* better hold on," said Kronk.

"I have paws! I can't hold on," Yzma said.

"I'll hold you," said Kronk. "But don't scratch!"

Kronk grabbed Yzma and down they plunged.

"AAAAAHHHH!" screamed Kronk.

"MEEOOOWWW!" howled Yzma.

"In Squirrel that's pronounced 'chit-chit-chitter-chit'," said Kronk.

"Who cares!" yelled Yzma. "Here comes another hill!"

"*Yikes*!" yelled Kronk as they raced around a corner.

Then they saw the broken track. Kronk jumped out of his seat and landed in front of the roller coaster. Bracing himself against the car, he used his feet as brakes. The car slowed and finally stopped, just inches away from a giant hole in the track.

"Ouch, ouch, ouch!" Kronk cried, dancing up and down on his smoking feet.

"Serves you right for pulling that lever," said Yzma.

"Yeah," said Kronk with a goofy smile. "But, when I fix the brakes and the track, this'll be the hottest thrill ride ever!"

*Walt Disney's*
**Lady** and the **TRAMP**

# A Rainy Night Out

"Yip!" Scamp barked at the squirrel nibbling on an acorn in the grass. His brother and sisters were taking a nap under the big oak tree, and there was nobody else around to have fun with.

"Yip!" Scamp barked again, and the squirrel darted across the lawn. Scamp gave chase. The squirrel zipped up a lamppost and leaped onto a nearby tree branch. With a whimper, Scamp sat down and thumped his tail on the sidewalk. That was the problem with squirrels. They always got away too easily.

Disappointed, Scamp trotted along the pavement, stopping when he got to an open space. The grass here was tall, and butterflies flitted from wildflower to wildflower.

"Yip! Yip!" Scamp raced through the tall grass. He chased the butterflies to the end of the open space and back again.

It was getting dark. Scamp decided it was time to head home. He hadn't caught a single butterfly, but he'd had fun trying. He couldn't wait to get home and tell his brother and sisters about the new game he'd invented. They'd be so impressed!

Scamp trotted up to the front porch and tried to get through the doggie door. *Thunk*! His nose hit the wood, but it didn't move. The door was locked!

"Yip! Yip! I'm home!" he barked. "Let me in!"

Scamp sat there for several minutes, barking. Nobody came to the door. Suddenly – *boom*! – thunder echoed overhead. Lightning flashed and rain began to fall.

Scamp bolted over to the big oak tree, sat down and covered his eyes with his paws. Thunderstorms were scary!

"I'm not going to cry," he told himself as his eyes started to mist over. He shivered in the dark. He'd probably catch a cold by morning!

Scamp let out a little whimper and moved even closer to the tree trunk. He buried his wet nose in his wet paws and closed his eyes.

Scamp was just falling asleep when a sound made him start. Somebody was coming up the drive!

By the time Jim Dear and Darling were out of the taxi, Scamp was dashing across the lawn as fast as he could go. He bolted through the door just as it opened.

"Scamp, you're soaking wet!" Darling declared as the puppy found his brother and sisters napping in front of the fire. And, as he lay down among them, Jim Dear came over with a warm towel to dry him off.

Home, sweet home, Scamp thought happily, as he drifted off to sleep.

Walt Disney's
# Peter Pan

# We're Going on a Picnic

"Cap'n?" Mr Smee knocked softly on Captain Hook's door. There was no answer. The chubby first mate pushed his way inside, carrying a breakfast tray. "I've got breakfast, Cap'n."

"I'm not hungry!" Captain Hook replied. "Go away!"

"But, Cap'n. You have to eat." Smee was getting worried. The Captain hadn't eaten in days. In fact, he hadn't even got out of bed! "I know you feel bad about Pe–" Smee stopped himself from saying the dreaded name just in time, "–that flying boy. And the croc – I mean – that ticking reptile, too." Captain Hook was really angry about being beaten by Peter again. Even worse, Peter had set the crocodile right back on Captain Hook's trail. "But we haven't seen hide nor scale of either of them for a week. I think the coast is clear."

There was no reply from Captain Hook.

Smee thought for a minute. "I know how to cheer you up!" he cried. "We'll have a nice old-fashioned picnic! Won't that be lovely!"

Again, silence from Captain Hook.

"Ah-ah-ah! No arguments!" Smee left the breakfast tray and hurried down to the galley. A picnic on Mermaid Island was just what the doctor ordered!

Smee whistled merrily as he made herring-and-pickle sandwiches (Captain Hook's favourite) and packed them in a wicker basket. This was Hook's day! Smee carefully folded a gingham tablecloth and placed it in the basket, along with his tin whistle. He was going to make sure that Hook had a good time, whether he wanted to or not!

Once the picnic basket was packed, Smee called down to Hook, "It's time to go, Cap'n!"

After a while, Captain Hook finally appeared on deck, blinking in the sunlight. "Fine," he said grumpily. "But I know I'm not going to have fun!"

Smee let the rowing boat down into the water and Hook began to climb down the rope ladder. Once he was safely in the boat, Smee picked up the picnic basket.

*TICK TOCK TICK TOCK TICK TOCK.*
"Smee!" cried Hook. "Help me!"

Smee peeked over the side of the ship. The crocodile was about to take a bite out of the boat!

In a panic, he threw the only thing he had on hand – the picnic basket. It landed right in the crocodile's open mouth. The crocodile stared at Smee in surprise. Then, without a sound, it slipped back under the water.

"My picnic!" cried Smee. "My tin whistle!"

"Next time you have any smart ideas about cheering me up," said the Captain, glaring at his first mate, "keep them to yourself!"

# The Journey Begins

Bernard couldn't believe this was really happening. Even though he was a caretaker, he had been selected by the Rescue Aid Society to come to the aid of a little girl named Penny, who appeared to be in grave danger. And what's more, he, Bernard, had been selected over all the other mice to be partners with the very beautiful and clever Miss Bianca. It was Bernard's first rescue mission ever and, even though he was very nervous, he was excited to get started.

Bernard had got himself packed and ready to go in minutes, and now he had arrived to pick up Miss Bianca.

"I'll just be a few more moments, darling!" she called to him as he waited outside her door.

"Uh, okay, Miss Bianca!" he called back, glancing quickly at his watch.

Just as soon as Miss Bianca had finished packing, they'd be on their way . . . .

"Uh, Miss Bianca?" called Bernard after a while. "We really ought to be going, I think. We don't want to miss our flight!"

"All right, darling!" said Miss Bianca. "Come give me a hand with this suitcase, please!"

Bernard found Miss Bianca trying to close her overstuffed suitcase. She had already packed several boxes as well. "Are you quite sure you'll be needing all those evening gowns,

Miss Bianca?" Bernard panted as he sat on the bag and tried to zip it up. "And that tea set? And 14 pairs of shoes?"

"A lady must be prepared for anything, darling," she crooned. "Now, I'll just put on my hat and we'll be off."

Bernard gave a final bounce on the suitcase and was able to snap it closed. After what seemed like hours, Miss Bianca appeared at last in a cloud of dizzying perfume. She was wearing a beautifully cut travelling cape and a stunning little hat.

"I'll take that!" said Bernard as Miss Bianca reached for the suitcase. It felt as though it was full of bricks, but Bernard managed to manoeuvre it through the door, where he grabbed his much lighter bag in his other hand.

"Darling," Miss Bianca said sweetly as they headed to the airport, "please don't fret. Everyone knows that flights are always delayed!"

Even when the plane is an albatross? Bernard wondered to himself. Yes, Miss Bianca and Bernard certainly made an unusual team. But he was sure now that they would get the rescue job done.

Just as long as he didn't drop her suitcase on his toe!

# DISNEY'S THE LITTLE MERMAID

# In Hot Water

Ariel could hardly believe that her plan was going so well. She had convinced Ursula, the sea witch, to change her from a mermaid into a human. Even though Ariel had paid for the transformation with her voice, she had already found her beloved Prince Eric. The only problem was that he didn't recognize her. And Ariel couldn't speak to explain who she was.

But Ariel wasn't worried. She knew he would fall in love with her, voice or no voice. And then they would be happy together forever.

"Come along, my dear," a female servant said, leading Ariel into a spacious room with sky-blue walls.

Ariel almost tripped on the edge of a rug, but caught herself just in time. She still wasn't used to her brand-new legs.

She put one hand into the pocket of her sailcloth dress to make sure that Sebastian was still inside. She was glad he was with her – having him nearby made her feel more at home.

"All right, let's get you cleaned up first," the woman said. "It'll be time for dinner soon."

As the woman bustled about, Ariel had a chance to look around the room. There were large windows along one wall and an ornate lantern hanging from the ceiling. There was also a large, shell-shaped bath filled with water.

Ariel watched curiously as the servant threw some white powder into the bath. Suddenly, the water fizzed with a huge pile of bubbles! Ariel gasped, delighted, as bubbles floated up out of the water towards the ceiling. She raced forward and leaped right into the bath, splashing water and bubbles everywhere.

Forgetting that she couldn't breathe under water any more, she dived beneath the bubbles. She came up coughing and wiped the water out of her eyes.

"Ahhhh!" Sebastian sputtered, swimming out of her pocket. He spat out a mouthful of bubbles. "What do these humans do to nice, clean water?"

The servant looked alarmed. "Oh, my! Did I see something move in there?"

Ariel shook her head, quickly shoving Sebastian back into her pocket.

"Well," the servant said. "You can't take a bath in that dress. Let's hang it up to dry."

Ariel was a little worried about Sebastian, but she did as the woman said. Soon the sailcloth dress was hanging on a towel rack.

Oh, well, Ariel thought. I'm sure Sebastian can take care of himself. Knowing him, he'll probably go and find the kitchen. I wonder what the cook is like? I hope he doesn't like seafood!

# Hot on the Trail

"Over here!" Simba said, sniffing the trail. "It's going this way!"

"Yup, this way," Nala said with a nod, sniffing a stick. "And not long ago."

"I saw that stick first," Simba said. Nala was a good tracker, but Simba had learned from an expert – his mum. She was one of the best hunters in the pride.

"Hmm," Nala said with a sniff. "So what are we following then, master tracker? Can you tell me that?"

Simba was silent. They had seen some footprints, but they weren't clear enough to read. They'd also seen some dark wiry hair on a log, but that could belong to lots of animals.

"Something that isn't very graceful," Simba said. They had seen lots of crushed grass and broken sticks.

"Mmm-hmm." Nala nodded impatiently.

"A rhino!" Simba said confidently.

"A rhino?" Nala rolled onto her back, laughing. "Simba, you crack me up!"

"What?" Simba couldn't hide the hurt in his voice. It *might* be a rhino!

"The footprints aren't big enough," Nala said. "It's Rafiki, the baboon."

Now, it was Simba's turn to laugh. "Rafiki likes the trees, he doesn't use trails like a hyena!" The giggle died in Simba's throat and he felt the fur on the back of his neck stand up.

Hyenas were clumsy and had dark wiry hair . . . .

Nala didn't say anything, but her fur was standing up a little too.

The two lions walked in silence. Ahead of them they heard noises – thrashing and grunting.

"Simba," Nala whispered, "maybe we should turn back."

"Just a little further," Simba whispered. They were almost there!

The young lions crept through the grass on their bellies as quietly as they could. The grunting and thrashing grew louder. They could see a dust cloud rising. Simba stifled a growl. Something about the smell and the sound was familiar, but Simba could not put his paw on it.

As they crept closer, two bodies came into view by the side of a termite mound. Simba pounced!

"Pumbaa! Timon!" he shouted, landing between his friends.

"Simba!" the warthog said, grinning. Termites dripped out of his muddy mouth. "Want some?"

Timon held a handful of wriggling insects towards Nala. "There are plenty to go around."

"Uh, no thanks," Nala said as she came out of the grass, giggling. She shot a look at Simba. "I think I'll wait for the master tracker to hunt me up some lunch!"

# Snow White's Thank-you Present

"I don't know how I can ever thank them," Snow White said to her new husband, the Prince. The two of them were on their way to visit the Dwarfs and give them a special present – a meal fit for seven kings!

Snow White looked at the dishes and hampers filled with delicious food. "It just doesn't seem like enough," she said with a sigh. "They saved my life!"

"I'm sure seeing you happy is thanks enough," the Prince said, putting his arm around Snow White. "They don't want riches, and they seem quite happy living the way they do."

Snow White had to agree and, as the cosy Dwarf cottage came into view, she perked up. She could not wait to see her little friends! "Yoo-hoo!" she called as she dashed from the coach. "Sneezy? Happy? Bashful?"

Snow White knocked on the door, but there was no answer. "They must not be home yet," she said to the Prince. "We'll have just enough time to get everything ready."

Snow White went inside and set the table and tidied the house, humming while she worked. She was so excited to see her friends that she couldn't help checking the windows for a sign of them every few minutes. As the sun set, the princess began to worry.

"They're awfully late!" she said. The

Prince agreed. It was getting dark.

"Perhaps we should go and find them." The Prince strode outside and unhitched one of the horses from the coach. Together the Prince and Princess set off to find the Dwarfs.

At last they reached the mine. Holding up lanterns, they saw at once what the trouble was. A tree had fallen over the mine entrance. The Dwarfs were trapped!

"Snow White, is that you?" Doc called through a small opening.

"Are you all right?" Snow White asked.

"We're fine, dear. Just fine," Doc told her.

"No, we're not," Grumpy said, rather grumpily. "We're stuck!"

"Don't worry," the Prince said. "We'll have you out in no time."

Hitching his horse to the big tree, the Prince pulled it away from the mine so the Dwarfs could get out.

Snow White embraced each dusty Dwarf as he emerged. She even hugged Dopey twice! "Now let's get you home," she said.

Back at home, the Dwarfs were thrilled to see the fine meal laid out on their table.

"How can we ever thank you?" Doc said, wringing his hat. "You saved our lives."

"Don't be silly." Snow White blushed. "Seeing you happy is thanks enough."

# Walt Disney's
# Bambi

## Winter Nap

Bambi nosed under the crunchy leaves, looking for fresh grass. There was none. He looked up at the trees, but there were no green leaves there either. Food was getting scarce in the forest.

"Don't worry, Bambi," Thumper said when he saw the confused look in Bambi's eyes. "We'll get through the fall and winter. Dad says we always do. We find what we can when we can, and we always make it until spring."

Bambi sighed and nodded. Thumper's dad was smart. He knew lots of things about the forest.

"Besides, it's better to be awake than napping all winter. Yech!" Thumper hated to go to bed, even at bedtime.

"Napping?" Bambi didn't know that some animals slept through the winter months.

"Sure. You know, like Flower, and the squirrels, and the bears. They hole up for months. Haven't you noticed the chipmunks putting their acorns away the past couple of months?" Thumper pointed towards an oak tree.

Bambi nodded.

"That's their food for the winter. As soon as it gets cold enough, they'll just stay inside and sleep," Thumper explained.

"But how will they know when it's time to wake up?" Bambi couldn't imagine life in the forest without all the other animals.

Thumper tapped his foot to think. It was a good question. And, since he had never slept through the winter, he wasn't sure of the answer. "Let's go ask Flower." They headed for the young skunk's den.

"Hello," Flower said.

"Flower, you sleep all winter, right?" Thumper asked.

"It's called hibernation." Flower yawned a big yawn. "Excuse me," he said, blushing.

"So, Bambi wants to know who wakes you up in the spring," Thumper said.

"You'll be back, won't you, Flower?" Bambi asked worriedly.

The little skunk giggled. "Oh, we always come back. Just like the grass and the flowers and the leaves," Flower explained. "I never thought about what wakes us up before. It must be the sun, I guess."

Bambi smiled. He didn't know the grass and leaves would come back in the spring too! He was feeling much better about the forest's winter nap.

Suddenly, Thumper started laughing. He rolled on his back and pumped his large hind feet in the air.

"What is it?" Bambi and Flower asked together.

"You really are a flower, Flower!" Thumper giggled. "You even bloom in the spring!"

# DISNEY'S POCAHONTAS

## A Big Buzz

Flit let out a big sigh. Pocahontas was spending so much time with John Smith that she never had time for him any more! He buzzed along behind the pair, following them everywhere. But Pocahontas was too distracted to play with him.

*Buzzz, buzzz.* Flit was grateful that his speedy wings made a noise when he flew. At least Pocahontas could hear him – even if she pretended she didn't.

"Look at this, John," Pocahontas said, crouching down in the path. "Fresh deer tracks."

John leaned over to inspect the prints left behind in the mud. Flit buzzed down too. There were two sizes of prints – large and small.

"A mother and her fawn," John said. He leaned forward for a closer look, accidentally pushing Flit out of the way.

"They're probably looking for food before the snows come, so they'll be fat enough to make it through the winter," Pocahontas explained.

John got to his feet. "I hope they find it."

Pocahontas smiled up at him, then stood too. Flit buzzed up a second later, just as John lifted his hand to push a lock of hair off Pocahontas's face. Once again, Flit was shoved away.

*Buzzzzzzzz! Buzzzzzzzzz!* That was it! Flit had had enough of being ignored!

Flit flapped his buzzing wings faster and faster. Then he began to fly in a circle around John and Pocahontas. *Zzzzzzzzzzz!*

"Do you think he's trying to tell us something?" John asked, leaning towards Pocahontas.

"I don't know," she replied. She leaned in closer to John too. Soon they were nose to nose, looking into each other's eyes.

Flit gave up. He stopped buzzing and flopped to the ground, landing in one of the deer tracks. He was exhausted.

"What was that about, Flit?" Pocahontas asked, scooping him up with a laugh.

Flit was still panting. He wasn't even sure he could fly any more. He gazed up at Pocahontas, his eyes wide and his shoulders slumped.

"That is one exhausted hummingbird," John said.

Pocahontas stroked Flit's blue feathers, then leaned forward and kissed him on the end of his long, pointed beak. Then she set him gently on her shoulder.

"You just ride here for a while," she told him. Flit grinned happily as John and Pocahontas continued on through the forest. Mission accomplished!

# Come Out, Whatever You Are!

The toys in Andy's room were in a panic. There was something in the wardrobe – and it was alive!

Passing by the slightly open door, Rex had seen some red lights blinking in the darkness. "Buzz, Woody, come quick!" he had called, terror in his voice.

The cowboy and the space ranger approached the wardrobe, the rest of the toys crowding behind them.

"What do you think it is?" asked Jessie. She picked up Lenny and pointed the binoculars at the wardrobe door, but it was too dark to see.

Woody walked right up to the wardrobe and called, "Hello in there, and welcome to Andy's room. Come on out. There's nothing to be afraid of."

But the thing with the red blinking lights stayed right where it was.

"I get it, a shy type," Hamm guessed. The piggy bank jingled the coins in his body. "Show your face and there's a reward in it for you."

When there was no response, Jessie grabbed her lasso. "I hate to drag you out, cowpoke, but you leave me no choice," she said. The cowgirl swung her rope into the darkness. But, when she tried to pull it back out, it wouldn't budge.

"Oooh, the strong, silent type," said Bo Peep.

Buzz tried next. "In the name of Star Command, I, Buzz Lightyear, space ranger, demand that you show yourself! I have a laser out here, and I'm not afraid to use it," he said in an official-sounding voice.

The stranger in the wardrobe didn't move. Buzz turned to Rex, who looked as though he might faint. "Clearly, the intruder is not threatened by the sheriff or myself. It's up to you as the dominant predator to go in and get him."

"Me?" asked Rex, his knees trembling.

"Yes, you," insisted Buzz. "Just use the techniques I've been teaching you. You can be very intimidating if you set your mind to it."

"Go on, you big lizard!" Hamm yelled. "Make him wish he was extinct!"

"Oh, all right," Rex said. "Here goes." He ventured into the darkness of the wardrobe and gave a spine-chilling roar. "I got him!" shouted Rex. He emerged from the wardrobe pulling on a shoelace. Everyone stared in disbelief.

"It's – a sneaker," Buzz said.

"With lights in the heel," added Woody.

Rex burst into tears. "My big moment, wasted on a shoe!"

"Well, look on the bright side," said Hamm. Rex looked hopeful. "There's a bright side?"

"Yeah," the pig assured him. "At least it didn't stick its tongue out at you!"

Walt Disney's
## Sleeping Beauty

# The Gift Horse

"**I** can hardly wait to see her!" Prince Phillip told his horse, Samson. He had just met the woman of his dreams singing in the forest. And she had invited him to her cottage that very evening.

Suddenly, the Prince pulled his horse's reins up short. Samson jerked to a stop and chuffed angrily.

"Sorry, boy," said the Prince. "But I just realized that I should bring her a gift tonight – something to show her how much I love her. Let's go to the village."

Samson shook his mane and refused to move a hoof. Shopping wasn't his idea of fun. He was tired and wanted to go back to the castle for some oats!

"C'mon, boy," pleaded the Prince. "I'll give you some nice crisp apples."

*Apples*! Samson's eyes widened. Suddenly, he wasn't so tired any more! With a bright whinny, he kicked up his hooves and took off.

When they reached the village square, the Prince scratched his head in thought. There were so many shops.

"What sort of gift do you think she will like?" he asked.

As a horse, Samson didn't care all that much. Yet he did his best to answer.

"Red roses?" asked the Prince, passing a flower shop.

Samson shook his head.

"Yes, you're right," said the Prince. "She lives in the forest. She must see flowers every day."

They passed a dress shop and the prince peered in at the window.

"How about a new dress?" he asked Samson.

Samson shook his mane in irritation.

"No, huh?" said the Prince. "Girls like to choose their own dresses, don't they?"

They passed more shops: a bakery, a hat shop and a blacksmith's.

Samson sighed. If he didn't help the Prince find a gift soon, they could be here all day! With a whinny, Samson took off down the street.

The Prince yelped in surprise. By the time he'd taken back control of the reins, Samson had stopped in front of a jewellery shop.

"Samson, you're a genius!" the Prince cried at the sight of the gems glittering in the window. "That sapphire ring sparkles as beautifully as her blue eyes."

The Prince bought the ring, slipped it in his pocket, then mounted Samson again.

"To the castle!" said the Prince. "I've got to tell my father I've found the girl of my dreams."

Samson whinnied and took off at a gallop. He didn't know what the King would say to the Prince, but one thing he was sure of – he had certainly earned those apples!

# Wild Life

Tod the fox had just arrived at the nature reserve, a vast, beautiful forest where wild animals were protected from hunters. Widow Tweed had brought him there to keep him safe, since her next-door neighbor, Amos Slade, had vowed to hunt him. Amos was angry with the fox because his beloved dog, Chief, had been injured while chasing after him.

At first, Tod didn't understand why his kind owner, Widow Tweed, had left him in the middle of this strange forest, alone and afraid. But she had seemed to be as sad about leaving him as he was about being abandoned.

The first night was dreadful. It had poured with rain and, although he tried to find shelter in different hollows and caves, they were always inhabited by other animals. There was no room for the poor, wet little fox. But the next morning, things began to look up. Tod met a pretty young fox named Vixey. She showed him around the forest, which had many beautiful waterfalls and streams full of fish.

"I think I'm going to like it here, Vixey," said Tod. Having lived his whole life with the Widow Tweed, he had never met another fox before, least of all one as lovely as Vixey.

But Vixey had lived the life of a wild fox, and she knew more about the world than Tod. "You must be very careful, Tod," she warned him. "Remember, we're foxes, and we have many enemies. You must always be on the alert for danger!"

"Come on, Vixey," scoffed Tod. "We're in a game preserve! I heard the Widow Tweed say that there's no hunting allowed in this forest. What could possibly happen to us here? We don't have a care in the world!"

Suddenly, a huge shadow fell over the two foxes. A look of great fear crossed Vixey's face. Turning around slowly and cautiously, Tod saw why. A huge bear was standing up on its hind legs. And it was staring straight at them!

"Grrrr!" the bear growled.

"Run!" yelled Vixey.

Tod didn't need to be told twice. The two foxes dashed away from the bear, scampering over hills, racing through a hollow tree and jumping over a narrow stream. When they were well away from the bear, they stopped and leaned against a rock, panting hard.

"Okay," Tod said, when he had caught his breath a bit. "I see what you mean about the dangers, Vixey. From now on, I'll be a lot more careful."

"Mmm-hmm," she replied. Then she smiled. "Come on," she said to Tod. "Let's go fishing!"

# A Yummy Dream

Winnie the Pooh stepped into his house and sat down with a sigh. He and Piglet had been out on a long walk through the woods. Now Pooh was tired. And, more importantly, he was hungry.

"My tummy feels very rumbly," Pooh said aloud.

Pooh got to his feet and went over to his honey cupboard. There was only one pot of honey inside.

"Oh dear," Pooh said. One pot of honey was not very much. He sat down and began to eat. He ate every last sticky drop. But, when he was finished, his tummy was still feeling a tiny bit rumbly.

"Well, I suppose there's nothing left to do but go to bed," Pooh said sadly. He put on his nightshirt and his nightcap and climbed into his cosy bed. A minute later Pooh's snores filled the air. And dreams began to fill his head – dreams of honey, of course.

Pooh stood before the honey tree. It was so full of honey, it was oozing out of the trunk!

"Yummy, yummy," Pooh said. He began to fill his honeypots.

Then, suddenly, a purple heffalump appeared behind him.

"Mmmm," the heffalump said, licking his lips. The creature stuck his long trunk into one of the honeypots and gobbled up all the honey.

"Those are my honeypots!" Pooh cried.

He tried to sound brave, even though he was just a little bit scared. The heffalump looked very big and very hungry.

The heffalump just stared at Pooh.

Pooh looked at the honeypots. There were a lot of them. Some were full, but most were still empty. Pooh looked at the honey tree. It was still overflowing with honey.

"I have an idea," Pooh said. "Let's fill the honeypots together, then share a nice snack."

The heffalump nodded excitedly. He picked up a honeypot with his trunk and carried it over to the tree. Pooh did the same, and the sweet, sticky honey dripped into the pots.

When all of the pots had been filled, Pooh and the heffalump sat down together. They ate and ate until all the pots were empty and their tummies were full.

"Thank you, Pooh," the heffalump said as he got to his feet. "That was fun. We should do this again soon."

Pooh nodded in agreement and watched the heffalump walk away. Getting to his feet, he patted his tummy.

When Pooh awoke the next morning, to his surprise, his tummy wasn't the slightest bit rumbly. Then he remembered his strange dream. It had been a dream, hadn't it?

WALT DISNEY'S
ALICE
in
WONDERLAND

# A Refreshing Cup of Tea

*"Twinkle, twinkle, little bat!*
*How I wonder what you're at!*
*Up above the world you fly,*
*Like a tea-tray in the sky."*

The song came from just around the tall tree with the funny, mitten-shaped leaves. Alice knew it could only have been sung by one person: the Mad Hatter!

"Oh, bother!" Alice sighed. Truly, the Hatter and his friends were among the last creatures she wished to see. They were so . . . so very mad, after all!

"And yet," Alice went on, again to no one but herself, "a nice cup of tea would be quite refreshing . . . ." And who in Wonderland knew where else a person might find tea?

And so, with a bold shrug, Alice made her way around the shady bend.

In the clearing, the Hatter, the March Hare and the Dormouse were sitting, much as they had been upon Alice's last visit, around their ample tea table, singing, and ranting, and sleeping, respectively.

"A-hem . . ." Alice made her presence known to them by clearing her thirsty throat.

"Well!" exclaimed the Hatter. "If it isn't our dear, dear old friend! I say, what was your name again, dear old friend?"

"Alice," Alice patiently replied.

"Well, have a seat, Alice, dear!"

"Thank you," said Alice. "But, you know, I can only stay a minute – though I could use a cup of tea."

"And how would you use it?" the Hatter asked. "Carefully, I hope."

"Very carefully," Alice assured him.

"Ah, well, that's good. And that's also bad."

"Bad?" Alice asked.

"You heard him!" said the March Hare. "Can't you see? We have no tea!"

"No tea?" asked Alice, gazing about at the table full of empty cups and saucers.

"No tea?" sobbed the Dormouse, stirring from his sleep. "No tea!"

"There you go upsetting him again!" shouted the Hare.

"I didn't . . ." Alice began. Then she remembered how useless it was to argue with a hare who was mad. Instead, she left the March Hare to his shouting, and the Dormouse to his crying, and the Hatter to his . . . whatever it was he was doing . . . and walked over to the stove, where a kettle was cheerfully boiling. Finding a tin of fragrant tea leaves, she dropped some into an empty teapot and filled it with hot water. Then she reached for the cleanest cup she could find and filled it.

She was tempted to offer her hosts a cup as well. But on second thoughts, she decided that perhaps it was better to just . . . go.

# Manners, Mowgli!

A strange but delicious smell drifted past Mowgli's nose. Turning around, he spied several platters of food. A moment later, people filed in and sat in a circle around the food. Mowgli was excited. He had just come to live in the Man-village, and he was about to have his first meal!

Mowgli lunged forward and grabbed a piece of meat. He shoved it in his mouth and chewed. He had never tasted cooked meat before, and it was delicious! As the juice dribbled down his chin, he grinned at the humans surrounding him.

They did not grin back. In fact, they were looking at him in disgust. Surprised, Mowgli's mouth dropped open. A piece of half-chewed meat fell out. Why was everyone staring?

"Disgusting," said an elderly woman.

"Why, he eats like an animal!" said a girl.

Mowgli didn't understand a single word they said. But it suddenly dawned on him that he didn't live in the jungle any more. Humans did things differently from the jungle creatures. Mowgli sighed. Would he ever fit in here?

Smiling sheepishly, Mowgli finished chewing and wiped his mouth with his arm. Then he sat back and watched the others eat.

They used strange, sharp sticks to cut with and flattened, paddle-like ones to scoop the food into their mouths. They took small bites and chewed with their mouths closed. Why, they didn't even seem to enjoy the meal at all! How odd!

Mowgli tried to copy them, with little success. The sharpened stick didn't cut nearly as well as his teeth, and half the food fell off the paddle.

"He's as clumsy as a baby," someone said.

"Maybe he really is an animal," said a girl.

At the next meal, Mowgli watched for a long time before he began to eat. The food was strange to him – warm liquid with soft vegetables. Holding his bowl in one hand, he tried to scoop the soup into his mouth with the paddle. But it kept slipping off, leaving him with almost nothing.

Mowgli put his bowl and paddle down with a frustrated sigh. Then, ever so slowly, he picked up the bowl a second time and lifted it right to his lips. Then he took a big gulp of soup, swallowing and smacking his lips.

The others stopped and stared yet again. Then the village elder nodded and lifted his bowl to his mouth and took a long sip, finishing with a lip smack of his own. He smiled at Mowgli. Soon everyone was gulping the soup, slurping and smacking away.

Mowgli grinned. It looked as though he might fit in after all!

# Knock, Knock! Who's There?

Standing in her brand-new bedroom, Lilo grinned. The walls were almost complete. In her mind, Lilo could see it all finished. Her bed would be against one wall, and Stitch's little bed would sit right beside hers. Lilo hugged herself with excitement. She wasn't quite sure that the wardrobe was in exactly the right place, but she loved everything else, so she didn't mind.

"Lilo, I want you to stay out of the workers' way," Nani said. "And keep an eye on Stitch! He keeps licking our nice new windows!"

Nani was worried. Cobra Bubbles was coming today to see how they were doing.

"We'll stay out of trouble," Lilo smiled angelically. "Right, Stitch? Stitch?" Lilo looked around.

Stitch wasn't exactly staying out of trouble. He had a tool belt around his waist, and his mouth was full of nails. With amazing force, Stitch spat the nails into the floor, accidentally fastening the end of his own belt to the ground.

"That'll keep you out of trouble." Lilo shrugged. Just then there was a knock at the door. "I'll get it!" Lilo called. She opened the new door. Cobra Bubbles filled the door frame.

"Hello," he said, without removing his sunglasses.

"Hey, come on in and see our new digs!"

Lilo cried, happy to see her friend.

Cobra Bubbles stepped over a power cord and walked around a pile of flooring. "You don't actually live here yet, do you?" he asked slowly.

"Not yet," Lilo chirped. "It's supposed to be finished next month."

"And where is . . . Stitch?" Cobra Bubbles peered around Lilo's room.

"Lilo?" Nani asked with a fake smile.

Lilo frowned. Stitch was no longer nailed to the floor.

Suddenly, they heard a knock. Lilo and Nani looked at each other. It wasn't coming from the front door – in fact, it sounded as if it was coming from Lilo's room!

"Who is it?" Lilo asked quietly.

With a monumental crash, Stitch burst through one of the new walls in Lilo's bedroom. "Here he is!" Lilo shouted.

"I see." Cobra Bubbles tried to keep frowning, but couldn't.

"Yes," said Nani nervously. "Stitch sure is, uh, helping out with the construction. Why, here he's decided on a new spot for Lilo's closet. We didn't really want it there, anyway." Nani gave Cobra Bubbles a weak smile, then turned to look at Stitch's handiwork.

"Actually," Nani said with a real smile, "this is a much better spot for the closet. Thanks, Stitch!"

Walt Disney's
# Pinocchio

# Imagine That!

The carnival was in town. Pinocchio grabbed his friend Jiminy Cricket and off they went. Pinocchio was amazed at the marvellous sights. There were jugglers to see and games to play. He even saw an elephant doing tricks!

"That elephant is amazing!" Pinocchio cried.

"I suppose," said Jiminy politely.

Next they came to a lion's cage. The big cat opened his mouth and roared.

"Look at those teeth!" Pinocchio marvelled.

Jiminy Cricket nodded. "They're pretty big, it's true."

Then they saw a giraffe.

"What a long neck!" Pinocchio exclaimed.

"Giraffes are all right, I guess," said Jiminy with a shrug. Pinocchio was confused.

"If you don't like elephants, lions or giraffes, what kind of carnival animals do you like?" Pinocchio asked.

"Fleas," said Jiminy.

"Fleas?" Pinocchio said, even more confused.

"Come on! I'll show you," said Jiminy.

Jiminy led Pinocchio to a tent with a sign that read FLEA CIRCUS.

Inside Pinocchio saw a tiny merry-go-round and little swings. There were small animal cages and a little trapeze. There was even a tiny Big Top with three miniature rings. But no matter how hard he looked, Pinocchio could not see any fleas.

"That's because there *aren't* any fleas," Jiminy explained.

"What's the point, then?" Pinocchio asked.

"The point is imagination," said Jiminy. "Why, you can do anything with your imagination," he continued. "You can even see the fleas at the flea circus."

"But I don't see them," said Pinocchio, confused.

"You have to pretend to see the fleas, and pretty soon you can," said Jiminy. "Like that juggling flea over there. Oops, he dropped his juggling pins."

Pinocchio laughed and joined in the game.

"That flea is going to jump through a ring of fire," Pinocchio said. "I hope he makes it!"

"Now the fleas are doing acrobatics," Jiminy declared.

"They've made a flea pyramid," said Pinocchio. "And the flea on top is standing on his hands."

Finally, it was time to go home.

"What did you think of the Flea Circus?" asked Jiminy Cricket.

"It was the most amazing circus I ever saw, and I didn't really see it at all," Pinocchio replied.

"Yes, indeed. You imagined it," said Jiminy Cricket. "Imagine that!"

WALT DISNEY PICTURES PRESENTS
# DINOSAUR

## Adventures in Babysitting

Aladar and Neera loved being parents. Their baby son was adorable and sweet and funny – and very active! In fact, from the moment he woke up in the morning to the moment he went to sleep at night, it seemed as if that little iguanadon didn't stop moving.

Zini came to visit often. "I love kids and kids love me!" Zini liked to say. "Any time you want me to babysit, you just say the word and it'll be Uncle Zini to the rescue!"

One day, the couple finally took him up on his offer. "We're just going to go for a walk," Neera explained. "Send someone after us if you need us." They strolled off, with Neera looking back every few steps.

Zini looked up at the baby dinosaur, who towered over him. "What do you say you and me go find some lunch, little guy?" he suggested. Instead, the baby made a beeline for the mudhole.

What if it's too deep and he can't swim? Zini thought. What if he gets stuck and can't get out? The lemur took a running leap and belly flopped in. Zini tried to grab on to the baby, but the dinosaur was much too slippery. While the babysitter flopped and flailed, the baby climbed out of the puddle and wandered towards some vegetation.

"Go ahead and start on lunch without me!" Zini called. "I'll be right there."

By the time Zini managed to pull himself over to the trees, Aladar's and Neera's son had already eaten halfway through a tree trunk. The lemur settled down under the shade of the tree with a nice bunch of leaves. The pair munched contentedly. Then, all of a sudden, Zini heard a loud *creak* and a *crash* as the tree fell to the ground. The baby had eaten right through the tree trunk!

Zini breathed a sigh of relief. That was a close one! This babysitting stuff was harder than he thought. "You know what, little guy? After the refreshing mud bath and that big lunch, I could use a nap. How about you?"

The baby dinosaur's lower lip stuck out. It began to tremble. Then he stamped his foot as hard as he could. The ground shook. "Waaaaaah!" he wailed. "Waaaaaah!" Zini did everything he could to calm him down. Finally, the baby wore himself out and collapsed on the ground, snoring.

When Aladar and Neera returned, their son was still sleeping peacefully. "Would you look at that?" said Aladar. "Zini, how did you manage to get him to nap?"

"Nothing to it," said the exhausted lemur. "I just have a way with children!"

# Stuck in the Mud

"Come on, Rob!" Little John called as he stepped over a fallen log. The two were out for a misty morning romp in the forest, but Robin Hood was lagging behind.

"Shhhh!" Robin put a finger to his lips. "I think I hear something."

"Let's have a look-see," said Little John. A minute later, they stopped at the edge of the forest and peered out from behind a bush. There, stuck in a muddy ditch, was a fancy coach.

"I'd know that coach anywhere," Robin whispered. "It belongs to Prince John."

"That snivelling coward," Little John said. "Serves him right to get stuck."

"Get me out of the mud, now!" a voice whined from inside the coach. It certainly was Prince John.

The driver's shoulders slumped. "But sire, the coach is laden with gold. I'll never be able to push it out by myself. Perhaps Your Highness would consider stepping out of the coach so as to lighten the load? Just until the wheels are free of the mud, of course," he added quickly.

"Step out of the coach?" Prince John bellowed. "And stand in the rain? I most certainly will not. And now I order you for a second time: get me out of the mud!"

The driver wiped the rainwater from his brow and walked to the back of the coach.

"I believe I have a plan that will help Prince John and that driver," Robin said. "Not to mention the poor."

Little John nodded with a grin. He knew exactly what sort of plan his friend had in mind. Robin reached into his satchel, pulled out a few items, and put them on. Little John did the same. Now they looked like two ordinary hunters. Little John stepped onto the road.

"Need some help there?" he asked the driver loudly. "I'd be glad to lend a hand."

Meanwhile, Robin sneaked around to the side of the coach. He was just opening the door when Prince John leaned out of the window on the other side.

"Hurry up, you fools!" he hollered.

Little John sidled up to the window. "You'll be out in a jiffy," he assured the prince.

Robin saw his chance. While the prince was distracted, he opened the other door and removed several bags of gold.

"Get pushing, then," Prince John snapped.

"I said, be glad to," Little John replied. He strolled to the back of the coach and, along with the driver, gave a single push. And, while Robin slipped into the woods with the gold, Prince John and his muddy-wheeled coach rolled down the road to Nottingham, the load a little lighter than before.

# Flik's Big Date

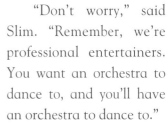

Flik loved Queen Atta very, very much. So, he decided to plan the most romantic evening for the two of them an ant could possibly imagine.

"I'll pick you up at eight tonight," Flik told Atta when he met her in the anthill early in the morning. Then off he hurried to get ready for their big date.

First, there was the dinner to prepare: sprouted wheat with sunflower seeds and wild truffles; free-range millet on a bed of dandelion greens; and Queen Atta's favourite dessert: gooseberry mousse.

The perfect menu! Flik thought. It was sure to impress Atta.

Then Flik went down to the stream to find the perfect leaf for a romantic moonlit cruise. "This elm leaf should do," Flik said as he tied the leaf to a root near the shore. "And I'll use this twig for my oar. Yes, Atta's going to love this."

But that wasn't all that Flik had planned.

"How's it coming?" he asked the circus bugs, who were back for a visit and busy practising their instruments just up the hill from the stream.

"Brilliant!" Slim replied. "Just brilliant. Don't worry about a thing. It's all under control. We'll have Atta's favourite song

memorized by tomorrow night, no problem!"

"But our date is tonight," said Flik.

"Oh," said Slim sheepishly.

"Told you so," said Francis.

"Don't worry," said Slim. "Remember, we're professional entertainers. You want an orchestra to dance to, and you'll have an orchestra to dance to."

"Are you sure you wouldn't like some magic instead?" Manny the Magician asked. "I have found that nothing inspires romance in a lady quite like cutting her in half."

"Um, I think I'll stick with the dancing," said Flik. But, speaking of inspiring romance, he'd almost forgotten all about the fireflies!

"Come on, guys!" he called to the dozen or so he'd hired for that evening. "I want some of you in the trees, some of you along the water, and the rest of you over there by the picnic blanket . . . perfect!" he said as their thoraxes lit up the quickly falling night. "Dinner is ready. Boat is ready. Music is . . . almost ready. Everything is set to go!"

Suddenly, Flik looked down at his watch, and his heart skipped a beat. "Oh, no! It's eight o'clock!" he yelled. "I've really got to go!"

Can you believe it? Flik was so busy getting everything ready, he'd almost forgotten to pick Atta up for their date!

# The Sky's the Limit

Captain Amelia and Dr Delbert Doppler were a smart couple. Amelia was a veteran of many dangerous voyages to faraway galaxies. Delbert was a noted astrophysicist. Even at a very young age, their quadruplets – three girls nicknamed Matey, Jib and Tillie (short for 'Tiller') and a boy, Sunny, named after his father's favourite star – began to show evidence of having inherited their parents' intelligence.

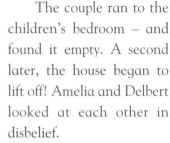

Unbeknownst to their parents, little by little, the Doppler quadruplets were using their talents to make changes to the house where they lived with their parents.

"Jib!" called Amelia, one windy afternoon. "Why are there large sails flying from the roof?"

"I thought they looked pretty up there," answered Jib.

"Tillie, what is that you're building in your room?" wondered Delbert.

"A rocket booster," she answered.

"Well, be careful!" her father warned. "Jet propulsion can be a tricky thing."

Amelia really became suspicious when she found Matey installing a giant steering wheel in front of the attic window.

"And this would be . . . ?" she asked her daughter.

Matey looked at her mother innocently.

"Something that's fun to spin?" she asked.

"Very curious," Amelia said to herself.

Then one night, after the children went to bed, the house began to shake.

The couple ran to the children's bedroom – and found it empty. A second later, the house began to lift off! Amelia and Delbert looked at each other in disbelief.

"We did it!" cried Sunny's triumphant voice. It was coming from the attic.

Amelia and Delbert rushed upstairs. "What's going on here?" demanded Delbert.

"I'm steering," said Matey, from behind the giant wheel.

"I'm controlling the sails," said Jib, as she pulled some levers.

"I blasted us off," Tillie admitted.

"And I designed the whole thing," bragged Sunny.

"What thing?" asked Amelia.

"Mum and Dad, welcome to your new motor home!" Jib announced.

Amelia and Delbert stared at their children.

"Well, what do you think?" Matey asked eagerly. "Do you like it?"

Her parents both broke out in proud grins. "Aye, aye, Captain!" boomed Amelia.

# Scrooge's Nature

"Would you look at that!" Huey pointed to a picture of a Junior Woodchuck relaxing in a hammock, while another camper fished in a nearby lake.

"And that!" Dewey's eyes widened. He pointed at a picture of a star-filled sky in the same brochure.

"Camping at Faraway Lake sure looks fun," Louie agreed. "Do you think Unca Scrooge would . . . ?"

"You never know. He might pay for us to go," Huey said. The three boys looked at one another.

"Nah!" they said in unison. Uncle Scrooge may have been the richest duck in the world, but he did not part with his money easily.

"Let's show him, anyway," Huey said. "It's worth a shot."

The other boys followed Huey into their uncle's study.

Dewey nudged Huey forward. "Look at this, Unca Scrooge." Huey thrust the brochure into his uncle's lap.

"Humph." Uncle Scrooge scowled at the glossy photos. "What have we got here, lads?"

"It's a camp, Unca Scrooge. It's educational," Huey stammered.

"Looks like a waste of my hard-earned money," the old duck said.

"But . . . but we could camp out under the stars," Dewey said.

"And cook over a fire," Louie put in.

"And see nature," Huey added.

Uncle Scrooge's eyes narrowed. He looked from the brochure to his nephews' hopeful faces and back to the brochure. So, they wanted to learn about nature, did they?

"Here you are, boys," said Uncle Scrooge a short time later. He smiled from the safety of the screened-in back porch. "You have tents . . ." He indicated the three small leaky tents set up in the garden. "You can see the stars . . ." In fact, only one or two stars were visible through the branches of the tree the tents were under. "And you're cooking over a fire," Scrooge finished, pointing at the tiny, smoky little flame.

Huey slapped at a mosquito on his arm. Dewey shook his head to chase away a cloud of gnats. Louie yelped as he was dive-bombed by a bat. Who knew the garden had so much nature in it!

"This is much better than that Junior Woodchuck nonsense, isn't it, boys?" Uncle Scrooge asked, with the smile of a duck who has saved himself a penny.

"Yes, Unca Scrooge," Huey, Dewey, and Louie said. Then they turned back to the fire.

"I think . . ." said Huey.

". . . next time," continued Dewey.

". . . we ask Unca Donald!" finished Louie.

# A Helping Paw

The dairy barn was warm and cosy, and 99 exhausted, hungry pups were taking turns to drink warm milk from the motherly cows.

"We'd nearly given up hope that you would get here," the kindly collie said to Pongo and Perdita, who had just arrived with the puppies.

"We're so very grateful to you for your hospitality," Perdita murmured wearily.

"Just look at the little dears," said one of the cows. "I've never seen so many puppies in one place before!"

Pongo, Perdita and the puppies had just come in from a long and weary march in the cold. It was very late, and the pups waiting for a drink of milk could barely keep their eyes open. The puppies had recently managed to escape from the dreadful old house owned by Cruella De Vil. They had been held prisoner there, guarded by two villains named Horace and Jasper. Cruella was planning to make a fur coat out of their lovely spotted fur. Luckily Pongo and Perdita had rescued them all just in the nick of time.

The pups had their dinners and gathered around the collie, thanking him for his hospitality.

"Not at all, not at all," the collie replied.

"Do you have warm milk for supper every night out here in the country?" asked Rolly.

The collie chuckled. "No, but we do eat very simple country fare. I'm sure it's plainer than the food you eat in the city, but we eat big meals because of all the chores we do."

"And is it always this cold in the country?" asked Patch.

"Well, now," replied the collie. "I suppose most of you come from the city. No, it isn't always this cold, but there are plenty of differences between living in the country and living in the city. Take leashes, for instance. We don't keep our pets on leashes here, the way you do in the city, since our pets have a lot of wide-open space to roam around in. There aren't as many dogs nearby, but there are certainly other sorts of animals that one doesn't see in the city. Take cows, for instance. And then there are sheep and horses and geese, and . . . ."

Suddenly, the collie stopped talking. A tiny snore escaped one of the pups he had just been talking to. He looked around and realized that every one of the pups, as well as Pongo and Perdita, had fallen into a deep sleep.

"Poor little things," he said quietly, as he trotted outside to stand guard. "They've been through so much. I do hope they get home safely soon."

October
# 19

# A New Friend

Imagine Mulan's surprise when, while out in the meadow picking flowers for her grandmother, what should she spy in an old cypress tree, but a tiny grey kitten.

"Oh, you poor thing. Are you stuck?" Mulan said.

"Meow," replied the kitten.

So Mulan grabbed hold of the lowest branch, and pulled herself up into the tree. The climb was not easy, but at last she reached the kitten. Cradling it in one arm, she climbed back down to the ground.

"There," said Mulan, catching her breath. "Now you can go back home."

Gently, she lowered the kitten to the ground. With a quick tickle behind her ears, Mulan nudged her on her way.

But the grateful little kitten barely moved an inch – instead, it sat there, blinking up at her and purring.

"Go on," Mulan said, smiling. "I'm sure there's a bowlful of milk waiting for you."

But still the kitten would not budge.

"Very well, suit yourself," said Mulan, scooping up her flowers. "I'm late already and really should get home. Try to stay out of trees, little one!" She turned to go.

"Meow, meow, meow!"

Now, imagine Mulan's surprise when she looked down at her feet to find her new kitten friend trotting close beside her.

"Well, well!" Mulan laughed. "It appears the Fas are going to have a little house guest!"

But not everyone at Mulan's house was pleased to have company. Namely, Mulan's dog, Little Brother. Especially when the kitten walked in and lay down on his silk cushion!

"Ruff! Ruff! Ruff!" he barked.

"Now, now," Mulan said. "Our friend here has just been through quite an ordeal. Be a good host and let her rest, won't you?"

But then the kitten did something even harder to forgive. She walked right over and drank out of Little Brother's dish!

"Grrrr! Grrrrr! Grruffff!" protested Little Brother.

"Oh, dear," said Mulan. "She's probably thirsty too. Here, kitty," she said, setting down a bowl of milk. "Have some of this."

Now, imagine Little Brother's surprise when that tiny kitten pushed the dish of milk all the way over to Little Brother with her little black nose.

"Meow," said the kitten, giving it one more push.

"Look, Little Brother!" exclaimed Mulan. "She wants to be your friend."

And, from that moment on, that's what they were!

Disney's *Aladdin*

# The Great Garden Mystery

For the first time in many years, the Sultan of Agrabah had spare time. With Jasmine and Aladdin helping him run the kingdom, the Sultan could spend his afternoons in his vegetable garden. He grew aubergines, chickpeas, parsley, cucumbers, tomatoes and lettuce.

"Vegetables, yuck!" Iago the parrot squawked, perching on a beanpole as the Sultan watered his aubergines. "Give me a fig any day. You can keep your lettuce and parsley. Blech!"

One day, the Sultan came out to his garden and found that there was not one vegetable left in it! The chickpea plants were bare, the lettuce was gone and the tomatoes had vanished. There wasn't even one lonely sprig of parsley!

The Sultan, Jasmine, Aladdin and Rajah searched high and low for any clues. Finally, they found one: a set of muddy claw prints. The prints could belong to only one creature – Iago!

"I can't believe it," said the Sultan. "That parrot must hate vegetables so much that he decided to get rid of each and every one of them!"

They followed the claw prints over the garden wall and into the city. The royal family wound their way further and further into the city, until Aladdin recognized his old neighbourhood.

"I wonder why Iago would bring those vegetables here?" he said. "If he wants to sell them,

he's out of luck – no one here has any money."

Aladdin got his answer soon enough. Rajah led the family around a corner, and there, in a courtyard, was a poor family having a picnic. It was a jolly affair – they were talking and laughing and passing dishes around. And in the middle of it all was Iago.

"Iago!" cried Jasmine. "You gave my father's vegetables away?"

The father of the family stood up. "My apologies, Your Highness," he said. "We did not know that the vegetables belonged to the Sultan. This parrot saw how hungry we were and said he would give us something to eat. We would give them back, but we have already made *falafel* out of the chickpeas and parsley, and *baba ghanoush* out of the aubergines. However, there is plenty to go around, if you would like to join us."

Jasmine thought she had never received such a nice invitation. So they all sat down, and tucked in. The *baba ghanoush* was rich, and the *falafel* was tasty, and went very well with the Sultan's tomatoes and lettuce.

"I am delighted," said the Sultan, "that my garden is such a success. I think, however, that it would be even better if the garden was in the city, and belonged to everyone. Perhaps I will move the garden to this very courtyard."

Everyone thought that was a wonderful idea, except for Iago. "Vegetables, yuck!" he said.

# Dumbo's Daring Rescue

Dumbo stood on his platform high above the floor of the circus Big Top. Below him, the clowns looked the same size as peanuts. He could hear them calling for him to jump.

"All right, kid. You're on," Timothy said from the brim of Dumbo's hat.

Dumbo was ready. He knew what he had to do because he did the same thing every night. When the firefighter clowns called, Dumbo would leap from the platform and plummet towards the ground. Then, at the last possible moment,

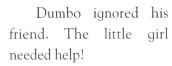

Dumbo would spread his tremendous ears and fly. The audience would cheer. And the show would be over.

"Hey, kid, that's your cue!" Timothy squeaked in Dumbo's ear.

Taking a step forward, Dumbo began to fall. He sped faster and faster towards the floor of the tent. The audience swam into view. They were screaming and laughing. Then, all of a sudden, Dumbo saw something else.

There, in the first row, was a little girl sitting all by herself. She was crying and holding on to a stick of candyfloss.

In an instant, the little elephant forgot all about the act. Spreading his ears, he swooped away from the shouting clowns. He scanned the seats intently. Why was the girl all alone? Where were her parents?

"Dumbo! What are you doing?" Timothy clung to Dumbo's hat as he soared towards the peanut and popcorn sellers. "We don't have time for a snack now!"

Dumbo ignored his friend. The little girl needed help!

At last, Dumbo saw what he was looking for. There, next to the candyfloss stand, were two very worried-looking parents.

"Clara, where are you?" the father called. His voice was lost in the hollering crowd. His daughter would never hear him calling to her!

Dumbo circled the tent again, turning back towards the bench where the little girl sat sobbing. How could he tell her that her parents were looking for her? He had to bring them together. Swooping low, Dumbo stretched out his trunk and scooped up the little girl.

"Dumbo, what are you doing!" Timothy cried again.

Dumbo sailed back and placed the girl gently beside her parents.

Immediately, the little girl's tears were dried. She was safe in her parents' arms!

The crowd went wild as Dumbo soared high over the arena. Even the clowns were smiling.

"Nice work, kid," Timothy said. "Good show."

# A Whale of a Tale

"**H**op aboard, explorers!" called Mr Ray. Nemo, Tad and the rest of the class jumped on the back of the big manta ray. It was special-guest week and they were going to the Drop-off.

When they reached the reef's edge, a royal blue tang fish swam up to meet them.

"And here is today's special guest," Mr Ray announced.

"Hello, everyone," said the blue tang. "I'm Dory . . . um . . . am I? Yes! Just kidding! I'm Dory, and I'm very happy to be here!"

"Dory, can you teach us something about whales today?" asked Mr Ray.

"Well, let's see . . . whales are very big, but they eat little creatures called krill. And I should know. One whale I met *almost* ate me – "

"So it's not true!" blurted Tad.

"*What's* not true?" Dory asked.

"Sandy Plankton said Nemo made up that story about how you and Nemo's dad got *eaten* by a whale!" said Tad.

"I did not make it up!" cried Nemo.

"Well," said Dory, "technically, Sandy Plankton is right. We weren't actually *eaten* by the whale – "

Tad smirked, until Dory added, "We were just *in* the whale's *mouth* for a mighty long time!"

"Whoa!" said the class. They were quite impressed.

Tad frowned.

"You see, the whale was just giving us a ride to Sydney. I find if you talk to a whale beforehand, it clears up most ingestion issues," Dory explained.

"Excellent lesson!" said Mr Ray. "Now teach us a few words in whale."

"Oh, okay," said Dory. "Now repeat after me. Haaaaavve aaaaaaaaaa nnnniiiiiice daaaaayyyy!"

"Haaaaavve aaaaaaaaaa nnnniiiiiice daaaaayyyy!" the class repeated.

"Very good!" said Dory.

"This is stupid," said Tad. "You didn't really . . ."

Suddenly, Tad stopped talking. Everyone just stared at Dory in horror.

Slowly, Dory turned around. A blue whale was right behind her!

Dory simply shrugged and told the whale, "Weeeee weerrrrre juuuuuuuuussst praaaaactisinnnng!"

With a loud bellow, the whale wished her a nice day anyway, then swam off.

"So, Tad, do you believe Dory now?" asked Nemo.

"Wow, that was *so* cool!" cried Tad. "I can't wait to tell Sandy Plankton how I was almost eaten by a whale!"

Nemo and Dory just sighed.

DISNEY'S
BROTHER
BEAR

# The Good Spot

"I'm tired. Where are we going to stop for the night?" Koda whimpered.

"You're the one who's supposed to know where we're going," Kenai growled in response. Their trip to the Salmon Run was taking much longer than he expected, and his bear cub 'guide' was driving him crazy. Kenai wished he could get away from him, even if it was only for a few hours. "Hey, is that a cave ahead?" he asked.

Koda scampered ahead to check it out.

"It *is* a cave!" Koda shouted. His energy suddenly returned. He ran inside and trotted back, twining around Kenai's feet and nearly tripping him. "And it's empty. Can we stop there? Can we?"

Kenai lumbered inside and slumped against the wall at the back. He didn't bother to answer Koda, but the little bear didn't seem to notice. He continued talking.

"It's not very big, is it? My mum and I had a huge cave. We always slept in the back too. It's warmest there. My mum called it the 'good spot'. Are we going to sleep in the good spot, Kenai?" Koda crawled on top of Kenai and started to make himself comfortable.

"I am," Kenai growled, shoving Koda off. "You're going to sleep over there." He pointed a paw towards the cave entrance.

Koda, for once, was quiet. He walked slowly away without looking back and lay down alone.

"Hmph," Kenai snorted and closed his eyes. A second later, they were open again. His ears twitched. Something was clicking. It was Koda's teeth. The cub was shivering by the cave opening. "Fine. You sleep here, and I'll sleep over there." Kenai stood and swept Koda towards the back of the cave with his paw.

"You're giving me the good spot? Thanks!" Koda grinned and curled up in the warm spot where Kenai had been lying.

Kenai grumbled and lay down. He was willing to do almost anything to keep Koda quiet. And the spot by the entrance couldn't be that bad, could it?

Kenai closed his eyes. He tucked his cold nose under his paws. But he could not sleep. The wind got in his ears, and the chill seeped up from the ground.

In the back of the cave, Koda rolled over, snoring peacefully.

Kenai shivered. He glanced at Koda. The cub looked so warm that the big bear crawled to the back of the cave. Being careful not to wake him, Kenai lay down beside the cosy cub.

"I guess you're right sometimes, little bear," Kenai whispered to Koda. "This *is* the good spot."

# One Part Hakuna, One Part Matata

"Why are you so sad?" Pumbaa asked Nala.

"I'm not sad," Nala said. "I'm just a little more on the serious side than the two of you."

"I think you could use a little *hakuna matata*," Pumbaa said.

"A whona mawhatta?" Nala asked.

"You really think she can handle it?" Timon whispered to Pumbaa out of the side of his mouth.

"Of course I can handle it!" Nala said, raising her voice. "I just need to know what it is first."

"Ahhhh, *hakuna matata*," Pumbaa said dreamily. "It's the problem-free way of dealing with all of life's inconveniences."

"It means, 'No worries'," Timon explained.

"Oh, I get it," Nala said. "Instead of dealing with your problems, you pretend they don't exist."

"*Hakuna matata* helps you relax," Pumbaa offered.

"It sounds like your *hakuna matata* is just another way of saying 'uninspired and lazy'," Nala continued.

"I think she might have just insulted us," Timon whispered to Pumbaa.

"There you are." Simba came walking towards them. "What are the three of you up to?"

"I was just learning about a strange little notion called *hakuna matata*," Nala explained.

"Isn't it great!" Simba said with a grin.

"Well, sure," Nala said. "If you don't ever want to get anything done."

Simba frowned. "It's not like that. *Hakuna matata* helps you get through things."

"Sure," Nala continued. "*Hakuna matata* – I don't have to worry. I don't have to try."

"I guess you could look at it that way," Simba said. "But, for me, it means, 'Don't worry about it right now. It's okay.' It gives me the strength to get through the bad times."

"Wow, I hadn't thought about it like that," Nala said.

"So, are you ready to join us now?" Timon asked.

"Absolutely!" Nala smiled.

"Bring on the crunchy beetles!" shouted Pumbaa.

"Let's go tease some elephants!" cried Timon.

"Everyone to the mudhole for a mud fight!" Simba yelled, and the three of them started off.

"Oh, dear," murmured Nala, "this isn't exactly what I had in mind." But she smiled, and ran after her carefree friends. "Last one to the mudhole is a rotten egg!" she cried.

WALT DISNEY'S
## *Cinderella*

# The Missing Slipper

"Oh, what a lovely morning!" cried Cinderella as she sat up in her bed in the royal palace. The sun was shining. The birds were singing. And the delicious smell of freshly baked cinnamon buns was drifting up from the royal kitchen.

"Mmm, breakfast," said Cinderella. She smiled down at the mice gathered on her satin bedspread. Then she stretched over and slipped on the dressing gown that lay at the foot of her bed. "Now, where are those slippers . . . ?"

"Here's one, Cinderelly!" said Jaq, jumping down to drag a silvery bedroom slipper closer to Cinderella's foot.

"Thank you, Jaq, dear," said Cinderella as she slid her toes inside. "But . . . where's the other one?"

Jaq turned and looked around. "I don't see it, Cinderelly!" Quickly, he bent down and peeked under the bed. Still nothing. Uh-oh!

"Mert! Bert!" Jaq shouted to his friends. "Has anybody seen Cinderelly's slipper?"

The other mice shrugged and shook their heads.

"Don't tell me I've lost my slipper," Cinderella said with a sigh. "Not again!"

"Don't worry, Cinderelly," a mouse named Suzy told her. "We'll find it."

Together, Cinderella and her friends searched her room from top to bottom. They peered under tables, behind bookcases, inside wardrobes and dressing tables – everywhere a missing slipper could possibly be.

"I'm beginning to think it walked away," Cinderella said sadly.

"Hmm," said Jaq. "That slipper was here last night . . ." Suddenly Jaq stopped in mid-sentence. "Gus-Gus!" he exclaimed, smacking his forehead. "That's right!"

"What's right?" said Cinderella.

"Follow me, Cinderelly," Jaq said.

With one slipper on, Cinderella followed Jaq as he tiptoed across the room and nodded towards a little mousehole. "Look here, Cinderelly," he said.

Curious, Cinderella knelt down and peered inside . . . and sure enough, there was her missing slipper – with a soundly sleeping Gus nestled cosily inside.

"Oh," said Cinderella, "what a little dear."

"Wake him up, Cinderelly!" said Jaq.

"Oh, no!" replied Cinderella. "Let's let him sleep."

"But Cinderelly needs her slipper!" he cried.

Cinderella thought for a moment. "Actually, no!" she told her mouse friends as she kicked off her other slipper. "I've just decided it's the perfect day for breakfast in bed!"

# Family Reunion

**M**eg paced up and down the room. "What's wrong?" Hercules asked his girlfriend.

"We're going to visit your parents," Meg told him. "I want to make a good first impression."

"You're smart and kind and intelligent," Hercules said, smiling. "How could you make anything other than a great impression?"

"All right, all right!" Phil cried. "Enough with the sweet talk. I have a cavity already. Can we get out of here?"

"Absolutely!" Hercules exclaimed. Pegasus galloped over and whisked them away.

Meanwhile, Hercules' parents, Amphitryon and Alcmene, were getting ready for their son's visit. Amphitryon was pacing too.

"Is everything all right?" Alcmene asked.

"Yes, of course," Amphitryon answered. "Why wouldn't it be?"

"Maybe you're nervous because your son is coming home and you haven't seen him in quite a while," Alcmene said.

Before Amphitryon could answer, they heard a sound.

"Look!" Amphitryon cried. "It's Hercules!"

And, sure enough, Hercules came charging up to the door. He leaped off Pegasus and gave a hearty hug to each of his parents. Then he introduced Phil.

"Mighty fine to meet you," Phil said as he slipped them his business card. "Fine boy you raised! Feel free to contact me if you find any more like him."

"And who's this?" Amphitryon asked.

"This is my friend Meg," Hercules said, blushing.

Just then, Pegasus snorted. "Oh, and how could I forget my pal Pegasus?" Hercules cried.

"All right, all right, enough with the niceties," Phil interrupted. "It's been a long trip. I'm hungry. Where's the grub?"

"Wait!" Hercules said. "I know you have prepared a wonderful meal, but first, I want to tell you what has happened since I left." He took a deep breath. "I've learned that I'm the son of Zeus and Hera. That's where I've got all my physical strength. But, without everything I learned from you, my adoptive parents," Hercules continued, "all that would mean nothing."

Amphitryon and Alcmene beamed with pride.

Then they all sat down for a feast worthy of the gods. Amphitryon and Alcmene were glad to have Hercules home; Hercules was happy to be home; Meg was honoured to be their guest; and Phil was thrilled to finally get to eat some home-cooked food!

# Enchanted Stew

Belle hummed to herself as she strolled through the castle. She had been living in the castle for a few months now and was finally beginning to feel at home. The enchanted inhabitants were truly good to her, and even the Beast seemed to be softening a bit.

Finishing her song, she stepped into the kitchen for a chat with Mrs Potts and the Stove. They were always pleased to see her, and Belle enjoyed talking to them while learning new recipes.

"Well, hello, dear!" Mrs Potts and the Stove called out together as Belle stepped into the large kitchen. The smell of roasting meat and vegetables greeted Belle as well, and her mouth watered. Dinner would be delicious, as usual.

"Hello," Belle replied.

"You're just in time for a spot of tea," Mrs Potts said.

Belle smiled as Chip hopped across the counter, stopping right in front of her. "I'll be your teacup," he said. "And no bubble tricks, I promise," he added seriously.

"All right then," Belle agreed. Mrs Potts filled Chip with steamy tea and dropped in a sugar cube.

"How was your morning in the library, dear?" Mrs Potts asked.

"It was wonderful!" Belle exclaimed. "I finished my book about knights in shining armour and started one about a prince who's disguised as a frog."

"A frog!" the Stove exclaimed. "Oh, my!"

Suddenly, black smoke began to billow out of the sides of the oven door.

"Oh, my!" the Stove said again, throwing open the door. Smoke poured into the room. When it finally cleared, Belle spied a scorched roast and crispy black vegetables inside.

"Oh, my!" the Stove exclaimed again.

"What are we going to feed the Beast for supper?" Mrs. Potts fretted.

The kitchen door opened, and Lumiere rushed into the room. "What is that awful smell?" he asked. A moment later, he spied the roast. "It's absolutely scorched!" he shouted. "We can't possibly feed that to the Beast! What will we do?"

Belle got to her feet. "Enchanted Stew," she said calmly. Taking down a large stew pot and a few vegetables, she began to chop and simmer. The last ingredient was the scorched roast.

"It adds the perfect smoky flavour," she explained. Just then the Beast came into the kitchen. "What smells so delicious?" he asked.

"Supper," Belle replied with a smile and a wink at the Stove and Mrs Potts. "It's called Enchanted Stew, and we cooked it together!"

# Like Father, Like Son

Tramp had a whole new life. He had gone from being a stray to becoming a member of the Dear household. And now, he and Lady were proud parents.

But Tramp was finding it difficult to change some of his old ways.

"Tramp," Lady said gently, "you need to set an example for the puppies – especially Scamp."

Scamp had an adventurous side just like his dad. So, it wasn't surprising that father and son often got carried away when they played together. They couldn't resist the urge to roll in a puddle of mud – and then chase each other across the clean kitchen floor.

Soon, Aunt Sarah and her two troublesome cats, Si and Am, were going to be visiting. Lady was worried.

"Don't worry. I promise to keep Scamp away from those troublemakers," Tramp said.

"And?" replied Lady.

"And I promise to stay away from them, too," Tramp added.

When the big day came, Lady and Tramp herded their pups into a bedroom and told them to stay put. But Scamp was curious. He slipped out of the room and hid behind the living room settee. Then he sneaked up behind the cats and swiped at their tails as they flicked back and forth. The cats turned and chased Scamp up and over the settee, under a table and into a cupboard.

Well, Tramp thought, I suppose I'm going to have to chase those nasty old cats whether I want to or not!

He enthusiastically dived into the cupboard. Seconds later, Tramp and Scamp emerged. Much to Aunt Sarah's horror, Si and Am were later found inside tied together with a scarf. When no one was looking, Tramp and Scamp shared a victory wink.

Tramp and Scamp were banished to the garden for their antics. When Lady came out that evening, she found that they had dug up the entire garden looking for bones. Father and son saw the look on Lady's face and knew that they were about to get a lecture.

Tramp looked at Lady innocently. "You want him to get exercise, don't you?" he asked.

"Try it, Mum!" Scamp cried. "It's fun."

"What am I going to do with you two?" Lady said, laughing.

Tramp and Scamp dragged a huge bone out from behind the kennel.

"Join us for dinner?" Tramp replied.

"Well, all right," Lady said. "But, as soon as we're done, we're cleaning up this yard."

"Yes, ma'am!" chorused Tramp and Scamp, looking very pleased with themselves.

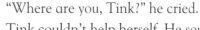

# Tink Learns a Lesson – Or Does She?

Tinker Bell was cross. She and Peter Pan had made plans to explore Skull Cave, but he was still playing "Pirate Treasure" with the Lost Boys. When she jingled impatiently by his ear to let him know it was time to go, he said, "Just a minute, Tink." So, she decided to teach him a lesson. She flew inside a hollow tree.

"Help, help me!" she jingled as loudly as she could. "I'm stuck!"

A moment later Peter appeared. He was out of breath from flying at top speed.

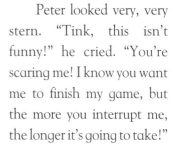

"What is it, Tink?" he gasped. "Are you in trouble?"

Tinker Bell couldn't help laughing at the worried expression on his face. She laughed so hard that she fell right out of the tree.

Peter Pan frowned. "That's not funny, Tink," he said. "I really thought you were in danger! And you interrupted my game!"

He flew away. Tinker Bell stopped laughing. Obviously Peter hadn't learned his lesson yet. He was still leaving her behind to play with his other friends!

She flew to the lagoon and hid among the reeds at the edge.

"Help!" she jingled. "I've got wet!"

Peter rushed over to the lagoon as quickly as he could. He knew how dangerous it was for Tink to get her wings wet.

"Where are you, Tink?" he cried.

Tink couldn't help herself. He sounded so worried. She laughed and laughed, until she rolled right out of the reeds.

Peter looked very, very stern. "Tink, this isn't funny!" he cried. "You're scaring me! I know you want me to finish my game, but the more you interrupt me, the longer it's going to take!"

He flew off. Tinker Bell stopped laughing. (Peter was really testing her patience!)

Tink sat down under a mushroom and thought about how to get even with Peter. One last scare would make him sit up and take notice.

But, as she thought, she became sleepier and sleepier. She leaned back against the mushroom stem and closed her eyes . . .

The next thing Tink knew, she was suddenly snatched up by a hungry hawk! Tink jingled and jingled – but Peter didn't come!

"I'm not fibbing this time, Peter!" she jingled. "I'm about to become lunch! I'm sorry I ever tried to fool you. This time it's real!"

Then she woke up. Tink was very relieved to discover that she was safe and sound under the shady brim of the mushroom.

Tink took a deep breath. That was very scary, she thought. I think perhaps I learned my lesson. . . .

Then she thought about it again. Nah!

TIM BURTON'S
NIGHTMARE
BEFORE
CHRISTMAS

# Bring on the Scare!

"No, no, no!" Jack Skellington cried, swooping down on a small ghoul carving a grisly face into a pumpkin. "That's much too scary! Didn't I tell you that Santa Claus is coming today?"

"Sorry, Jack." The ghoul started to carve a fuzzy kitten face into a fresh pumpkin.

"That's better." Jack beamed at her, then moved on. He walked through Halloweentown, overseeing the preparations for the next day's Halloween celebration.

"This year will be even better than last year," Jack said to himself. "We've learned so much from dear Santa Claus!"

The year before, Jack and the rest of Halloweentown had tried to take over Santa's holiday, Christmas. But they had learned that it was better to stick to what they knew best.

Jack peered into the graveyard and gasped. Several citizens were dressing up the ghosts in chains and tattered rags.

"Oh, this won't do at all!" he exclaimed. "Poor Santa got enough of a fright last year!"

"Sorry, Jack." The Halloweentown citizens quickly exchanged the chains for garlands of flowers.

Jack laughed. "Much better!"

Finally it was time for Santa's arrival.

"Welcome, Santa!" the Mayor cried. "Welcome to Halloweentown!"

"Thank you," Santa said. "I'd love to see what you have prepared for all the little boys and girls this year."

"Of course!" Jack clapped his hands, and the townspeople paraded past Santa. They showed off their pretty pumpkins, flowery ghosts and all the rest of their work.

Santa looked a little disappointed.

"What's the matter?" Jack asked anxiously. "Was that too scary? We tried to make sure you wouldn't be frightened. . . ."

"Is that what's wrong?" Santa cried. "Don't be silly! You can't de-fright Halloween."

"But we thought you didn't like what we did to Christmas last year," Jack added.

"I didn't," Santa explained. "But that's because it was Christmas – the children were expecting sugar plums and teddy bears, not ghouls and goblins. But at Halloween, it's just the opposite! You can't disappoint them!"

"He's right . . ." Jack mused. "All right! Let's get back to work!"

Instantly, the townspeople produced an array of horrifying tricks and treats – scary jack-o'-lanterns, moaning ghosts and more.

"Ho, ho, ho!" Santa cried as a gang of shrieking banshees chased him out of Halloweentown. "That's more like it! Happy Halloween, everyone!"

Disney·PIXAR
# MONSTERS, INC.

# Happy Halloween!

"Boo?" James P. Sullivan whispered, poking his head through the door. "Hey, Boo, are you here? I came to wish you a Happy Halloween. Boo?"

There was no answer. The big, furry blue monster took one step into the quiet bedroom, then another. He saw the familiar mobile dangling from the ceiling. Toys, books and games were put away neatly on the shelves, and the bed was made. But there was no sign of his little human friend.

Sulley sighed, his shoulders slumping. "Oh, well. Guess you're not here right now," he murmured.

He couldn't help feeling disappointed. He'd been looking forward all day to visiting his favourite human child that evening. There was no Halloween in Monstropolis, but Sulley knew that it was the one day of the year when human children actually *liked* being scared. It seemed like a good day for a visit from a monster – especially a friendly monster.

Sulley yawned. It had been a long day on the Laugh Floor at Monsters, Inc. – his best friend, Mike Wazowski, had broken yet another laugh record that afternoon – and Sulley was tired.

"Guess I could just sit down here and wait," he murmured, sitting on the edge of Boo's bed. His eyes drooped. He leaned back on the bed and yawned again.

"Guess I could just rest my eyes for a little . . ." Sulley mumbled as he drifted off to sleep. "*Zzzzz.*"

The next thing Sulley knew, a cool breeze was tickling his fur. He felt someone poking him in the foot. "Not yet, Mike," he grunted. "It's too early to get up for work, I– AHHHHH!"

He had just opened his eyes. Instead of Mike's familiar round green body, he saw . . .

"A GHOST!" he shrieked. He leaped up and started to run out of the room to escape the horrifying, flapping white creature standing at the end of the bed. "Oh, nooooooo!"

The ghost giggled. "Kitty?" it said happily.

Sulley stopped in his tracks. "Er, what did you say?"

"Kitty!" the ghost cried again. It reached up, grabbed its ghostly white hood, and pulled it back from its face.

When Sulley saw what was under the hood, he broke into a smile. Suddenly he felt very foolish. He'd completely forgotten that every Halloween, human children dress up in costumes to try to scare each other. It had certainly worked on him!

"Boo!" he exclaimed joyfully, reaching out to hug her. "It's you! Happy Halloween, you little monster!"

# "Stackblackbadminton"

After dinner at Prince Eric's castle, Ariel, Eric and Grimsby went into the drawing room to relax.

"My dear, do you play?" Grimsby asked Ariel. He pointed to a table. On it sat a red-and-black chequered board.

Of course, Ariel could not answer because she had exchanged her voice for legs. But she nodded eagerly.

"I'll make the first move," Eric said, and slid a black disk from one square to another.

That seems simple enough, thought Ariel. The game seemed similar to a merpeople game called 'Conch.' She reached over and pushed the same black disk to a third square.

Eric laughed. "No, no. I'm black. And you're red. *You* move the *red*. Understand?"

Ariel gazed at Eric and sighed.

"Perhaps I should show the young lady?" suggested Grimsby.

He took Ariel's seat, and the two men moved the disks all over the chequered board. But Ariel still didn't understand what they were doing – this game wasn't like Conch at all!

Suddenly, she heard a flapping sound on the windowsill. It was Scuttle!

Ariel pointed at the men and mouthed, *What are they doing?*

"They're playing Stackblackbadminton, a popular human game," said Scuttle.

Ariel's eyes widened. That sounded like something she had better learn if she wanted to fit into Eric's world.

"You see those disks?" asked Scuttle. "Those are *chips*. At the end of the game, players stack their chips. Then the dealer – the person *not* playing – "

*Me?* mouthed Ariel.

Scuttle nodded. "Yes. It's up to you to end the game by collecting all the chips off the board."

Ariel smiled. She would show Eric she *did* know how to play.

She walked right over to the two men. They seemed to have finished playing. They were staring hard at the board – and there weren't many chips left on it. So she bent down and swept all the pieces off the board.

Eric and Grimsby yelped. The little mermaid grinned. Eric didn't think she knew how to play his game but, from the stunned look on his face, she'd given him quite a surprise!

Ariel smiled and began to lay the 'chips' out as if they were shells in a game of Conch. This "Stackblackbadminton" game was all right, but she couldn't wait to teach Eric and Grimsby how to play a *really* good game. She picked up the first 'shell' and showed Eric how to move it. He smiled at her, and her heart fluttered. Things were starting to go well at last.

Disney's
THE ARISTOCATS

# The Best Kitty-sitter

Duchess and O'Malley had planned a lovely dinner at Paris's finest restaurant. There was just one problem – they had no kitty-sitter!

O'Malley sighed. "Well, I guess we're just going to have our date night another time," he said. "It's too late to find a kitty-sitter. Too bad."

"Oh, honey, don't be so blue," Duchess said.

"Did I hear someone say 'blue'?" a voice called from the front door. It was Scat Cat, who had been passing by. "Sorry, the door was open."

"That's fine, Scat Cat," O'Malley said. "Come in."

"Did I overhear you say that you couldn't find a kitty-sitter?" Scat Cat asked. "Well, dig it – you found him now!"

Duchess and O'Malley told Toulouse, Marie and Berlioz to behave for Scat Cat. After they left, Scat Cat said to the kittens, "Listen up, cool cats. I'm not the regular kitty-sitter, so this isn't going to be a regular kitty-sitting evening. Got it?"

"Yeah!" they all shouted.

Scat Cat had brought three instruments with him: an upright bass, a trumpet and a small piano. "Gather 'round, cool cats. We're making music!" Scat Cat exclaimed. He showed Toulouse where to put his fingers on the bass. Next, he gave Marie the trumpet and put Berlioz on the piano. Together they jammed for over an hour, having a grand old time.

"Okay, let's go," Scat Cat announced.

"Go where?" Marie asked.

"We've got a gig and we don't want to be late," Scat Cat said. "You're going to *perform*, dig it?"

Scat Cat led the three down the street to a club, where he had signed them up for the weekly open-mike jazz show.

"I don't think we can perform tonight," Berlioz said, shaking his head. "We're not very good."

Scat Cat looked at the three kittens. "You have to play from here," he said, pointing to his heart. "You all have soul – you can't teach that. If you miss a note, just keep playing. *Feel* the vibe."

The kittens smiled. "All right," they said. "Let's rock!"

As they strutted onstage, the familiar faces of Duchess and O'Malley greeted them from the crowd. They had been about to return home from their evening when they saw Scat Cat leading the trio into the club.

"One, and a-two, and a-three," Scat Cat counted and they all began to play. Throughout the club, heads were bopping and paws were tapping. The crowd was mesmerized.

"This is the best jazz group I've ever seen," O'Malley whispered to Duchess, and the happy couple sat back and let the music take over the night.

# Rise and Shine!

"All right, Dwarfs!" Doc called one morning. "Is everyone ready to leave for work? Let's see. We've got Happy, Dopey, Sneezy, Bashful, Grumpy and Sleepy." Doc looked around. "Sleepy?" No answer. Sleepy was nowhere to be found.

"Oh, no, not again," Doc complained, leading the other Dwarfs up the stairs to their bedroom. There, just as Doc expected, they found Sleepy, dozing peacefully in his bed.

Doc walked to Sleepy's bedside. He pulled the covers off the sleeping dwarf. "Come on, Sleepy! Rise and shine!" Doc called. But Sleepy just rolled over and dozed on.

"Oh, this is ridiculous!" exclaimed Grumpy. "We go through this every single morning, dragging Sleepy out of bed, and I'm tired of it."

"Me, too!" said Dopey.

"Me, three!" said Sneezy. *"Ah-CHOO!"*

The Dwarfs stood around Sleepy's bed, looking down at him, wondering what to do.

"I have an idea!" said Doc. "We'll have to take the day off from the diamond mine and stay here today to work on my plan, but I think it will solve our problem – once and for all!"

The Dwarfs gathered into a huddle around Doc as he outlined the details. Then they got their tools and set to work. Soon the bedroom was filled with the sounds of

hammering, sawing and metal working. All of the activity centred on Sleepy's bed. Despite the racket, Sleepy slept on . . . .

He slept all morning. He slept all afternoon. He slept all evening. He slept through the night.

Then, bright and early the next morning, an alarm clock perched on top of Sleepy's bedside table sprang to life; its bell jangled noisily, shaking the clock.

With a rope tied to its handle, the clock bounced across the top of the table until it fell off the edge. The falling clock tugged on the rope, yanking a broomstick at the other end. When the broomstick moved, the large weight it was propping up dropped to the floor, activating a pulley that pulled up sharply on Sleepy's headboard. The head of Sleepy's bed lifted off the floor, and Sleepy slid down and off the foot of the bed, onto a smoothly carved wooden slide that carried him out of the window, down to ground level and – *splash*! – right into a wooden tub filled with cold water.

Wide awake, Sleepy sat in the tub, blinking and wondering what had just happened.

The other Dwarfs crowded around the bedroom window and peered down at him, grinning cheerfully (except Grumpy, of course).

"Good morning, Sleepy!" cried Doc. "Do you like your new alarm clock?"

DISNEY'S
THE HUNCHBACK OF NOTRE DAME

# The Four-legged Festival

Quasimodo was a kind young man who was always quick to offer help to anyone in need. He was especially drawn to those who were alone in the world. After spending years confined to the bell tower of the cathedral, Quasimodo knew just how terrible loneliness could feel.

It wasn't surprising, then, that Quasimodo had a growing collection of orphaned animals. First he had taken in a stray kitten, and then an abandoned puppy. Next he adopted a lamb, an old donkey, a baby bird and an ox. Esmeralda and Phoebus helped him build a pen. But they weren't sure how he could afford to continue feeding so many pets. "I'll find a way – somehow," Quasimodo told the couple. "They're counting on me!"

The Festival of Fools was coming up, and Quasimodo was a little worried about how his pets would react to all the noise and excitement. "While you're helping Clopin with his puppet show at the festival," said Esmeralda, "why don't we have Djali keep an eye on the animals?" Djali was Esmeralda's clever little goat. He was used to crowds, and often danced with Esmeralda in the village square.

"Why, thank you, Esmeralda!" replied Quasimodo. "That's a wonderful idea."

The day of the festival arrived. Esmeralda brought Djali and put him inside the pen with the other animals. The square quickly filled with people wearing costumes and masks. Delicious smells drifted through the air from the sellers' stands. The animals pushed at the sides of the pen, wanting to investigate the new smells and sounds. Djali also wanted to join the fun. He nibbled at the latch of the pen and the gate flew open.

Djali heard the tinkling of Esmeralda's tambourine on the far side of the square and ran towards the sound. The other animals followed – even as the goat crashed through a stall full of masks for sale! Everyone turned to see the animals, which were now disguised as jesters and kings, songbirds and queens. The masked animals danced right past Clopin's puppet wagon and onto Esmeralda's stage. Quasimodo watched in amazement as Djali and the others joined in the gypsy's merry dance. The crowds cheered and showered the performers with coins.

When the show ended, Esmeralda climbed down from the stage and delivered the money to Quasimodo. "This should take care of whatever food you need to buy," she said happily.

Quasimodo felt like dancing for joy – but he decided to leave that to the animals!

# Walt Disney's Bambi

## First Frost

Slowly, Bambi opened his eyes. Curled next to his mother, he was toasty warm in the thicket. Bambi blinked sleepily, peering past the brambles. Something was different. The forest did not look the same. The air was crisp and cold, and everything was frosted and sparkling.

"Jack Frost has been here," Bambi's mother explained. "He's painted the whole forest with ice crystals."

Bambi was about to ask his mother who Jack Frost was and how he painted with ice, when he heard another voice, an impatient one.

"Get up! Get up! Come look at the frost!" It was Thumper. He tapped his foot impatiently. "We haven't got all day!"

Bambi stood and looked at his mother. When she nodded approvingly, he scampered out of the thicket. Bambi looked closely at the colourful leaves on the ground. Each one was covered in an icy white pattern. He touched his nose to a big orange oak leaf. "Ooh, it's cold!" he cried.

"Of course it is!" Thumper laughed.

"I think it's beautiful," said Faline, as she stepped into the clearing.

"Me, too," Bambi agreed.

"Well, come look at this!" Thumper hopped away and the two young deer followed, admiring the way the sun sparkled on the frost-covered trees and grass.

Thumper disappeared under a bush; then Bambi heard a new noise. *Creak, crack.*

Faline pushed through the bushes with Bambi right behind her. There was Thumper, cracking the thin ice on a puddle with his feet.

Bambi had never seen ice before. He pushed on the icy thin puddle covering with his hoof. It seemed to bend. Then it shattered!

Soon the three friends were stomping on the ice-covered puddles. When all the ice was broken, Faline had an idea. "Let's go to the meadow!"

Bambi thought that was a great idea. The grass would be sparkling! They set out at a run, bounding and racing each other through the forest. But when they got to the meadow's edge, they all stopped.

They looked, sniffed and listened quietly. They did not sense danger – no, the trouble was that in the meadow, nothing was different. There was no frost.

"What happened?" Bambi asked.

"Frost never lasts long," Thumper explained. "It melts as soon as the sun hits it. But don't worry. Winter is coming, and soon we'll have something even better than frost. We'll have snow!"

# Orator Owl

On their way home from a leaf-collecting excursion on a cold, blustery autumn afternoon, Pooh, Rabbit, Piglet and Eeyore made their way past Owl's house. They could not help but notice the cheerful light glowing in all the windows – a light so warm and so inviting that the chilly group seemed to thaw just looking at it.

And so it happened that they soon found themselves warm and cosy in Owl's living room.

"Owl, thank you for having us in to warm up," said Pooh. "It's awfully windy and cold outside today."

"Well, it *is* getting on towards winter," Owl replied. "Naturally, that means it will only get colder before it gets warmer." Owl went on to explain the difference between the sort of blustery autumn cold that they were experiencing and the winter sort of cold that was to come. He explained it in very great detail, using words like *frost*, *frosty* and *frostily*. It turned out to be quite a long explanation. Owl was just beginning to expound on the particular subject of frost*bite* when Rabbit interrupted, hoping to give someone else a chance to talk.

"Yes, Owl," he said. "I know that Piglet was very glad to have his scarf on today, weren't you, Piglet?"

"Oh yes," Piglet said. "Kanga knitted it for me."

Owl cleared his throat. "Ah yes, knitting," said Owl. "An admirable hobby. Did you know that knitting is done with knitting *needles*? But they aren't sharp, as one might assume. They are not, for example, as sharp as sewing needles. Or cactus needles . . . ." Owl continued with a comparison of many, many different types of needles. An hour later, when Owl seemed ready to jump into a discussion of pins, Rabbit again tried to change the subject.

"Speaking of pins," Rabbit began, "how is your tail today, Eeyore? Suitably secure and well attached?"

"Seems secure," Eeyore replied with a shrug, "but it always falls off when I least expect it. And I certainly wouldn't expect it to fall off now, when it seems so secure. So I suppose that could mean it's about to fall off."

Rabbit saw Owl sit up in his chair and take a deep breath – a sure sign that he was preparing another speech about tails, or expectations, or Rabbit knew not what – so Rabbit decided it was time to go.

Goodbyes and thankyous were said, and soon the four visitors were outside, making their way home through swirling leaves.

And all the way home, Rabbit tried to decide who was windier: the great autumn wind . . . or long-winded Owl.

# Great Minds Think Alike

Tito the Chihuahua stopped suddenly in the alley and sniffed the air.

"Why'd you stop, shorty?" Einstein the Great Dane complained, shoving the smaller dog with his huge paw.

"For your information," Tito said, "I was locating our next meal."

Einstein looked confused. "You were what?"

Tito sniffed again. "Check it out, *amigo*." He pointed to a window two storeys above them. "Up there!"

Einstein lifted his nose and sniffed. "Meat loaf!" he exclaimed hungrily. Sure enough, a meat loaf was cooling on the windowsill. "But how are we going to get it? It's way up there!"

"Leave it to me," Tito said.

Einstein looked insulted. "I could get that meat loaf if I wanted to," he said.

"Oh, yeah?" Tito said. "Put your money where your mouth is! Come on – first one to the meat loaf gets the first bite."

Tito raced across the alley and climbed up a pile of crates. His plan was to reach a clothesline stretching between two buildings and use it as a tightrope to the windowsill. A clumsy animal like Einstein would never be able to do that!

Meanwhile, Einstein noticed a dumpster skip pushed up against the wall of the block of flats. If he climbed up there and stood on his hind legs, perhaps he would be tall enough to reach the windowsill. A pipsqueak like Tito would have no chance of doing that!

"Ha," Einstein said. "I'll show you that bigger is better, my little friend."

"Oh, yeah?" Tito glared at Einstein. He grabbed the clothesline and began to wriggle his way across. He neared the window . . . .

Einstein clambered on top of the skip. He carefully stretched up, up, up . . . .

Both dogs reached the windowsill at the same time.

"Hey!" Tito yelped. "Where'd dinner go?"

Someone had taken the meat loaf inside!

"Darn," said Tito. "But hey, Einstein, that was a good trick with the dumpster. Do you think you could do it with me standing on your head? Because there are a lot of clotheslines that are too high for me to reach."

"Sure!" said Einstein. "I could lift you up to a clothesline, and – hey! I smell chicken pie!"

Sure enough, there on another windowsill was a steaming dish. And right under that window was a clothesline – a clothesline that would normally be too high for Tito to reach by himself. But with a little help . . .

Tito looked at Einstein. "Are you thinking what I'm thinking?"

Einstein grinned. "Great minds think alike!"

# Off-road Adventure

"Lost toys!" announced Mr Mike the microphone.

"What's wrong?" said Woody.

"Who needs help?" asked Buzz Lightyear.

"It's the Green Army Men!" Hamm the piggy bank cried from the windowsill. "Andy left them outside and it's raining. Now they're stuck in the mud!"

Buzz and Woody hurried to the window and peeked through the rain-splattered glass.

"How are we going to help them?" Woody cried.

"What about RC Car?" Hamm suggested.

"Great idea!" Woody exclaimed. Buzz and Woody climbed inside, and the racing car took off.

RC Car raced out of Andy's bedroom and down the hall. At the top of the stairs Buzz and Woody held their breath.

"Here we goooo!" Buzz cried.

*Bump! Bump! Bump!* They bounced down the stairs.

"Ouch! Oof! Oww!" yelped Buzz.

"Oof! Ouch! Oww!" said Woody.

RC Car raced to the kitchen and through the swinging dog door.

"There they are!" cried Woody.

"Situation critical!" shouted the Green Army Men. "Need help!"

"We're coming, guys!" Buzz shouted.

RC Car veered into the mud.

They parked near the Army Men. With a loud "Yee-hah!" Woody swung his lasso and looped the rope around the Army Men. They tied the other end of the lasso around RC's bumper and pulled the Green Army Men to safety. Then they all crowded into the car.

"All aboard?" asked Woody.

"Roger that," said the sergeant with a crisp salute.

RC Car drove up the pathway and through the dog door. But, when he got to the stairs inside, everyone groaned.

"How can we drive back up?" asked Woody.

"Don't worry!" Hamm yelled from the top of the steps. "We're on it."

It took a while, but soon the toys upstairs had pieced together an ultra-long road out of train tracks, leading right up the stairs. RC Car gunned his engine and up he went, just as Andy's mother pulled into the drive.

The toys all worked together to pull the tracks back into Andy's room. They took them apart and tossed them into the toy box.

"That was close!" said Woody. "But I think we got away with it."

"Of course," said Buzz. "Andy's mum will never suspect a thing."

Downstairs, Andy's mother scratched her head. "I wonder where all this mud came from?" she said.

# Small Fairies Come in Big Packages

Princess Aurora's wedding to Prince Phillip would take place in just a few days. The three good fairies, Flora, Fauna and Merryweather, wanted to give Aurora the perfect gift. They stood in front of an enormous box, trying to decide what to put in it.

"How about a pretty dress for Princess Aurora to wear on her honeymoon. Something pink!" Flora said decisively.

"What about a grand carriage?" Fauna put in with a smile.

Flora shook her head. "King Stefan is already having a carriage made for them. No, let's give her a dress."

"I've got it!" Fauna cried. "A flock of doves that we'll release just as Aurora and Phillip come out of the church. Perfect!"

"A tiara to wear with her wedding gown – that's what Aurora needs," Merryweather piped up. "With three jewels: one red for Flora, one green for Fauna and one blue for me. It will remind our sweet Briar Rose of how much we love her."

"A dress is much more practical than a flock of doves, dear," said Flora firmly.

"But a flock of doves is much more romantic than a dress," Fauna insisted.

Merryweather put her hands on her hips. "A tiara! What's wrong with a tiara?"

But neither Flora nor Fauna even glanced her way. That made Merryweather mad.

"It's settled. We're giving her a dress," Flora said.

"Doves," said Fauna.

"Why can't we give her a – " Merryweather began but, as she waved her arms, trying to get the other fairies' attention, she lost her balance and fell right into the big box. Flora and Fauna did not notice.

"We'll give her both!" said Flora.

They pointed their wands at the box, showering it with sparkles. A huge piece of satin ribbon appeared, wrapped itself around the box, and tied itself into a big bow.

Flora and Fauna put on their capes, ready to deliver the gift to Aurora. But where was Merryweather?

"Oh, well, perhaps she went on ahead," said Flora. "Let's be on our way."

At the palace, Flora and Fauna placed the gift before the Princess. When Aurora untied the ribbon, Merryweather burst out of the box. She presented the Princess with a beautiful tiara that sparkled with red, green and blue jewels.

"Oh, thank you, my dears! It's perfect!" Aurora said with a gasp.

Merryweather smiled. "That's exactly what I thought!" she said.

Walt Disney's
# ALICE
## IN WONDERLAND

# The Queen's Way

"Goodness!" Alice took a few steps back She had no idea a queen could bellow quite so loud! Alice had been excited to meet the Queen of Hearts, but the Queen was always shouting, "Off with his head!" It really wasn't very friendly.

"I guess since she's the Queen, she can do what she likes," Alice said to the flamingo croquet mallet she held firmly by the feet.

The flamingo nodded.

"Perhaps she'll be friendlier when we begin playing." Alice sighed.

"Only if she wins," the flamingo replied.

Alice didn't care if the Queen won. Besides, she wasn't really sure the game had rules. And the hedgehog she was supposed to use for a ball did not look as if he would stay put long enough for her to knock him under any of the playing-card wickets, anyway. Standing back, Alice watched the Queen take her turn.

Her Royalness bent over the hedgehog ball, swung her flamingo mallet high into the air, and brought his beak down with a whoosh. The prickly creature was off on a rolling run. He tumbled through wicket after wicket, getting dizzier as he went. He had nearly finished, when one of the wickets bent over the hedgehog's path too late. The hedgehog rolled off course, and the Queen's turn was over.

"Off with his head!" the Queen roared.

She pointed her terrified flamingo at the card.

"Oh, this is so unfair," Alice lamented to her own flamingo. "It wasn't his fault that the hedgehog got dizzy. And that is no way to treat anyone!"

"It *is* a way," her mallet whispered, looking terrified. "It's the Queen's way."

Unfortunately, the Queen had heard Alice. She turned to Alice. Her face was redder than a tomato. Alice knew what had to be coming. She cowered beside a rosebush and waited for the horrible order.

"Off with her – "

"M-m-my dear." The small King appeared from behind the Queen. "The wickets are out of line." He pointed at the cards that were nervously shuffling themselves off the croquet field.

"Get back here!" the Queen shouted. "I'll have your heads!" Forgetting all about Alice, the Queen marched towards the cards.

Alice breathed a sigh of relief and straightened her collar. "She wants everyone else to lose their heads," she whispered very softly. "But, clearly, she has already lost her own!"

At this, Alice's flamingo laughed so hard, she nearly lost her grip on it. Alice smiled. The Queen might be a living terror, but at least Alice had a friend in this crazy court – even if her friend was a croquet mallet!

# Dawn Patrol

One day, Mowgli went to the jungle to visit his old friend Baloo the bear.

"Why so sad, Mowgli?" asked Baloo.

"It's the dry season, and the river is getting low," said Mowgli. "My friends in the village are worried about running out of water."

"Oh," said Baloo. He scratched his head. "But what about the spring in the jungle? It never goes dry."

Mowgli shook his head. "The spring is much too deep inside the jungle. It would take all day to get there from the village."

Just then, Bagheera the panther padded over. "Mowgli, I have an idea: Dawn Patrol."

The next morning, Bagheera, Baloo and Mowgli all waited by the spring. Before long, the ground shook with the approach of Colonel Hathi and his elephants.

"Hup, two, three, four. Hup, two, three, four," chanted the Colonel as the herd marched behind him.

"Here they come," said Bagheera. "Dawn Patrol."

Quickly, Bagheera, Baloo and Mowgli hid in the bushes. They waited for the elephants to stop at the spring and take a long drink.

"Ready to try my plan?" Bagheera whispered to Mowgli. The boy nodded, then the two sprang from the bushes crying, "To the river!

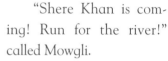

Quick! Everyone, as fast as you can!"

The elephants looked up in alarm.

"W-what's the m-meaning of this?" stammered the Colonel.

"Shere Khan is coming! Run for the river!" called Mowgli.

"Company . . . RUN!" cried the Colonel, and the elephants stampeded through the jungle.

Bagheera and Mowgli watched the herd knock down every tree between the spring and the river. When Mowgli reached the river, he turned around and saw a clear, easy path straight to the big spring!

Now it was time for Baloo to play his part.

"Hey, whoa!" cried Baloo, running up to the herd. "False alarm!"

"What's that?" asked Colonel Hathi.

"Shere Khan isn't coming after all," said Baloo. "Human hunters are after him, so he's heading far away. We're all safe!"

The Dawn Patrol sighed with relief. Then Colonel Hathi called, "Forward, march!"

As the elephants marched off, Mowgli grinned. "With this new path to the spring, my friends will never run out of water."

Bagheera nodded. "Good work," he said.

"Yes, it was," said Baloo with a laugh. "And you know what was good about it? Somebody else did the work for us!"

Walt Disney's
# Pinocchio

# Slugger

Pinocchio, as you know, was not always a real boy. Once, he was a puppet. And before that, he was a log. And before that, he was the trunk of a tall, shady tree. But that's of no great importance to our story . . . it's simply to remind you that Pinocchio was not always a boy – and that to him, being a real boy was indeed a dream come true.

*Our* story, in fact, takes place some time later, when Pinocchio was walking home from school one day. He had just been thinking to himself of what real-boy play he would enjoy that afternoon – climbing trees, or skimming stones, or maybe just stomping in the mud – when suddenly he spied a whole group of real boys gathered in a field just down the road.

"What are you doing?" asked Pinocchio.

"Playing baseball," said a red-haired boy.

"Baseball?" Pinocchio hadn't heard of that game before. But it sounded like fun.

"Can I play?" he asked.

The boys nodded.

"Did you bring a glove?" one boy asked.

"A glove?" said Pinocchio.

"That's okay," said the boy. "You can use mine while I bat." He tossed a big, brown leather glove into Pinocchio's hands. "You can play first base."

Pinocchio grinned. First base! That sounded important! This game was going to be fun. Now, if he could just work out which base was first . . . .

Luckily, the other boys ran off to their bases, leaving just one empty. Pinocchio trotted out to the dusty square. Then he waited to see what came next.

"Batter up!"

*Whoosh!*

*Crack!*

It didn't take long. One fast pitch, and before Pinocchio knew it, a ball was sailing over his head, and a tall boy was running full-speed at him!

"*Ahhhhh!*" Pinocchio screamed, covering his face with his big glove. The boy was safe. And Pinocchio moved to right field. But on the very next pitch, where should the ball fly, but up . . . up . . . up . . . and down to right field. This time, Pinocchio tried to catch it – but it landed with a *plop* on the grass behind him.

But Pinocchio never gave up and, when it was finally his turn to bat, he stepped into the batter's box and held his head high. To Pinocchio's surprise, the bat felt strangely natural in his hands . . . almost like a part of his old, *wooden* self. He watched the pitcher carefully . . . and on the first pitch – *crack!* – he sent the ball high and away, into the sky.

"Hooray!" the boys cheered. A slugger had been born! And a real boy had learned a new game.

# Kida's Surprise

Although it was Kida's 8,500th birthday, she honestly didn't want anyone to make a big fuss about it. There were much more important things to think about. Rebuilding the city, for one thing! And yet, as the day wore on and Milo still had not said even "happy birthday" to her, Kida was beginning to feel a little down.

I threw a big party for Milo a few months ago *and* gave him his very own pet ugobe, thought Kida. And that had just been for his measly 30th birthday. Now it was Kida's big day and, if she didn't know better, she'd think Milo had completely forgotten . . . .

Wait a minute . . . Kida *did* know Milo! And come to think of it, he probably *had* forgotten. And not just him. For the first time in her life, Kida sadly realized, no one in Atlantis had remembered her birthday. Obviously there were much bigger things for Atlanteans to think about. She really didn't want to seem selfish, but would one little seaweed cake with a few candles have been too much to ask for?

Anyway, Kida tried as hard as she could to not feel sorry for herself, and concentrated instead on tuning up her Ketak speeder. It was hard, though, when Milo finally came up to her later that afternoon and asked if she'd like to help him take his slug-like ugobe for a walk.

"Oh, I don't know." Kida sighed. "I'm a little tired."

"Ah, come on, Kida," said Milo. "I thought it would be such a fun thing to do on this special day."

"Special?" said Kida, suddenly perking up. Had Milo remembered her birthday after all? "Of course." Milo grinned. "It's exactly eight and a half months since we met!"

"Oh," Kida replied.

"So are you coming?" Milo asked her.

"Oh, why not," she finally agreed.

So, Milo put a lead on his ugobe and took Kida by the hand. He led them through the palace courtyard, out onto the street. But, instead of turning right, Milo went straight on, heading towards the city centre.

"Where are you going?" Kida asked. "There's no place for an ugobe to run this way."

"No?" said Milo. "Are you sure?"

"Positive," said Kida. "There's only – "

"SURPRISE!"

Kida's mouth fell open as thousands of smiling Atlanteans greeted her with a thunderous cheer and a cake the size of a Ketak. The entire kingdom had gathered beneath the great crystal Heart of Atlantis to surprise her!

"Happy birthday, Kida," said Milo. "You didn't really think we'd forget it, now, did you?"

Disney's
# ROBIN HOOD

## For Old Times' Sake

At last, good King Richard had returned to Nottingham and sentenced greedy Prince John and his cronies, the Sheriff of Nottingham and Sir Hiss, to hard labour in the rock mines.

"Brave Robin Hood," said the King upon summoning Robin to the castle one day soon after his return. "In light of the fact that Prince John has harassed and overtaxed the good people of this kingdom, and in recognition of all you have done to defend and protect them while I was gone, I ask if you would do the honour of returning this money to the citizens of Nottingham, to whom it rightfully belongs."

Robin Hood beamed. "Your Majesty," he replied, "it would be my honour."

The next day, at the appointed time, Robin Hood arrived at the castle, ready to perform his duty. He had brought Little John to assist him. They found King Richard waiting for them just inside the main gate. Next to the King was a wagon overloaded with bags of gold coins.

"Well, my boy," the King said to Robin Hood, "here is the people's money. I trust you to distribute it fairly."

Robin Hood smiled and looked at the wagon. He looked at Little John. He looked at the King. He looked back at the wagon.

Then his smile faded.

"Something doesn't feel right," Robin Hood said, turning to face Little John. "Something is . . . *missing*."

"Missing?" Little John said, surprised.

"Of course!" Robin Hood cried. For all those years under Prince John's rule, he had *robbed from the rich* to give to the poor. That was his thing. Giving to the poor without the robbing part felt somehow . . . incomplete. Now that generous King Richard was back, there would be no need to rob from the rich. Naturally, thought Robin, that was a good thing. And yet . . . it *was* the end of an era.

"Your Majesty," Robin Hood said to the king, "I don't suppose you could make this handing over of the money a bit more . . . oh, I don't know . . . *challenging*?"

King Richard wrinkled his brow. "Challenging?" he replied, puzzled.

Robin Hood turned to Little John, who also looked confused. "What do you say? One last heist . . . for old time's sake?"

Little John smiled.

King Richard also understood, which is how it happened that, later that afternoon, Robin Hood and Little John 'stole' a wagonload of gold from the castle yard.

And wouldn't you know it – King Richard did not seem to mind at all!

# A Silo Scare

Flik took a step back and gazed up at the giant silo he and a troop of ants had just finished building. Now that the colony was using his harvester, they had a surplus of wheat. The silo would store the wheat safely.

"Nice job, Flik," Queen Atta said.

Flik blushed. A compliment from Atta always made his face feel warm. Atta was the smartest and prettiest ant in the colony. She was also its new Queen.

"Thanks, Atta," Flik said, trying to sound casual. "It should keep our wheat dry all winter."

Suddenly, a voice called down from the top of the silo. "Hellooooo," it said.

Flik and Atta looked up. It was Dot, Atta's little sister. She and her Blueberry friends were sitting on top of the silo.

"The view up here is amazing!" Dot called.

"Dot! Be careful!" Atta said worriedly.

Dot grinned down at her sister. "We will!"

"Don't worry," said Flik. "I built in several safety – "

Atta interrupted him. "I have a meeting," she told Flik. "Stay out of trouble," she added in a louder voice. For a second Flik thought Atta was talking to him. Then he realized that she was talking to the Blueberries.

"I'll keep an eye on them," Flik said.

"Come on up, Flik," Dot called as Atta hurried away. "You just have to see the view!"

"Coming!" Flik replied. He did want to see the view, and he also wanted to keep a close eye on the Blueberries.

But, just as Flik got to the top, one of the Blueberries leaped into the silo.

"Wheeeeee!" she cried as she zoomed down towards the pile of wheat.

"The silo is not a playground," Flik told the other girls. "It's for storing wheat, and I built in all these extra safety devices – "

"Come on, Flik," Dot interrupted. "We don't need any safety devices!"

Grinning, she jumped into the silo and slid to the pile of wheat at the bottom. Two other Blueberries followed. But then – *whoops!* – another Blueberry accidentally pushed down a lever. A big pile of wheat tumbled into the silo, heading straight for the Blueberries below!

Panicked, Flik hit a switch. The falling wheat was caught halfway down by a handy-dandy wheat stopper – one of the safety devices he'd built into the silo.

The Blueberries stared at Flik. Just then, Atta walked by. "Dot, what are you doing?" she asked.

"Uh, Flik was just showing us his great safety devices," Dot said sheepishly.

"And they really work," said Flik, sighing with relief.

322

## Walt Disney's
## 101 DALMATIANS

# Special Delivery

Now that their family had grown so large, Roger, Anita, Nanny and the Dalmatians had moved to the country, or to the "Dalmatian Plantation", as Roger liked to call it. A weekly delivery of dog food came from the city. It arrived every Thursday at 3pm, and Rolly looked forward to it with eager anticipation.

One Thursday, Rolly and Pepper noticed that the back of the van had been left open. "Are you thinking what I'm thinking?" Pepper asked Rolly.

Rolly nodded. "Snack time!" Rolly and Pepper made a dash for the van and leaped into the back. Pepper clambered up onto the pile of bags and sniffed around. There had to be some loose food somewhere . . . .

"Bingo!" Pepper cried. "Rolly, up here!"

Rolly was there in an instant.

*Slurp, slurp, crunch*! The two puppies were so busy eating that they didn't see the van driver come out of the house.

*Slam*! He closed up the back of the van. A second later it was rumbling down the drive.

"Uh-oh," Rolly whispered.

Finally, after what seemed like a very long time, the vehicle lurched to a halt. The back door opened, and the driver began unloading bags of food.

Pepper and Rolly jumped off the van while he wasn't looking. They ran and hid behind the house.

"What do you two think you're doing?" a gruff voice asked.

The puppies spun around. A big bulldog was looking down at them. "This is my property," the dog said. "It is time for you to scram."

The two puppies stared at him.

"Now!" he barked.

"You don't scare me," Pepper said boldly. "You're not half as bad as Cruella."

The bulldog's mouth fell open. "Do you mean Cruella De Vil?" he asked. "You must be Pongo's and Perdita's puppies! I heard about your adventures over the Twilight Bark! You live on the Dalmatian Plantation, right?"

"Yes!" cried Rolly. "Can you take us there?"

"You bet!" the bulldog said. "Let's go!"

Luckily, Pongo and Perdita were out that day and didn't realize what a pickle Rolly and Pepper had got themselves into. But there were 97 puppies waiting in the garden as Rolly and Pepper arrived with their escort.

"Wow," said Lucky, after he had heard their tale. "Were you scared of that big mean bulldog?"

"No way!" Pepper spoke up. "That bulldog was all bark and no bite!"

# Abu's Wild Ride

It was midnight in Agrabah, and all the kingdom was fast asleep – all, that is, except little Abu. Perhaps it was because of the extra-long nap he'd had that day. Or perhaps it was the giant piece of chocolate cake he'd eaten that evening. Whatever the reason, Abu simply could not fall asleep. And so, hours later, when the palace was so quiet you could hear a veil drop, Abu was looking around for something to do.

Of course, he could have made himself a midnight snack. But he really wasn't hungry. Or he could have played with Rajah's tiger toys. But no . . . they were covered with tiger slobber. Yuck! There was, it seemed, nothing at all in the whole, entire palace for a wide-awake monkey to do . . . . And then, there in the corner, Abu suddenly spied a patch of bright wool hovering in the moonlight. Aladdin's Magic Carpet!

Now that, Abu thought to himself, was something to do! And so, with a happy little squeal, Abu hopped aboard.

*Whoosh!* Before Abu even knew what hit him, the Carpet was off, zipping towards the ceiling, then zooming to the floor. Eek! Abu clung to its fringes for dear life – and grinned. This was great! Obviously, the Magic Carpet wasn't very sleepy either. In fact, it was acting as if it had eaten some chocolate cake too!

The Carpet carried the little monkey through the castle corridors . . . whizzing in and out of doorways, twisting around columns, skidding down staircases, as fast as it could fly . . . until at last it zoomed right out of an open window.

Uh-oh, thought Abu. This wasn't good. Where in the world was the Magic Carpet going? Soon the palace was just a tiny dot behind him. Where would he end up?

Just as Abu was really starting to worry, what should reach out and grab a tassel, but a giant blue hand.

"Whoa, now, pardners!" a hearty voice boomed. "Slow down!"

It was the Genie. Abu sighed with relief.

"Taking a little joyride, are we?" he said.

The Carpet nodded and, if it's possible for a carpet to look sheepish, well then, it looked very sheepish indeed.

"Well, time to go home now, oh Flat, Fuzzy One," the Genie said, giving the Carpet a gentle little pat. "Hmm, I can't say I blame you, Abu. I've always wanted to drive one of these too. Whaddya say we take her home together?" He gave Abu a wink. "Scoot over! And, hey, Abu, I won't tell Aladdin about tonight if you don't."

Abu shook the Genie's hand. It was a deal!

# Eeyore's New Old House

One blustery, cold November day in the Hundred-Acre Wood, the blustery, cold November wind blew so strongly that it knocked Eeyore's house right over!

So Eeyore went to Pooh's house. "Well, Pooh," Eeyore said, "it seems that November just doesn't like me. Or my house. So I'm afraid I will have to stay here with you. If you don't mind, that is."

Pooh assured Eeyore that he didn't mind and offered him some honey.

"I'd prefer thistles, if you have any, which you probably don't," Eeyore said. "Oh, well. Perhaps Rabbit has some."

Well, Rabbit did have some thistles, so Eeyore settled down to stay with Rabbit. But Rabbit's house was so full of vegetables and gardening tools – rakes and shovels and baskets and twine – that there was scarcely room in the burrow for Eeyore. "I suppose Piglet might have more room, though I doubt it," said Eeyore.

Piglet told Eeyore he was welcome to stay with him, and even made Eeyore a little bed next to the pantry, which was full of haycorns. But Eeyore was allergic to haycorns, and soon his sneezing almost knocked Piglet's own house down.

"One house knocked down today is more than – *ah-choo*! – plenty," said Eeyore. "I'll just have to try Kanga and Roo."

Kanga and Roo were happy to put Eeyore up in their house. Roo was so excited to have a guest that he couldn't stop bouncing. Soon Eeyore was feeling dizzy just from watching him. But, just as Eeyore was about to try Owl's house, Piglet, Rabbit and Pooh arrived.

"Eeyore, we've found you the perfect house to live in!" Piglet cried.

"I doubt that," Eeyore said as they led him through the Wood. "The perfect house would have thistles, and enough room, and no haycorns, and, above all, no bouncing. But where am I going to find a house like that?"

Soon, they arrived at a snug little house made of sticks, with a pile of thistles in it. "Here it is, Eeyore," said Piglet.

"That's *my* house," said Eeyore, hardly able to believe his eyes. "But my house got knocked down."

"Piglet and I put it back together again," Pooh said, "and Rabbit donated his thistles, so now you have a house with thistles, and enough room, and no haycorns, and, above all, no bouncing."

Eeyore looked at his house, and then at his friends. "It looks like November doesn't dislike me so much after all," he said. "Maybe, that is."

# The Meaning of Thanksgiving

"Here, Stitch," Lilo said. "Hold up this Pilgrim man while I tack up his wife."

Stitch was confused. He didn't understand why Lilo was running around hanging up decorations. What was so special about tonight's dinner?

"Hungry," he said.

"Quit complaining, Stitch," Lilo scolded. "It's Thanksgiving. You're supposed to be very, very hungry before we eat. Just like the Pilgrims, you know."

Stitch didn't know. In fact, he was more confused than ever.

"That's where Thanksgiving comes from," Lilo explained. "The Pilgrims were hungry, so the Indians made them a big dinner, and so they were all thankful."

"Pilgrims?" Stitch repeated uncertainly.

"Pilgrims," Lilo said firmly. "The Pilgrims were some people who came across the ocean in these big boats, and . . ." She sighed as she noticed that Stitch looked more confused than ever.

Suddenly Lilo had an idea.

"I know how to explain it!" she cried. "Stitch, the Pilgrims were sort of like you — remember how you came to Earth in a spaceship, far, far away from your old planet?"

Stitch nodded. He definitely remembered that.

"Okay," Lilo said. "And remember how you were lost and all alone, and you weren't sure what to do, and everything seemed strange and unfriendly, and then you joined our family?"

"Family!" Stitch cried happily. He nodded again.

"Well, that's the same thing!" Lilo said. "You're like a Pilgrim. And now you're thankful to be here, right?"

"Right," Stitch agreed.

"That's how the Pilgrims felt too," Lilo said. "They were thankful. So now we celebrate Thanksgiving to remember that. Get it?"

Stitch nodded. He understood about being thankful. He still wasn't sure why Lilo was hanging up so many decorations, and he still wasn't sure why they had to wait so long to eat the turkey he could smell cooking in the kitchen, but he decided it didn't matter. When Lilo left the room to get more decorations, Stitch took a small bite out of the cardboard Pilgrim. It tasted pretty good. He took a larger bite, then another.

By the time Lilo returned, the whole Pilgrim was gone. She looked around in confusion.

"What happened to the decorations?" she asked Stitch.

Stitch grinned at her. There was a tiny piece of Pilgrim's hat stuck in his teeth. Lilo stared at it suspiciously.

"Happy Thanksgiving!" Stitch cried.

# A Talented Mouse

"Look, Dumbo," Timothy Mouse said, pointing to the newspaper. "There's another article about us in here!"

That wasn't unusual. Ever since Dumbo had become famous for being able to fly, everyone was interested in him.

Mrs Jumbo, Dumbo's mother, peered over Timothy's shoulder. "What a nice story," she cooed. "Too bad the picture isn't better – why, I can hardly see you, Timothy!"

Timothy peered at the paper. "Hey," he said, scanning the story. "This article doesn't mention me at all!"

"It's all right," Mrs Jumbo said soothingly. "Everyone knows how important you are."

Timothy puffed out his chest proudly. After all, he had taught Dumbo to fly!

Then he sagged again. "Am I really that important?" he said. "It's Dumbo who has the talent – not me."

Mrs Jumbo and Dumbo tried to comfort him, but he wandered away sadly. He was so smart, so talented – he should be famous too!

"I have to figure out a way to get famous on my own," he muttered. "But how?"

Suddenly he snapped his fingers.

"I've got it!" he cried. "I'll learn to fly too! That way Dumbo and I can be famous together!"

He quickly climbed to the top of the tallest circus tent. Dumbo had learned to fly by jumping off things. Timothy just hoped it would work for him too. He rubbed his hands together.

"Here goes nothing . . ." he muttered.

He leaped off the tent and looked down. The ground seemed very far away.

"Uh-oh!" Timothy gulped. What had he done? The ground got closer and closer. Timothy squeezed his eyes shut . . . .

Suddenly, Timothy felt himself being whisked upwards. Opening his eyes, he saw that he was clutched in Dumbo's trunk.

"Whew!" he gasped. "Thanks, chum!"

Dumbo smiled at his little friend. He set Timothy in his cap.

Timothy settled into the familiar spot. Flying was much more fun when Dumbo's ears did all the work!

Soon they landed beside Mrs Jumbo.

"Oh, Timothy!" she cried. "You're safe! When I saw you fall, I was so worried . . . . Dumbo and I don't know what we'd do without you."

Timothy blinked. "Never thought of it that way," he mused. "Maybe I'm not front-page news every day. But who cares? I know I'm important, and my friends know it too. That's what matters!"

He smiled. He had plenty of his own talent, and that was good enough for him!

DISNEY'S
MICKEY MOUSE

# Spring Cleaning

Mickey Mouse hummed as he straightened up his messy house. He swept up some leaves that had blown in through the front door. Then he shook the mud off his doormat.

He was picking up some old magazines when one of them caught his eye.

"'Make a Fresh Start with Spring Cleaning,'" Mickey read aloud. "Hmm. Spring cleaning, eh?"

He looked out of the window. It wasn't spring – it was autumn! What was he doing cleaning his house?

"Whew!" he exclaimed as he dropped his broom and flopped onto the sofa. "Looks like I have a whole day free now. I think I'll see if Minnie wants to come over!"

A short while later, Minnie Mouse rang the doorbell. "Hi, Mickey!" she said cheerfully. "What do you want to do to – "

She gasped. Mickey's house was a mess! There was mud on the floor, dust on the shelves, dirty dishes on the table, laundry piled here and there, books and magazines everywhere . . . .

"What's wrong?" Mickey asked.

"Mickey," Minnie said, "er, when was the last time you cleaned your house?"

Mickey laughed. "Don't be silly, Minnie!" he said. "I don't need to clean this place for months."

"M-m-months?" Minnie gasped. She couldn't believe it. In a few months, Mickey's entire house would be buried in mess!

"Sure!" Mickey shrugged. "Haven't you ever heard of spring-cleaning?"

Minnie wasn't sure what to do. She didn't want to be rude, but she had to convince Mickey to clean his house – and it couldn't wait until spring!

"You know, Mickey," she said casually, "I just read something about a fun new trend."

"Really?" Mickey smiled. "What's that, Minnie? Maybe it's something we could do today, since we have the whole day free!"

"Oh!" Minnie pretended to be surprised at the idea. "Why, I suppose we could! I hadn't thought of that."

"So, what's the trend?" Mickey asked eagerly. "Waterskiing? Rock climbing? Fondue parties?"

"No," Minnie said cheerfully. "Autumn cleaning! It's the newest rage."

"Autumn cleaning?" Mickey said doubtfully. He blinked, then smiled. "You know, that's so crazy, it sounds like fun! Come on, let's try it!"

Minnie smiled and picked up the magazine with the spring-cleaning article in it. "Good," she said. She stuffed the magazine into the dustbin. "I'll start right here!"

# A Real Sleeper!

"Time for bed, Nemo," said Marlin. "It's a school day tomorrow," he added. "You need to get your rest."

"Okay, Dad," said Nemo. "But can you tell me a story? How about one when you were younger?"

"Well, just one then," said Marlin, swimming back over to his only child. He thought for a moment, then smiled broadly. "Did you know that when I was younger – much younger, actually – did you know that I wanted to be a comedian?"

Nemo's eyes widened with surprise. "*You*? A comedian? Aren't comedians supposed to be . . . funny?"

"Well, you see, son," said Marlin, "life is not easy for a clownfish. You may as well realize that right now. See, when you're a clownfish, everyone you meet assumes that you are funny. It's a common mistake. Anyway, years ago, I figured that as long as everyone expected me to be funny, I would try being funny for a living."

"But, Dad," said Nemo, "you aren't funny at all."

"Hey, now! Wait just a minute!" Marlin said, a bit huffily. "In my day, I was known as quite the crack-up! Let me see. I'm sure I can remember some of my old routine, if I just think about it for a minute." He thought for a moment. "All right, it's all coming back!" He cleared his throat. "Good evening, ladies and jellyfish! The ocean sure is looking *swell* tonight. Would you like me to give you a coral report about the latest happenings on the reef? Get it?" he said, looking down at Nemo. "You see, there's something called an oral report, and the words coral and oral sound quite a bit alike."

Nemo gave his father a pained look.

"So, the other day my appendix nearly burst," Marlin went on. "So I decided I'd better go to a sturgeon!"

Nemo blinked. "Dad, these really aren't that funny," he said with a yawn.

"A *sturgeon*. Get it? Rather than a surgeon?" Marlin sighed and continued his routine. "A funny thing happened on the way to the show tonight. I met a guy, nice fish and all, but he seemed to be a bit down on his luck. He told me he was living on squid row."

Nemo's eyes were starting to droop sleepily.

"Do you know why the whale crossed the ocean?" Marlin continued. "Now, don't try to guess. I'll tell you: the whale crossed the ocean to get to the other tide. The other *tide*."

Nemo's eyes were now completely closed, and a tiny snore escaped from him. Marlin smiled at his sleeping son.

"Works every time," he said with a chuckle.

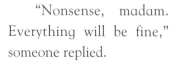

## Surprise!

Basil of Baker Street looked up from his newspaper. He sniffed the air. A mysterious smell was wafting through the room. There had also been some strange noises in the hallway, and the front door had been opened and closed an unusual number of times.

"That doesn't smell like Mrs Judson's usual tea," he muttered grimly. "I sense there's trouble afoot . . . ."

He hurried to the kitchen. His housekeeper, Mrs Judson, was standing near the oven.

"Er – what is it, Basil?" she asked quickly.

Basil narrowed his eyes. Was it his imagination, or did she have a guilty expression on her face? Just then, he noticed a dab of a mysterious blue substance on the counter.

"Nothing," he told Mrs Judson, quickly wiping up the substance. "Nothing at all."

He retreated to his study, his mind churning. Could this be a mystery – in his own house?

He quickly set up a complicated array of beakers and test tubes, then dropped the blue substance into his new contraption. The little dial at the end spun around. The arrow landed on the words UNKNOWN SUBSTANCE – EDIBLE.

"Confound it," he muttered. "That doesn't tell me anything!"

He decided to search for more clues. Tiptoeing into the hall, he heard voices.

He followed the voices to the kitchen. Leaning against the door, he listened carefully.

"Oh, dear, I'll never be ready!" Mrs Judson cried.

"Nonsense, madam. Everything will be fine," someone replied.

"That's my dear friend Dawson's voice!" Basil whispered. "Blast it, don't tell me he's in on this dastardly plot!"

Just then, Dawson opened the door and spotted Basil. "There you are, old chap," Dawson said. "There's something that requires your attention, if you don't mind."

"There is?" Basil asked suspiciously.

Dawson chuckled. "Yes, I need to have a word with you in the drawing room."

Aha! Basil thought. Perhaps now I will get to the bottom of this mystery!

Dawson threw open the doors of the drawing room.

"Surprise!"

Basil stared in shock. His family and friends all stood there, smiling at him. Even Olivia Flaversham and her father were there. And Mrs Judson was holding a bright blue cake with candles on it!

Basil laughed out loud. What kind of detective am I? he thought. I didn't even remember my own birthday!

# Why Worry?

Zazu didn't know what to do with Timon and Pumbaa! Ever since they had come to the Pride Lands, he'd been trying to find the perfect jobs for them.

"Zazu," said Simba, "I think you should forget it. Timon and Pumbaa are used to taking life as it comes. *Hakuna matata* – no worries – that's their philosophy."

"Well, it's certainly not mine!" said Zazu.

That afternoon, the hornbill told Timon and Pumbaa that they would be in charge of watching the cubs while the lionesses went off to hunt. "No problem!" said Timon.

"Can we go to the water hole by ourselves?" asked Kiara, Simba's daughter.

"Sure," said Timon. "Have fun!"

"Do we have to take a nap?" wondered another cub.

"Not if you don't want to," said Pumbaa.

The cubs thought Timon and Pumba were the best babysitters on Earth. But Zazu didn't. He was furious.

"Aw, Zazu," said Timon. "Loosen up!"

"Things are loose enough around here as it is." Zazu sniffed. "Too loose, if you ask me."

The next day, Zazu put Timon and Pumbaa in charge of clearing the brushes around the water hole. As they uprooted each plant, they found an insect feast in the soil underneath. Pretty soon they were stuffed. It was time for a nap.

"What's this?" shouted Zazu. "Sleeping on the job?"

"Don't get your feathers in a ruffle," replied Timon. "What is it with you, anyway? You seem kind of tense all the time."

"Tense? Of course I'm tense!" Zazu shouted. "I'm Simba's right-hand man. It's up to me to see that the kingdom is in perfect order!"

Pumbaa spoke up. "And you do a very good job of it too."

"Thank you," said Zazu.

"But," added Timon, "what good is an ordered kingdom if you never stop to enjoy it?"

Zazu admitted that Timon had a point. The other members of the kingdom always seemed to head in the other direction every time they saw Zazu coming. Maybe he was too hard on everyone, including himself.

"Gentlemen," Zazu said. "I finally have the perfect job for you. I'm making you the ministers of *hakuna matata*. You are in charge of keeping things from getting too serious around here."

Simba was delighted when he found out. "Zazu, you're a genius!" he said.

"Thank you, sire," said Zazu. "I always said there was something special about those two!"

# The Masquerade Ball

"Where could she be?" Cinderella asked. She looked around the grand ballroom. Hundreds of happy citizens were gathered there, each dressed in a splendid costume.

Cinderella and her new husband, the Prince, were holding a Masquerade Ball. Cinderella had sent a special invitation to her Fairy Godmother, who had promised to come.

But the ball had started almost an hour ago, and Cinderella still hadn't seen any sign of the plump, cheerful little woman.

"Don't worry, my love," the Prince said. "I'm sure she'll – what's this?"

A messenger handed Cinderella a note.

*Never fear –*
*I'm here, my dear.*
*Just seek and you will find*
*Which mask I am behind!*

Her Fairy Godmother was playing a trick on her! "I'll find you," Cinderella whispered.

Was her Fairy Godmother wearing that beautiful unicorn costume? Was she the princess with the pink mask? The dancing harlequin clown? The fuzzy brown bear? Cinderella felt a little dizzy as she turned around and around. How would she ever find her Fairy Godmother in the crowd?

Cinderella stared at a masked milkmaid with twinkling eyes standing near a fountain.

Could that be her? she wondered.

Cinderella looked around thoughtfully. When she turned back to the fountain, the milkmaid was gone! Instead, someone in a butterfly mask was standing there.

"Looking for someone, Princess?" the butterfly said in a deep voice.

"No – never mind," Cinderella said.

She wandered away, still searching. But she kept thinking about the twinkling eyes behind the butterfly mask. Then she remembered something – the milkmaid had the same twinkling eyes! Could it be . . . ?

She hurried back to the fountain. But there was no sign of the milkmaid or the butterfly. The only person standing nearby was wearing a beautiful white swan costume.

"Oh, dear," Cinderella whispered.

She stared at the swan. Mischievous eyes twinkled behind the feathered white mask.

Suddenly, Cinderella laughed out loud. "Aha!" she cried. "I caught you!"

She pulled off the swan mask. Her Fairy Godmother smiled back at her. "You win!" she exclaimed. "How did you find me?"

"I almost didn't, the way you kept magically changing costumes," Cinderella said. "Then I remembered how you magically changed *my* outfit not too long ago – and I figured it out!"

# Jazzing It Up

"Now, that's what I call a beat!" Thomas O'Malley cried. He tapped his paw to the lively rhythm of Marie's singing. The kitten was really learning to jazz up her musical exercises.

"Nice jivin'," Scat Cat purred when Marie was finished. "You keep it up, little lady, and you'll be rockin' the whole house at your recital next week!"

Marie smiled happily. O'Malley and his friends were so funny! She was glad O'Malley had come to live with her mother and brothers and Madame Bonfamille in the big Paris house.

She was also glad that there was a recital coming up. All of Madame Bonfamille's friends were coming, and some of her mother's and O'Malley's too. There would be tea and crumpets and salmon and fresh, creamy milk. It was going to be a gala event.

And there was more. None of the guests knew what Marie was going to perform. It was going to be a total surprise, and completely different!

Normally, Marie performed a classical piece by Brahms or Mozart – something sweet and delicate and ladylike. But not this time . . . .

Finally, it was recital day. Marie peeked out from behind the velvet curtain and felt her heart race. The parlour was packed with fancy ladies, gentlemen and cats from all over Paris.

"I hope they like it," she said to herself as she took the stage.

Scat Cat gave her a quick wink before he began to pound away on the piano. A few of the ladies in the audience gasped, and one waved a handkerchief in front of her face.

"It's too late to turn back now," Marie told herself. She tapped her foot, took a deep breath, and began to sing . . . .

Her voice was loud and clear and slid across the notes like honey.

Madame Bonfamille and all the cats smiled and nodded in time with the rhythm. But most of the ladies and gentlemen did not look as pleased.

Scat Cat's eyes narrowed as he pounded his paws on the ivory keys. The romping music echoed off the parlour walls.

Marie belted out the refrain. She closed her eyes and let the music carry her away. And, when she opened them, it was her turn to be surprised. Everyone in the audience was moving to the beat, tapping their feet or nodding their heads. They were in the groove!

Marie did a little flip before she and Scat Cat finished the song. And, as soon as she stopped singing, the audience was on its feet. Marie and her jazzy performance received a standing ovation!

Disney·PIXAR
## MONSTERS, INC.

# Tough Audience

The sticker on the door read: ENTER AT YOUR OWN RISK. But Mike wasn't scared. He always collected the most laughs on the floor and he had never met a child he couldn't crack . . . up. Tossing his microphone from one hand to the other, Mike sauntered through the wardrobe door to face his audience.

"Hey, how ya doin' tonight?" Mike greeted the child. The boy in the racing-car pyjamas just glared. "Did you hear the one about the monster who made it in show business?" He really clawed his way to the top." Mike paused for a laugh, but the boy was silent. "Talk about making a killing!" Mike added. Still he got nothing.

"All right. I can see you're a tough audience. Enough of the B material." Mike pulled out the stops. He told his best jokes. He worked the room. He was on the stool, off the stool, hanging on the curtains, standing on the bedstead. But the child didn't even crack a smile.

Mike prepared to let the one about the seven-legged sea monster fly, when he heard tapping on the wardrobe door.

"You know you really ought to get that checked." Mike pointed at the wardrobe. "You could have skeletons in there." The child didn't blink.

Mike pulled the door open a crack. "I'm working here," he whispered.

Sulley poked his head in. "Mikey, you're dying. You've been on for 20 minutes and you're getting nothing. There are plenty of other kids to make laugh tonight. You can come back to this one later."

"No way," Mike hissed. "He loves me. When he laughs he's going to laugh big. I can feel it." A teddy bear sailed through the air and hit Mike in the eye. "See? He's throwing me presents."

"Cut your losses, Mikey. Let this one go." Sulley put a large hairy paw on Mike's head and urged him back through the door.

"I'm telling you, I've almost got him," Mike spoke through clenched teeth, and barely flinched when the unamused boy tossed a banana peel at him.

"And I'm telling you to give . . . it . . . up." Sulley pulled harder on Mike. Mike grabbed the door frame and braced himself. Suddenly Sulley lost his grip, and Mike flew backwards, skidding on the banana peel and falling flat out.

"Why, I oughta . . ." Mike leaped to his feet ready to charge Sulley but was interrupted by the sound of laughing. In fact, the child was laughing so hard tears streamed down his face. Mike high-fived Sulley. "You know, some kids just go for the physical comedy," he said with a shrug.

# The Father of Invention

There was never a dull moment in the castle of Belle and the Prince. Friends came and went, Mrs Potts and the other members of the household bustled about, and Maurice, Belle's father, was always tinkering away on a new invention.

One morning, Maurice wheeled a complicated-looking contraption into the kitchen, and presented it to Mrs Potts. "Just a little something to make your life easier," he said proudly.

"Thank you, Maurice dear, but . . . what is it?" the housekeeper wondered.

"I call it a 'plate pitcher'," answered Maurice. He took a pile of clean plates and loaded them onto a mechanical arm. Then he positioned the machine in front of the open china cabinet. He pressed a button and stood back proudly. With a couple of loud clangs, the machine sprang to life.

The plate pitcher began to hurl plates this way and that. They smashed against walls and onto the floor.

"Look out, Mrs Potts!" shouted Maurice as a plate whizzed by her head. He crawled along the floor, reached up and hit the off switch. "I'll just go work out the kinks," he said, wheeling the machine out of the room.

The next day, Maurice had another surprise. "It's for cleaning the carpets," he explained as he pointed to a large metal box with a big hose coming out of it. "No more beating heavy rugs for you!"

"Well, it looks harmless," Mrs Potts decided. "How does it work?"

"Like so!" exclaimed Maurice. He picked up the hose and flipped a switch. Instantly, curtains, pillows and lamps were sucked towards the nozzle – and it looked as if Maurice himself was in danger of disappearing! Luckily, Mrs Potts came to his rescue and turned off the machine.

"Must have made it a tad too powerful," Maurice admitted.

The following day Maurice had yet another time-saving device for Mrs Potts. This one was a laundry machine that flooded the entire ground floor of the castle with water and soapsuds.

"Maurice," Mrs Potts said gently, "it is very sweet of you to want to make my job easier. But I enjoy it. By taking care of the castle, I'm taking care of the people I love." She looked thoughtful for a moment, then added, "But I have to admit, the one thing I would love is something that would make me a nice, hot cup of tea at the end of the day."

"I have just the thing!" Maurice replied with a twinkle in his eye.

Mrs Potts looked slightly worried. "You do?" she asked.

"Yes," Maurice answered. "Me!"

335

THE EMPEROR'S
*NEW GROOVE*

# Kronk's Feast

"One more time!" Kronk cried. The Junior Chipmunks looked at their leader, took deep breaths and launched into "We're Not Woodchucks" for the fourth time. "We're the ch-ch-chipmunks. We're not w-w-woodchucks," the kids sang, halfheartedly puffing out their cheeks.

The tired troop sagged on their log. Next to them, Bucky the squirrel and three of his friends sang along too – in Squirrel. "Squeak sq-sq-squeak. Sq-sq-squeak squeak, squeaker, squeak." The furry animals' tails drooped.

"I'm hungry," Tipo whispered to his sister Chaca.

"Keep singing," Chaca said behind her hand. "He's got to be done soon."

While the children began another verse, Kronk stood at the fire. He mixed, flipped and seasoned in a frenzy. He had been cooking for hours, and the smells drifting towards the tired troop were delicious.

"I'm . . . almost . . . ready." Kronk struggled to balance several plates on his arm before spinning around to present them to the troop. "Voilà." The big man grinned. "Bon appétit!"

The troop leaned forward and smiled. The food looked as good as it smelled. They began to help themselves.

Kronk stood back modestly. "I do pride myself on being a bit of a gourmet," he said.

Everyone was pleased. Everyone, that is, but Bucky and the squirrels. Where was *their* food?

"Squeak! Squeaker, squeaker, squeak," Bucky mumbled behind his paw. He gave a quick nod, and all of them ran off towards Kronk's tent. This was an outrage! The squirrels were Junior Chipmunks, too!

Bucky held open the tent flap and the squirrels ducked inside. "Squeak," Bucky commanded as he pointed at Kronk's sleeping bag. The other squirrels nodded. They knew what they were supposed to do – chew holes in Kronk's bedding! Just as the squirrels were about to get to work, they were interrupted.

"Oh, squeeeaak," Kronk's deep voice crooned from outside. "Squeaker squeeaak!"

The squirrels peeked outside the tent.

There was Kronk, holding a new plate. Balanced upon it were a golden-brown acorn soufflé and a bowl of steaming wild-berry sauce.

Bucky shrugged sheepishly at the leader.

"Thought I forgot you, huh? Would Kronk do that?" The leader set the tray down. "How about a hug?"

The four squirrels grasped the large man's legs and squeezed. All was forgiven. Together all the Junior Chipmunks enjoyed their meal.

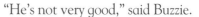

# "Hey, Hey, We're the Vultures!"

"Nothing exciting ever happens around here," Buzzie complained to his vulture singing buddies.

"That's not true," said Flaps. "What about that fight we had with the tiger Shere Khan last week?"

"Blimey, you're right," said Ziggy. "That was pretty exciting."

"But what are we gonna do now?" asked Buzzie.

"Let's sing," suggested Ziggy.

"Hey, good idea!" said the other three vultures.

"Only one problem," said Dizzy. "We need a tenor."

"Awww, you're right," said Ziggy. "That little Man-cub fellow, Mowgli, would have been a great tenor. Too bad he left the jungle."

"So, what are we gonna do?" asked Buzzie.

"How 'bout we hold an audition?" suggested Ziggy.

"Good thinking," said Flaps.

So the vultures put the word out in the jungle and, a week later, there was a line of animals ready to try out for the group.

"Name?" Buzzie asked the first applicant.

"Coconut," the monkey replied.

"All right, Coconut, let's hear ya sing," said Flaps.

Coconut shrieked for a few minutes, and the four vultures huddled together.

"He's not very good," said Buzzie.

"And he's a monkey," added Flaps.

"Next!" said Dizzy.

The vultures auditioned a lemur, two sloths, a wolf, a hippo, a toad and an elephant. None seemed like the right fit. Finally, the last animal stepped up.

"Name?" asked Buzzie.

"Name's Lucky," said the vulture. "Hey, aren't you the four fellows that helped that little Man-cub scare away that tiger Shere Khan?"

"Yeah," said Buzzie. "We are."

"Then I guess you four might be called 'lucky' yourselves!" cried Lucky. He began to laugh at his own joke.

"Go ahead and sing," said Ziggy, rolling his eyes.

Lucky sang for a few minutes and the four vultures huddled together.

"He's not bad," said Dizzy.

"Plus, he's a vulture," said Ziggy.

"And he's the last one left," pointed out Flaps. That settled it.

"You're hired!" the vultures sang.

"See, told you I was Lucky!" cried the vulture.

"But only with auditions," said Dizzy.

"Yeah," said Buzzie. "When we meet Shere Khan again, we'll see how lucky you really are!"

Walt Disney's
## Peter Pan

# Tinker Bell's Bedtime Story

"Shove over!"

"No. You shove over."

The Raccoon Twins were at it again. Peter Pan knew the bickering wouldn't stop until one of the boys had pushed the other out of the hammock.

"Hey!" Cubby yelled. The twins had tumbled out and landed right on top of the bear-suited boy.

Peter sighed. Every evening had ended like this ever since Wendy left.

As the tussle grew, Peter had an idea. He went to look for Tinker Bell.

"Say, Tink," Peter said when he found her, "how'd you like to be the new mother to all of us boys?"

Tink looked at Peter as if he was crazy.

"Aw, c'mon," Peter said. "You've seen the guys since Wendy left. They're fighting something awful. They need someone to tuck them in at night and tell them a bedtime story."

Tink was silent for a moment.

"I guess I could ask Wendy to come back," Peter said, looking at Tinker Bell slyly.

That did it. The last thing Tink wanted was for Wendy to return! The little fairy flew into the hideout and shook a finger at the Lost Boys.

"Gosh, Tink. What is it?" Slightly sat up, straightening his fox ears.

"Tink is going to tell us a bedtime story," said Peter.

The boys settled down. "Go ahead, Tink," Peter smiled. His plan was working perfectly!

Tink sat down and crossed her arms over her chest. She began to jingle.

"Once upon a time," Peter translated, "there was a beautiful fairy who, against her better judgement, lived with a pack of dirty, unruly, silly boys. And the dirtiest, unruliest and silliest of them all was Peter Pa– hey!" Peter interrupted his translation. "That's not nice, Tink!"

Tinker Bell jingled spitefully at him. "Okay," Peter said with a sigh, "I know it's your story. Go ahead." Tink continued and Peter translated, "One day, as the lovely Tinker Bell was minding her own business, the very smelly and unpleasant Peter Pan – *Tink*! – asked her to tell a bedtime story. Well, Tinker Bell didn't know any bedtime stories, so she went to fetch Captain Hook, so *he* could tell one."

With that, Tinker Bell flew out of the window.

"Tink! Tink, come back!" Peter cried. Tinker Bell returned and hovered in the window, jingling with laughter. "That was a dirty trick!" Peter scolded. "And besides, that's no way to tell a bedtime story." He sat down next to the boys' beds. "You have to do it like Wendy did. Like this."

Now it was Tink's turn to smile. While Peter told a bedtime story, and the Lost Boys drifted off to sleep, Tink curled up in her own little bed and closed her eyes. Her plan had worked perfectly!

# Disney's THE LITTLE MERMAID

## Ariel's New Move

"Whoa." Prince Eric brought the carriage to a stop. Beside him, Ariel barely managed to keep from sliding off the seat. She had been human only for a short time, and she wasn't used to her legs yet.

"Are you hungry?" the prince asked. Eric gestured towards a restaurant and looked at Ariel expectantly.

Ariel smiled and nodded. She could not speak, and she was a little wary of eating. Humans ate fish, and she could not help but think of her best friend, Flounder, whenever she saw something scaly lying on a plate. But she wanted to please the prince.

The restaurant was nearly empty. Eric and Ariel sat at a table for two as the owner approached.

"What'll it be, dear?" a woman with warm brown eyes and white hair asked, looking kindly at Ariel.

"She'll have . . . the soup?" Eric looked at Ariel for confirmation. Ariel nodded. "And I will have the speciality of the house."

Ariel was glad that Eric didn't seem to mind talking for her, though she desperately wanted to speak for herself and tell him how much she enjoyed being with him.

When the owner walked away, the silence in the room seemed to grow. Ariel tried to communicate with gestures, but Eric didn't seem to understand and, after a few minutes, the poor girl started to feel foolish.

With a sigh of relief, Ariel noticed the owner coming back with their food. Eric seemed relieved too.

After she set down their plates, the white-haired woman walked over to a tall wooden piece of furniture near the wall. She sat down in front of it and placed her hands on the black and white keys.

Ariel had never seen a piano before. And she had never heard one either. She was enchanted by the music. She let her spoon drop into her bowl. The song was lovely – happy and sad at the same time. She wanted to sing along! But, of course, she could not. Still, she could not break away. The music reminded her of the rhythms of the ocean. She stood and began to sway, but her new legs were so awkward, she stumbled.

Suddenly, Eric's strong arm was around Ariel's waist. With his other arm, he took Ariel's hand in his. Ariel looked startled. "Haven't you ever danced before?" the prince asked.

Ariel shook her head shyly.

"I'll show you," the prince said, smiling at her. He whirled Ariel around the floor. The Little Mermaid was a natural. She spun and smiled, glad that they had found a way to communicate without words.

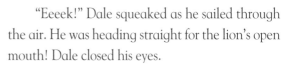

# Death-defying Dale

One morning, Chip and Dale woke up to find a giant red-and-white-striped tent just outside their tree.

The chipmunks scampered over to the tent and peeked through the door. Inside, a man was shouting through a megaphone.

"Ladies and gentlemen!" he cried. "Welcome to the World's Greatest Circus!"

The chipmunks tiptoed inside. They watched a silly clown with orange hair and a big red nose do somersaults. Nearby, a lion tamer cracked his whip at a lion. And high overhead, trapeze artists tumbled though the air.

Just then Dale smelled something delicious. There on the ground, right by the centre ring, was a bag full of peanuts!

Dale's tummy rumbled. He needed a snack. Chip and Dale hurried over to the peanuts.

Chip was about to take a bite when he realized that someone – or something – was standing behind him. He turned around and his eyes opened wide. It was a huge elephant! Chip squeaked in surprise, but Dale was face-first in the sack of peanuts . . . and didn't hear him.

The elephant reached into the sack with its trunk, looking for a peanut. But it didn't grab a peanut. It grabbed Dale!

"Arooooo!" the elephant trumpeted. With a flick of her trunk, she flung Dale away.

"Eeeek!" Dale squeaked as he sailed through the air. He was heading straight for the lion's open mouth! Dale closed his eyes.

*Whoosh!* Suddenly, something scooped Dale out of the air. He opened his eyes. One of the trapeze artists had accidentally grabbed Dale as he flipped through the air. Dale sighed with relief.

But a second later the trapeze artist let go. "Eeeek!" Dale cried as he fell.

Just then a clown stepped beneath him. *Boink!* Dale bounced off the clown's red rubber nose. He flew into the audience.

*Crash!* Dale landed in a carton of popcorn.

Dale popped out of the popcorn. Suddenly, a spotlight shone down on him.

"Ladies and gentlemen," the ringmaster announced. "Please give a round of applause to our surprise guest, the Death-defying Chipmunk!"

The whole audience began to cheer. Dale looked around, surprised. Then he took a bow.

"And, as a reward for this chipmunk's bravery, I'd like to offer him a special treat," the ringmaster went on. "One hundred circus peanuts!"

A clown walked up to Dale, holding a huge bag of peanuts.

"Eeeek!" Dale cried. No more peanuts for him! And he dashed out of the circus tent as fast as his little legs would carry him.

# Berry Blunder

Madame Medusa thrust a bucket into Penny's hand. "I only want the plumpest, juiciest berries!" she screeched. "And don't come back until the pail is full!"

"Yes, Medusa," Penny replied. Carrying Teddy in one hand and the bucket in the other, she started off into the swamp. Picking berries was a regular task for her, and one she didn't mind. It got her away from the ship and from Madame Medusa.

Penny pushed a reed aside and looked over her shoulder. They were there, of course. Medusa never let Penny go anywhere without sending Nero and Brutus – her horrible pet crocodiles – to watch her.

Penny looked around. It wasn't easy to find her way through the swamp because everything seemed to grow together. Luckily she knew where to go.

A few minutes later, Penny stood before a bush heavy with plump berries. She set Teddy down in a tangle of branches. "You'll be comfy here while I pick," she explained.

Penny was just plucking the first berry off the bush when Brutus lumbered forward and opened his massive jaws, grabbing Teddy and tossing him into the murky water.

"Teddy!" Penny cried. She snatched up her friend, hugged him to her chest, and glared at Brutus who was munching on the berries.

"You creep!" she said. "You could have hurt Teddy. And these berries are for Medusa!"

Brutus responded by snatching another several dozen berries off the bush. Then Nero joined him, chomping away. Soon, half of the branches were empty.

Penny was furious. She would never fill her bucket – much less eat some berries herself – if Brutus and Nero ate them all.

Scowling and holding her dripping Teddy, Penny looked around. When she spied a patch of bright red fruit growing several yards away, she smiled to herself.

"Nero, Brutus!" she called cheerfully. "There's another berry patch over there!"

Lifting their massive heads, the two crocs looked where Penny was pointing. A second later, they had crossed the swamp and were gulping down the plump red fruit.

Penny began to giggle. Their eyes wide and their nostrils flaring, Nero and Brutus were desperately gulping down gallons of swamp water. The nearby 'berries' looked like berries, but they were actually hot peppers!

"You shouldn't eat so fast, boys," she said sweetly as they squirmed in the water.

Penny picked until her bucket was full. Then, taking Teddy by the arm, she headed back to the ship. How *berry* sorry I am! she thought.

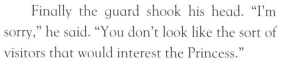

# A Visit to the Castle

"Gosh," Bashful said bashfully. "Do you think the Princess will be glad to see us?"

"Of course!" Happy chuckled.

"All right, men," Doc said. "Here we are. Now, all we have to do is go up and dock on the floor. That is – knock on the door!"

The Seven Dwarfs had just reached the castle where Snow White lived. They had been so busy in the mines that this was the first time they'd had a chance to visit since Snow White had married the Prince.

Sneezy looked up at the beautiful castle. "*Ah-choo!*" he sneezed. "Wow. This place sure is pretty."

"Time's a wastin'," Grumpy muttered.

He knocked firmly on the tall wooden door. A moment later a guard opened it.

"Er, good day," the castle guard said. "New servants around the back, please."

"Oh, we're not flu nervants," Doc spoke up. "Er, we're not new servants. We're here to see the Princess!"

"Yes! The Princess!" the other Dwarfs agreed. Dopey nodded eagerly.

The guard looked doubtful. "*You're* here to see the Princess?"

He looked them over. The Dwarfs stood up straight, glad that they'd remembered to wash that morning.

Finally the guard shook his head. "I'm sorry," he said. "You don't look like the sort of visitors that would interest the Princess."

"Oh, but we are!" Sleepy yawned. "She'll be interested in us."

"Sorry," the guard said. "You'll have to go."

But Grumpy held the door open. "Mark my words," he growled. "If you don't tell the Princess we're here, there'll be trouble."

"Who is it?" a sweet voice called from inside the castle. "Who's at the door?"

"Never mind, Princess!" the guard called. "It's just some strange little men who claim they know you."

"Little men?" Snow White cried, rushing forward. She peered around the door past the guard, and her lovely face lit up with joy. "Why, Doc – Grumpy – Sleepy – Dopey – Happy – Sneezy – even dear Bashful!"

Bashful blushed deeply. "Gosh," he said. "Hello, Princess."

The guard looked surprised. "You mean you know these fellows?" he asked the Princess. "I thought they were just riffraff."

"Riffraff?" Snow White cried. "Why, no – they may look a little different, but they're just like royalty to me! They're my very best friends!"

The guard apologized to the Dwarfs. Then Snow White invited her friends into the castle for a nice, long visit.

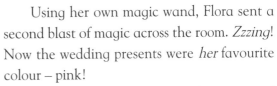

# Pink or Blue?

On the wedding day of Prince Phillip and Princess Aurora's no one was happier for them than the three good fairies.

"Such a happy day!" exclaimed Flora from a balcony overlooking the crowded ballroom. "Fauna, don't you agree?"

When Fauna didn't answer, Flora looked over to find her weeping.

"Fauna, why are you crying?" asked Flora.

Dabbing her eyes, Fauna said, "I love weddings even more than happy endings! Both make me cry for joy!"

"It is a joyful day," said Merryweather. "Everyone in the kingdom is here. And look at all the wedding presents!"

"Oh, my!" said Flora. "It will take days for the bride and groom to open them all."

"Point them out again, dear," Fauna asked Merryweather. "I had tears in my eyes."

Without thinking, Merryweather used her magic wand to point, and when she did – zzzing! – she accidentally turned all of the white packages her favourite colour – blue.

"Merryweather!" snapped Flora. "Change those packages back this instant."

"I don't know," said Merryweather, tapping her chin. "I like them this way."

"Oh, do you?" said Flora. "Well, look again!"

Using her own magic wand, Flora sent a second blast of magic across the room. *Zzzing!* Now the wedding presents were *her* favourite colour – pink!

"Now, dears," said Fauna, trying to make peace. "Today is not a day for bickering."

"I'll stop, if she will," said Merryweather, after she'd already changed the pink packages back to blue again!

"You call that stopping?" said Flora. Then *zzzing!* went Flora's wand. And the presents turned pink again!

Fauna had had enough! Taking out her magic wand, she waved it around in a circle, and chanted:

"*Presents changing pink and blue,
wed your colours, then stay true!*"

With a final *zzzing!* Fauna sent her magic spell across the room, and the presents changed again.

"What did you do?" cried Flora and Merryweather.

Fauna shrugged. "I simply mixed your colours together and locked them in. Pink-and-blue-striped wrapping paper is all the rage this year," she said. "Now let's all go eat some wedding cake."

"Wedding cake?" said Merryweather. "Hmm... I wonder what colour the frosting is."

# DISNEY'S POCAHONTAS

# My Side of the Story

Perhaps you know the story of how Pocahontas and John Smith made peace between their people. Well, I've got a much more interesting story for you – mine.

My name is Percival, but my friends call me Percy. Once upon a time, I was the pet pug of a very important man named Governor Ratcliffe. I lived a life of luxury. My meals were served in sterling silver bowls. I had ten different kinds of bones to choose from. I wore perfume, for goodness' sake! But life felt, well, pretty boring.

That all changed the day we arrived on the shores of America. Ratcliffe was after one thing and one thing only – gold. And Ratcliffe didn't care about the people who lived in this new land. John Smith did, but I didn't care much for John Smith. He was always trying to pat me on the head. "Grrrrr!" I would growl at him. You have to be firm with these humans. Make sure they know their place.

Not long after we had arrived in the New Land, I was having a bubble bath when suddenly – *splash*! – a raccoon landed in my tub! Well, if there's one thing my mother taught me, it was to avoid all animals without a pedigree. This wild creature could be rabid! The raccoon ate my cherries and then ran off. After that I had one thing on my mind – revenge!

The next time I saw the raccoon, he was eating bones out of my personal bone collection. So I had to chase him – it was a matter of pride! But wouldn't you know it, the brazen little devil trapped me in a hollow log. There I was, stumbling around the woods with a log stuck on my head. It was hours before I got that thing off.

That's when I ran into John Smith and Pocahontas. And guess who was with them – that bone-thieving raccoon! He grabbed a little hummingbird and started waving him at me like a sword. It would have been funny if it wasn't so annoying!

And then the weirdest thing of all happened – a tree talked to me! Grandmother Willow said I shouldn't chase Meeko. By chasing him, I had started trouble between us; now, it was time to stop the fighting. Of course, I understood immediately. I'm pretty clever, you know.

It took the humans a little longer to get the picture, and John Smith got hurt. But it all worked out okay in the end. I decided I didn't need my fancy, high-falutin' life, so I became a settler with my new friends!

John, however, had to go back to England. I knew he would miss me. So when he reached out to pat my head, I actually let him.

After all that he had been through, I felt he finally deserved it.

# A Mouse in the House

Alice was a daydreamer. When her older sister tried to read Alice her lessons in the meadow by their house, Alice did everything but pay attention. Once, she fell asleep and dreamed of a silly place called Wonderland.

When Alice woke up from her dream, her sister gave up on lessons for the day and suggested they have tea instead.

Sitting at the dining room table, Alice began to tell her sister all about Wonderland. "I know I was only dreaming," said Alice, "but it all seemed so real!"

"What happened?" her sister asked.

"Well," said Alice. "I attended the strangest tea party at which the Mad Hatter and the March Hare – they were the hosts of the party – kept offering me tea, but refused to serve me any." Alice picked up the teapot to refill her own cup. "And you won't believe it, but inside the teapot lived a little–"

The lid of the pot Alice was holding flew open and a little whiskered face popped out. "Eek!" yelled Alice, slamming down the lid. Her mind raced. How could the Dormouse from her dream have crossed over into her real life?

Alice finished her tea and biscuits as quickly as possible. When her sister went to pour more tea, Alice grabbed the pot and insisted, "I'm sorry, but there isn't any more!"

"My goodness!" Alice's sister declared. "Now *you're* acting like the Mad Hatter and the March Hare!"

Alice slipped outside with the teapot as soon as she could. With her kitten Dinah following close behind, she went straight to the tree where she had fallen asleep that very afternoon. "Maybe if I doze off again," she told Dinah, "I can dream this little fellow back where he belongs."

But Alice couldn't fall asleep. She tried counting sheep, and reading the boring book her sister had left by the tree. Nothing seemed to work. Finally, she lifted the lid of the pot. "I'm sorry," she told the Dormouse. "I'm not sure what else to do." But the Dormouse knew. He jumped out of the teapot – and was chased by Alice's kitten! The Dormouse ran into the stump that led to the rabbit hole of Alice's dream, but Dinah stayed behind. The inside of the stump looked too dark and scary to the little cat. Alice waited, but the Dormouse did not come out again.

That night, as she slept, Alice dreamed of Wonderland again. She was back at the un-birthday party, waiting to be served a cup of tea. The Dormouse threw open the teapot and gave Alice a sleepy grin. "Thank you, miss!" he said. "And, whatever you do, please don't dream about your cat!"

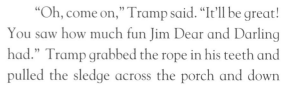

# Sledging

Lady stood on the porch as Jim Dear and Darling walked up the front path. Jim pulled a sledge and Darling held their son. They were all covered in snow, rosy cheeked and smiling from ear to ear.

"That was fun! Wasn't it, Darling?" Jim asked.

"I don't know the last time I had so much fun," Darling agreed, patting Lady on the head.

"But we should get out of these wet clothes before one of us catches a cold," Jim said, leaning the sledge against the side of the house.

"I agree," Darling said. And the three of them hurried inside.

Just then, Tramp came walking up the front path. "Hey, Pidge," he said to Lady. "What do you say we take this old thing for a spin?"

"What is it, anyway?" Lady wanted to know.

"A sledge!" Tramp told her.

"What do you do with it?" she asked.

"You ride down hills," Tramp explained.

"That sounds dangerous," Lady said hesitantly.

"Nah, it's fun!" Tramp cried. "So, what do you say?"

"It's awfully cold out here," Lady said. She wasn't convinced at all.

"Oh, come on," Tramp said. "It'll be great! You saw how much fun Jim Dear and Darling had." Tramp grabbed the rope in his teeth and pulled the sledge across the porch and down the steps.

Lady took off after him. "Wait for me!" she cried anxiously.

"Come on, Pidge!" Tramp encouraged her. "Jump on!"

Lady jumped onto the sledge, and Tramp pulled her down the snow-covered street and up to the top of a nearby hill. "What a view, huh?" he said.

"What a view indeed," Lady agreed. "What now?"

"Now, we ride," Tramp said. He pushed the sledge forward and took a running leap onto it, sending them racing down the hill.

"Oh, dear!" Lady yelped as they plummeted down the hill, the wind blowing her ears back.

"Just hold on!" Tramp instructed.

Lady squeezed her eyes shut, and Tramp barked with excitement. But suddenly they hit a patch of ice, the sledge spun, and they went flying – right into a snowbank!

Tramp jumped to his feet. "Pidge, are you okay?" he asked anxiously.

"Okay?" Lady asked. She was already pulling the sledge back up the hill. "Hurry up, Tramp! Let's do it again!"

# Hanukkah Fun

"Happy Hanukkah, Pooh Bear!" Roo exclaimed as he opened the door for his first guest. It was the first night of Hanukkah, and Roo and Kanga were having all their friends over to participate in some Hanukkah customs.

"Happy Hanukkah, Roo!" Pooh replied. Just then a delicious smell wafted by his nose. "Something smells yummy!" Pooh cried.

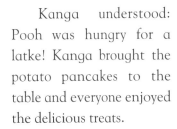

Kanga was making little potato pancakes called *latkes*, a special Hanukkah treat. "Try to be patient, Pooh," Kanga said with a smile. "We'll have these latkes a little bit later."

Before long, Piglet, Eeyore, Rabbit, Tigger and Owl had also arrived and it was time to light the Menorah, a candleholder that could hold nine candles.

"First," Kanga explained, "we light this centre candle, called the *shammosh*. Then, we use the shammosh to light one other candle for the first night of Hanukkah."

Tigger noticed that there weren't any candles in the other seven candle holders of the Menorah. "When do we light the other candles?" he asked Kanga.

"Well, Tigger," Kanga said, "Hanukkah lasts for eight nights. So tomorrow, on the second night, we will light two candles with the shammosh. On the third night, we will light three candles, and so on . . . until, on the eighth night, we will light all the candles!"

Everyone watched the candles burning. Then Pooh said, "Um, Kanga? Is it a little bit later . . . now?"

Kanga understood: Pooh was hungry for a latke! Kanga brought the potato pancakes to the table and everyone enjoyed the delicious treats.

When they were all eaten, Roo said, "Now let's play *dreidel*!" He got out a four-sided, clay spinning top. Kanga made a pile of sweets, nuts and pennies in the centre of the floor. She also gave a little pile of goodies to each guest.

Roo explained the rules, then each player took turns spinning the dreidel. Depending on what side the dreidel landed on, the player might win more treats from the centre pile, or lose treats from their own pile and have to add them to the centre pile.

"This is fun!" Piglet exclaimed. "And to think: there are seven *more* nights of Hanukkah!"

"Hey, Mama," said Roo, "there are eight of us and eight nights of Hanukkah. Can our friends come over every night of Hanukkah, and take turns lighting the Menorah?"

Everyone, including Kanga, thought that was a wonderful idea.

So that was exactly what they did.

# Walt Disney's Pinocchio
## The Greatest Gift

Pinocchio was the luckiest boy in the world – and he knew it. No longer a wooden puppet, at last he was a real, live boy! And Pinocchio knew he owed it all to Geppetto for believing in him.

"I wish I could give Papa something in return," Pinocchio said to himself one day.

Pinocchio didn't have any money, so he decided to make a gift for Geppetto.

"Perhaps I should use Papa's tools and carve a present for him out of wood!" said Pinocchio.

So, one afternoon, while Geppetto was out, Pinocchio sat down at the woodworking bench. The only problem was, Pinocchio did not know the first thing about woodworking.

"That looks dangerous," said Pinocchio, eyeing a chisel. "I don't think Papa would want me to use that on my own." He decided he needed another gift idea. "I know!" he said. "Maybe I can cook something for Papa!"

Pinocchio went over to the hearth, where Geppetto did all of the cooking.

But he soon realized that he didn't know how to cook either. "And Papa is always telling me to stay a safe distance away from the fire," he reminded himself.

Pinocchio looked around the little house and spotted Geppetto's accordion sitting on the table.

"Of course!" cried Pinocchio. "Papa loves music. I could write him a song as a gift and then perform it for him!"

So Pinocchio picked up the accordion and began to play. But the sounds that came out were . . . well . . . just awful!

"Hmph," Pinocchio said in frustration. "I don't know how to play the accordion or write a song." He put the accordion down and stood in the middle of the room. Tears were welling up in poor little Pinocchio's eyes when Geppetto came in through the front door.

"My dear boy," Geppetto said, hurrying to Pinocchio's side, "what is the matter?"

Through his tears, Pinocchio explained how he had wanted to make a gift to show Geppetto how much he appreciated everything his father had done for him.

As Geppetto listened, his look of worry softened into a smile, and then *his* eyes welled up with tears. "My son," he said, "don't you know that you, and you alone, are the greatest gift a father could ever want?"

"I am?" Pinocchio asked.

"You are," replied Geppetto.

"Well, in that case," said Pinocchio with a sly grin as he hugged his papa, "you're welcome!"

Then Geppetto picked up the accordion and they sang and danced all the rest of the day.

# Royal Help Wanted

Prince John and Sir Hiss had just finished repaying their debt to society in the rock mines. They discovered that Robin Hood had given back the citizens' hard-earned money. And that meant that Prince John had not a penny to his name and no one to boss around any more – except Sir Hiss, of course!

"Well, it's quite obvious that you will need to get a job," the Prince told Hiss. "Jewels and fancy carriages and servants cost money, you know."

"Me, sss-ire?" hissed the snake.

"Of course!" John replied. "You can't very well expect *me* to get a job. Princes don't work, they sit around and look noble!"

And so Hiss set out into the town. He spent the entire afternoon looking for a job. First, he went to Friar Tuck's church.

"Everyone deserves a second chance," Friar Tuck told him. "And I just happen to need a bell ringer." He pointed to the huge bell that hung in a tower of the church.

And so, every hour, Hiss grabbed hold of the rope and pulled with all his might. The sound of the bell was deafening! It wasn't so bad at one o'clock, when he had to ring the bell once. Or two o'clock, when he had to ring the bell twice. But around six o'clock, the clanging started to give him a colossal headache. At twelve o'clock, he left and went looking elsewhere.

Hiss tried the bakery, but they told him he needed hands (or at least paws) to knead dough.

Then he went to the blacksmith and asked him for a job putting horseshoes on horses. But the horses were terrified of snakes, and Sir Hiss nearly had his tail squashed when he tried to get near a nervous palamino.

Finally, Hiss gave up and returned home.

Prince John was not pleased. "Now what are we supposed to do for money?" he demanded. "I refuse to beg! Those wretched commoners would give anything to see me humiliated."

"You're absolutely right, sire – they would!" exclaimed Hiss. "That's it! Follow me!"

Before Prince John could protest, Hiss had the lion locked in stocks in the middle of the village square. "Pay a farthing and pelt the Prince with a tomato!" called Sir Hiss. In minutes, a line of adults and children stretched into the distance. Most of them had a pretty good aim.

"Wah!" cried Prince John, his face dripping with tomato juice.

"But, sire," Sir Hiss said, "look at all these coins!"

# Tod's Homecoming

Tod the fox wanted to show his fox friend Vixey where he grew up. He took her to the top of a hill where they could look down on a beautiful valley.

"I grew up on Widow Tweed's farm," said Tod, pointing with his paw at a farm nestled in the valley. "She took care of me when I was just a cub.

"And that's my best friend Copper," Tod said, pointing to a handsome hound. "Copper lives at Amos Slade's farm. His house is right next door to Mrs Tweed's."

As the two foxes watched, Widow Tweed, Amos Slade, and Amos's cranky old dog, Chief, climbed into an old banger. With a puff of smoke, they drove off.

But Copper was still at home. He was near the fence, snoozing under an old barrel.

"Let's go visit Copper," said Tod.

"Not me!" Vixey declared. "I'm a fox, and I'm not fond of hounds. I'll catch some fish for our dinner. See you later."

Alone, Tod scampered down the hill, excited about seeing his old pal. But, when he got there, he spotted a strange man sneaking into Amos Slade's henhouse.

"Wake up, Copper!" yelled Tod. "A chicken thief is raiding the henhouse!"

Copper woke with a start and leaped into action. But the rope around his neck held him back.

"You'll have to stop that chicken thief yourself!" cried Copper.

"But I can't stop him alone!" Tod replied.

"We'll help," someone chirped. Tod looked up and saw Dinky the Sparrow and Boomer the Woodpecker sitting on the fence.

"Let's go!" said Tod.

Tod burst into the henhouse first. The thief was there, holding a squawking chicken in either hand.

Tod bit the man in the ankle.

"Ouch!" howled the thief.

Boomer flew through the window and pecked at the chicken snatcher's head. The thief dropped the chickens and covered his head.

Meanwhile, Dinky untied the knot that held Copper. Now, Copper was free – and angry too! Barking, he charged at the burglar.

Eggs flying, the chicken snatcher screamed and ran. As he raced down the road, Dinky and Boomer flitted around his head, pecking him until he was out of sight. The fox and the hound trotted back to the farm.

"Good to see you, Tod," said Copper, wagging his tail. "What brings you here?"

"I just stopped by for a quiet visit," Tod replied.

"It was real quiet, all right!" said Copper.

# Red Alert!

"Nice work with the wheat husker," Flik said. He smiled with satisfaction as he watched a troop of ants lower the contraption that lightly smashed the wheat kernels. How had the colony got along without his clever inventions? Flik wondered.

"How's it going with the berry masher?" called a voice. It was Atta, the colony's Queen.

"I was just heading over to take a look," Flik said, smiling at Queen Atta. "Care to join me?"

"Sure," Atta said as she led the way to the berry-mashing area. Mashing berries was messy, so the ants did it in a special part of the anthill.

"Cowabunga!" called a large ant. Ten dozen ants leaped off a rock onto a giant lever. The lever lowered, pressing a flat rock onto a pile of berries. Sweet red juice squirted out from the sides and dripped into carved wooden bowls.

When all the juice was squeezed out of the berries, Atta dipped her finger into a bowl for a taste.

"Delicious," she said. Red juice stained her mouth and chin.

"The berries were especially sweet this year," Flik said modestly.

"And with your new invention we should have plenty of juice for this year's feast," Atta said. "As long as Dot and the Blueberries don't drink it all first," she added.

Flik laughed. Dot and her Blueberry friends loved berry juice and were always trying to dip into it before the feast. They had been shooed away from the berry masher more than once in the last week. Three times, in fact!

"Good work, masher ants!" Flik called to the horde that was climbing back up to their jumping rock. Another group was making a pile of fresh berries.

They had nearly finished piling a huge mound of berries, when suddenly the alarm sounded.

"Alert, alert!" a guard ant called through a megaphone made from a rolled-up leaf. "Red fire ants are storming the colony!"

Flik, Atta and the masher ants fled the food area as fast as their legs could carry them. Sure enough, they soon ran into half-a-dozen red ants. Flik was about to charge when he heard a familiar voice.

"Flik, it's me!" it said. The voice sounded like . . . Dot's.

"Hold on!" Flik shouted. The ants stopped. Flik quickly wiped the first red ant's sticky face. "These aren't fire ants," Flik explained. "They're Blueberries – covered in berry juice!" He smiled at Atta. "Maybe we should call them Redberries, instead!"

Walt Disney's
# IOI DALMATIANS

# Having a Ball!

"Ten days until Santa!" the spotted puppies barked, bouncing into one another as they tumbled down the hall.

"Ten days until presents!" Penny barked.

"And ten days until Christmas dinner!" Rolly added.

"Ten days to stay out of trouble!" Pongo said with a smile.

"Do you puppies know what comes before Santa and dinner and presents?" Perdita asked.

"Umm. . . stockings?" Lucky asked.

"No, before that," she said.

Patch wasn't sure. He sat down on the hall rug to think.

"We have to decorate and sing carols," Perdita said, wagging her tail. At that very moment, Roger and Anita threw open the door to the study and invited all the dogs inside.

Patch blinked. He couldn't believe his eyes. "What's a tree doing in the house?"

"Just watch." Perdy gave Patch a quick lick.

While the dogs looked on, Roger and Anita began to decorate the tree. They hung lights and angels, snowmen and tinsel. Of all the decorations, Patch liked the glittering glass balls best. Balls were one of his favourite things! He could not take his eyes off them.

When the tree was ready, Anita brought in cocoa and dog biscuits. Munching on a biscuit in front of the fire, Patch didn't think the evening could get any better. Then Roger sat down at the piano, and everyone began to sing.

Patch howled along with the others, but he could not stop looking at the balls on the tree. A large red one was hanging near the floor.

Patch reached over and gave the ball a pat with his front paw. It swung merrily above him. Looking at his reflection, Patch started to laugh. His nose looked huge!

"What are you doing?" Penny stopped singing to see what was so funny. Then Freckles joined them, then Lucky. The puppies took turns knocking the ball and watching it sway, then – crash! – it fell to the floor, shattering.

The singing stopped. Poor Patch was sure the special evening was ruined.

"Oh, dear." Anita scooped the puppies out from under the tree. "Careful, now," she said. "Those balls aren't for playing with."

While Roger swept up the glass, Patch cowered. He knew he was in trouble.

"Maybe I should give you all one gift early," Anita said with a grin. Patch couldn't believe his luck. Instead of a firm talking-to, each puppy got to rip open a small package. Patch tore off the paper. Inside was a brand-new red rubber ball!

## Disney's Aladdin

# Jasmine's Jewel Thief

"This is so much fun!" cried Jasmine. She and Aladdin were flying all over the desert on their favourite flying carpet.

Jasmine leaned back against Aladdin and reached up to smooth back her windblown hair. But, as her fingers brushed past her ears, she noticed something missing. Sitting up, she felt again. One of her gold earrings was gone!

"What is it?" Aladdin asked when he saw Jasmine searching the Carpet.

"It's nothing. Just an earring," Jasmine said. She tried to be casual about it, but her eyes gave her away.

"Just an earring?" Aladdin said. "Didn't your father give them to you?"

"Yes," Jasmine confessed. "They are my favourites. At least, they were."

"Are," Aladdin said firmly. "We'll find the other one. Home, Carpet," he instructed.

Back at the palace, Aladdin and Jasmine looked everywhere. They searched their chambers, the gardens, even the fountains. They were about to search the kitchen when Abu scampered by.

Aladdin looked at the monkey suspiciously. "You haven't seen a shiny gold earring, have you?"

Abu shrugged, but did not look Aladdin in the eye. Aladdin knew he was on to something.

The monkey was crazy for anything that glittered. He'd spent too many years as a poor thief.

"Are you sure?" Aladdin asked sternly.

Slowly, Abu motioned Aladdin to follow him.

When he saw the monkey's bed, Aladdin almost started to laugh. Why hadn't he noticed before how lumpy it was?

When Abu pulled back the covers, Aladdin could not help himself. He laughed out loud. Abu's bed was covered with shiny objects! There were spoons, goblets and coins. And, from beneath his small pillow, Abu pulled out Jasmine's earring.

Aladdin shook his head and smiled at Abu. "You don't have to scavenge any more. We live in the palace!"

So they took the earring to Jasmine. "You found it!" she cried. She leaned down and gave Abu a kiss. The little monkey blushed.

"Here, Abu, take this ring as a reward for finding my earring," Jasmine said. She removed a gold ring from her finger and gave it to the monkey, who gave a happy jump and tucked it into his hat.

"Actually, Abu didn't really–" Aladdin began. But just then he caught Abu's deadly glare. "Well," he continued, amused. "Yes. Um, good job, Abu."

*Walt Disney*
**DINOSAUR**

# Teamwork

Aladar smiled at his dinosaur baby. The little iguanodon was growing fast.

"Come on, Daddy!" the little tyke called. He jumped to his feet and took off towards a rocky hill.

"We've been out all morning!" Aladar replied. "I need a little rest." He watched his son clamber up the big rocks.

"Be careful!" Aladar's mate, Neera, called out.

"I will, Mum!" the baby dinosaur called back. "I just want to see what's on the other side of this hill. I won't be long!"

"He'll be fine," Zini, their lemur friend, reassured Aladar and Neera. "He's been off on his own dozens of times."

Neera sighed. "I know," she agreed. "It's just that he's my . . . baby."

Aladar lay in the sun, waiting for the tiny iguanodon to reappear. And waiting, and waiting . . . .

"Son?" Aladar called. "Where are you?"

Zini leaped up onto a nearby boulder and looked around. "I don't see him," he said.

"We have to go find him," Neera said.

The three friends were unusually quiet as they searched for the baby iguanodon. They scoured the dry lake bed near their Nesting Grounds and climbed hill after hill. But no luck.

Neera's eyes were full of worry. "Baby, where are you?" she called.

"Shhhh," Zini said. His ears twitched. "I think I heard something."

They all listened. Zini was right. There was a noise coming from a nearby cliff. Zini squinted. "There's a cave up there," he said. "It looks like the entrance has been blocked off."

The lemur bounded easily up the steep hill and through a small opening at the mouth of the cave.

"I found him!" he cried from inside.

"I'm okay!" the young iguanodon added. But his voice sounded a little shaky.

Aladar and Neera were already climbing up the steep incline. The going was slow, and they tripped on several boulders before they got to the mouth of the cave. But, working together, the iguanodons and Zini pushed the rocks blocking the entrance out of the way.

"Mummy! Daddy!" The baby iguanodon scampered forward and gave his parents a hug. Then the foursome made their way home.

"I'm never going exploring again!" declared the young dinosaur. "Well, almost never. Well, maybe just a little. Hey, look at that dry riverbed! Can we go explore it?"

Aladar and Neera smiled at each other. "Maybe tomorrow, son," Aladar said. "But I think one of us will be going with you!"

## The Show Must Go On

The wind whistled around the Big Top, pulling the canvas tent Dumbo was holding out of reach of his small trunk. "I'll get it," Dumbo's mother said as the tent flapped over their heads.

If the weather hadn't been so terrible, Dumbo thought, he could have flown up to grab the edge of the tent. But the whipping wind was too much, even for Dumbo's wing-like ears.

At last, standing on her back legs, Mrs Jumbo caught the canvas in her trunk. She pulled it taut and let the roustabouts tie it off. But Dumbo noticed several new rips in the fabric.

"Quit your clowning!" the Ringmaster barked at the clowns. He noticed the rips too. He ordered the clowns to sew them up. "The repairs must be finished by showtime!"

Dumbo felt terrible. All the circus performers, animals and roustabouts were working hard in the storm. He had gone and made even more work, by letting the canvas get torn. And now the Ringmaster's mood was as foul as the weather!

Just then Dumbo noticed another blast of cold air whirl the Ringmaster's black top hat off his head.

"That does it!" the Ringmaster shouted. "There will be no show tonight!"

Dumbo could not believe his ears. The announcement was even enough to wake Timothy Q. Mouse from his nap in a nearby bale of hay.

"No show? I can't believe it!" Timothy cried. The rest of the circus folk couldn't believe it either. They silently continued to set up.

"What a fuss over a hat." Timothy shook his head. "The show must go on."

Dumbo nodded. Then something caught his eye. The Ringmaster's hat was caught on the flagpole, high over the Big Top. Perhaps he could get it for him.

Bravely, Dumbo took off. The wind was strong, but he tucked his head down and flapped his ears hard. When the wind calmed for a moment, the small elephant saw his chance. He grabbed the top hat and flew quickly to the ground.

Shyly, Dumbo held out the hat to the Ringmaster.

"Thank you, Dumbo." The Ringmaster took his hat gratefully. He looked around at all the people and animals still hard at work. He looked a little embarrassed. Then, as he placed the hat on his head, he shouted, "The show must go on!"

Everyone cheered.

"What'd I tell ya?" Timothy asked, winking at Dumbo.

# Old Man Octopus

"You're it!" Nemo tagged Sheldon, who was hiding next to a mollusc.

"Aw, man!" Sheldon swished his tail. "I'm going to get you next time, Nemo."

"Only if you can find me," Nemo teased. Then he called louder, "Ollie, ollie, all swim free!" The rest of the fish who were playing hide-and-seek returned to the giant barnacle they were using as base. When they were all there, Sheldon began to count again.

Nemo swam away, scanning the reef for a good hiding spot. Sheldon would be out to get him for sure. Nemo swam past a large empty abalone shell. "Too easy," he muttered. He darted into an anemone. "Way too obvious." Finally he came to a dark cave in the coral. "Too dark," he shivered, looking into the spooky opening. "It'll be perfect."

Mustering his courage, Nemo swam inside. At first he couldn't see anything. Then, as his eyes adjusted to the dark, Nemo saw a large eye open on the cave wall. What could it be?

Another eye opened. Then the entire wall began to move.

"O-O-Old Man Octopus!" Nemo stammered as eight long arms oozed off the cave wall. Nemo and his friends told stories about Old Man Octopus at sleepovers. In the stories Old Man Octopus sneaked up on little fish and gave them a terrible scare.

"S-sorry to disturb you, sir." Nemo swam towards the cave entrance. Then he noticed something amazing. The octopus's arms were changing colour . . . and texture! Instead of matching the brown bumpy cave wall, now they looked more like the reddish coral at the bottom of the cave.

"You didn't disturb me, boy. Tell me what brings you to this corner of the reef?" The octopus's voice was slow and kind, and Nemo's fear melted away.

"Hide-and-seek, sir," Nemo answered politely. "But I wouldn't need a cave if I could camouflage myself like you!"

Old Man Octopus laughed. "Hide-and-seek, eh? One of my favourites. The camouflage does come in handy, but nothing beats a cloud of ink when you want to make a break for the base!"

"You can shoot ink clouds too?" Nemo was so excited he forgot to be quiet.

"I hear you, Nemo!" Sheldon shouted.

"Are you ready to swim for it?" Old Man Octopus whispered with a wink.

Nemo nodded. He high-fived one of Old Man Octopus's tentacles. Then in a burst of inky blackness he darted out of the cave, past Sheldon, and all the way back to the barnacle base. Safe!

Disney's
## TREASURE PLANET

# Jim Hawkins: Space Cadet

On the first day of his second term at the Interstellar Academy, Jim Hawkins stepped aboard a solar sloop. For a second, he felt as if he was back on board the *Legacy* – the vessel where he had become a real spacer. But the feeling vanished as his classmates pushed past him, eager to begin the fun part of training.

Jim allowed the more confident students to crowd in front of him. Just a few days ago he couldn't wait to get back to the Academy and resume studying to be a captain – especially since the second term was when pilot training began. But now he felt as if he'd lost his space legs.

"Tie up." A multilegged purple boy beside Jim handed him a lifeline. "We're out of here."

As Jim secured his rope, the instructor showed one of the more daring students how to navigate away from the port. Several other students anxiously waited their turn at the helm. One by one, the instructor let them take the wheel.

They were good. Really good.

The instructor looked up, spotted Jim and waved him over with a catlike paw. Her almond eyes reminded Jim of Captain Amelia. So did her way of barking orders. "You there! Stop skulking. Come take the wheel."

Jim shuffled over and flipped his hair out of his eyes. Here was his chance to show them all what he was made of.

Grasping the wheel, Jim pulled to the right. He wanted to try something tricky. The craft lurched.

A few students chuckled, and the instructor raised an eyebrow.

The awkward ship was not at all what Jim was used to. He liked speed. And, to make matters worse, with his clumsy manoeuvre he had pointed them towards a pod of enormous Orcus Galacticus!

"Look out!" an insectoid alien shrieked.

"Turn!" someone else yelled.

*Take the helm and chart your own course.* Silver's voice echoed in Jim's head.

"Trim the sails!" Jim yelled loudly. He must have sounded commanding because three students sprang into action.

Jim held the wheel steady. He did not turn and, as the sloop picked up speed, he manoeuvred between two giant space whales, smoothly emerging on the other side.

The students near him breathed a sigh of relief, and Jim felt a hand on his shoulder.

"Unconventional," the instructor said sternly, "and well beyond your years, Hawkins. But one thing – never, ever do that again."

Jim smiled. He knew a challenge when he heard one.

Disney's
THE
LION KING

# All Wet

Timon pounded his tiny chest and gave a mighty yell as he swung out over the lagoon. He let go of a vine and threw his arms out wide, hitting the water with a small but very satisfying smack. He popped to the surface, shouting: "Ta-da!"

Pumbaa was next. "Look out below!" he called. He backed up on the rock ledge, then charged. The warthog's splash sent water flying high into the air. The lagoon was still rippling when he surfaced.

"Not bad," Simba said. "But I bet Nala could do better." The Lion King looked up at Nala, who was sunning herself on a rock as far from the water as possible.

"Ha!" Nala laughed. "You know I don't like to get wet."

"Oh, come on, Nala. Give it a try. The water's fine!" Simba said.

"The water *is* fine," Nala replied slowly, rolling over and licking her paw, ". . . for drinking."

Pumbaa and Timon sniggered. Simba frowned. Nala was making him look silly in front of his friends. Was he King of the Pride Lands or not?

Using his most commanding voice, Simba gave Nala an order. "You will come swimming with us right now, or else!"

Nala did not even lift her head. She closed her eyes. "Or else what, Your Mightiness?"

Simba couldn't come up with anything, so the argument was over. And Nala, as usual, had won.

Accepting his defeat, Simba ran to the edge of the rocky ledge, sprang high in the air and tucked his paws in for a royal cannonball.

Pumbaa and Timon were drenched. Slinking slowly out of the water, Simba signalled to them. He pointed at his dripping mane and then up at Nala's rock.

Timon winked, and he and Pumbaa began a noisy mock water fight to distract Nala. While they hollered and splashed, Simba climbed up to Nala's warm spot in the sun. He walked quickly but silently. Drawing closer, he crouched, his legs coiled to pounce. Nala did not move.

Then, with a triumphant roar, Simba jumped onto Nala's rock and gave his sopping mane a mighty shake. Nala was drenched.

Nala leaped to her feet with a snarl. Simba rolled onto his back, laughing.

"You're all wet, Nala!" Timon guffawed. Pumbaa was laughing so hard, he could barely breathe.

Nala tried to glare fiercely at Simba, but she couldn't. She had to laugh too. "King of the practical jokers," she said.

# Walt Disney's
# Bambi

## Night-time is for . . . Exploring!

As the moon rose above the forest, Bambi snuggled close to his sleeping mother. What a day it had been! Exploring new places, learning new words and meeting new friends. Bambi yawned and closed his eyes . . . .

"Bambi! Oh, Bambi!"

Bambi slowly opened his eyes. "Thumper?" he whispered. "Why aren't you asleep?"

"Asleep? Come on!" cried Thumper. "Sleep is for the birds! How can you sleep when there's so much to see and do at night?"

"But everybody knows that night-time is for sleeping," Bambi said.

"Oh, brother," Thumper said. "Do you have a lot to learn! Follow me, Bambi, and I'll show you how the night is a whole new day!"

And suddenly, at the prospect of an all-new adventure, Bambi's sleepiness disappeared. Quietly, he stood up and let Thumper lead the way.

Thumper was right – the forest was as busy at night as it was during the day, but with a whole new group of animals. Owls, opossums, raccoons and badgers – all those animals that Bambi thought spent most of their lives asleep – were now as lively as could be.

"Wh-wh-what's that?" Bambi exclaimed, as a dot of light landed on his nose.

"Don't worry, Bambi, it's just a firefly,"

Thumper said with a giggle.

"'Firefly'," Bambi said. Then suddenly, the little light disappeared. "Hey, where'd it go?"

"There it is!" cried Thumper, pointing to Bambi's tail. "No, wait. It's over there."

Happily, Thumper and Bambi chased the firefly as it flitted from one friend to the other. "I think he likes us!" Thumper cried.

But their game was soon interrupted by a flurry of sound. Thousands of leathery wings were suddenly beating overhead.

"Duck, Bambi!" hollered Thumper, just as the whole group swooped around their heads.

"Boy, that was close!" said Thumper.

"Were those fireflies too?" Bambi asked.

"Naw," Thumper laughed. "They didn't light up! Those were bats."

"'Bats'," repeated Bambi. "They're really busy at night."

"You can say that again," agreed Thumper, trying to stifle a yawn. And, since yawns are contagious, Bambi's own yawn was not far behind.

"This was fun," Bambi told his friend. "But what do you say we go home and go to bed?"

But there was no answer . . . for Thumper was already fast asleep!

# Such a Shame

Mulan nudged Khan into a gallop and kept her eyes straight ahead. She was on her way to town to go to the market for her family. It was a regular trip for her, but the people working on the sides of the road did not seem to think so. Without even looking at them, Mulan knew that she was causing whispers. But they weren't just talking about her. They were talking about the man riding with her – Captain Li Shang.

The captain didn't seem to notice the whispering, even as they entered the town and a group of girls giggled behind their fans. Mulan did her best to ignore it. Everyone had been making a fuss over her since she returned from the Emperor's palace. They all said she was a hero, but inside she just felt like . . . Mulan.

Shang swung down from his horse and offered to go inside to buy the rice. Mulan was about to object. She didn't need Shang's help at the market. The only reason she'd brought him along was because he wanted to see more of her town. But Shang was already inside the tiny shop.

Mulan sighed. She held the Captain in high esteem. She liked him – she really did. But she was always disagreeing with him. Even when she didn't need to.

"Shame!" Across the street, an older woman pointed at Mulan, startling her out of her thoughts.

"Shame!" the woman said again. "Don't think I have forgotten you."

Mulan blushed, recognizing the woman. It was the Matchmaker! Mulan looked at the ground as her cheeks grew even hotter, but they were not as hot as they had been on the day that she first met the Matchmaker – the day she accidentally set the woman on fire!

The Matchmaker continued, pointing and screeching at Mulan as she waddled across the street. "You!" she scolded. "Just because all of China thinks you are a hero does not mean you can escape your fate. I predict you will bring shame to your family. I feel it."

Mulan did not know what to say to the old woman.

"There is not a matchmaker in the world who could ever find a match for you!" the woman screeched.

"Then it is a good thing she will never need one," Shang said. As he walked past the Matchmaker, he accidently stepped in a puddle, splashing the Matchmaker from head to toe!

The Matchmaker was speechless, her face twisted into a scowl. Mulan could not think of a thing to say either. But, instead of wearing a scowl, her face was set in a wide smile.

# A Merry Christmas

"Merry Christmas!" Ebenezer Scrooge crowed as he watched the Cratchit children open the gifts he'd brought.

"A teddy bear!" Tiny Tim exclaimed. His sister had a new doll, and his brother was busy playing with a new train set.

"And there's another present too," Scrooge said with a twinkle in his eye. "I'll be right back." A moment later, he reappeared, carrying a big package wrapped in red paper and tied with a giant green bow.

The children ripped off the paper and squealed in delight.

"Father, it's a sledge!" they cheered.

"I can see that," Bob Cratchit replied, looking up from the turkey he was carving. Scrooge had brought the turkey over that very morning.

"Can we go sledging? Can we? Can we?" the children chorused.

"Of course," Cratchit replied. "But not until after dinner."

"And dinner is ready right now," Mrs Cratchit said.

"Dinner!" the children shouted as they scrambled to their seats at the table.

Mrs Cratchit sat down at the table. "I can't remember when we've had such a feast, Mr Scrooge," she said happily. "Thank you."

Scrooge raised his glass in the air. "That's what Christmas is all about," he said warmly. "Happiness and goodwill."

Everyone clinked glasses, then got busy eating.

"Now, how about that sledging?" Mr Cratchit said when they had eaten.

Minutes later, everyone was wrapped up. Scrooge pulled the children all through town, singing Christmas carols at the top of his lungs.

"Why is everyone staring at Mr Scrooge?" Tiny Tim whispered to his father.

Mr Cratchit smiled down at his son. "Because they like him," he said.

"I like him too," Tiny Tim said, as Scrooge pulled the sledge to the top of a hill. Everyone climbed off to look at the steep slope.

Scrooge picked up the sledge and walked several paces away from the top of the hill. Then, taking a running start, he jumped onto the sledge and raced to the bottom.

"Whoopeeee!" he cried.

Then Scrooge pulled the sledge back up the hill. "Who's next?" he asked, panting.

"Me!" Tiny Tim shouted. Everyone else got a few turns too.

Later, as he pulled the children back to their house, Scrooge felt warm despite the chill in the air. This was the merriest Christmas he could remember.

# Under the Tree

"He's approaching the tree." Immediately after the report came through, the monitor in Woody's hand began to crackle. It wasn't static, though; it was the sound of wrapping paper being torn open.

As he waited for the next report, Woody looked around at the terrified faces of his fellow toys. Christmas morning was always difficult for Andy's toys. They all lived in fear of being replaced by something bigger and better.

"Let it be a new video game!" Rex the plastic dinosaur wrung his tiny hands.

"As long as it's not another spaceman," Buzz Lightyear said.

"It's a . . ." The toys leaned closer. "It's a . . ."

Sarge began his report, but before he could finish, Woody shut off the monitor.

"What are you doing?" Hamm cried.

"Woody, we need to be debriefed in order to face the enemy!" Buzz sounded alarmed.

"Now hold on a minute, guys." Woody put his hand up to silence the toys. "Let's just think a minute. I want each of you to remember what it was like when you were unwrapped. Remember when you first met Andy."

"He chose me from the shelf himself," Rocky Gibralter boasted.

"And it was a great day, right?" Woody asked, looking around at everyone.

"I was a birthday present," Rex said, smiling. "I even got to wear a bow."

The other toys all chimed in, smiling and laughing as they told each other about their arrival.

"And we're a team, right?" Woody interrupted.

"Sure we are." Buzz nodded. "We can fight the new enemies together."

Woody shook his head. "No, Buzz. That's what I'm talking about. These new toys aren't our new enemies. They're our new friends!"

Slowly Woody's words began to sink in. "You mean, they come in peace," Buzz said.

"Exactly!" Woody cried. "So, how about, instead of sitting around here moping, we get busy planning a welcome party!"

"Great idea!" Rocky Gibraltar said.

"Oh, Woody," Bo Peep said. "I love it when you show your soft side."

Woody blushed. Then he turned the monitor back on. "Sarge, I want you to stand down. I have new orders. I repeat, new orders."

"Yes, sir. What can we do for you, sir?" the sergeant barked.

"Gather your troops and come upstairs. Andy's toys are throwing a hoedown for the new toys. It'll be our first annual Christmas Welcome Party!"

DISNEY'S
## BROTHER
BEAR

# The Bear Facts

Koda the cub loved to tell stories. But sometimes he got a little carried away. One day, he was telling a group of cubs about the fishing expedition he and Kenai had been on the day before.

"And then we caught about 100 fish! I mean, that pile of salmon must have been as tall as a tree. Of course, I caught most of them, but Kenai caught some too," he said.

"What did you do with all of them?" asked one little grizzly.

"We ate them all. Yup, we were mighty hungry after all that work," Koda declared.

Just then, Kenai lumbered up to the circle of cubs. "Hey, Kenai," asked one. "Is it true that you and Koda caught 100 fish?"

Kenai shot Koda a stern look. "Well, not exactly," he said. "Here, I brought you guys some berries for lunch."

"Hey, everybody!" Koda exclaimed. "Did I tell you about the time I ate so many berries that my whole body turned purple?"

"Can that really happen?" one of Koda's pals asked Kenai.

"Well, not exactly," Kenai answered. "Your tongue can turn purple for a while, though."

Later that day, Kenai and Koda went walking in the woods. After a while, it became clear that they were lost.

"Kenai," Koda said, "we're goners."

"Koda! Would you please stop exaggerating all the time?" Kenai scolded. "We're not dead, we're just lost!"

"Look . . . over . . . there," said Koda, gesturing. A strange male grizzly was approaching – and he did not look friendly.

"You're right," said Kenai. "We're goners."

"Not yet we aren't," Koda answered, suddenly sounding brave. The cub sprang into action. "Look out, you big lug . . . I'm a ragin' ball of fur!" Koda cried. The cub darted back and forth, throwing kicks and punches at the air. He shrieked and whooped. He jumped up and down and spun around.

The grizzly stood absolutely still, looking completely confused by the cub's odd behaviour. Eventually, he turned and walked off.

"Koda, that's the craziest thing I ever saw," said Kenai, shaking his head in disbelief. "Thank you for saving us."

Safely back at the bear camp that night, Koda recounted their hair-raising adventure to the rest of group.

"Kenai, did it really happen that way?" one of the cubs asked.

"Yes," said Kenai, smiling. "That's exactly how it happened, believe it or not!"

# The Perfect Gifts

The holidays had always been Cinderella's favourite time of the year. Even when she lived in a cold attic room in a house with two mean stepsisters and one truly evil stepmother, Cinderella had loved the cheer and good feeling of the season. She had cooked delicious holiday treats and made small decorations. And she had always managed to set aside time to make some small presents for her mouse friends.

Now that she lived in a beautiful castle, Cinderella found that she enjoyed the holidays even more. She decorated the castle, planned an elaborate holiday menu with the cook, and even threw a holiday ball. But this year Cinderella wanted to give especially wonderful gifts to her mouse friends, who had helped her so much.

First, Cinderella went to the royal kitchen. "My mouse friends like cheese," she told the cook. "Could you make some cheese pudding?" The cook assured her that the cheese pudding would be the best in the world.

Then Cinderella went to the royal tailor. "My mouse friends are each about three inches high. I don't know what size that makes them – maybe extra-extra-extra-extra small," she said. She told him their favourite colours, and he helped her pick out rich, beautiful fabrics. "I will make mouse outfits the likes of which have never

been seen," he said, rubbing his hands together.

Finally, Cinderella went to the royal carpenter. "My mouse friends haven't got any nice furniture. Can you help me?" she asked. The carpenter said he would gladly make tiny beds and chairs and tables for the mice.

The next day, as Cinderella and Prince Charming were having tea, the cook, the carpenter and the tailor arrived to deliver the presents for Cinderella's mouse friends. Cinderella thanked them and sent them each on their way with a kind word. Then she and Prince Charming looked at the gifts for the mice. The pudding was a beautiful colour, the clothes were artfully sewn and the tiny furniture was grand and elegant. But none of it seemed quite right for Cinderella's mouse friends.

"I don't understand," Cinderella said sadly. "The cook and the tailor and the carpenter are the best in all the land. So why don't I like what they made?"

"Well," answered Prince Charming, "You know your mouse friends better than anyone else. Maybe *you* should make their presents."

"You know, that's a wonderful idea." Cinderella was delighted. "I'm going to make my friends the nicest gifts they have ever received."

And she did.

Disney·PIXAR

**MONSTERS, INC.**

# Something Different

Sulley groaned and shifted in his reclining chair. "Ate too much again," he sighed, rubbing his big blue belly.

"Oh, me too," Mike moaned, reclining beside him in front of the fire. "It's the holidays," he said with a sigh. "All we do is sit around and eat."

"And eat and sit around," Sulley agreed. "Ain't it great?"

"Great if you like the same thing all the time," Mike said glumly. Then his tone changed. "What we need," he decided, "is to get away. We need to go someplace, do something different." Mike grew more and more excited. He had good ideas all the time, but this one was really great.

"Sit down. Have another chocolate." Sulley waved a box of sweets at Mike.

"Someplace with snow!" Mike pounded his fist in his palm. "That's it!" Ignoring Sulley, Mike walked towards the telephone. "I'll call Yeti. He'll know where we can find a little winter wonderland to call our own!"

"Go ahead and call, little buddy." Sulley yawned and looked into the fire. "But I'm not going anywhere . . . except to take a nap after another piece of chocolate . . . ."

\* \* \*

"I don't know how you talked me into this," Sulley said a short time later. He and Mike stood at the top of a steep hill, with snowboards strapped to their feet. "Can't I use a sledge instead?"

"Come on," Mike said. "Sledges are for old monsters. You'll be great!" The round green monster took off down the hill. He did turns, he caught air, he went fast and, in a spray of snow, he came to a halt. "Your turn," he called up to Sulley.

"Why do I know I will live to regret this?" Sulley asked under his breath. "Actually, how do I even know I will live?"

He slid slowly across the top of the mountain. He was moving. This wasn't so bad! But when he tried to turn down the hill, things got tricky. His board had a mind of its own . . . and it had decided to go back to the lodge!

\* \* \*

Sulley groaned and shifted in his chair. He propped his sprained ankle up on a pillow and rubbed his stomach. "Ate too much again," he sighed, rubbing his belly.

"Me, too." Mike groaned in a reclining chair beside him. In front of them a glowing fire hissed and popped. "All we do is sit around and eat." He sighed happily.

"Ain't it great?" Sulley smiled sleepily.

"Sure is." Mike sipped his hot chocolate. "I told you we needed to get away and do something different!"

# Disney's HERCULES

# The New Neigh-bour

Pegasus grazed peacefully outside the house where Hercules and Meg lived. Now that Hercules was a mortal and not a god, life was a little quieter than it used to be. This morning, however, there was some excitement in the village. Some new neighbours were moving in.

"Let's go over and make them feel at home," Hercules told Meg. They gathered some flowers and headed over to meet them.

A little while later, Pegasus heard a soft whinnying. He turned to discover a beautiful mare approaching him. His heart soared. But then Pegasus remembered the time that Pain and Panic had disguised themselves as a filly and captured him. He was determined not to fall for their trick a second time. He spread his wings and charged, shooing the horse down the hill.

The mare raced past Meg and Herc as they returned home. "Pegasus, what are you doing?" asked Meg. "That's no way to make our neighbours' horse feel welcome." Pegasus gulped. The beautiful horse who had tried to meet him really *was* a beautiful horse!

"If I were you, I'd get over there and try and make it up to her," suggested Hercules.

Within minutes, Pegasus pranced across the neighbours' field, stopped in front of the mare and struck a noble pose. He doubted any filly would be able to resist a stallion as handsome as himself. The lovely horse was unimpressed. She turned so that her tail swished right in Pegasus's face! Herc's horse knew he would have to do something amazing to impress this beauty. He flapped his wings and rose into the air. Then he dipped and swooped and somersaulted across the sky. When the filly started to walk away, he flew alongside her – and crashed right into a tree!

Hercules was watching from the hillside. Pegasus certainly does need some help, he thought.

Meg had an idea. "The right gift might convince that mare to forgive him," she said. She piled a basket high with apples and oats and tied a huge red ribbon around it.

But, when Pegasus went over to deliver the gift, holding the basket handle in his teeth, the female horse kicked it over. Then the mare whinnied and stomped, letting Pegasus know exactly what she thought of him.

Finally, Pegasus realized what he had to do. He sheepishly walked over to the filly with his head bowed. Then he gently nudged her with his muzzle. She neighed and nuzzled him back. All she had wanted was for Pegasus to say he was sorry. Now she understood that even though he was a bit of a birdbrain, her new friend had a good heart.

**DISNEY·PIXAR**
**MONSTERS, INC.**

# Something Different

Sulley groaned and shifted in his reclining chair. "Ate too much again," he sighed, rubbing his big blue belly.

"Oh, me too," Mike moaned, reclining beside him in front of the fire. "It's the holidays," he said with a sigh. "All we do is sit around and eat."

"And eat and sit around," Sulley agreed. "Ain't it great?"

"Great if you like the same thing all the time," Mike said glumly. Then his tone changed. "What we need," he decided, "is to get away. We need to go someplace, do something different." Mike grew more and more excited. He had good ideas all the time, but this one was really great.

"Sit down. Have another chocolate." Sulley waved a box of sweets at Mike.

"Someplace with snow!" Mike pounded his fist in his palm. "That's it!" Ignoring Sulley, Mike walked towards the telephone. "I'll call Yeti. He'll know where we can find a little winter wonderland to call our own!"

"Go ahead and call, little buddy." Sulley yawned and looked into the fire. "But I'm not going anywhere . . . except to take a nap after another piece of chocolate . . . ."

\* \* \*

"I don't know how you talked me into this," Sulley said a short time later. He and Mike stood at the top of a steep hill, with snowboards strapped to their feet. "Can't I use a sledge instead?"

"Come on," Mike said. "Sledges are for old monsters. You'll be great!" The round green monster took off down the hill. He did turns, he caught air, he went fast and, in a spray of snow, he came to a halt. "Your turn," he called up to Sulley.

"Why do I know I will live to regret this?" Sulley asked under his breath. "Actually, how do I even know I will live?"

He slid slowly across the top of the mountain. He was moving. This wasn't so bad! But when he tried to turn down the hill, things got tricky. His board had a mind of its own . . . and it had decided to go back to the lodge!

\* \* \*

Sulley groaned and shifted in his chair. He propped his sprained ankle up on a pillow and rubbed his stomach. "Ate too much again," he sighed, rubbing his belly.

"Me, too." Mike groaned in a reclining chair beside him. In front of them a glowing fire hissed and popped. "All we do is sit around and eat." He sighed happily.

"Ain't it great?" Sulley smiled sleepily.

"Sure is." Mike sipped his hot chocolate. "I told you we needed to get away and do something different!"

# The New Neigh-bour

Pegasus grazed peacefully outside the house where Hercules and Meg lived. Now that Hercules was a mortal and not a god, life was a little quieter than it used to be. This morning, however, there was some excitement in the village. Some new neighbours were moving in.

"Let's go over and make them feel at home," Hercules told Meg. They gathered some flowers and headed over to meet them.

A little while later, Pegasus heard a soft whinnying. He turned to discover a beautiful mare approaching him. His heart soared. But then Pegasus remembered the time that Pain and Panic had disguised themselves as a filly and captured him. He was determined not to fall for their trick a second time. He spread his wings and charged, shooing the horse down the hill.

The mare raced past Meg and Herc as they returned home. "Pegasus, what are you doing?" asked Meg. "That's no way to make our neighbours' horse feel welcome." Pegasus gulped. The beautiful horse who had tried to meet him really *was* a beautiful horse!

"If I were you, I'd get over there and try and make it up to her," suggested Hercules.

Within minutes, Pegasus pranced across the neighbours' field, stopped in front of the mare and struck a noble pose. He doubted any filly would be able to resist a stallion as handsome as himself. The lovely horse was unimpressed. She turned so that her tail swished right in Pegasus's face! Herc's horse knew he would have to do something amazing to impress this beauty. He flapped his wings and rose into the air. Then he dipped and swooped and somersaulted across the sky. When the filly started to walk away, he flew alongside her – and crashed right into a tree!

Hercules was watching from the hillside. Pegasus certainly does need some help, he thought.

Meg had an idea. "The right gift might convince that mare to forgive him," she said. She piled a basket high with apples and oats and tied a huge red ribbon around it.

But, when Pegasus went over to deliver the gift, holding the basket handle in his teeth, the female horse kicked it over. Then the mare whinnied and stomped, letting Pegasus know exactly what she thought of him.

Finally, Pegasus realized what he had to do. He sheepishly walked over to the filly with his head bowed. Then he gently nudged her with his muzzle. She neighed and nuzzled him back. All she had wanted was for Pegasus to say he was sorry. Now she understood that even though he was a bit of a birdbrain, her new friend had a good heart.

# A Wintry Walk

"It's so beautiful," Belle murmured as she gazed out of the castle window. Snow had been falling for hours and hours, covering everything in a deep blanket of white. "You know what would be nice? A wa – "

Suddenly, a heavy red cape was draped over her shoulders. "How about a walk?" the Prince asked.

Belle smiled into his blue eyes. "I was just thinking that!" she said.

"Aha," he replied mischievously. "But were you thinking of a walk on these?" He pulled a pair of large showshoes out from behind a chair.

"Snowshoes!" Belle cried, clapping her hands together. She and her father used to go showshoeing together in the woods when she was a little girl, and she loved it. No matter how deep the snow was, the special shoes allowed her to walk over the huge drifts.

Minutes later the pair were in the castle courtyard, strapping the snowshoes onto their boots. Belle walked forward gracefully, heading through the gate towards the forest, pausing to scatter birdseed for the neighbourhood birds.

But the Prince was having trouble, tripping over the giant shoes with every step.

"When I was a beast, I just walked through the snow," he said, panting. "I didn't have to bother with silly contraptions like these!" He stepped forward and tumbled head-first into a deep snowbank.

Belle laughed. At first, the Prince scowled but soon he was laughing too.

"You're thinking too much," Belle said. "It's actually a lot like walking in regular shoes. You just have to keep your feet a little further apart so they don't get caught up on each other."

"Hmm," the Prince said. He stepped forward. But, when he lifted his other foot, it caught on the icy top layer of snow, and he fell again.

Belle stifled a giggle as she helped him to his feet. "Step lightly," she suggested.

"I'll say," the Prince grumbled. He stepped more lightly this time, and moved easily across the snow. Soon he was keeping up with Belle, who led him all the way through the forest. It was a wonderful, wintry walk. And, when they got back to the castle, they found hot chocolate and biscuits waiting for them in front of the fire!

"Oh, good," said the Prince. "Eating! This is one thing I'll always be good at." He picked up a biscuit, which broke and fell with a *plop*! into his cup.

"Aw," he said, crestfallen.

"You know," Belle said with a teasing smile, "you aren't so different from the clumsy beast I fell in love with!"

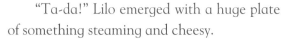

# Countdown to Midnight!

"No sleep till midnight!" Lilo and Stitch chanted, bouncing up and down on Lilo's bed. It was New Year's Eve, and Nani had agreed to let them stay up late.

"Okay, okay." Nani held her hands out. "It's only five o'clock now. Don't wear yourselves out. You still have seven hours until the new year."

Lilo and Stitch looked at each other. Wear themselves out? Impossible! "Look, Stitch," Lilo said, looking as serious as possible. "We only have seven hours. What do you want to do first?"

"Surfing!" Stitch cried.

"Sunset surfing it is!" Lilo gave the little alien a high five before turning to Nani. "Okay?" she asked sweetly.

Nani shook her head again. I must be nuts, she thought. "I'll go get my suit." She sighed.

The three surfed until sundown. Then they headed for home.

"So, what's next?" Lilo asked Stitch. Stitch smacked his lips. "Dinner!"

"Don't worry," Lilo said. "We'll cook."

"And I'll clean," Nani muttered.

When they got home, Nani lay down on the couch with her arm over her eyes. Five hours until bedtime. She switched on the TV and tried to ignore the crashing noises coming from the kitchen.

"Ta-da!" Lilo emerged with a huge plate of something steaming and cheesy.

"What is it?" Nani asked cautiously.

"Pizza, Stitch-style!" Lilo said. "With anchovies, peanut butter and fruit cocktail!"

Nani cringed. "Don't worry, Nani," said Lilo. "We left the toothpaste on the side this time. Plus, there's a milkshake for dessert!"

The three ate the gooey mess while Lilo and Stitch discussed what was next.

"How about that milkshake?" Nani suggested before Lilo could come up with a noisier, messier or more dangerous idea.

Stitch grabbed the blender and dumped the milkshake on his head. Nani shooed the two into the living room and began to tackle the mess in the kitchen.

The washing-up took forever. Nani could not figure out how they'd managed to use so many pots and pans. She was still elbow deep in suds when her eyes grew wide with alarm. Something was wrong. It was too quiet! Nani rushed into the living room. Lilo and Stitch were sound asleep! Nani looked at her watch.

"Five-four-three-two-one," Nani counted down. "Happy New Year," she said softly, as she covered the pair with a blanket.

She smiled as she looked at the clock. It was only 10pm!